Earth and Mars

Wayne Wignall

Prologue

Just after that the jeep veered sharply to the left then down a slope before turning upwards. The contents in Martin's stomach didn't give him any comfort. *Perhaps, he thought, a ciggie will iron out that nausea?* The soldier could see him touching his upset region. He still laughed as he exhaled a cloud of smoke. Martin gestured a hand as finger scissors and placed them onto his lips. The soldier took some time to acknowledge him. He felt himself from the bottom upwards. "Where did I place those damn fags?" He muttered to himself.

"It's about time you stopped smoking Jenkins!" the driver snapped after gaining a bit more speed, and the shock of his driving became more apparent.

"The way you're going, it's no wonder Capt. McCormick is feeling sick."

The driver chuckled. "Bull! He's sick of your company, private."

The vehicle joined onto a dirt track and onwards, a dark-green mess tent could've been seen, and the going was a lot more smoothly.

"Well ask the dude if he still wanna smoke?"

Jenkins flattery replied, "The dude in the back is an important officer meeting our commanding officer."

There wasn't a response other than him cursing the track diverting away from his general direction. There was another soldier at the front that was reaching forward for his radio. "We've sight of the tent."

"Affirmative," the radio crackled briefly.

Jenkins gave Martin one of his cigarettes and lit it.

The friendly soldier continued. "I must say that since you're an astronaut, I bet Washington is looking to strengthen their hold on space exploration."

Since the driver was able to tame their journey. Martin shifted his attention away from Jenkins. He was once a fighter pilot but transferred to launch space shuttles. Of course, he had accepted it but the future of NASA was under threat by programmes being scrapped and the workforce reduced. He knew that there had already been cuts too in the air force so it was puzzling to understand his significance. A thump and a sudden swerve and Martin's train of thought collapsed. He peeled ahead and managed to see small craters scattered all over the place.

"We use this field for artillery exercises. Amongst other things: cavalry; testing launchers; infantry pushes; air support. But we don't usually tailor for astronauts. I thought we abandoned the Star Wars project. Oh yeah and the—"

"Don't you ever shut up?" The driver asked.

"I cannot see what else it could be but why out here in the middle of nowhere?" Martin now asked.

"Like I said to you earlier, this terrain is for military exercises. He'll be here and you'll be meeting him at that observation-post."

Martin puffed out a smoke ring.

"I know what you're thinking. What do the armed forces have in common with you? Besides, the White House has assigned the General on this project."

"Which is?"

"Satellite surveillance I guess since you're an astronaut."

"Is this supposed to be a secret gathering?"

"We only know what you know but if you wish to share with me the juicy details, I will still be here for the ride back."

"Tell me," Martin started to question, "what do you think about America nowadays?"

"I think this is an exciting and challenging time. We will always be strong in this demanding world so—"

"I mean the lack of fund to NASA?"

"I'm only a soldier doing the bidding of a commanding officer: I haven't really an opinion."

"That's a pity. So you never thought that it's unusual that I'm—"

"I'm only making conversation. I'm not that smart to understand what is actually going on. I only hope I haven't caused you any alarm. I'm just as curious as you are on where this will lead us."

The four-by-four was now getting closer to the point-of-interest that held everybody's desire on what the astronaut had to do with warfare.

Book 1

Chapter 1
—Unplanned births—

*A*S A CHILD, Leo came from a warm-hearted family. His British mother raised him with a distant and religious father. His dad was married, to somebody else, but had a fling with her. It all started after the Jamaican election of the Prime Minister in the late sixties that went a little too far. After his father heard of her expecting him, he quickly promoted her as his personal secretary within his embassy in London.

His father insisted that his secret lovechild must follow good morals, which meant not getting mixed-up in music offering profanity in sex, drugs and violence. It was impossible to imagine Leo's involvement to being horny, taking hallucinogenic substances, and whom he might see fall behind a gun. However, his father walked in on him when Leo was in his bedroom playing *forbidden* music. Through his shock, he prayed to the Lord for sheer forgiveness that evil lurked within. "Jesus Almighty! Please forgive me!"

He turned his attention onto the boy. "And what do you think you're doing?"

"Dad, I was just checking out my sound system."

"Are you trying to give me a heart attack? I cannot cope having a son who won't listen."

"Of course I do listen."

"Then why are you listening to that music before I walked in?"

"I was just tuning to—"

"So I should listen too?" his father asked abruptly, but decided to leave the room.

In its aftermath, his parents placed a ban that he mustn't use his sound system for six months, and it prevented his curiosity to listen to radio stations that were airing explicit material. It wasn't enough. He couldn't help to hear profanity at a London tube station. He was observing punk rockers, having their hairs spiked-up and the sides of their heads shaved, playing their loud stereo that had many sexual references. Leo's ears were picking up every single word in the song and thought of mistaking it, yet, they were singing the dirty chorus too. He felt unfairly treated, by his parents, to being shielded away in the glorification of marijuana, violence and sex. Still his nagging parents decided that he must attend a Catholic boarding school to be reformed. Young Leo loved the idea because he would be sent away to freedom; it was also where he adored his extra-curriculum in a musical band of the Air Cadets.

Once Leo reached into adulthood, he took on Astronomy at Cambridge University. His entrance was inspired through his teenager years of watching *Flash Gordon* – it had a very distinctive music theme that rejuvenated his thirst for life. After he graduated, jobs to appreciate the universe were very hard to come by. Although, Leo found a place in the Royal Air Force to become a fighter pilot. It was sheer luck, and strictly speaking, competition is always ferocious. One in every several hundred will be able to be successful and Leo pulled through.

***

Leo was at the military airbase, in Turkey, during the possible war with the Soviets. He was part of a joint military effort with America where he met a man who could tickle his fancy, Bill Kaiser. He had a medium build and his complexion was Caucasian. Bill Kaiser had piercing blue eyes, dark thick short black hair and sported a horseshoe beard. Plus, he spoke with a heavy southern American accent, as he hailed, from the back countries of Texas. Evidently, Leo was a black gentleman who kept together bronze dark brown eyes – it was hard to see into his pupils. Also, the Briton had a short haircut, a trimmed beard too. Moving on, their friendship started in the mid-1980s since working to test a decoy system to counter a Soviet attack. The equipment was believed to make their enemy think that their target flew from the west, but it was actually eastwards. Therefore, allowing them the critical edge to win dog fights.

Bill Kaiser had shared many short stories with Leo on his teenage years. To recapture them all:

His youth was on his daddy's horse ranch, and his papa wanted him to continue their longevity of running it. The place was beautiful and enormous which had many tall birch trees spread along the outskirts; they would whisper to one another by the gentle wind. He was a go-getter who felt that the ranch had little to offer. His buddy claimed that it all began when he drunk his first beer keg at a friend's party; he enjoyed it. After Bill returned home, with a terrible hang over, he saw that life there wouldn't exceed his leisure. By a thumping headache, he imagined thousands of party revellers were gathering together on the horse field, and they danced until the early morning. However, few people lived within ten miles of that ranch. After he earned his college degree, he signed up for the United States Air Force. It alarmed his father; he saw his own flesh and blood had abandoned his family's long running in agriculture. He was angry at first, but became supportive and patriotic.

Leo and Bill had a few drunken conversations about Russia. One time, they were knocking back cold bitter-sweet beer in an empty bar. They were sitting around a table after a game of pool too.

After a swig, Leo addressed his counterpart. "God, it was the space race of going to the moon. Isn't it strange that we can casually drink Bud, while they'll be drinking vodka?"

"That's absolutely true. You should be considering that the powers that be may call upon us to strike their frontlines."

"God only knows that to attack them will result in millions dead."

Bill was a little diffident. "I wish," he continued, "I knew what I was doing joining the air force. It makes me sick to think that we're like a moth led to the flame."

"Why don't we approach this in a casual way?"

9

Bill belched under his breath. "What are you suggesting? Are you able to diffuse the whole thing?"

"Only God knows," Leo continued, "you've heard of the domino-effect theory?"

"Of course, it was that which got America involved in the wars in Asia."

"Well, let's use it."

"Go on."

"You do understand using the model on the human race?"

Bill laughed. "You mean," he concluded, "we knock down a Soviet. Then a cosmonaut and one-by-one a Russian will fall over!"

Leo attempted to be serious – he was drunk though. "I don't mean that exactly, but let's look at Jesse Owens, for he's the first African American who won the gold medal at the Olympic Games." Leo astonished himself if he was lucid. "From there on," he continued, "we may move along to Martin Luther King and Nelson Mandela."

"Not sure that I follow you."

"They were like a domino-effect. One was the first Black Olympian, the other a pacifist and then there's the combatant."

"So how are they going to help solve the Cold war?"

"Well, let's consider the pacifist. We don't attempt to attack first."

"It's not that simple as they will see an opportunity to strike."

"That's true. He did sacrifice his own life for a greater good."

"So we allow the Russians to walk all over us?"

"Martin Luther King believed in it."

Bill pardoned Leo. He got up to order another round of Budweiser. He thought to himself if his drink buddy was becoming absurd, if not too drunk. On his return, he gave one of his bottles to him. "I must say that he's a brave man, but I can't see Reagan being a pacifist."

Leo was silent for a short moment. "Thatcher too. I suppose the next option is Nelson Mandela."

"We could follow him but we won't be covering a lot of ground quickly."

"It's the element of surprise. We have the intelligence on the Soviets...just think about...our stealth fighters."

"Come on!" Bill said loudly, "it's surely isn't easy for our guys to gather military intelligence, is it?" He drank a little. "I mean," he carried on, "that Moscow could play us as fools to strike, and then we have a nuclear war. Besides, I thought Nelson Mandela was a Commie, isn't it?"

"I don't think he publicly declared that. But few people assumed too much on his passion on humanity. Anyway, I can easily recall JF Kennedy being a left-wing, and he stood up against the Soviets."

Bill replied sarcastically, "He was shot by a left-wing."

"Yes but the shooter was a Commie."

"So then," Bill mentioned to gather his thoughts, "so to consider *striking first*, our Generals don't have a clue how."

Leo thought on that. "I do remember America campaigning in Korea and Vietnam. Basically, Russia wasn't too bothered."

"So what you're saying is that we ought to strike small countries like Cuba? You really haven't solved the Cold war because the Soviets still see us as fascist."

"You mean when the Nazis made an unprovoked attack against them?"

"Exactly, let's keep it short that violence to solve the Soviet problem came a little too late."

"I suppose the fascists have really ruined aggression."

Bill laughed loudly. "Oh really? Yet how is a sprinter going to solve the Cold war?"

Leo had the giggles too. "I think," he added, "it's safe to say that my domino-effect theory isn't fool-proof!"

Chapter 2
—Orchestrate—

*T*HE PAPER WAS tossed across his desk before leaning back in his chair. It seemed to swirl to his right but kept his posture forward. Kaiser had a moment to think how the world had changed. After a sigh, he reached for that Washington Post dated 10th November 1989. The front cover had been read repeatedly and the news columns were starting to fade. The headline, of course in big letters, wasn't as jet black as before:

Two Germanys unite

He welcomed prosperity and four years in the making; Germany had become a substantial economic power. Kaiser saw America a lot stronger as a military force; an affluence; and the world's political broker. He had been General of an air force base at Edward's but now the Chairman of the Joint Chiefs of Staff. Across his desk was the large portrait of President Frederick Bungles. The picture was framed in varnished oak and he smiled purposefully to anyone who glared upon him. Nearby were flagpoles draped with the Stars and Stripes on either side. Like most senior desks in the government, his had a formidable size that he could lay dozens of documents to analyse; it had an unbelievable shine which reflected its surroundings such as the windows to the lighting above it. To his left was a computer terminal that held classified information on weapons still under development. He held a position, in the Pentagon, many soldiers relish to have yet he wanted more.

That paper was symbolic to him since it marked the end of the iron curtain but at a price. Before becoming the Chairman of the Joint Chief of Staff, he had to make harsh decisions: There were people who stood to *fight the good fight* against communism but now they weren't required any longer. He wasn't comfortable to face them in person; still wasn't at ease when letters were sent to see hundreds depart with his photocopied signature. Kaiser had been told that the end of the cold war caused the recession but he couldn't believe that. His country had a hallmark of being the most opulent in the world. Russia wouldn't have considered *Glasnost* if America was in turmoil he thought to himself. He had wanted to blame the Bungles administration; they had failed to see and prevent shortcomings.

He stirred from his deep thought when his buzzer became alive. "What is it?"

"President Bungles wants to see you in the Oval Office this afternoon around one."

"Fine," he replied and ended that call.

He still saw that paper in front of him. It had a photograph of Germans using sledgehammers wanting to take a piece of the wall, and it was their breakthrough to enjoy the wonders of capitalism. *A breakthrough,* he considered. It didn't take long for him to recall when he took up a scholarship to study economics at the Air Force Academy. Obviously, taking time to study, and work in the air service, wasn't in a grand scale but he felt adamant to question Bungles. He believed that America was only successful because of the forces: Its Independence led by General Washington; war against the Japanese and in Vietnam. He remained headstrong that the American military brought prosperity, and nothing else really mattered. It might seem strange that Kaiser could loath his President and feel oblige to see him that afternoon (Bungles offered him the post). He was now part of that administration so why see him? Himself and Bungles did portray themselves as keen golfers; they would play at Andrews Air Force Base; the pair would also spend time together at the clubhouse and mingle with its members. That was why he was given the position to run as the Chairman of the Joint Chiefs of Staff because of his membership. No-one could just join unless you held some form of prestige to that club be that you were the most powerful man in the world to a powerbroker at Wall Street:

The elite reside there.

Kaiser was making himself ready to see Bungles. Bill picked up his treasured paper and placed it in his desk draw. He hesitated a little. The General returned to the draw and read the headline again. Kaiser thought of the Pentagon and the White House working together for a good cause; his cause; his future; his ambition. Bill Kaiser had a reverie about the clubhouse:

General Cedric Bran was his economic tutor who had introduced him to become a member. The place was like no other club for it consisted of a secret ritual: drinking a cup of pig's blood mixed with red wine. It was a mark of respect to become part of that order which wanted to thrive in the world. There were manufacturer executives that won government contracts due to being members at that club; financial investors benefited too; newspaper editors along with various figures from the church. Of course, statesmen and senior figures in the military were part of the fold. Those in the fraternity enjoyed how wealth wasn't a real issue for them, even in times of economic strife. As a club member, he alone initiated a catchy phase Hog's Head; It was his way to receive respect.

Kaiser grinned to himself that certain figures in the White House were uniting in secret with his Pentagon office. He thought about having Bungles his President for another four years. He dropped his smile and looked at the portrait of him. Kaiser couldn't understand why he would even consider re-election after the cuts he had made. The General could only perceive him as cold-hearted, yet the old paper brought him an aspiration to run for the White House. He turned around to fetch his light blue double blazer coat and cap to see him. There wasn't any need to debrief Bungles on the military might of Russia; China nor in Cuba. It was only to try to win the President over that further cuts would jeopardise the country...From whom? To make a bold claim that Britain was going to become a western threat; Germans to create a new war machine; or Mexicans would declare war on the entire continent? Of course not!

He was at the loser's end. *Yes, Mr Pathetic*, he patronized to himself, *you'll be able to make deeper cuts.*

Chapter 3

—Gate crashing—

*L*EO WASN'T AWARE of the dark surge of power, yet, his curiosity nearly took the better of him after Bill Kaiser was promoted to General, and the Joint Chiefs of Staff at an alarming rate. Before it sank in, he and his wife were invited to see him at a party. For Leo, it meant rubbing shoulders with senior politicians for the first time ever. Evidently, he felt sanguine to build better bridges across the pond, and progress quickly as the Chief Commander of the British armed forces. Leo was straightening his tie for that important occasion. He was wearing his military uniform, which had the rank of Squadron Leader. His wife, Carly, was wearing her long black silk slit dress.

Leo felt his eye-lids slightly heavy from staying up late in a bar. His mind made an escape from reality. *Oh my God*, Leo thought, *I'm at the Pharaoh's banquet in Egypt...*

He felt a sharp jab on his side, and roused to look around at the reception area in the White House. When he came to, it was Carly poking him in his chair. She squinted her eyes to take hold of her husband's sight, and looked away for him to glance upon somebody. Bill Kaiser, in his full air-service uniform, was waving and advancing towards them. Leo got up to embrace him, as if, the pair was long lost brothers.

Bill said, "What on Earth were you doing? Daydreaming? God, it has been far too long."

"Too right."

"Leo, things here are going to change, and I like to thank you for taking the—"

"This is my wife," Leo said, as he got her up, "Carly."

"It's nice to meet you, Carly," General Kaiser acknowledged her before grabbing Leo by his shoulder, "I want to see you in one of the back rooms after the

President's speech. You're gonna love every moment to what I've gotta say."

The Briton found the evening very lively, and so urged him to discourse. Bill nodded and Leo was able to chase his dream to understand the heavens; to become an Astronomer. The news made him feel light-headed and his knees nearly gave way, yet, felt the urge to punch into the air. He always longed to work in astronomy, but opportunities were scarce to fulfil. His wife was astonished, and had a good heart for her husband. She was a remarkably beautiful, black woman with relaxed hair to her shoulders. Carly possessed narrow slit eyes, and her waistline was slim. There were seats nearby and both husband and wife made good use of them after Bill took his affairs elsewhere. As they sat before the entrance to the dining hall, they hardly believed his sheer luck to chase his dream. For the pair; they thought of themselves in a fairy-tale.

"Is he really serious, Leo?" Carly asked.

Leo took hold of her hand. "I've known him far too long," he said, "Kaiser already knew that if we win the Cold War, that I want to take-up astronomy. For if he's lying, I shall fight the Joint Chiefs of Staff in this house, and then I shall fight the Chief on the streets, and I shall never surrender."

Carly shared on his light humour. "You can be rather dramatic."

In spite of all the champagne and razzmatazz, Leo still hadn't any suspicion that Bill could pull strings in space observation. All he saw was a man highly-regarded, and if Bill wanted him to work anywhere in America, he sure as hell could!

The couple was to wine and dine, amongst two hundred other invitees, to listen to President Frederick Bungles. He was the 41st President of the United States of America and he was going to start his Presidential re-election in 1993. It was seven in the evening when all the invitees had to report to the dining hall. The tables were covered in the finest pressed cloth, laid with silver cutlery and were candle-lit. The manservants and maids did their best to prepare the room, only earlier, clanging sounds of the finest cutleries and the clash of crockery were made. Much later, the invitees took over the atmosphere. The ceiling was high giving room for chandeliers. The walls had oil paintings of past American leaders too. At the far side of the grand dining hall, President Bungles was preparing his speech, and he received a rosy applause as he stood up to face his guests–

"Good evening, everybody," he said, "it's nice to see old faces and it's even nicer to see faces that I do not remember." He could hear his guest being jovial. "I've brought you all here," he resumed, "so that we can have a terrific meal, and leave this dining hall that my chef is better than yours–"

His guests were giggling, clapping and cheering for him.

Momentarily, Bungles got their attention. "As you may already know, we are heading straight into another recession thanks to newly discovered bullions of gold under the White House. In other words, our stockbrokers are worthless! But, my beloved friends, we're now stronger than before..."

Olly was Bill Kaiser's wife. She noticed his boredom as he looked expressionlessly at the President. She took his right hand, looked into his eyes, and spoke in a gentle tone. "What's the matter?"

"It's just isn't funny as I already heard his jokes during his rehearsals."

After the President completed his ten minute speech, dinner was served in earnest. The menu was universal for the diners: Spicy smoked haddock and saffron soup; roast chicken legs with sea salt and thyme and finally for dessert, raspberry cranachan. As the guests were busy eating, a musical band was to play out hits of latin jazz.

Bill Kaiser didn't appreciate his host. At times, he was looking above the President at the chandeliers – wanting them to crash to lighten up his evening – he never liked Frederick Bungles. President Bungles didn't even like Bill Kaiser, and he had plans to let him go. He believed it was best to oust the General via his scheduled report on military expenditure. He would address the public, on television, that Bill Kaiser wasn't feasible.

Chapter 4
—In the limelight—

*I*T WAS REFRESHING, the drink oozed down his throat. He held the empty glass high; rich patterns of etched glass made easy to grip. Bill Kaiser made a sigh and slammed it on his oak desk. He was more than thankful of the White House having a great bartender, for he had his first Mint Julep Cocktail. Also, the General was making himself ready, to visit the Pentagon, after taking over the Oval Office on Wednesday, 13th October 1993. His military motorcade was waiting at the front of the White House when he emerged with one of his top military men. He was certain to inspire support in his *State of Public Safety* AKA *Supreme Revolution*. Beforehand, he had already hardened his heart since becoming a Non-Executive Officer in a weaponry company – the actual Executives were his confidants who appointed him to secure military contracts in the Pentagon. Yet his business nearly folded when Bungles was insinuating that he was looking elsewhere to secure contracts. Bill scorned President Bungles, and ordered his confidants not to trade for an entire fortnight. As the stock market seemed less active, Hog's Head believed that it should cause top leading shares to plummet, and trailing shares would take on a knock-on effect. A further act, several financial magazines were to slander him. All in all, the knave act would create no confidence in their US President. As the propaganda gained a lot of momentum, Bill believed that a fortnight was long enough to deal with his scapegoat.

***

On his arrival, several dozen news journalists were waiting in a small Press room. The General was already late to address them, and he headed straight to the podium:

"Good Afternoon. I'm General Kaiser, Joint Chiefs of Staff," he said and paused for a moment. "You're most likely aware," he continued, "of the military being stationed throughout DC. It's under the orders of the State of Public Safety. It's because the Supreme Court decided that the US Administration shall be held accountable for the continuous turmoil. As you may already know, the former President has broken our nation, and it was due to his tentative handling. Therefore, we only seek to obviate him and Congress. After that, we're to determine a new system that will be stable, reliable and accessible for the American people. We've asked the Supreme Court to accept the resignation of the former President, and to monitor the progress of our new constitution. All state departments like Justice, the Treasury, Agriculture and the likes are to continue as normal. However, as from now, former senior state officials in the White House and Congress have been removed due to their mismanagement on the economy, nose-diving the dollar and their insensitivity with the American people.

"At present, under the approval of the Supreme Court, I'm fully responsible for the swift shift of that government, and I accept the resignation given to me by the former President. Unfortunately, I may not be able to answer many of your questions."

All of the journalists, at the conference, confounded on who should be held accountable for the revolution, and how long was the state of emergency going to last? Yet Bill Kaiser left the limelight and his Lieutenant-General replaced him.

Later on, during the day, the American people would be watching the start of an economic boom on the news. Henceforth, Bill believed that his new power was only going to get easier.

21

Chapter 5

—Better or for the worse—

*L*EO'S EYES TURNED watery after opening an envelope:

Bureau of Consular Affairs
Washington D.C
September 12th 1993

Dear Mr Rockford.

We would like to thank you in taking a sincere interest to work in America.

We must emphasise that we've no jurisdiction in the Space Observatory in Orlando has it is currently run by the University.

However, we understand that General Kaiser, the Joint Chiefs of Staff, gave recommendation for you to work in the United States. Given that you were placed as a high-priority to improve our standing in the world, we've enclosed a cheque of $100,000 which will help you get settled in Florida. Furthermore, we've granted your visas to work here for the next three years.

Finally, we thank you again for taking an interest in our great nation.

Yours Sincerely

Donald Richardson
Bureau Executive

"Carly," he shouted, "you won't believe what I've got!"

She entered the living room. "What are you talking about?"

Leo shown her the letter and she gasped at the amount of money.

"This is what dreams are made of," Leo said.

Being a family man, he did have three children between the ages of ten and thirteen. The eldest were twin daughters, Christina and Niobe. The youngest one was their son, Donno.

***

He decided to gather his family together for a meal at a busy and exquisite restaurant. It was a large place with over one hundred tables to book. There were also many large pictures of Orlando's landscapes hanging on the walls. There was even many enormous fish and lobster tanks dotted between the tables, which made it looked like an aquarium.

Leo raised his champagne flute fondly to his wife and children. "Carly, we've come a long way in our lives, and I'm surely happy to be with you...Kids listen to your father! I'm proud of this family, and I'm pretty sure that I hope you're all proud of our achievements."

It couldn't be a spoilt occasion as the cuisine had the right texture. The sea food had a glossy look, it was served at the right temperature, and the taste of the salty flaky bits did seem to melt in their mouths. The Rockfords were full of praise of themselves, and they continued their praises by tipping the waiter, handsomely.

***

The following morning, Leo was driving through a run-down district. He had the latest GPS gadget installed in his car. Strangely, his navigational system was indicating to being close to home, but he wasn't. After fifteen minutes of driving around haplessly, he spotted an alley to stop and gather his thoughts. He turned into it from his fear of being lost. He still kept his engine running as the car rolled along the long and quiet alley. The driver looked upon several people blocking the route ahead with their backs on him. Leo's anxiety was raised whilst imagining being in a red-light district – there were neither prostitutes, nor pimps as he got closer. His heart was pounding slightly, because he was putting himself into a peculiar situation, and he still got nearer behind them. The men were minding their own business, and they didn't notice Leo's silent approach. Still he continued to drive onwards. The unusual awareness of the street-wise escalated rapidly from being peaceful to abusive.

Three men put up a front across the alley. "Sir! What ya lost, officer?" one of them shouted.

"Sorry!" Leo replied after winding down his window. His heart was beating faster to his misfortune, and thought to manoeuvre a U-turn.

The brawlers saw Leo as an intruder and they pointed their handguns on him. "Get out of that fucking car, sir!"

In Leo's mind, he knew that they were to claim ownership on his Ford Thunderbird. The drama happened very quickly, and it left him in a state of shock after he moved away from the car. Also, they made their final demand to leave his car keys in the ignition before driving away. Leo tried to remain calm as he headed back out. He looked on, in disbelief, that he was stranded.

Yet things only turned from bad to worse as he emerged onto the main street corner. Plain-clothed police officers had a suspicion that he was drug-pushing. They drove in an unmarked police car moving closer towards him. Then, the officers bailed out to continue their approach.

"So hi there, "one of them asked, "are you new here?"

"Yes but–"

"So who is in your crew?"

"What are you talking about? My car got stolen!"

The officer asked, "You sound like you're from England. Are you visiting for business?"

"Are you undercover cops?" he wondered.

"Yes, in a way, but we wouldn't be telling you! So what are you doing in this neighbourhood, sight-seeing?"

"I haven't any intention of being here. My navigational system had a malfunction."

The second officer decided to make his presence known. "You have," he asked, "a navigational system? What's that?"

"Look my car is stolen, aren't you going to file the crime?"

"We would," he continued, "after we understand that system you're going on about?"

"Cutting-edge navigator," Leo replied.

"How come I never heard of it?"

"Look my car has just gone–"

"Wait just a minute...Are you now saying that your space-boogie is missing?"

"So what are you carrying?" the first officer now asked.

Leo got a little angry. "What kind of cops are you?"

"We're vice," he said showing his police shield, "this area is swarming with petty criminals that make excuses about aliens."

The officers shook their heads. They didn't believe him that there was such a device, and they suspected that he was only putting up a front of being car-jacked – it was in the early nineties, after all.

"Are you concealing any weapons?"

"No."

"We'll need to frisk you, sir."

"Aren't you listening to a single word that I just said?"

"It's routine–"

"You're not," Leo snapped, "doing your jobs properly!"

"Look, if you won't cooperate, we'll have to arrest you."

Leo saw that the two officers were being a little too weary against his concern, and he got a lot more rowdy. "What makes you think that I'm not the victim of a crime?"

Unfortunately, his dramatic mood-swing placed him under arrest for disturbing the peace.

***

Leo was released with a caution, and the police filed his auto-theft. He returned to his four-bedroom home by taxi. It would still remain a dreadful day when he thought of not seeing his stunning new car again. Also, he felt that his car insurance premium was certain to increase dramatically. Leo told of his awful ordeal, to his wife, but Donno was crying and screaming. Leo's son could be heard complaining of school bullies that have dubbed him too posh to earn their respect, and they were teasing him on the American Independence. Donno continued whining that they must return to Britain. Carly wanted to hear her husband but she comforted Donno first.

Leo was perturbed and quietly retreated to his bedroom. He had an introspective on his Catholic school teaching against Satan. *Oh my God*, he thought to himself, *surely the beast is contriving in making my life a living misery.* He had another fear that evil would be lurking around at his new job. Leo made a prayer that his new colleagues weren't going to conspire against him for being different. The man sat on his bed. He continued pondering if his workload was unpleasant, and faced doing more work than his counterparts. His countenance didn't appear to show grief when he heard screams downstairs becoming louder. He got upon his feet, and found himself outside to take a stroll around the block. In doing so, it only made him feel vulnerable; a racist resident might shoot him in an almost white suburban area. Yet, he was able to clear his mind when he circled back home safely.

***

13th October 1993. Leo hired a car on his first day at work. Whilst driving, he found no amusement on how his financial budget had rocketed on his way to the Robinson Space Observatory – the premise was situated on university grounds. It was shaped like a dome and it was built right in the middle of a large stretch of lawn. On his arrival, he'd see a few white-coats making some commotion near the entrance. Leo parked his car to get out, and headed towards them.

"Bejesus! We're at war!" A worker said – to anybody close.

Leo couldn't compute what he meant. "Sorry," he commented, "but I don't understand what you're talking about? Could you explain yourself?" He stared at him. "The US Army," he added, "has taken away our liberties!"

Leo was still unable to comprehend his remark, but he rightly anticipated where he ought to go. From within, Leo asked a passing person about those dotted outside. "It may sound weird," she replied in a white-coat, "but it's all over the news channels. It has been reported that there's some kind of terrorist threat being planned on Washington, because they're trying to shut our government down."

By her revelation, Leo felt that life couldn't get any worse. He contemplated that Satan had other plans than himself.

"Are you a student?" She asked him.

"No, I'm not, but I was."

"Oh you must be Leo Rockford," she added, "the Briton, isn't it?"

"Yes that's right."

"Don't suppose you're looking for Professor Nunn? He's straight ahead on the last door on your left."

The new Astronomer thanked her, and he took the chance to look around his immediate surrounding. He saw a narrow corridor having several doors scattered along it. Immediately afterwards, the Professor, Duncan Nunn, came up to greet him. Yet, he informed, in so many words, that the Space Observatory was under threat. He stated that there were reports of US soldiers bursting into the White House to reprimand President Bungles. Therefore, critical funds might be at stake. After Leo listened to the verbose nature of his new employer, he hardly believed the news, and his annoyance became clear, that his career change, due to the eloquence of his American friend, was a bad one to make. He feared his marriage was doomed.

Despite the havoc, Duncan Nunn gave Leo some scientific marvels. Their space observation had a newly installed electromagnetic telescope. Duncan explained that his team were investigating the possibility of life on

Mars, and to sustain human life there on. It was those typical insights that Leo longed to hear since his time at university. Technically speaking, the wave projection reflected back from the Mars surface, which gave them the ability to identify a rock to a nut. It was a very powerful device in the heart of Orlando, and he was part of that team. Leo felt certain of having his feet firmly on the ground. He would be able to challenge his mental resolve than to test his physical agility. So as it stood, it had to be his ideal job, which matched his passion, his adventure and his ultimatum.

The male who was outside earlier, formally reintroduced himself. "Sorry about the hysterics," he mentioned as he shook his hand, "it's just that you don't get to hear Washington being besieged. Anyway, my name is Clifford."

"Nice to meet you, Clifford. My name's Leo Rockford and as you may guess; it's my first day here."

"I suppose you never saw America having these terrible crises: Wall Street and now D.C."

"I knew America is always the centre of attention of the world. This country will pull itself through. So what is actually happening in Washington?"

"What we know for certain is that the US military is controlling DC. Now the new development may have been ordered by the President, unless he was caught napping," Clifford said humorously.

"A lady reckons it might be something to do with a terrorist attack, don't you agree?"

"You would if the news story didn't keep changing at a moment's notice. Anyway, there's going to be a press conference at the Pentagon. I think they'll know more what's really going on."

Leo was led into a self-catering canteen, which had two small microwaves, hot-drink vending machine, six small tables, and of course, a television-set perched on the top-corner wall. Clifford was anxious, like everybody else, to find something plausible since the news stories kept on fluctuating: It was a terrorist attack; a dangerous cult that paid homage to their religious apocalypse, or the military personnel taking action on pay! None of those reasons offered any sound explanations. Leo sat around one of the tables with Clifford and Duncan, and there were other tables being occupied.

Leo noticed Duncan looking rather relaxed about the whole Washington crisis. "Don't you think this is serious?" Leo asked.

Duncan returned with a smile. "This is America. All kinds of weird stuff do happen here."

"Nothing like this, surely?"

"You'll be amazed of the stories, I've heard, what goes on in Washington."

Leo felt a little uncomfortable to continue his conversation. Just then, he looked at his watch and it read 12.05pm. The conference was running late.

Clifford wanted everybody to be quiet. The only sound made was the newsreader continuing his speculations. What soon followed was General Kaiser who took his position at the stand. He gave his acknowledgment that he was the Joint Chiefs of Staff, which left everybody on edge.

"I know him!" Leo said astonished.

"We've all heard of him. That's General Kaiser," Clifford replied.

"It's a small world, I've a friend who knows him. It was he that recommended you to me, Leo," Duncan said.

Clifford asked, "Leo, so you met him?"

"He's trying to say something," Duncan said regardless and pointed at the TV.

The General left the stand box. Now the newsreader wasn't making many speculations on the military.

Clifford turned to face Leo, and coughed to gain his attention. "So how did you know him?"

"It's nothing. It was a training exercise in Turkey."

"Training for what?"

"NATO," Leo explained, "it was during the Cold War."

"Did you know about this?"

Leo could see that Clifford and everybody else were staring at him. He firmly shook his head.

Professor Nunn asked, "Do you believe General Kaiser will continue funding this complex?"

Leo replied, "I only knew him through a mate in the joint exercise in Turkey—"

"Hi there," a women greeted Leo and was sitting at a table nearby, "has your mate got anything to do with this?"

He found himself in a right muddle, and noticed how Bill departed in a short space of time. He attempted to shift his attention. "It must be the Supreme Judges, isn't it?"

The workers could only perceive it as plausible. At that moment, Duncan gave pardon to leave the canteen. Leo felt, deep inside, that something else must be at play than the unfolding drama. He began wondering if the Supreme Court had actually made that injunction. Leo found that the only way to settle his nerves was to imbibe with the General himself.

Much later, Duncan returned to the canteen. "I've just made contact with NASA," he said, "about the large investment on our project. It looks likely that we'll still be fully operational until next summer."

Afterwards, Duncan Nunn permitted Leo and his employees to take leave.

***

On his arrival home, he noticed the television set in the lounge was on fairly loud.

"Has he gone mad with power, or a new power is taking over him?" Carly asked.

"I thought," he reacted, "I knew him but I'm not sure what's going on."

Later that evening, the Rockford household got livelier than usual. Niobe and Christina heard about the news development, from school, and they compared General Kaiser to *Ming the Merciless* – an infamous character in Flash Gordon.

Donno Rockford looked in good spirit. "Dad, I told those bullies that you knew the Buffalo Bill, and the bullies are my friends now!"

Leo congratulated his son and thought that the unfolding events might be for a greater good.

Furthermore, the television had been reporting of a bull market on Wall Street.

Leo and Carly retired to their bedroom after their children got tucked into their beds.

"Leo, so you think Bill's wife knew about the coup?"

Leo hummed in thought. He hadn't the slightest idea what was going on. When he thought of Bill, it meant drinking a brew, and went downstairs to grab a beer – yes, he mindlessly went away to get one! Leaning against the fridge, he began drinking in quick and large gulps. Once that was done, returned upstairs.

"Do you think Bill's wife knew anything?" Carly asked patiently.

"Perhaps she knew something was up, but I'll page Bill."

Chapter 6

—Eureka!—

*T*HE GENERAL WANTED to welcome foreign Heads of State to his official residence - *The Supreme White House*. His first Christmas invite went to the British Prime Minister, but his gesture was seen as abhorrence in London. MPs were debating that Kaiser wanted them to follow his lead. There were ugly scenes at the House of Commons before stewards and the police were called in to remove MPs. Leading the uproar, the Prime Minister assured everybody that he wouldn't give in to economic strife, and he blatantly refused the visit. Then Kaiser invited the French President, but the Frenchman feared a new republic on the cards. Also, newspapers were making their own headlines like *Democratie est non tyrannie!* Other words, tyranny plays a bad image, after both the German Kaiser and Furher were trying to destroy theirs. Henceforth, France refused. After the bitter chill and snowfall in January, the French behaved less defensive against General Kaiser. They saw a man with an open and gentle charisma. France observed him attending meetings with American banks for better customer protection. They also noticed him visiting workplaces, and he had an interest in the welfare in the workforce. As the General could be described as the *man of the people*, the French admired him. He was a phenomenon similar to General de Gaulle. Therefore, the President of France accepted his second invitation to Washington, amongst them, the British felt obliged to accept. Kaiser was now able to stand side-by-side with world leaders — unfortunately, for him, in America, he had a stigma of being depicted as Ming the Merciless.

General Kaiser was busy, in the Oval Office, after meeting up with the two leaders. The room had been refurbished since the Presidential Seal was removed for Supremacy: the lion took the place on the marble floor than the eagle. He kept the furniture being the oak desk and red cushion-seated chairs with golden arm-rests. Kaiser imagined a special treat beyond the double doors, pass the exit onto the long corridor, which led to his great bartender. Basically, he still acquired a taste for Mint Julep. Kaiser used his intercom to order his drink.

As he sat on one of his empty chairs, he took a sip from his glass. Also, began checking his pager when he came across Leo's. Leo's might seem trivial in Washington, but it gave him an idea to improve on his public standing. He just thought of an US President that took the odd-chance of pioneering Stars Wars, so why shouldn't he send a man to Mars. Bill decided to read Leo's message and it asked about the nature of the Supreme Revolution. The man couldn't keep his emotions in check, as he was convincing himself, to launch mankind to Mars.

"You're a sight for sore eyes!"

The General decided, there and then, to see his old friend again. Kaiser replied back wishing to see him, and his wife at the Supreme White House in the foreseeable future. On his mind, Leo and Carly were invited to dinner.

Restless Bill was on the move by exiting his office. In the reception area, he spotted his Press Secretary.

"Mike, could you be kind to get Harry back here. He only left a few moments ago."

"I'll get on it."

***

Harry headed towards the helicopter pad at the back of the Supreme White House. Once he boarded, one of the pilots approached him. "We got the Press Secretary on the line."

"What the hell does he want?"

"Something to do with General Kaiser."

Harry moved forward to take the call. "Hello?"

"Hi there, are you airborne?"

"No."

"Don't suppose you could return back inside."

33

"Is this really the Press Secretary?"

"Yes, it's me, Mike. General Kaiser wants to have a quick chat."

"I'll be right back," he said and hung up.

He then ordered his pilot to stay put before making his exit. It was a long walk moving up the sloped lawn, which was tiresome. He wondered on the significance of seeing him face-to-face as he got closer.

Once Harry was directed to the Oval Office, he saw Kaiser smiling behind his desk. "What's the matter?"

"It's to do with you. I want you to arrange a party."

Harry took a seat at his desk. "You called me in here for that?"

"You know from the start that I've a problem with my persona."

"You mean about Ming, right?"

"You spoke about engaging with Hollywood. Well, how about engaging with NASA."

Harry gave it some thought. "So you're thinking of sending a rocket to the moon?"

"I got something much better than the moon. It's Mars."

Harry stalled a moment. "If feasible," he replied, "it might just do the trick. So how did you come to that?"

"It's Leo! He kind of gave me a rush of inspiration."

"Who?"

"He's a dear friend of mine during my time at an airbase in Turkey. Look, since it was your idea that I should improve public relations, I thought to give you the honours on arranging a banquet here."

"You want this banquet with NASA?"

"Well sort of, but I want to surprise Leo that we'll be investing in Florida. The funny thing is that he works on those telescopes looking straight at Mars. He sent me a text which triggered it."

Harry laughed. "That's divine intervention. I suppose we could roll out a red carpet for him too."

"He's my answer to my prayers, but let's just keep this information between ourselves."

"So we're having a special banquet, and I guess you want me to invite Leo?"

"...And his wife!"

"Consider it done." Harry said, shook his hand and left.

Harry Trump was the Adjutant-General for the *Supreme Commander* - General Kaiser. Before his promotion, he was the Lieutenant-General. He was raised in New York and belonged to an Estonian Jewish linage. His great grandfather Vadim Kask, immigrated to America, and changed his surname to Trump to adapt to his new way of life. As a young boy, Harry Trump was known as *Two-Face* because he had the knack of getting his friends out of trouble with his other friends. Little Harry also gave his sincere attention, in the classroom, than most boys of his age, and gradually, he attended Harvard University to study Economics. After he gained his first-class honorary degree, he enlisted with the US Army to become a commissioned officer at Fort Drum, and it was a gigantic military base in New York: It was the home of over 10,000 soldiers.

Chapter 7

—Space programme—

*I*T WAS JUNE 1994. Leo, along with his wife, was invited to attend a banquet at the Supreme White House. He wore a black tuxedo and Carly was wearing her velvet puffy frock. She was also wearing her mother's old pearl necklace, which made her feel like a million dollars.

It was officially a fundraiser event for a Children's Space Academy. There were Wall Street investors, Supreme Judges, senior government officials and Generals mingling altogether.

Leo and his wife stood by a table which had a servant offering them punch. It tasted bland and they thought to hunt down another serving champagne.

General Kaiser made his approach and extended his arm. "It's nice to see you, Leo. It's good of you to turn up."

"Thank you," Leo said, shook his hand and kept a straight face, "I thank you for having me."

"Would you believe that I got some good news?"

Leo got a little weary – of his good news antics. "Are you now offering me a position in the Space Academy?"

"No but I hope you're prepared to hear me out."

"Go on."

He said, "Harry is my Adjutant-General. He has been snooping around and noticed that your Space Observatory might be facing closure. As you know, we were strapped for cash but the economy is picking up. As you can see here, we're raising awareness to prevent closure of a school." Kaiser placed a hand on Leo's shoulder. "Let me cut to the chase," he continued, "for NASA will be prepared to invest further into your Space Observatory."

Leo's countenance was constant. "That's fantastic."

"You don't seem jolly about it, right?"

"Well, it was kind of daunting moving here. First I experienced a car-jacking. Afterwards, I was told that the Observatory doesn't have a long-term future – mainly lack of student enrolment and funds. This may sound funny, but we've been doing an awareness campaign, and a bit of fund-raising to ensure our future for a further 12 months. God! It has been painful. However, I'm happy to hear that NASA will be investing a lot of interest in us."

"I never said it was going to be easy."

Leo sighed. "I shouldn't be selfish. But NASA to really show interest in us will improve our profile a lot more. The staff at work will find great comfort in it."

"You must be hurting? But NASA sees potential of probing the Mars planet for water. Basically, they're preparing for *Operation Scarlet*, and we need your telescope to chart the surface. As you may not have already gathered, the Space Agency will be securing your future for the next decade."

"Of course," Leo responded, "the students and staff will be most definitely happy."

***

Leo's science team were to devise a planetary chart. The project was enormous, tedious and tiresome to electronically collect and integrate the telescopic images for NASA. The Astronomers knew they had a boring task of collecting spatial data, double check it - even treble-check sometimes. Such boredom could deteriorate anyone's role at work, but those employees loved understanding the heavens. The new project allowed Leo to manage his own team as the Senior Surveyor.

Miraculously, *NASA* was full of surprises in the design of the new space shuttle. They were following-up on ideas that six astronauts should sit in the cockpit, and they were to use the state-of-the-art fuel engine. The engine consisted of two X-ray machines that faced one another to emit waves, which caused resonance. Via the amplified wave, it caused an ignition in an anti-matter to dissipate new and powerful energy. Therefore, pushing the envelope on alternative fuel, and the engine was called *Prima Donna*. Additionally, the craft contained twin jet-rocket engines, which enabled the craft to perform VTOLs and CTOLs (Vertical Take-Off and Landing & Conventional Take-Off and Landing). They also refined their understanding on Einstein's theory of relativity: The ship could journey along, the sun's and other stars', spatial tension causing artificial gravity along its hull. NASA set a launch date, in advance, of nine years because the space shuttle won't be fully operational. Also, the elegant ship was to take up the name as *Orion*. Her fuselage could easily carry a hundred people, which had plenty of space along its three decks. The top deck was the cockpit, and ultra-speed flights had to be done by three astronauts at the helm. Astronaut A had the tasks of designating paths, monitor the fuel engine, and the life support system. There were Astronauts B & C piloting the ship too. The deck below was to be the living quarters, and each crew member was able to sleep, eat and rest there. At its rear, a gym and a sanitation-room. The lower deck contained spacesuits and vehicles to cover the Mars surface. In addition, lots of space for food storage, life support and a battery generator. The wings of the fuselage took up a triangular shape for lift and speed. According to NASA experts, Orion could commence launch at 50,000 feet above sea level. Henceforth, it was going to have many unique features.

Chapter 8
—The shortlist—

*E*IGHT YEARS HAD passed by, and it was December. General Kaiser had a handicap by not drafting a team to Mars. He had even gone to meetings, with the NASA Advisory Panel, on the issue. General Kaiser wanted a celebrity to venture into the space programme. He went further that the space exploration couldn't go on without Leo Rockford. However, the Advisory Panel recommended the 45th Space Wing to only take up the mission, and they wanted Capt. Martin MacCormick in command. Also, they believed that the top pilot should only decide on who he wanted in his team. They were unanimous that Capt. Martin MacCormick would take the position as the Orion Commander. Also, they agreed that Capt. MacCormick should draft his own crew, but he had to bring forward his shortlist to Kaiser. Nevertheless, the General demanded a celebrity, along with Leo, into the mix – it was his hope that Americans would be inspired to believe he was fair and just.

Before such a team was drafted, Leo had moved into a five-bedroom house. It had a long drive with palm trees planted at either sides of it. He had a narrow garden and along the front of the house was a veranda with many hung baskets of flowers. The house was painted in brilliant white throughout. Leo was alone in his armchair watching a wrestling match when his telephone began ringing. He had been drinking several cans of beer and felt lucky that the phone wasn't far away. He leant forward. "This is Rockford's residence."

"Is that Leo Rockford?" A strange voice asked.

"Yeah."

"It's Harry Trump, Adjutant-General of the Supreme Council."

"Who?" Leo asked rudely before it sunk in, "I'm sorry, Harry. I was just watching Booker-T on the television."

"Please I do understand. I wanted to catch up with you, for General Kaiser wishes to see you within the next seven days," Harry acknowledged. "You know what? I call you when you're—"

"Please don't," Leo reacted as he was straightening up in his chair, "I can take leave from work next week Monday."

"That will be great, Leo. I'll charter you a nine o'clock plane at the Orlando airport with overnight stay. Also, you'll be picked up from your house around 8am."

***

The following Monday, Leo got himself ready to board a plane on the runway. He froze when he saw the Adjutant-General sitting and waiting for him inside.

"Hi there, I thought you would like some company."

"Goodness me," Leo responded, "you really do want me on this plane, don't you?"

"Enjoy the comfort."

Indeed, the interior of the plane reminded Leo a little bit of his television lounge as it was spacious, air conditioned, a television set and it had recliner leather chairs. Leo thought it was best to sit opposite Harry. "This is great," he said, "you didn't have to ascertain yourself, that I'll see Bill."

"You're a very important person today, here fancy some morning scotch?"

"Why not, indeed. You usually see me at the Observatory every once in a while."

"True but this is a lot more different than your updates."

Leo accepted his drink. He thought to himself of his importance, while they flew to the Capital.

***

At the Supreme White House, Leo entered part of the building known as the Blue Room. Kaiser greeted and congratulated him on his efforts. He also offered him a seat across his desk. Leo accepted and looked around — room wasn't blue. It was very large and it seemed ideal to host summits. There were many chairs along the walls with huge hung oil paintings of former Presidents. Right in the middle of the hall was the General's desk and an Atlas sculpture close by.

The General said, "I couldn't help believing the great abilities of Robinson Space Observatory in providing necessary data for *NASA*."

"Thank you, Bill."

"You see. You would do us proud if you joined the space crew on the Mars mission."

Leo had circumspection of finding heaven – he had found hell instead. He had thought it was congenial of having a great future just before his car got stolen, followed by his job insecurity and his son's school bullies. Furthermore, the Observatory had a number of setbacks before completing the map, and now Kaiser wanted him to join a space crew, which could take months and it seemed dangerous. "It's great that you've been considering me for that position, but I do have a family to consider."

"Don't talk crap! If we were at war with the Soviets, do you expect your superiors to understand that?"

Leo was slightly taken back by his military drill. "You do too much for me Bill."

"Nonsense! It's you that hasn't done much for us! I want to see you on the launch to Mars, as you'll be one of the most important figures in American history."

Leo wasn't sure how to react to Kaiser's strong request, but noted that the launch was less than eleven months away. He might be able to prevent his name being drafted in, yet, he couldn't be certain on how to go about it.

Whilst Leo tried to diminish his Mars prospect, Bill walked a short distance to his wooden figurine of the Atlas. From there, he fixed himself a stiff drink of bourbon whiskey. "I think I want to make you some kind of ship commander as you held a senior pilot rank once. I'll need to discuss this further with the NASA Advisory Panel, but Capt. MacCormick is likely to become the ship's Commander. How does Assistant Commander sound?"

Leo nodded slightly – but he was shaking his head as well.

Bill said, "You're aware that the launch isn't until September. However, as part of the crew, you're to receive immediate and extensive training, isn't it?"

"Sure I do, Bill, but why me? What's so great about me? I ain't American, although, I'm British."

Bill sipped into his drink before taking a seat. "That's simple," he said, "you've an interesting background. You began your new job here at the start of the Supreme Revolution." He began running his pinky finger along the rim of his glass. "You're a symbol of what's good about America. You may not be American born but I want to prove to my critics that we aren't in the game to play narrow-minded politics. This will drive democratic countries even closer to the Supreme constitution, so you got to do this for me."

"Say Bill, as your friend," Leo wondered, "I never had the chance to ask you about your relationship with the Supreme Judges, is it closer than ours?"

Bill looked at him and began to imagine Leo having a snare behind his question. "What are you driving at? Are you suspecting something? That I'm really Ming who was cooking a scheme through the mass media, the stock market, the job losses and what about the crazy idea of a gentleman's club having dark powers?"

"I've known you since Turkey and we had sworn an oath on military secrecy. We aren't known to reveal secrets, are we? So tell me, how did you do it?"

Kaiser sarcastically asked, "Are you now working for British Intelligence? Look here, I do not have time for your little games."

"Bill, if you could oust the President with the Court's injunction, then what makes you think that some disillusioned American couldn't do the same to you?"

"Do the same?..I see...So you the type that wants me to believe in paranoia."

"I'm the type that wants you to keep an open mind."

"Do you know what you're saying? It's about national security and you aren't my Adjutant-General to advise me of some plot to get rid of me."

"True," Leo responded, "but as a friend, I want you to be frank."

Bill chuckled a little. "Frank! Listen up, all you got to worry about is that the Supreme Judges—"

"That's the problem! Supreme Judges gave you an order to control this country."

The General took his time to re-evaluate him and moved away from his desk. Again he filled his glass before he sat down again. "Come on! It's just politics."

"Bollocks, Bill! How did you do it?"

"Well, if you must know, I had a golf game with some Supreme Judges at Andrews. It was there that evening when we decided that America was facing a very serious economic meltdown."

"So you're admitting that the conspiracy theory is true," Rockford said smiling – he thought of him as Ming.

"Suppose I am but it isn't what you think."

"You were playing a game with executive members at a golf course; which neither I nor the general public have access to."

Bill asked softly, "Do you want me to support the Robinson Space Observatory?"

"I just want the truth?" Leo asked.

"You want to claim the truth on the Supreme Revolution," Bill replied, "then you're entering a dangerous territory about the security of this nation. It's a classified matter."

"Top secret like the stealth fighter in Turkey?" Leo exclaimed sarcastically.

Bill noted that his old friend didn't ask for a drink; the man in front hadn't the will to drink with him. It seemed likely, to him, that he might walk out of his office, and abandon everything he fought for.

"Great!" Leo pressed on, "please forgive me, for I've enjoyed the rollercoaster ride in America. However, I'm still prepared to return to Britain and ask for my job back with the RAF. While I'm doing that, please enjoy your well-earned status as the Supreme Judges' elected leader."

Leo got upon his feet to face the exit, but Bill quickly held him back on his left shoulder.

"Look," the General said, "I mean every word that you'll be entering dangerous territory, and you'll be a traitor if you decide to breach the security of this great nation. Listen, this isn't the room to hold such discussions, and I would feel more relaxed if you were a member at the Andrews Clubhouse."

Leo turned around to acknowledge Bill. "I expect Harry will be making preparations for my membership."

"And I'll be expecting you to follow orders."

***

The following morning, Leo stirred from his bed. He heard the noise of water dripping ahead. However, the Adjutant-General was paying him a visit. Leo stopped the night in one of the many guest-rooms. The room itself was large and it didn't seem to have much furniture. Harry raised his concerns that he signed papers on the Trainee Astronaut and Pilot training course, along with his application to join the Andrews Clubhouse. Once completed, he jokingly informed him that he had better pass his NASA training on time. Then Harry advised him of authorising Leo's temporary leave from the Space Observatory. He went further still to advise that a helicopter was ready to pick him up for Orlando.

When Leo was alone in the room again, he had to reflect back to see if he was taking the right course of action: He noticed his morning happening too fast and was certain that Harry had coerced him – to sign the papers while half-asleep. Nonetheless, if Leo was to refuse signing them, it would only lead to further complications. After all, he had to return a favour, or lose his NASA contracts: The Space Observatory and even his small Public Relations Agency.

***

Shortly afterwards, it was broadcasted that a NASA official had misplaced his briefcase on a train, which contained Martin MacCormick's shortlist. The rumour prompted Kaiser to publicly announce his own, and Leo

Rockford was the new Commander of the Orion. (Hog's Head was behind the security lapse to recommend Leo. Furthermore, his application to join Andrews was accepted too)

Chapter 9
—Lift-off—

*T*HE REVOLUTIONARY SPACE shuttle was newsworthy. General Kaiser could easily close his eyes, thinking on the craft's design inside-out. He was mesmerized by it, and had already requested it to take-off at Orlando International Airport.

The astronauts had stayed at the Kennedy Space Centre the night before. Early in the morning, started their day by freshening-up; having breakfast and to fit into their space suits. En route, the crew was to arrive at the airport by minibus. Photographers were waiting outside to get the best shots of them. Plus, numerous broadcasters were on stand-by too, spectators were gathering outside, and the police was monitoring the situation. After their transport found a place to park, the astronauts climbed out, and revealed their wear being all red.

They were waving continuously into the crowd, and felt like rock-stars in ruby-encrusted embroidery.

"Hey space cadets!" a peculiar voice said as the crew headed towards the terminal. "You got to fix the air-conditioner!"

Leo heard the rude awakening and stopped to look along the direction of the outburst. He saw a male news reporter holding a microphone, but Leo vindicated the man. He looked further ahead of the journalist; he saw airport maintenance staff wearing jumpsuits that were identically red, and they were laughing and saluting him. The immediate vicinity turned into a thunderous roar, which left the other astronauts wondering on the amusement behind them.

Security was upbeat throughout the airport. An important figure was standing nearby a terminal bay: The Supreme Commander, General Kaiser. He stood firm and tall with the sheer purpose of greeting them. It was to be a military precision as the crew would meet at 10 am sharp.

Leo saw the General standing in complete attention, and their families were waving and smiling.

"General Kaiser," Leo uttered to Bill, "hope we haven't kept you waiting."

The General shrugged off his concern. "Not at all," he clasped Leo's hand, "I've just dashed back here from my coffee break." Then he faced the others to shake theirs.

The General gathered Rockford and MacCormick together. "I'll be expecting you back here safe and sound."

"We for one, will hope so." Rockford and MacCormick said simultaneously.

Kaiser, his Adjutant-General and the space crew stood motionlessly for a photo session. There were questions firing at the line-up if Martin was happy to go to Mars. They even asked Leo on his career change.

The General turned to face the space crew. He said, "Good luck."

By his good riddance, the crew gave their farewells to General Kaiser, their families, and the spectators. Amusingly, Leo's American born daughter, Alicia, decided that her father couldn't do with being cold in space, and she presented him her gift of a hot water bottle. Leo kindly accepted her gift and the astronauts entered onto the dock bay, through its arm extension, that led them into the ship itself, Orion. Commander Rockford took the honour to seal the hatch door, and led his crew to the cockpit on the upper deck: Alpha Control.

All commercial flights were grounded, which would give Orion free-reign to launch into ultra-speed. Commander Rockford wasn't instructed to follow a flight path, get a weather report, nor permission to take off by air traffic control. The only orders he ought to obey would be from Kennedy Space Centre. They had the responsibility to keep regular contact with the Orion during her exploration. Also, the Centre was to monitor the integrity of the ship against possible space anomalies.

In the cockpit, the crew was completely suited-up. Commander Rockford moved up to the front to take his position. "Kennedy Space Centre," Leo said, through his installed mouthpiece, "this is Commander Rockford reporting in for duty. We're good to go."

"This is the Kennedy Space Centre. We hear you loud and clear. We'll advise you to take your time to familiarize with the eagle. I'll repeat, we recommend before you perform take-off to familiarize with the controls."

"Copy Kennedy, all systems are go," Leo mentioned to waive his advice, "we're to take-off immediately and commence the launch at 50,000 feet."

The Orion began to roll out along the runway to pick-up speed and her nose rose as to ascend into the air. Leo sat at the helm and alongside him, on his right, his Assistant Commander was going to aid him.

A third person was responsible on monitoring the critical stages. That astronaut was Capt. Chris Tallon, a Coordinator. He'd be faced, a small distance, behind Rockford and MacCormick. He was answerable to Leo, but Chris thought of the time when Capt. MacCormick had the gig on running the ship. He knew that Capt. MacCormick had had a successful pace in the air force, and in the Space Wing. Yet, Chris easily sensed him wanting to rip Leo's heart into shreds. The earliest sign was at their Training Facility when Rockford made a request, to MacCormick, to record the first three-days of the Prima Donna readings into a manual logbook. However, Martin MacCormick challenged his authority that he preferred to write to his wife. The difference in their opinions was going to blow into a nasty exchange, but Capt. Tallon intervened to volunteer.

MacCormick asked, "Capt. Tallon, is the Prima Donna on standby?"

"Engine is on standby. We'll be ready on your command."

Leo wished to see that all the members of his crew, were strapped in their seats, before the mid-air launch.

So he helped himself to turn his head and body around to get a good view. Leo raised his thumb to show his support on his reserved staff: Lieutenant Emily Walters, Tasha Chayton and Jay Kaiser. The reserved staff returned Leo's gesture, and they were at the rear end of the cockpit. The Commander turned to face his view-screen, and made himself certain of being strapped up as well.

"This is Commander Rockford to Kennedy Space Centre, do you copy?"

"This is Kennedy. How may we assist you?"

"We'll be commencing the jump-sequence for outer space. Is traffic clear?"

"We report no bogeys in your pathway. You're clear to proceed."

"Capt. Tallon," Leo said, "initiate the Prima Donna."

During mid-air, the new engine was set to perform her remarkable high output as Chris started it.

"It's warming-up," Chris responded.

"Select the pathway for the nearest plasma-line to Mars," Leo said

"Pathway has been selected for the Beta plasma-line," he replied.

"Start the launch sequence," Leo requested.

The Prima Donna engine would replace the jet ones. It was unique as the component sounded like a diva singing la-la-la at a smooth rhythm. Rockford gave his new order and the aircraft took on a magnificent transformation to become a speeding-bullet, and the speedometer was recording a steady velocity of 48,300 kph. Alarmingly, the Prima Donna engine could go a lot faster, yet, NASA's safety protocols weren't to be overlooked.

"This is the Orion," Leo announced to Kennedy, "we've successfully cleared the Ionosphere and we're on schedule of tracing the Beta plasma-line."

"We copy, Orion."

It was a successful launch into space without a glitch. The astronauts were all smiles inside the cockpit, for they were coming to terms that they were the first to test the engine during flight. With their self-congratulations, the Orion continued her pursuit for the sought after plasma-line. Those lines held the secrets why the universe maintained a pull on the planets. So to go along them should cause artificial gravity along their hull.

Seven hours into flight, and the crew was still looking for it. The space shuttle had whisked by the moon at a steady velocity of 48,300 kilometres per hour. Straightaway, the crew realized their own greatest of making a giant leap.

Eventually, Capt. Tallon's control panel was indicating that the Orion was drawing closer to the Beta plasma-line. Suddenly, the astronauts experienced gravity around them. All of the crew sensed a relief that the Orion was on course, and it had completed her successful launch. Also, the shuttle seemed to prove a scientific theory that small atomic fibres of plasma caused the pull throughout the universe.

All formalities on deck was casual as Leo un-strapped himself. "Great," he said, "I'm off to the loo!"

At the rear end of Alpha Control, Jay Kaiser unfastened himself to get onto his feet. "God! I just want to get out of this suit, and chill out in the living-quarters. Besides, what was all that fuss about?"

"What fuss?" Emily asked.

"That this is far better than a commercial aircraft."

She giggled and they could hardly believe their luck of a space shuttle having such luxury.

Chapter 10
—Close company—

*I*T WAS THE ninth hour after the launch and Capt. MacCormick sat alone in Alpha Control. He was in awe of the Orion, slipping inside a plasma-stream, which was leading to Mars. Capt. MacCormick was enjoying to man the Orion – he could have placed her under auto-pilot, or relieve the controls to the Space Centre as well. He gathered his thoughts on how he should have been the Commander. As he pondered on, he had hoped to become the first astronaut to set foot on Mars, and the first to plant the flag of the United Supreme of America. He was still a little bitter of Rockford, but he praised the rigorous recommendation by the Advisory Panel to keep him on the team. He believed that if Kaiser took steps against him, the General risked damaging his relationship with the Space Wing and the Air Force. After which, the American people would speculate that all wasn't well, which would cause resentment against autocracy – so he thought,

He recalled the first time he met Leo Rockford; that he was an attention-seeker whom hadn't any real interest in the welfare of the crew. Martin felt very strongly that the special bond between Kaiser and Rockford had cost him his rightful place.

***

The middle deck was the living quarters. It was known *as Beta Control* and the Supreme American flag was fully spread and decorated against one of the walls in the common room. The flag itself contained horizontal red and white lines, but had a large white star that replaced the fifty others. The ideology behind the new flag was that the *large star* spoke highly of the Supreme Commander, while the *red stripes* meant the number of

Supreme Judges. Furthermore, the *white stripes* were speaking for the senior figures in the military.

The common room was where the astronauts could send electronic mails, hold video-phone conferences with their families and friends. Plus, the crew might eat, drink and relax. At the rear of the deck was a sanitation room. Not so far, an infirmary, a small gym area, a small kitchen and sleeping-quarters.

A non-commissioned astronaut, Jay Kaiser, was in the common-room, which was at the front of Alpha Control. He wanted to discuss about the impact of their Mars mission with Leo. They were both wearing their navy blue overalls. Jay saw a great future to become a film director. "Leo, Flash Gordon is the flagship that gave America the vision of venturing further into space. Just look at this symbolic ship."

"I suppose you could be right but surely it isn't the point, is it?"

"It's huge," Jay said, "the general concept that Flash Gordon did inspire General Kaiser will generate billions of dollars. It has real potential and remakes would be sensational." Jay took a slip of his coffee. "Also," he continued, "imagine a screenplay which the archenemy is further afield. Just think about it because it may send us on a trip to Saturn."

"You appear a little optimistic—"

"Where else in the world can people be a little optimist?" Jay interjected. "I hope that you're considering Kaiser, aren't you?" he asked but continued anyway, "and what of NASA's regards on the universe and space travelling? How about you, are you not optimistic for being the first Briton to venture into deep space?"

"I'm sorry, you're right," Leo said embarrassed. Subsequently, he excused himself to check on Martin MacCormick.

Out of the six astronauts, Jay Kaiser was the most recognisable figure. He was a film actor appearing as Major Tyus in the Flash Gordon franchise. He played a macho character with a popular one-liner: "strike the Martians before they strike us!" In one of his screenplays, his foe, Ming the Merciless, declared a cease-fire for peace. Yet, Major Tyus was certain that Ming was a liar. In the confusion, he faced a court martial as he disobeyed a direct order not to strike an alien humanitarian ship. Just before his court verdict, Flash Gordon had new evidence that the ship was heavily armed for an attack and he got acquitted. Jay Kaiser's character epitomized as an action toy figure, on breakfast cereals, cell phones, children's clothing, video games, in comics and on animation. In his personal life, he had a unique taste of his wife, Kitten Taylor, wearing wild berry flavoured lipstick, and she was an actress too. Besides acting, he loved abstract art and was critically acclaimed in the art world too. Jay requested to NASA to put together paint brushes, oil paints and canvas sheets before the launch. He had an athletic build and stood at five feet and ten inches. His birthplace was San Diego and he was 45, but he looked a lot younger than he foretold people. He had light brown eyes and dark, short and curly brown hair. The mystique and physique of Jay Kaiser allowed Harry Trump to pay him a visit to become an astronaut. Oddly enough, it was a blessing in disguise as Flash Gordon was losing its box office appeal. So Jay Kaiser found hope that Flash Gordon would bounce back. After Kaiser succeeded on the shortlist, he moved away from Hollywood to attend his nine month training course at Cape Canaveral. Whilst there, he took up the pace in free falling, space-walk simulation, first-aid training, map reading, space-boogie driving, agility and mental enhancement. In addition, he took time to enrol as a pilot alongside his Commanders, Capt. Chris Tallon and Lieutenant Emily Walters. Unfortunately, it was becoming impossible for Jay to grasp his pilot training course on time. Nevertheless, he was certain that his presence would be resourceful and exhilarating.

***

Leo arrived in Alpha Control. He saw Capt. MacCormick humming to himself, and was still in his full head and space-gear. Leo took a seat by him. He said slowly and loudly, "Extraordinary!..Being the first!...To land this advanced ship!...On another planet!"

Capt. MacCormick replied, "You're correct and I can hear you fine without shouting, sir."

"No need for formalities."

"I'm sorry, Leo," Martin said and took his helmet off. "I've looked at your career-record; it's very impressive and I'm glad that you're part of this team."

"I agree," replied Martin. "When I was the Commander," he added, "I'd read of yours too."

Leo said, "Of course, Martin, it was out of my hands once Kaiser made his decision to appoint me."

"I agree, Leo," Martin insisted, "if I were on the Supreme Council, I would've done the same, but not in favour of civilian astronauts."

"I've spoken to the General," Leo continued, "he told me that he wished a civilian to pilot this ship. To prove that we do not need a military outfit in doing great wonders for the new constitution."

"I understand," Martin said regretfully.

Tasha Chayton entered. "Does anybody want a hot drink?"

"No thank you. I'm good!" Martin and Leo said simultaneously.

Tasha saw life a little strange when doing her usual work on Earth. Her nostrils had breathed in the pollen of plants. Yet, others she was forced to hold – that horrendous smell used for her study too. Dr. Tasha Chayton was a brilliant Botanist. She was doing journals on how plant life might interact in space. Furthermore, she was a Professor at Yale University with her own botany department. Beforehand, she worked on genetic modification, which led to crops to tolerate growth in hostile terrains. Tasha was 34 years of age with green-hazel eyes, and she had long curly ginger hair. Even more, kept a superb physique, which was through her regular exercises at the university gym. She was married to Quency Chayton, a native Indian-American at the same university. Her husband lectured on American history and he took great pride of his heritage, which he hoped to pass on to his children. Yet, she had a hectic lifestyle of running special errands like lectures, her research papers for NASA and she did write textbooks on her specialty. (Harry Trump didn't approach her for an interview as an astronaut. It happened to be her, through a friend on the NASA Advisory Panel, to put in a good word to the then Commander, Martin MacCormick. She sensed that her application would be successful since General Kaiser had been making his open plea of sending civilians to Mars)

Chapter 11
—Bitter taste—

*T*HE AVERAGE DAILY speed was 64,400 kph. So far, it had been three weeks since the launch from Earth. The crew hoped to arrive on Mars to mark the day of the Supreme Revolution.

Whilst in flight, there was a little scuffle between Leo and Martin about the showers. Both appeared to accuse each other at not cleaning after themselves, but once again, Chris Tallon diffused the situation because he illustrated that Jay Kaiser was the culprit.

During the three weeks in space, Jay had found it hard to continue his artistic work. He lost his cool and tolerance once he realized that he couldn't be close to Kitten Taylor. Apparently, he felt rejected at not seeing his wife for few months. Jay had a further complication as he couldn't understand his temptation for Tasha who regularly sat in Beta Control.

For Tasha, she was fully aware of his advances, but made it pretty clear that he shouldn't gain any ground. Both Tasha and Jay were sitting in Beta Control.

"Tasha," he asked, "how do you and your husband hold it together?"

"Simple Jay, have an active lifestyle," Tasha said bluntly and she might seem rude concentrating on her memoirs; for she was writing of her relationship with all of the members in the crew and the conditions of her plants on the three decks.

"You need to teach me how to be more like you because your husband doesn't know what he's—"

"Please I'm busy," she told him firmly.

Jay was thinking ahead. In the next 48 hours, he knew that a colleague would volunteer on an internet pod-cast. Basically, it allowed Earth the chance of interacting with the astronauts on how they were coping, discuss their personal lives, and what they planned to do in the future. Jay had already done those pod-casts when his interest in Tasha Clayton seemed to blossom. Some of his hardcore fans left messages trying to provoke him to register a desire for her: *she's hot.* He tried ignoring but saw himself tossing and turning in bed. As far as his fantasies were going, if the Orion was stranded in space and they found a habitable planet to live on, it was paradise to be with her. He wanted to believe that it had to be worth the risk of cheating on his wife, and lose his clean image. However, Jay decided to leave her alone.

Tasha found it amusing that a famous star from Hollywood would want to risk losing everything, if she were to kiss and tell. Besides, she didn't see any good reason why she should compromise her long-term relationship with Quency. Furthermore, the way she saw Jay in a parallel universe was one with hormone problems.

Martin MacCormick walked into the common room. He nodded in acknowledgment of Jay leaving. He took a seat and pushed his chair closer to a computer terminal. He spotted Tasha being busy on her memoirs, and thought it was best not to draw her attention. He began writing his email to his wife.

Tasha asked, "Why don't you use that conference video, it's more realistic than writing messages, right?"

Martin turned her way and gave a smile. "That's true but it's midnight."

"God no!" Tasha cried, "I promised to call my hubby earlier! Well, I suppose, he might be still awake."

Martin laughed lightly. "Suppose I could do the same."

Tasha giggled as well and moved a short distance away to make her late night call.

Martin sent his message to his wife. Yet, there it lingered inside him – his hatred. He detested Leo for being in charge. He still reckoned he had more to offer than ten *Leo Rockfords.* Furthermore, all he perceived was a *prick* who had a telescope on a hill, getting sucked up into space. More so, he believed that the British ex-patriot had far too much say on American affairs.

Anyway, his career began at the Edwards Air Force Base before his transfer. Within nine years, he obtained his captaincy. Anytime Martin attended special functions between the Air Force and the Space Wing, his chest was covered in medals, as if, he was the highest ranking officer in the entire fleet. In his eyes, his accomplishments meant that nothing stood in his way, and when he had the Mars assignment, it seemed very likely of a quick promotion to Major. However, his de-selection would only slow his progress. He was certain that Leo was going to be an impediment to earn him further stripes. The way he saw it, if a Major position was available through an early retirement, resignation or sudden death, then his chance to become the successor was overstated. Martin clearly recalled the moment when he and his wife were in their kitchen making dinner, yet all of a sudden, their television set had the Supreme Commander announcing Leo as the Commander – *the son of the bitch*, he thought.

Chapter 12
—The Landing—

*1*3TH OCTOBER WAS the morning when the Orion spotted the red planet, which was drawing closer towards them. It also marked the day when General Kaiser swept into power. Leo Rockford, Martin MacCormick, Chris Tallon, Emily Walters, Jay Kaiser and Tasha Chayton were seated in Alpha Control. They were wearing their spacesuits as the ship continued to get closer. Furthermore, the ship had left its plasma-stream, which meant the crew was experiencing weightlessness.

"This is Commander Rockford," he was saying to Kennedy Space Centre, "we're continuing our advance onto the red planet, and we'll be landing along the crater."

"This is Kennedy Space Centre speaking, and we acknowledge your descent."

The Commander gave his order to MacCormick to enter the Mars' atmosphere. Both Rockford and MacCormick were working together to bring the Orion's nose up, which was to allow the ship to glide along the red planet's atmosphere during descent.

Martin couldn't believe how red Mars was on his approach and it remained red whilst the Orion flew into the airspace. He also noticed different shades of red along the ground. The Assistant Commander had already shared stories of orbiting Earth, that he saw mainly white clouds, green land and blue oceans. He jokingly commented of White being on the move to engulf Earth. Yet, Blue breaks through and pushes the White away, as if, fearing for its own life, and Green then attacks the White for its territory. It was always changing and Martin couldn't determine the dominate colour.

MacCormick said, "Look how red this planet is, Leo."

"Yeah, it's crimson," the Commander replied.

Jay sat next to Tasha at the back. "Think ya gonna find life on this rock because nothing fertile can ever survive here, isn't it right?"

"That's why we are landing near a crater opening, and who knows what we may find."

"Sure thing but our Commander is also an Astronomer, and he told me that he hadn't detected any life here."

"Did he also tell you that those telescopes aren't capable to see underground?"

"No," Jay replied.

"Shows how much Rockford loves you to be our new Supreme Commander," Tasha joked fondly.

Just as she mocked Jay, the Orion switched on her rocket engines and the ship continued her steady descent.

The Orion was drawing closer to the huge crater. Along the edge of it laid a possible cavern site, which meant the Commander was to lead four astronauts to venture into the tunnel and to bring back any samples. There were lots of speculations that an ice lake existed and the expeditionary team would be able to verify it. Also, the party was to plant the new United Supreme of America flag nearby.

"It's the Lord God doing his mysterious work for us to understand our existence," Jay said.

Capt. MacCormick did pick up what Jay mentioned via his headset. He wasn't fully wearing his seat straps and so glanced behind. In doing so, the Commander took his turn to look upon the preacher. Eventually, everybody trained their eyes on Jay Kaiser.

Capt. MacCormick asked, "What are you talking about? And what Scripture are you referring to?"

Jay replied, "Think about it. The Romans were explorers and they were forgiven through the blood of the Lamb. Basically, if we were to see ourselves like them; we'll find Redemption for our sins. Furthermore, our Creator is giving us a message that this universe was accurately designed by him."

Momentarily, Capt. Tallon thought quietly on Jay's belief. "Are you telling me that God made us explorers to better understand ourselves?"

"Of course I am! I just accepted our course of nature, that we're a God send, right?"

Capt. MacCormick turned to the front. Whilst searching for Christ in his heart, MacCormick realized that he hadn't any ground to dismiss his claim. He considered that the Romans were forgiven through Jesus and Jay's remark was consistent with the Bible. He only nodded to himself.

"OK, Jay," Capt. Tallon said, "you know that Mars was once a pagan God of war, and the soldiers did wear a scarlet uniform. Yet Jay, what you're implying is that Christians should lay down the cross and make prayer for this planet as–"

"No silly!" Jay said harshly, "Romans played their part in early Christianity, and if it were not for the Romans, we would not be having this conversation as the early Bible was in fact put together by them."

Tasha was listening. "I thought," she wondered, "the Bible was devised by the Jews?"

"Believe me when I say this," Leo said as he joined in, "what you're saying is being heard back on Earth! So do you really want to start a religious order in space?"

"We do have the churches for that!" Jay said wittingly.

Lieutenant Walters asked, "Come on Jay, why now? Why haven't you directed a movie of your vision of space?"

"For I'm an actor," Jay responded, "I do not command the actors' guild."

Silence filled the air. Leo and Martin were observing their view-screen to lower the ship. Eventually, the Orion found a convenient spot to land upon and it grounded to a halt.

"Orion reporting," Leo was confirming to Earth, "the eagle has landed and we are to venture out onto the surface."

"Copy, Commander Rockford, we are right behind you."

All the astronauts wore headsets when they heard Leo reporting in. They were already advised that after stepping out onto Mars, everything was going to be broadcasted live. They released their seat restraints, and were coming to terms of feeling lighter. Jay Kaiser made the mistake of banging his head on the ceiling after getting up too quickly.

Lieutenant Walter was laughing at Jay's misfortune with the rest to follow. "You must be the first astronaut to hit your head like that!"

Jay said sarcastically, "Chuckle all you want but remember this – I'm a featherweight just like the rest of you."

Tasha said fondly, "Yeah but we weren't the first to be light-headed. So please tell us how you did it?"

"Now listen very careful," Jay said to undermine their humour – but did it poorly, "it was lots of physical training back in Florida."

"Perhaps you've been pumping too much steroids!" the Commander said jokingly.

The party moved for the spiral staircase, which stood outside Alpha-Control and it led to Beta-Control. They all found the walk rather springy as they went down the steps, and their movements appeared to trick them that they were going back up. Jay Kaiser wouldn't be alarmed about his new lightness. Nevertheless, he nearly lost his balance.

Fortunately, Chris gave his support to prevent him tripping down the flight of stairs. "Jay, I hope you don't make a fool of yourself out there, because Earth will be watching you closely."

Jay was slightly embarrassed. "Thanks. NASA never put us through this type of training. You would have expected the experts were aware of the lightness here, and had laid that knowledge on us."

"Come off it," Capt Martin MacCormick reacted, "every time we come out of a plasma-line, haven't you ever noticed weightlessness?"

Jay replied, "If you do mind, my Assistant Commander, do you see things floating around because of weightlessness? I think not."

"Jay, remember this," Leo warned, "Earth is hearing exactly what you are saying. Once we've lowered ourselves upon the Mars surface; our wives, our neighbours and our neighbours' neighbours will be watching and listening to every move that we're going to make."

"It's very true," said a familiar voice from the Kennedy Space Centre. "You're bound to find Hollywood wanting you to star in the remake of Laurel and Hardy."

"Kennedy! Your training sucks!" Jay Kaiser said defiantly.

A short moment later, they arrived on Beta Control and the Commander was still taking lead towards Omega Control. The walk was quiet along the aisle. Most of the electronic equipment in the common room were switched off. The only sound that the astronauts could hear was a kitchen fridge further ahead.

Suddenly, an incident occurred along the middle deck that a light bulb fizzled out. Lieutenant Emily Walters spotted it from the corner of her eye, whilst everybody else was in oblivion. She made nothing of it and pressed on to follow the party. She was a shuttle pilot with a lot of flight experience. Her parents lived in Washington, and had supported her to go to New York University to read her degree in Air Traffic Management. She then took the decision to join the Air Force and then the Space Wing. Within seven years, she raised to the rank of Lieutenant to fly rocket planes before she took to flying shuttles. As a woman, she made sound achievements in the NASA space programme. As an astronaut, she worked on upgrading reconnaissance satellites. It was in the Air Force where she met her husband. Like Tasha, she had no children due to her lifestyle. She had short blond hair in a bob along with light blue eyes, and Emily kept her figure slim.

The astronauts moved along Beta Control to pass through their sleeping quarters. They walked on without an incident and continued walking pass the kitchen. Still the crew moved on steadily until they saw the air chamber to enter Omega Control.

Assistant Commander MacCormick spoke to his Commander when making partial sight of it. "Commander Rockford."

"What is it, Martin?"

"Who do you want in the two space vehicles?"

The six astronauts did have a quiet walk along Beta Control, and Rockford noted that he hadn't made his decision of who should be in whose vehicle. He paused slightly to think. "I'll have Tasha and Emily and you may have Jay."

Rockford continued to move towards the air chamber. He proceeded to open the hatch door, made his entrance, and then the astronauts put on each other's life reserves.

"Do you know how annoyed I am with the internal design of this ship?" Jay said whilst he was putting on Emily's.

"You mean that you have to go through this chamber procedure to bring a heap of food from the freezer vault."

"That's exactly the point! Why didn't they move that chamber door away from the main freezer?"

"That's because," Capt MacCormick replied, "it will compromise the design of the hull. You see, if there's a serious breach on the lower deck, at least we have the middle and the upper levels with sufficient supply of oxygen."

"What about the food, man?" Jay answered back. "What're we to live on?"

Leo reacted, "This ship has been tested for hull breaches way before we took this mission on. Also Jay, this ship has been developed over the last nine years with the best minds in space engineering. So believe me that the likelihood of a breach is close to zero-to-none."

"All those health and safety protocols for an air-tight ship isn't my vote of confidence."

Tasha replied, "Surely to work in Hollywood, you've health and safety procedures right?" She said, after he nodded, "You give Hollywood your vote of confidence but not this space programme. Jay, you're a hypocrite."

Nobody dared to continue that conversation about the design of the ship, and Leo closed the hatch door behind him. He saw a set of buttons and he extended an arm to press for the ground level. The chamber depressurized as to deplete the oxygen to match the air quality outside of the ship. Soon enough, Leo pressed a different button and the vents in Omega Control would suck any oxygen from the lower deck too, and the atmospheric pressure should balance with Mars.

Leo began to open another hatch door that led to a spiral staircase. He carried on leading his team: Martin MacCormick; Tasha Chayton; Emily Walters; Jay Kaiser and Chris Tallon until they were all facing two space vehicles.

Chris Tallon wouldn't be taking part on the Mars surface. Nonetheless, he was to operate at a terminal to lower the space vehicles, communicate with the expeditionary party and to monitor their life signs. Since he was staying behind, Chris would be routing their signals to Earth by Orion's extractable deflector dish. To take on his background, he was raised in Des Moines, Iowa. His father was from Edinburgh when he arrived to work on a hydraulic contract. He took on a joy for adventure in London, Tokyo and Cairo before he married his mother. Chris earned his college degree in Civil Engineering to be just like his father. However, he felt incomplete for real adventure; he signed-up for the US Air Force to become a commissioned officer. He did find adventure as he worked in the reconnaissance branch, and he took on secret missions around the Middle East, North Korea and countries that resented the new American constitution. Chris had been in the force for over eighteen years and joined the Space-Wing by Adjutant-General Trump.

At the front of Omega-Control, there stood the huge freezer. Jay believed to reiterate his concern. "Can you imagined that the all-powerful NASA could have been dumb by placing the showers in here, isn't it? What is health and safety if you have to wear your space suits to the shower cubicles?"

Leo, Martin, Chris and Tasha remained silent.

Lieutenant Walters replied, "Jay, we know that you are important to join us because you can obey orders. So let it be."

While Jay was trying to understand Emily's high regards, Leo headed towards the nearest electronic vehicle and he beckoned Tasha and Emily to hop on board. Jay took the initiative to sit in the driver's seat of the other one.

Martin approached him. "Are you," he said, "the chauffeur because what do you think you're doing?"

"Sir, I'm waiting for you," he answered and cleared some dust on the steering wheel. "Don't worry for I've been trained for this."

Martin thought about the impact of allowing the Hollywood celebrity his reins. He had already brunt his humiliation by a de-selection. Furthermore, he was starting to believe that Jay would cause more harm on his career. Nevertheless, he kept a cool head. "It's a Commander's vehicle and I will drive it, Jay."

Jay understood his rank and moved across to the passenger's seat. Martin sat at the helm and started the engine.

Leo was the first to drive his space buggy onto the elevator platform. He turned on the vehicles front and back view video cameras. Also, he put on the headlights for the unknown. He reported to the Space Centre. "This is Commander Rockford. You've my permission to allow our communiqué as a public live feed."

"Thank you Commander Rockford, all communications are in the public domain, until your return to the air chamber."

They all knew that whatever they were to say, the public would be the first to know. It also meant that they had to address each other in a formal manner under NASA's guidelines.

Commander Rockford used his headset to address Earth: "This is Commander Rockford of the Orion. It's a great honour to serve a country, which believes in putting the people first. Within minutes, we'll be descending onto the Mars surface as in commemoration for the United Supreme of America and her allies." Leo turned his head to one side to face Chris Tallon. "Lower the platform," he pleaded.

"Affirmative, Commander Rockford."

Commander Rockford, Lieutenant Walters and Mrs. Tasha Chayton were in complete awe at what they could see. All across the opened horizon, it looked to be a red day. They could see red rocks, a lot of red dust particles that were blowing in the wind and its red skyline.

"God, it's beautiful!" Lieutenant Walters said.

The Commander and Mrs. Chayton remained speechless as the platform continued its descent. After it came to a halt, the Commander drove the vehicle off and ordered Capt. Tallon to raise it. The platform started its ascent to collect the second vehicle above.

Suddenly, the astronauts were able to hear a familiar voice from Earth. "This is General Kaiser of the United Supreme of America. We for one believe it's a great honour to hear how beautiful it is on Mars. I would like to send my congratulations on your expedition."

"This is the Commander of the Orion, Leo Rockford, we as a crew wish to thank you, for proving that space is within our reach."

After his gratitude, he could hear a tremendous round of applause from the Space Centre. Leo took a little walk under the Orion before it faded away. He couldn't believe he was really on Mars. The vicinity seemed too peaceful; nothing else was stirring in the breeze. The second vehicle emerged from the ship and Capt. MacCormick drove off to join his Commander – who was on foot, obviously.

Capt. MacCormick made his request for the platform to be raised. Henceforth, the five astronauts were to be completely alone and shut off to gain any immediate access onto the Orion.

"Alright, team. I'll be your shoulder-angel advising you of your vital life signs." Chris said – of course, he was on the Orion.

"OK," the astronauts replied.

The Commander proceeded towards his vehicle with his two passengers. Martin was close behind. The track ahead had many loose red rocks making the ride bumpy as they got closer towards the huge crater. The Commander thought it was best to stop two hundred metres short from the entrance to look closely at the terrain.

"What a beauty," Leo said as he jumped out of the vehicle, "I've never in my entire life seen such a remarkable landscape."

Lieutenant Walters agreed, "It's so beautiful."

"It's surely something." Mrs. Chayton also agreed and took out a photography camera from the glove compartment. She jumped out of the boogie to capture some images.

The Assistant Commander stopped nearby. Both he and Mr. Kaiser climbed out of their transport to look on at the wonder.

"Man, what has been here before us?" Mr. Kaiser asked.

"I believe a meteorite had been here," the Commander replied.

Tasha continued taking her snap shots and Jay moved beside her at the top of the crater drop. The crater itself appeared to have a diameter of 25km, and it was dangerous to explore the drop below. Nonetheless, along the top-side of the crater laid a mountain, which the five-man-team was to explore its tunnel. The astronauts knew that NASA had a strong belief, for some time now, that Mars contained large pockets of water underground. Tasha only hoped to bring back some samples to study the possibility of life on Mars. Frankly, the Mars surface was a red planetary desert. Still, it was believed an underground oasis would be found. One of the main tasks would be to plant the new American flag. The latter being the tunnel. Afterwards, they were to return to the Orion, and the astronauts had no more than three hours before their oxygen depleted.

Momentarily, they were admiring the wonders along the edge of the crater. Tasha, Emily and Jay took snapshots of the horizon around them. Because of their inbuilt helmet cameras, they were able to transmit their images back to the Orion. From the shuttle, its powerful defector dish was to transmit across to Earth.

The Commander then gave new orders to move out. They also got a reminder from Chris to check their life-signs, which everybody did by their forearm-panel.

Once they were closer to the entrance, the astronauts jumped out of their transports, and the Assistant Commander received the honour of planting the flag. Martin MacCormick was to give a formal address for his nation and the world: "To the United Supreme of America, the world and my fellow crew. It's an honour to serve my country in space, and we all agree that this mission is a huge technological advancement in aeronautics. I plant this flag with the Commander's blessing to celebrate our Supreme Council: It's our tenth anniversary and may God save General Kaiser."

The astronauts could hear many claps and cheers through their headsets. Needless to say, the applauses came from the Space Centre.

"As an American," Jay announced as he was finding the courage within himself, "this experience is like none other I've ever taken before. I too will honour the courageous NASA team in their development of a key spaceship, and it's an honour to be an Astronaut and an American."

"Yes," Leo agreed, "it's true that I am a Briton and I came to America to fulfil my dream to discover the stars. So being here is like an icing on a cake and I honour General Kaiser in supporting an international effort."

Tasha cleared her throat. "As a woman," she said, "whose dream it is to find life on Mars. It's an honour to serve with the Orion as we have a great crew to honour this day."

Lastly, Lieutenant Walters gave her thanks to the Supreme Council and she praised the revolution.

Afterwards, Chris – their shoulder-angel – advised them to check their individual readings. It became apparent to Leo that they had approximately an hour of oxygen before turning about. Without further delay, they pressed a button on their forearm-panels to switch on their helmet torches. Tasha returned to her vehicle to reach for a metal case, which she would use for excavation and Jay did too.

Leo said, "Right, we're to enter into this tunnel in single file and I'll lead the way."

In the darkness, the tunnel hadn't a predictable path as it swayed from either side. They were moving to the right from the entrance, then it might go left. Even though, it was going downwards. Inside, it just led deeper and deeper under the Mars surface and as they flashed around, the rock face wall was reddish. Everybody was quiet as Commander Rockford continued to take point. As the team pressed on, they picked up a sound, it lingered in the air but faded, yet, a new gushing sound dominated its presence. They moved on in the tunnel and they knew that it was getting louder.

Chris reported, "Please may you check your level of oxygen?"

They acknowledged Chris. It still checked out fine and they went further down. As they pressed on, they had forty minutes remaining, and Leo had a long face that the tunnel wouldn't expose him to an opening. Nevertheless, they ventured into the unknown towards the sound of the echo.

The Commander noticed that the tunnel was becoming less steep and it brought him new hope. He continued to move forward to enter into a cavern. The astronaut looked left then to his right and saw that the dark room had a circular shape with a diameter of 20 metres.

The Assistant Commander was behind him and ventured into the room. He looked to his left while the Commander tried to glance above.

The Commander was looking up to determine the high ceiling but he couldn't. His helmet torch was at full beam but it wasn't enough to penetrate the darkness above him. The gushing sound was coming from the centre of the cavern and the Assistant Commander became curious. He moved on, but noticed Leo was waiting for the other astronauts to follow into the room. Martin saw that the ground surface was completely smooth and the further he approached, the more the ground surface mould upwards at its centre. The Assistant Commander proceeded to move even closer and saw what was making the noise. Ahead of him was a water spring, which had red and white reflections of his flashing white torch and the red walls of the cavern.

History was in the making: Assistant Commander Martin MacCormick discovered a water reservoir on Mars–

"Commander Rockford!" Martin shouted and was very congenial, "I've found a water spring."

"That's great news!" Mrs. Tasha Chayton said and was excited too, that life might have existed on Mars. One by one, they all made their entrance into the circular room. They all noticed the high ceiling and heard the water gushing within the cavern. Some of the astronauts tried in vain to determine any formation of stalactites but there wasn't any clear visibility.

"There's something peculiar about this spring water, Leo!" Martin reported and he wasn't paying attention to NASA's advice on addressing one another formally.

Leo was surprised by his conduct. *No matter*, he thought, *I'm sure to do this properly.* "Assistant Commander," he said, "this is Commander Rockford and what's the problem?"

"This looks like a manmade fountain."

Mr. Jay Kaiser started to venture towards the centre of the room, as the Assistant Commander continued his observation.

"What the fuck!" he swore.

Since two astronauts were breaking NASA broadcast-protocols, the others moved towards them to the centre of the room. As they all looked on, there was a circular rocky rim on the mould. More so, the rim had an unusual pattern of lines and curves along it; the appearance looked like some form of writing.

"So it looks like the water," Leo responded, "has been smoothing the ground."

Jay said, "Looks like some ritual writing."

Tasha disagreed, "Just because there's a straight line here and a curve line there doesn't mean it's a sign from God, nor can it be alien graffiti from Flash Gordon!"

"I agree with Tasha," supported Commander Rockford, "unless you are implying that Neil Armstrong was here before us."

They all laughed at one another. How silly they were of having an imagination that the lines and curves had to be a form of communication. Even though, those lines had fine deep cuts along the mouth, which no one was able to understand?

"Perhaps we should come back here," Tasha suggested to Leo, "to fully investigate this cavern in the near future. I'm pretty sure that the spring wall is a wonderful work of nature."

"Check your suits," Chris reported, "as I recommend return to Orion within the next twenty-five minutes."

"Thank you, Orion," Leo acknowledged and sought the attention of his crew, "OK. We must gather has much samples as possible as we're to return back."

Tasha opened her metal case and pulled out a flask to collect the water. The other astronauts looked around for any loose minerals along the smooth surface.

Lieutenant Walters cried, "What the hell is that?"

Commander Rockford tried to figure out from whence it came but he couldn't. Nevertheless, he spotted other astronauts moving towards the far side of the room. Leo approached them and saw a large amount of ruby stones scattered along the ground, which sparkled brightly under the light of his helmet. He laughed. "Take the loot," Leo said, "Lieutenant Walters."

"It isn't this," Emily said and pointed away, "but that's what I'm looking at!"

Leo made another look beyond the ruby stones and saw something very unusual. It was made of red stone and it was shaped with two stick arms, two stick legs and a head. It was a foot tall too – it seemed to be a human figurine.

"This is Kennedy...We have a problem...We're advising you that your live streaming has been disconnected. We advise further that you must leave that area."

The five astronauts looked at each other as they wondered on what was foretold.

"I'm Commander Rockford," he responded, "and I'll order my crew to return when I see fit. As the Commander, are you wishing to keep the public in the dark because of a crystallize rock?"

"Not at all. We do not want to panic the American people. That's sensitive," the communicator replied.

No one dared to say anything. It seemed that the Kennedy Space Centre was really in control of their actions.

"I think we should return back," Jay mentioned – as he had enough, "unless we want to suffocate here."

He collected the figurine and the others rounded up the ruby stones. They didn't make a sound and the only thing being heard was coming from the water spring. Of course, they were making themselves ready to move up–

"Sorry for the inconvenience," the communicator said, "we'd hope that you'll agree that that may cause tension. Some people may think that this mission is a hoax."

Leo cried, "Just under whose orders are we not to broadcast our findings?"

"That's me, Bill Kaiser."

"Why?"

"Because it's scandalous. After all, I'm seen as Ming the Merciless occupying the White House."

Leo turned to his crew. "OK," he said as to demonstrate that he was in control, "imagine those critics against the Supreme constitution that would love to gloat on our finding. So do we all agree that we ought to carry on with our mission?"

"Continue that we didn't see an odd-shaped ruby?" Jay Kaiser said sarcastically.

"You're aware that the Supreme Commander is under a lot of pressure from dissidents. Point being is that they may use that man-shaped rock against him," Leo said. "Basically," he continued, "he has done a lot of good in America and it's a shame that there are elements not satisfied."

"I think we should talk about that back on the Orion, sir," the Assistant Commander said after reading his air reserve.

"Right you are!" Rockford agreed and he turned to Tasha, "have we collected enough samples from the spring?"

"Sure, I collected a flask load and it's safely packed inside this case."

Leo looked upon Jay Kaiser. "Have you–"

"Yes I have," Jay stopped him in his pace, "I have the rock doll and I have collected those rubies as did Emily."

"Let's go back!" he said.

The expeditionary party went back up the steep tunnel, which was an uneventful walk. Nobody wished to comment about anything to anyone, as nobody had the will during the black-out. Of course, they had seen amazing things in the room: The water; the smooth ground surface that rose at the centre; plenty of a rich minerals and the ruby figurine. It was fair to say that they saw paradise in space.

The astronauts had eight minutes remaining when they reached the Mars surface outside. They were tiresome but relieved that they had got out in one piece.

Eventually, they heard a crackle in their headsets. "We're going to steam you live again," a man said from the Space Centre.

"OK," Leo replied.

Mrs. Chayton and Mr. Jay Kaiser had already loaded their space vehicles for the next stop. Chris reported in that they still had five minutes to return to the air lock. As quickly as they could, the Commander and his Assistant Commander drove straight back to the Orion.

As they were getting closer towards the ship, the platform-door began its descent and Leo drove his vehicle up the ramp to a complete stop.

Leo said, "You can raise the platform."

The platform began to move into motion. Soon enough, it would be the Assistant Commander's turn to call for his descent and ascent.

The duration of the expeditionary party before they returned to the shuttle was three hours and ten minutes, which meant they had broken one of their Safety Protocols. Once the platform was sealed, they marched straight for the air lock with their samples.

The last thing they heard after they left the lower deck came from Earth. "This is Kennedy Space Centre, we would like to thank you in allowing the live feed of your expedition to the world."

Chapter 13
The party host

*I*T LOOKS LIKE we're not quite dead!" Rockford said. "It's a good thing that we didn't exceed the critical level," Martin implied. "Thank God, it wasn't completely depleted."

"We would have been dead for sure, Commander," Tasha agreed.

"Since we're going–"

"Oi!" Jay interrupted Martin, "we should celebrate the loot once we've slipped into a plasma-line."

"Jay," Chris responded, "we're heading towards the cockpit."

"The Commander had said earlier that we must adhere to our Safety Protocols," Jay said and had an acute smile, "but it isn't to be. If we now are going to banter or congratulate ourselves, we'll suffocate inside our air-tight suits."

"We're going to the upper level," Leo responded, "and then we'll slip into a plasma-line. You shouldn't be complaining."

They continued moving, in complete silence, towards their designation. Eventually, Rockford was able to take his position at the helm.

Emily Walters invited herself to operate the Prima Donna controls. "Chris, I take it from here."

"Right you are," he concurred and moved to sit along the rear.

"Right then, Emily," Rockford acknowledged, "once we reach 40,000 feet, I'll advise you to commence the launch."

"Ready when you are."

Before the rocket engines were going to start, Leo checked on his crew to see if anyone wasn't wearing their seat straps. "I believe we can take off," he said.

The rocket engines were ignited and the Orion was going to have a vertical take-off. She rose above the ground and the wheels were placed into its bay pad. The engines changed its vertical ascent, above 2000 feet, along a diagonal incline. The manoeuvre took approximately twelve minutes as the craft achieved her ideal height.

Rockford said, "Start the Prima Donna engine."

Emily got ready his request as she warmed up the powerful engine. In a short while, she updated her superior. "Engine is online, Commander."

"Are we detecting anything unusual in our pathway?"

"Radar detects nothing. The skies are clear."

Rockford turned around to see if his crew was still in their seat restraints, but he was strapped to face only forwards. "Are we strapped up at back?"

"Of course, we're all strapped back here," Jay replied.

Rockford stopped his struggle to turn around. "Start the launch sequence."

Prima Donna began to match the lift-capacity of the rocket engines, after which, the former switched off. Henceforth, the Prima Donna was singing her reign, causing the Orion, to accelerate at an alarmingly rate, to outer space. Once the Orion was clearly beyond the gravitational pull of Mars, the Commander issued a new order to Emily to track a plasma-line. She detected one and coordinated the course onto her Commander. The whole process took several hours and there was relief and joy, thereafter.

"This is Commander Rockford," he reported, "we've successfully launched from Mars and we're heading home."

"Kennedy Space Centre copies you loud and clear."

Rockford said, "Since we've been to Mars and are now going home, I'll like to invite you all on the middle deck for our own little party."

Martin placed the ship under autopilot after he heard Leo's invitation.

"Rockford, you're the man!" Jay said and he un-strapped himself from his seat. He was the first to exit Alpha Control, and as for taking point, Jay arrived at the sanitation area for his shower. The other members, in the crew, followed him as they were all feeling sticky, sweaty and a bit smelly. Jay heard an alarm upon the forearm of his spacesuit – it warned that he would be subjected to a severe depletion of oxygen. Jay had pretence of dying. "If we had stayed any longer in that cave chamber looking for a foxy alien," he continued, "our party was bound to be dead quiet." While they were cleaning themselves in the cubicles, they were singing songs about how lucky they were to be the greatest team on gaining space supremacy.

***

The crew had dressed down into their casual overalls. A cork was pulled from a bottle. There was an overdrive of claps and cheers when champagne was poured into a flute. The astronauts had got together upon the concave sofa, and the table nearby had two bottles of champagne, beer cans and a bottle of Californian red wine.

Leo rose from his seat. He stood to face his crew, and raised his glass high. "You know what? I have been saving those bottles for this toast, and I thank you all for being patient to not open them sooner."

"Indeed, Commander, yet we still got plenty of frozen barrows in Omega Control," Jay said jokingly.

Leo laughed. "Really?" he pretended to ask. "Ladies and gentlemen," he continued, "as you all know, we've been in space for the last four weeks in this daring exploration known to the human race. We've proved that you do not need to be from a military background, and this will be part of American history and of the world."

Everybody was being congenial when they saw Leo raising his glass to Martin. "Speech, Speech, Speech!"

"I would like to thank Assistant Commander MacCormick for supporting his Commander, and taking great care of this ship," Leo said. He now was facing another astronaut. "Lieutenant Walters," he complimented, "you've been the backbone of this operation, and I cannot see how we could have manned this ship without your expertise.

"Chris Tallon," he said smiling, "I thank you for your constant reminders and to keeping our Prima Donna singing, and Tasha Chayton..." He looked into her direction and he raised his flute even higher. "You've been inspirational for us to understand that life can exist on Mars, and I hope that your research will continue to be fruitful in botany. And of course Jay Rhodes, you've been the morale on this ship and without you here, I dare say, it would have been bloody boring."

The astronauts showed their gratitude to their Commander. Leo drank his fill before he placed his empty flute onto the table. "I think I should fetch some glasses so that we can do this toast properly."

So the Commander went to the kitchen. Tasha also joined him to bring back some drink utensils.

"God," she said, "I want to take a closer look at some of our findings."

"Oh my God! I've almost forgotten the ruby-figurine."

They both decided to take another look at their find. To their perception, the ruby-figurine looked too realistic to not look anything else than a humanoid. It had a head, which contained two dents for eyes, a snout for a nose and a dent for a mouth.

Leo said, "What have we found on Mars?"

"Well, we didn't detect life but this is something else," Tasha replied. "Goodness me," she recounted, "the water." She headed nearby for another case and pulled out a metal flask. She decided to pour some of the water into a flute. What alarmed Tasha and Leo was that the flask content wasn't transparently clear. In the kitchen, their new insight was that the flask was pouring a light wine colour.

"This makes more sense than the ruby-figurine," Rockford said.

"Perhaps so but this is not the water, that we know of."

"Perhaps it's dirty water, dye."

Tasha was feeling slightly embarrassed because she did thought Mars had many deposits of light-wine-coloured natural water. "You could be very right, Leo." Tasha placed that flute to one side of the kitchen and returned the ruby-figurine to its metal case. She even placed the flask in its case too.

"I think you should clear the glass," Leo recommended, "as we do not know who might be capable of drinking from it."

Tasha got apologetic for her casual misplacement. She retrieved the flask, and emptied the flute's content into it. Afterwards, Tasha headed to the sink to clean the glass. She looked at Leo standing nearby. "Hope the sanitation system doesn't get affected."

The Commander caught her eye. "This ship has far too many Safety Protocols to concern ourselves of a slight hazard. So, I command you to wash it out now."

Tasha laughed lightly as the glass was already under a thin stream of tap water. "You could have given me that clearance earlier."

She dried the flute and raised it for a closer inspection. "This will be my drinking glass."

"You win," Leo said.

***

"You know what," Jay was saying to Chris in the common room, "I respect this mission by allowing real-time coverage of the expedition. Yet, why do we really have to hide the fact about the red figurine?"

"That's because Kaiser fears the public labelling him as a Martian – the figurine spells trouble."

"So we form a conspiracy of keeping that figurine away from the public eye?" Jay asked.

"No idea but surely the Commander will know, isn't it?" Chris wondered and they all were looking onwards to their party host.

Leo took a seat near Jay and began pouring some alcohol. "Jay, I'm sorry for putting you in this situation but it's a sensitive matter," Rockford said and gave Jay his drink. "I think," he continued, "that ruby-figurine will be denied of its existence for the immediate future."

Jay asked, "So we're like them?"

Leo was bemused by what he meant–

"You must have heard of the conspiracy theories out there," Jay said promptly," it's *them* that were rigging the financial markets, *them* behind the Supreme Council and it's still *them* that murdered President Bungles."

"Theories hold no proof," Leo said.

"That's right," Jay continued, "yet as we're concealing the truth of our extraction. Therefore, we may be spoken of as becoming part of the problem."

Quietness was in the room as his truth sank in. Leo Rockford knew full well that he was *part of the problem*. It was becoming apparent that his colleagues didn't know where their loyalties lie.

"General Rhodes," Leo said as to beguile, "may not be the perfect man and I'll raise these fresh concerns to him."

Jay said, "As a man who follows religion, it's up to God to decide not General Rhodes. I'm not so naïve at pointing out the existence of the Red Resistance Force."

Emily agreed, "They are indeed the enemy of the state."

Jay nodded and drank his fill. "Politics do make the water murky than it really is."

All of the crew had a filled flute, and Leo stood up to deliver his toast. "This will have to be the best team that Kaiser has put together. I just hope that you'd believe me that whatever Kaiser's decision will be: We're in this together."

Straightaway, Leo received loud cheers as the party went into full swing.

Tasha was sitting next to Emily. "I bet my husband misses me."

"I hope my husband misses me as well, Tasha."

"Been in space a full month," Tasha went on, "and now we can return within two weeks."

"That's if we ignore the plasma-lines," Emily reacted, "and we would be travelling at a greater velocity." She smiled. "Looks like the ruby-figurine is at the centre of attention for Jay. I think that doll has saved you of your marriage."

Tasha laughed. "I never knew Jay like that," she said, "as a person who will stand for American justice." She giggled further. "Can you see me and him together reassuring the public that adultery is for a greater good."

Both of the girls laughed a little at each other.

Tasha said, "I do support the Supreme constitution but are we supposed to just land on Earth and pretend that something didn't happen?"

Emily leaned towards her. "Believe me," she whispered, "if we go against Kaiser, we will be arrested for threatening the security of our nation."

"Oh my God, it's over a red rock."

"As strange as it sounds, yes," she said and took a swig of her bubbly wine. "We're not alone in this; think of the Kennedy Space Centre as we're all in this together."

"Jay's right about one thing: *Politics does make the water murky*," Tasha said.

"Perhaps so but the point is that I serve for my country, and I cannot undermine the constitutional ruling. I shouldn't be considering that I could take sides on the matter. Basically, it isn't legal for any military personnel to defy Kaiser."

"We're putting our husbands in the dark over our extraction. Would you agree that we're in fact cheating them?" Tasha asked.

"I'd imagine so Tasha, it's kind of like breaking our marriage vows in sharing."

Tasha looked at the men drinking, then turned to speak to her best friend. "I understand what you're saying," she said, "God, this party really sucks, isn't it?"

They both giggled some more.

A bleeping sound could be heard. Leo stood up; for he knew it was calling for him. He took another seat, away from his crew, to establish a link. "This is Commander Rockford, how may I assist you?"

"Sorry to ruin your moment but I couldn't contact anyone on Alpha Control."

"Nice to hear from you again, General Kaiser," Leo responded after his image materialized. "I'm guessing you want to talk more about the Mars incident?"

"Are you alone?" Bill asked.

"This link is secure and everybody else is celebrating—"

"That's the problem: Celebrating about that thing you found! That would be fuel for the Red Resistance Force. If I knew better, I'd never have considered this mission. For God sake, what were the stinking odds of finding that thing? Is it million-to-one, or a billion-to-one shot?"

"I've spoken to the team about that figurine and we've all decided to keep it amongst our—"

"I suppose we could invite more people into joining our occult," Kaiser interrupted. "New blood is good for the order, yet, do you think I should trust them?"

"All you need to worry about is that the figurine is secured. I'll be sending it directly to you. Besides, the chance that a member of this crew will be destroying your trust looks unlikely, and it'd be their word against yours. Anyway, they're fully aware that whistle-blowing is a threat to national security."

"I think I see your point but they must sign papers to keep that secrecy."

"That will be a good move for all of us," Rockford agreed.

"Well, I'll be seeing you on Earth," Bill said, "oh by the way, give my congratulations to the crew. I think it'll be honorary to mark your arrival."

"I will do, General Kaiser. I thank you for considering my thoughts," Leo said and closed the link politely.

Before Leo returned to the party, he considered himself a Samaritan: One who had saved his crew from possible surveillance, imprisonment, or even, liquidation. After he re-joined, he poured another glass of champagne and took his seat on the sofa. "That was General Kaiser and he wishes to congratulate you all for a job well done," Leo said, drank a little. "There will be," he added, "some kind of military commemoration once we get back, and I imagine that our findings will enter into some form of museum."

"I don't think that ruby-figurine will be on exhibition, isn't it?" Jay asked politely.

"Yes, you're right. I believe that the ruby-figurine will be finding its way within the Department of Defence."

"That sounds a little drastic," Martin added.

Leo nodded. "I agree with you, Martin," he continued, "it's one thing to create civil unrest and it's another to store the doll at Area 51. All that I'll say it's a harmful weapon. The truth being told: It's a sheer provocation for the Red Resistance Force."

Chris disagreed, "I've seen photos of a turnip that looks like a horse's dick and a dead fish for a human face. However, don't you just think that we're just overreacting?"

"Again Chris, the Red Resistance Force would neither see a good cause with the turnip nor the fish. Yet, all bets are on that the figurine will be their prime objective in their attempt to single-out and quash the Supreme Commander."

"I'm not a person known to keep secrets," Jay said.

"We must once we arrive back on Earth; we're to sign official government papers, which will forbid us to talk openly about the figurine."

Jay couldn't contain himself, and was moving backwards and forwards in his seat. "It's over a stupid, awkward looking thing! I swear Bill Rhodes has got to be the most paranoid leader I've ever heard of. So this is us: We go home...We see our loved ones...We kiss them on their cheeks...We watch a little television, and act as if we haven't seen it, isn't that right?"

"That will be the price of not telling another living soul. I too mustn't tell my wife and family."

Tasha said sarcastically, "Suppose the spring water will have to do."

"Wasn't that cavern area a little odd to decipher," Chris mentioned. "I'm sure I was seeing some form of written communication along the spring wall."

"What the hell was it?" Jay promptly asked.

"Just because we have the Roman alphabet doesn't mean that our style of writing has gone into space!" Leo said.

"I agree with you, Leo, but you must admit that the lines were kind of engraved on the stone wall, wasn't it?" Tasha now asked.

"If I remember correctly, we couldn't even see the roof of the cave. Let's think about it, we haven't got the full picture."

"You know what? Mystical writing may benefit in a feature film," Jay wondered.

"You're surely something, Jay," Emily responded, "was it you, just a moment ago, saying that the public have the right to know about the extraction, but you now want to make money out of them, right?"

"That's show business, madam!" Jay replied wittingly.

Martin noticed Leo looking under the weather, and confided in him. "You appear a little stressed out about our walk on Mars. You should relax as everything will be okay."

"I know I should but as the Commander, I must bring order in my crew as you do understand."

"True but I haven't seen you chilling out since the launch. If I were you; I'll take some time off for a while. I'll act as the Commander on Alpha Control, for you deserve your rest."

Leo laughed lightly. "I never knew you were a concerning type. I think I'll take you up on your offer."

"You should and the Orion will be in good hands," MacCormick tried to refill Leo's glass before realizing that it was empty. "Looks like we need to find another one."

Leo stood up. "I'll get another one. Oh, did you know that the extracted water is red?"

"Is it really red?" Martin looked to the ceiling as he tried to understand Mars having a red sky, red rocks and now red water too. "I thought I saw the last of redness. I could call it...*Martin's Devil.*"

Leo sat down again as to keep his balance. "*Martin's Devil?* That will go down well like Bloody Mary, do you agree?"

"I'm very serious. Finding that water, red, is a great scientific discovery, and since I'm the first to discover it, then I'll call it *Martin's Devil.*"

"You're not serious, are you?" Leo asked.

"You bet your bottom dollar!"

"You're a drunk man," Rockford said, "I think you had one too many."

"Not at all. It's the American dream and the fame will bring fortune."

Leo was at the point in his career where he was the first to set foot and drive a space vehicle on Mars. He saw the drunk as inferior, therefore, he shouldn't be remembered for anything else – than planting the flag. Leo attempted to play down his own appraisal. "Why don't we just call it our mineral water or something?"

"It's for fame and fortune. You might have gathered that you were an embarrassment to NASA. But now I do not doubt it."

"You really are drunk," Leo said and stood up again to get another bottle.

"You're really a confused nincompoop!"

Leo turned tail heading for the kitchen. As he passed through, he started singing:

I'm the Commander of this drunken spaceship
A drunken crew that follows its leader
I've a loyal crew but one for mutiny
That is Captain MacCormick
Martin wanted to rule the seas
He's a boaster that sails the galaxies
Only God can see he's full of crap
The space cadet is he, is he!

After finishing his song, he imagined that Capt. Martin MacCormick had to be the cheekiest person he had ever met. *He is too opinionated*, he thought. He stood silently and swaying a little in the kitchen. Leo imagined that since he hadn't discovered any of the extracted substances, he would be made a mockery to Kaiser. Whilst Rockford remained drunk, he perceived his Assistant Commander as crude, selfish and tight-fisted. He began playing with the idea of stirring shit against Martin. Leo stared at the cupboard containing the metal cases. By his impulse, he stumbled across. He opened a case to retrieve the flask. After which, he used his imagination to mock Martin; special wine cocktail with the main ingredients of red wine, bubbly champagne and a hint of the water from Mars. In another glass, he filled it with just champagne. After Leo held two clean and filled flutes in his hands, he headed straight back to the main party.

Martin was laughing on Leo's entrance. "Commander! I thought you were hosting the party for the six of us!"

"Sorry, but here's yours," he handed Martin his fill, "I think I gonna get some bottles."

Emily said, "I give you a hand, Leo."

"No need. I'm your host so don't spoil your leisure by giving me a hand."

"Seriously, you're drunk," Jay said.

"So you will be too," Rockford reacted quickly, "after I get those bottles!"

Leo headed straight back and was satisfied: Martin was knocking back his drink. He emerged into the kitchen and saw that the flask stood tall on the table. The unfastened flask cap was beside the opened bottle of champagne. Also, the metal case wasn't shut closed. It all might look a little too suspicious and he quickly cleared any evidence of his wrongdoing. After he got the table tidy, he returned to the party with two champagne bottles and bourbon whiskey in hand.

He reappeared in front of his revellers and Leo could see that Martin had a big grin on his face—

"Leo, could you please make me another one as you're a decent bartender."

"I aim to please," Leo said and placed the bottles on the table.

Chris said, "I know that we're celebrating, but don't you think that we're drinking excessively?"

"I think he's right," Tasha agreed, "you blokes are drinking far too much. So how on Earth are you supposed to get sober?"

Martin, Leo and Jay were the heavy drinkers as the rest were looking at them. They were rowdy and Jay attempted to stand upon his feet. He stumbled a little before grasping along the edge of the sofa. Then he looked on, in earnest, at the girls. Tasha could see his desire to change places with Chris to sit beside her.

"Hi, Tasha, I thought that I'd better show some respect in this party."

"You're drunk," Tasha said sternly.

"Please let me–"

"Tasha and I," Emily stressed, "are heading into Alpha Control to monitor the situation from there. You, Jay, stay put with Chris!" She collected Tasha.

As the party was dissipating, Tasha whispered, "Emily, that guy is a creep thinking that he holds the best specimen in his pants."

The Lieutenant agreed, "He even thinks that he is the superior ruler."

Chris believed, wholeheartedly, that he must take charge of Beta Control. He thought that the best way to get the louts sensible quickly was to make them ready-made meals. He especially felt responsible to keep an eye on the womaniser. "Jay, I need you to make some hamburgers with me."

In the common room, Martin looked up at his Commander standing over him. "I'm feeling as if I've drank something exotic."

"Watcha say? You're feeling odd?" Leo asked.

"It's my stomach...It's warming up...It's as if I've been drinking ginger wine."

Leo looked at him, and thought to himself of being the cause. "Does it hurt?"

"No, it's just a warm and glowing sensation."

Leo said, after noticing Martin's cheeks were turning rosy red. "You look like you have been drinking much, much more than I!"

"You look–" Martin turned to one side, choking heavily, before vomiting onto the floor.

"I think you should go to the infirmary."

"Leo you're the biggest bullshitter that I've ever come across! Who the fuck is gonna help me there?"

Picking up his colleague from his seat, he allowed him to place one of his arms around him. Leo wondered if it was worth the effort to spike his drink? Had he poisoned him? Was there anybody else to clean the floor? "Damn it, Martin! If I knew you couldn't handle your drink, I would have never brought in those bottles!"

Martin looked at his Commander from his side. "Okay, let's go."

Both Leo and Martin headed towards the infirmary. On their approach, Chris was the first to spot them whilst Jay was making microwave snacks.

"Do you need a hand?" Chris wondered.

"No, we're good," Leo answered, "just that Martin needs some quality air."

The pair arrived in the infirmary and Leo helped him to take a seat on the bed—

"Now, I'm going to ventilate this room because you've been drinking far too much."

He headed to a wall panel to turn a nozzle. "I'll be cleaning your mess in the play room."

Martin said, "Sorry, I'm just a little drunk that's all."

Leo moved to a small adjacent room, and found a mop and bucket to put into good use. Momentarily, Leo recollected why he must clean the floor. He was still certain of being the cause, nevertheless, Martin had been drinking heavily. He mopped the floor and his cleaning released a scent of critic lemon to remove any assumption of foul play. Afterwards, he began his journey to the rear of the ship to empty the mop and bucket before checking on him.

After he returned to the infirmary, he saw Martin facing the ventilation fan with his back on him, and Leo proceeded to walk nearer.

"Leo, I'm really feeling great."

"Impossible! You drank like a fish back there."

"That's the thing. I'd done but this ventilation is fantastic."

Leo got a little closer to face him abreast. He looked at his face and saw him with a rosy red nose, red steamy eyes and he still had those red rosy cheeks. "Martin, you look terrible."

"No, I'm feeling great."

"Look across the room."

Martin turned around to face the wall with the large mirror. He could see himself from head to toe, and he moved closer still. "This isn't normal has I'm not an alcoholic."

"I was told one time about white people can be receptacle to flushes by the influence of heavy drinking."

"But I am not a regular drinker and the last time I drank was last Christmas Eve. It's as if all of a sudden my body is more sensitive."

Leo wanted to confess his crime. "God, I'm very s—"

Chris and Jay entered into the infirmary and saw that Martin looked a little peculiar.

"What in God's name has been happening in here?" Jay asked.

Leo turned around to face his new arrivals; he shrugged his shoulders and shook his head. "Martin was puking all over the floor, in the common room, looking like that."

"I think I better check this with the medical terminal there," Chris said before moving towards the side of the bed. "Are you having stomach cramps?"

"I feel perfectly fine," Martin replied.

"Are you having any dizzy spells?"

"Chris, I feel great not ill what so ever."

"Do you or did you suffer from alcoholic abuse?"

"For the last time, I'm feeling perfectly fine, and that's a no!"

"Apparently, you got some kind of space sickness. So you should rest in here for the night."

"Let's pretend that the sun is around the corner to make us feel that we know the difference between night and day," Martin said sarcastically.

Jay was perplexed. "I never thought that you could get space sickness out here."

"Jay," Leo reacted, "he's tougher than leather."

Still Jay was looking puzzled. "I think you should rest in here because you might be having the same spatial sickness too, isn't it?"

"Leo, there are hamburgers ready to go if you're hungry," Chris said.

"Thanks," Leo replied and headed for the kitchen leaving Chris and Jay behind to watch over Martin.

"Sure hope that you don't return back to Earth that red!" Jay said.

Martin agreed, "I hope so too but I feel as if I could take on another bender."

"Sir, I recommend that you stay away from any further alcohol as our prime concern is to get to Earth in one piece!" Chris strongly advised.

Jay smirked. "Capt. MacCormick will return in one piece as long as he can get home sober."

Chapter 14
—Turn the tables—

EMILY FOUND HERSELF awake in Alpha Control, and realised resting in the Assistant Commander's seat. Tasha was close by in Leo's. Emily turned around to see if anybody else had slumbered with them but there wasn't anybody else. She then viewed the clock from an overhead panel, in front of her, it was 10 am.

"What are you doing?" Tasha asked.

"It is morning and we've been asleep in here all of this time."

Tasha rose upon her feet and stretched her arms and legs a little; she made a tiresome sound but won the battle to stay awake. "Thank God that party is over!"

"We aren't supposed to chill out in here. God, they were animals!" Emily recalled.

"Jay was the worst. All he seems to think about is sex."

"True, he should have packed a sex-doll for his troubles." Emily said and the pair giggled.

"Those men couldn't handle their drinks, could they?"

"Not from what I've seen. They were like rowdy school children drinking their first apple drink."

Both Tasha and Emily were looking at each other smiling. They wouldn't say a word as if they were telepathic. Eventually, they laughed. "School children drinking cider!"

Tasha said, "Chris wasn't much of a pirate on his rum, was he?"

"That's true; he's sweet."

"If I had to choose a husband from this crew, I think I go for Chris."

"Aren't you supposed to be happily married?"

Tasha still on her feet took a short walk, by stretching herself further, then sat at the back. She felt a little creepy to be in the Commander's seat, in fear of, being caught sleeping. "Of course, just that being in space for the last month makes you wonder a little."

"Not enough to sleep with Jay."

Tasha was jovial. "He belongs at Porn Valley where he can act out those fantasies."

Emily retired from the Assistant Commander's seat to join her. "That's a little harsh, isn't it?"

"You don't know what kind of animal he is. He sees himself as a skunk that can separate whom he wishes to charm or not."

"I kind of, see him OK but spoilt doing those heroic movies!" Emily smirked.

Martin entered and he saw both Emily and Tasha resting along the back.

"See you looking sober and well, Martin," Emily mentioned, "you were in a right state."

He joined the pair. "Emily, I think that's because I sat on the sofa for far too long. It really does affect your blood circulation to react slowly. Anyway, have you been in here all of this time?"

"Uncomfortable, isn't it?" Tasha said – despite her beauty sleep.

"Sorry if the lads were making too much noise in Beta Control."

"Forget about it, Martin, we're a team."

Martin leaned over towards Emily. "That's the point," he said in a soft gentle tone, "we're a team and we shouldn't have behaved like men from the dark ages." He took hold of one of Emily's hands. "I will make sure," he continued, "that wild parties shan't be authorize, and I would like the both of you to retire on Beta Control."

"Martin, what're you doing?"

"Emily," he said and was still holding her hand, "something strange had happened last night."

Tasha leaned forward slightly and gasped.

Martin wouldn't falter. "Yesterday, I was drunk but within an hour of being tipsy, I felt ready for another bender."

"That isn't funny and what are you doing holding my hand?"

"I believe in maintaining our integrity. Basically, I'm doing this to show you that you're not alone on this mission."

Emily turned to Tasha for her response. She saw her countenance, of course, looking bemused on Martin's *integrity*. Soon enough, Emily faced him. "Are you still drunk?"

"No, no not drunk. Just want to point out, that if you girls have any social issues regarding this crew, speak to me."

Tasha said, "Have you men been talking about us?"

Martin glanced onto Tasha and shook his head. "No, we haven't been talking about the pair of you, last night."

"What has Jay been saying?"

"Like I said," he went further, "nobody has been talking about you after the party. I do understand how difficult it must be, being thousands of miles away from Earth, and I will always be here, Emily."

She removed her hand from Martin's. "Why do you have those feelings for me? You're still drunk and you're a married man."

"You do not understand what occurred in the last 24 hours, Emily. I have feelings for you I never realized I had."

Tasha got up from her seat, wanting to lead Emily away to Beta Control. "Oh boy," she excused, "I think we'll all be feeling sorry with ourselves."

Just as the girls were about to leave, Commander Rockford entered into the room. He saw the two girls quickly moving away. "What seems to be the problem?"

"There's no problem, just having a casual conversation with Emily." Martin said.

The girls left Alpha Control. Therefore, Rockford and MacCormick remained on the upper deck.

"Are you feeling okay, Captain?"

"I've never felt better," MacCormick replied, whilst rubbing his eyes, "I'm starting to see things a little clearer."

Rockford sat beside him and was looking straight ahead. "I know that you've been sick and that you had remarkably sobered up within an hour. Also, you had some kind of red rosy fever."

Martin nodded. "It's true, very true. I must admit that ever since that party, I have new feelings for Emily."

"Are you under some form of aphrodisiac?" Rockford said astonished, "this isn't you, for I've known for the last nine months."

"Something strange has happened at the party."

Leo had a sneaky suspicion that he was responsible for his *new feelings*. Nevertheless, he didn't wish to confess. "All I saw was a man throwing up at the last moments of the party," he told him, "did you know that I had to mop your filth while you were standing around in the infirmary taking its air? Plus, you had turned red in the face like a proper drunkard."

"Perhaps you did but now I feel immensely better."

"Martin," he replied and did take offence, "I do hope that your professionalism won't be compromised because of that party."

"You do not have to worry about my professional conduct. I feel a lot more refreshed."

"That's good. I do not wish to have a team, on the Orion, for the next three weeks having a casual groove."

"Some reason," Martin said, "I'm beginning to see things a lot more clearly about the metal case, our Supreme Council and this Mars mission."

"What are you talking about?" he went on, for he was aware of his own handiwork, "because you aren't making any sense?"

"I am talking about them."

"*Them?* What do you mean?"

"Since I became sober, I'd a clearer vision on the Supreme constitution. It's how Kaiser became the force of reckoning, for he's funded by the need for money, and it's his money that sent us to space. Remember, money made our Supreme Commander one of the richest people in America. Even you're inspired by money."

Leo was part of an inner circle – he wasn't in the position to reveal anything to him of its extraordinary activities. All Leo saw was an ordinary person that had a strange idea on rich people. "Martin, you're scaring me."

"That's what I felt when I got sober. Yet, it's all beginning to make sense to me how the world turns."

"And what do you think that is?"

"It turns because man is inspired to better himself through the lust for money. The more you have the less lacklustre you become. You see, Leo, I was supposed to be heading this operation before you right?" Martin waited for Leo to acknowledge – he nodded. "All of a sudden," he added, "it's you and you're a man of sound wealth, right?"

"Martin, we've been together on this mission for the last four weeks. Furthermore, I do not have any interest of hearing paranoid delusions that you may believe are true."

"True but you'll have to agree that there are two sides of the coin. On one side, it's a theory whilst on its opposing side, it is practical," Martin carried on, "the coin also does the trick on science, for example, NASA had a theory that we could launch to Mars. Now we're practically understanding space travelling, isn't it right?"

Leo nodded. "I see that you're using science for your argument."

"We're astronauts, aren't we?"

"We're indeed."

"My theory balances that this space mission is a financial attraction for control of the world, and foreigners are seeing that dreams are made in America, and that's why foreign investors are likely to pour their fortune into our financial markets. By these foreign investors, we have those corrupt Americans that abuse the system by making them believe that they'll be gaining."

Leo was staring at his Assistant Commander for a long time. "You sound like you're in the wrong kind of job."

"No because that wrong kind of job only leads to the same goal."

Leo was perplexed. "What do you mean by that?"

"Yes, it's them with the goal that leads to many different areas in Washington. Just think about it, Leo, if we didn't have them being practical then we wouldn't have theories."

Leo remained dazzled. "I suppose you want to change the world by your conspiracy theories."

"No, I do not want to change the world. I just had that incredible thought when I became sober last night – if we can call it last night."

"Are you happy with the new constitution?"

"If it wasn't for Kaiser, we wouldn't be having this conversation and we wouldn't be astronauts, right?"

Reluctantly, the Commander nodded his head.

"Leo, you look like you need a strong cup of fresh coffee, let me fix you one."

"Okay, strong with two sugars and milk, MacCormick. I'll sit here as we'll need to plot on how we are going to get back to Earth."

"True but that can wait, as our autopilot is active."

Leo assumed that Kaiser would find Martin a flatter. Especially that he hadn't participated within their inner circle. He made up his mind to move towards the front of the cockpit to claim his Commander's seat. He spotted an adjustment; Leo tried to lift the seat up but found it a little too stiff to budge. Anyhow, Leo opened a channel for Kennedy Space Centre. "This is Orion reporting."

"This is Kennedy Space Centre. Glad to hear of you again and how can we be of assistance?"

"We will shortly be having a crew meeting on our route home. Of course, we're to discuss ignoring the plasma-lines to arrive home a lot sooner."

"We hear you."

"What's life like on Earth?"

"Quiet."

"Anything you spotted while we were away from Alpha Control?" Leo asked.

"Negative, it has been quiet. Your auto-pilot is working fine so we didn't see the need for an override."

"Great, speak soon."

Martin and Chris entered into the cockpit with three cups. Martin gave his to Leo.

Chris said, "Yeah, Martin, we need to talk about sorting our route back to Earth."

Leo nodded whilst sipping his coffee. "Nice cup of coffee, Martin."

The Assistant Commander took his seat beside his Commander.

Chris noticed that their backs were against him as they took their positions. Nevertheless, he said, "We know that the short cut back home is to be under weightlessness. So I think for the next seven days, we should consider this option. The sooner we get home, the better our morale will be. I even believe that the rest of the crew will also agree."

Leo took another gulp into his coffee. "This isn't a formal meeting," he said, "we should all decide together on that."

Chris agreed, "Sorry, just that we haven't decided on our long-term strategy of getting home."

Leo cleared his throat. "No apologies are necessary. We're all in this together because whatever action we take will affect us all."

Martin turned to his left. "You know what? Perhaps discussing this here isn't ideal. We should go to the deck below."

Leo agreed, "How silly are we? Why was I thinking of taking this form of conduct?"

Chris rose up starring into deep space. "I never said how beautiful the stars looked, have I?"

It was indeed beautiful; a unique view of the tinkling stars that were very small and millions of light years away. The sun is the biggest star that seemed isolated to the countless others. He stared at them for some time as if he had doubted their existence.

Martin stood up as well and looked through the front visor. "You must understand," he muttered, "that our livelihoods depend on this universe."

Eventually, Leo stood up and turned away from the front view visor. Chris was tidying around him, but looked at him in dismay.

"Leo, you're red orangey looking."

97

Martin looked directly at him. "What have you been taking?"

Leo noticed their odd reactions and he took a moment to look at Martin, then he looked straight at Chris. "I'm not in the best of moods by your prank!"

Chris moved closer to Leo. "I think you should follow us into the infirmary because you are showing similar symptoms that Martin had."

Leo froze; he wasn't sure on what was happening to him. He dashed for the stairs because there weren't any mirrors located in Alpha Control. As he was passing, his anxiety got the better of him that somebody had spiked him. Only earlier, Leo had been taking a cup of coffee after he woke up. Somehow, Martin had figured out that he was the culprit behind his tainted drink. Within moments, Leo stood in the common room–

"Not you as well!" Tasha cried, "and I thought Jay was kidding that the party was getting red hot!"

"What?" Leo asked, "don't you mean Martin?"

"I think you ought to go to the infirmary," Chris said as he caught up from behind, "until you're in the clear."

Jay entered – from the kitchen – and stood in awe. "Some kind of space bug is on the loose because Leo has got it too!"

Leo, Martin and Chris made their way to the infirmary. The Commander was the first to approach the infirmary door so he halted to turn around...His Assistant Commander was approaching. "I don't suppose," he continued, "you've any idea about this space bug?"

"I only know exactly what you know," Martin said before gesturing for him to enter.

"What's that supposed to mean?"

"You are now me."

Chris was third-in-line along the corridor, and saw the pair bickering. "It's not good enough for us to be standing out here. Get in there so that I can diagnose you."

Leo heard his formal request from his trustworthy employee. He accepted his entrance with the two men following. Secondarily, he received another request to lie on the medical bed.

Capt. Chris Tallon used the medical terminal. He knew that the rare symptoms of the facial flushes, vomiting and to becoming immediately sober weren't on the diagnostic system. However, all he could consider was to use the terminal – just in case. Chris turned up the ventilation. "What have you two guys been drinking? I don't suppose you feel fine, Leo?"

Leo looked at his quasi-doctor. "I do feel great."

"You have, in effect, becoming him."

"You're becoming me," Martin agreed.

Rockford looked straight at him and was irritated. "Martin, if you've nothing important to say: Say nothing."

"Only that I was drunk when I had that supposed red fever."

Chris saw that Martin wasn't helping, and so pointed to the door. "I think it's best that you leave Leo for the time being."

"I think you're right, Chris," Leo consented.

Martin used that moment to make his exit. Therefore, two men remained in the infirmary.

"God, it was Martin and it's you now. I don't suppose you've been doing anything unusual in the last twenty-four hours since the epidemic?"

"Chris, if I knew, I would have told you already."

"All I see is that the pair of you was drunk. Also, Martin miraculously got sober quickly. Now, it's you. It's you that is looking reddish and none of this makes any sense whatsoever. God forbid, all that I can imagine is that your space suits were damaged on the expedition. So, Leo, was your suit compromised?"

"Not that I'm aware of."

"I'll need to conduct an investigation to see if both of your suits were compromised." Then Chris thought on an idea that was troublesome. "God!" he said as he was approaching the door, "it might be those metal cases in the kitchen! I'll be containing those cases in Omega Control. We shouldn't have brought the contents upon this deck."

"Well, it was a risk we were willing to take as Tasha only wished to take a closer examination of the figurine," Leo recounted.

99

Chris made his way out to attend to his concerns. Leo thought back on his whole dilemma. His face appeared to be completely reddish, and his only plausible explanation was that Martin was messing with his morning coffee.

Tasha and Emily went to the infirmary to see their Commander – who was with Jay. They heard Jay mockingly insisting that Leo ought to remove his overall, and slip into a night gown.

"I feel superb really."

"What have you and Martin been up to?" Tasha asked.

"All I know is that we got drunk."

"Have you been drinking anything else than alcohol?" Jay continued, "perhaps red tonic?"

"That isn't at all funny!" Leo responded, "you mean the spring water from Mars, right?"

Jay nodded. "Right you are."

"I was drinking the same stuff as you, Jay."

"That's what I'm afraid of because I could be next to having those flushes. Besides, your condition is not heard of."

Tasha said, "Look, Jay, the epidemic comes and goes and look at Martin, Martin is fine. Plus, he's now more energetic than ever before. I think our Leo will pull through stronger than ever."

Emily said, "Chris has decided to place the metal cases in Omega and that he would be gone for the next thirty minutes or so. In the meantime, we're not going to change course. It's because you'll be floating out of your bed with that red face. The main point is that once you have fully recovered, we will be holding a meeting in the common room to discuss if we ought to continue using plasma-lines, isn't that right?"

"It's nice having plasma-lines," Jay said, "to experience artificial gravity. Yet, can we forget the luxury and just head straightaway home?"

"If we do that, our body strength won't be strong by the time we arrive on Earth. Besides, you'll not be able to walk for an entire fortnight."

Jay sat on Leo's bed. "Emily, it's so true. Either we arrive a lot sooner, or face the fact that we could have got home a lot sooner."

"It's why I would recommend," Emily continued, "that we have a mixture of situations. Let's say a week of artificial gravity and the other not."

Jay asked, "Weightlessness meaning that we are operating the Prima Donna engines at full capacity, right?"

"Right, it's a great piece of ware."

Tasha was shaking her head. "Commander," she went on, "I think you should continue your rest for the next couple of hours." She turned to face her other colleagues. "Let's leave him in peace,"

So the Commander should be completely alone for the next two hours. He was still bemused if Martin mixed his coffee by accident. His own rational explanation was that Martin saw him as a sod. However, did Martin really have so much hatred for him? As he was racing for the cause, Leo knew that his best answer was to conduct a one-to-one conversation with him. Incidentally, his thought to ask or confess made him feel too primitive. All because Martin could had done nothing on his part, isn't it? His counterpart might imply that he had lost his own mind, right? Leo's anxiety was taking a hold on him; he wanted to strip Martin of his position and promote Chris Tallon. He muttered, "Capt. Martin MacCormick, your career is through."

Three hours later, Leo was awake by Chris, Emily, Tasha, Jay and Martin.

"A fiver he's back to his old self," Jay said fondly, "just look at him, he's back from the dead."

Leo said, "Good to see you guys."

"Likewise, Commander," Chris responded, "I see that you're looking fine. We've taken the precaution of replacing your spacesuit, and we've decided to move the two metal cases into Omega Control. Only God knows who he will strike next."

"Do you remember what has been happening to you over the last twenty-four hours, Leo?" Tasha asked.

Leo recalled spiking Martin's drink, and he might have returned his favour–

Rockford was suddenly not in the infirmary; he was in a larger room where bright beams of light shone upon him. Leo was emitting a thermal glow, and heard a thunderous sound of drums. He had a peculiar body, of an alien life form standing tall and proud where people call him, Zetta–

Tasha touched him on his shoulder. "Are you fine?" she wondered, "do you remember what has been happening to you over the last twenty-four hours?"

"I was red, right?" Leo answered as he was shaking his head in disbelief – he thought his mind had gone.

"Just like me, Leo." Martin replied.

Leo was trying to see him, but he was behind Tasha. "What have you done to me?"

Martin's countenance expressed being oblivious, He was looking at everyone else before glancing down at him. "What have you done to me?"

The rest of the crew were quiet and saw that Martin and Leo were blaming each other.

"Now be straight with us," Emily said to take the initiative, "what have you two been up to last night?"

Martin and Leo simultaneously glimpsed at her. "Nothing," they said, "was going on."

"Sure looks like nothing," Jays said sarcastically, "the pair of you were left alone, while Chris and I were eating hamburgers in the kitchen. Tasha and Emily were also in Alpha Control gossiping over us. You see, the two of you have obviously been doing something with our backs turned away."

"All I remember last night," Leo stated, "is that Martin was drinking like a fish."

Chris nodded, yet speculated, along with the crew, at what really took place. "You mean that the pair of you," he went on, "accidentally drank the Mars spring water?"

Leo said angrily, "That is nonsense! Being drunk doesn't mean we couldn't tell the difference between a space-flask to a bottle of champagne! God, what planet do you really think you're from?"

"You were all pigs," Emily said and she shuddered a little. "That's why Tasha and I left that party."

"I'm sorry to hear that," Jay added, "but I thought you required a little affection—"

"Is that your charming answer? Lord, please give me strength! You need to spend a little more time with your wife!" Chris said.

"On this ship how?"

"Doesn't matter, I thought I knew what I was talking about. Obviously, I do not."

Leo said, "I think you can see that I am in perfect health. So if you will excuse me, I wish to be left alone with Martin to discuss our journey home."

They all left the infirmary, which meant that Martin and Leo were alone. With a knowingly eye, they looked at each other. Martin placed his back against a wall whilst crossing his arms. Also, he was nodding his head as if he was expecting Leo to understand.

Leo ended the silent. "So you drank anything that wasn't vinegar?"

"And there I was thinking that I was drinking wine. Yet, it tasted like a soft beverage, coke maybe? God, at the party, I thought I was drinking some kind of punch. I mean we are talking about making the best cocktail in space?"

"Last night at the party as I was fixing your drink, I was thinking of your discovery."

"*Fixing* is the right word, and I agree with you."

"You fixed me a decent cup of coffee, didn't you?"

"The point is this, have you been thinking about the water spring on Mars?"

Leo continued to look at Martin, and began to think about their time on the planet, the time they were in the cavern seeing few unexpected sightings. He boldly went further to understand his desire of spiking Martin. He ascertained that Martin spiked him back. "That does explain the coffee that you made."

"No, it doesn't but it will. You see, Leo, after I recovered from the party, I have been thinking about that water spring and my thoughts led me into some form of hypnosis. Just think about it."

Just after Martin advised him, Leo's mind seemed to give him a recollection. Aliens were singing, kneeling and praising him. He was their creator, and in his imagination, he was in the Mars cavern drinking the red water for it was potent. One would become superior, wise and the order of things to come. "What the fuck is happening to me!" he cried.

"That's exactly what I thought last night. To prove that I wasn't becoming mad, I had to return that favour of yours," Martin admitted.

"I see it's like some kind of crash course; I feel wonderful! How are we to explain this to the rest of the crew?"

"Despite you mixing my drink over your lust for power, I'm not sure they will approve. Besides, I hated you for taking my Commander position."

The sensation, in Leo's head, stopped, he could control it. He had the key to open the door into an alien civilization. "This is a conspiracy if we do not tell our crew, isn't it?"

"True! The crew may confide us in this infirmary for the rest of the journey, and God knows what will happen to us back home. This is ground-breaking science and I'll hope to share this with Emily for I know she will understand."

Leo shook his head, he laughed too. "People will envy us."

"Have you heard yourself trying to understand it?" Martin asked.

"Sort of saw something but a lot to take in."

"Well, basically, we're not alone in this universe."

Chapter 15
—Space travelling—

*L*EO GOT OUT of his bed to join the others. Slipped on his boots, and advanced towards the mirror to check his readiness. As he was doing so, Martin watched on in complete silence. Both Leo and Martin then walked together until emerging into the common area.

"Finally," Jay said whilst giving a thunder-clap, "Ming's flu is no more!"

"Hear, hear, Commanders," Chris cheered on, "hear, hear!"

"Now shall we go home?" Tasha smirked politely.

Leo nodded. "Yes, Tasha," he said, "and this time, there will be no delay."

Emily also showed her support for her superiors, but she was still a little wary of Martin.

Jay got nearer to Leo. "We should use full throttle to return home within nine days."

"We only just arrived in here," Martin intervened and was pointing at the concave sofa, "we'll need to gather around here to discuss this further."

Leo sat along the right side of it. Beside him, his Assistant Commander, Martin MacCormick, Tasha sat near him and Emily followed suit. Next were Chris and Jay.

Leo said, "Well, I would like to personally apologize for the way the senior staff behaved earlier with the rare case of being under the weather," light humour followed through. "As we all know, we have taken our time to arrive to Mars for the Supreme Revolutionary Day. Also, I believe that this trip has allowed us to understand the importance of being patient and tolerant.

"As we have accomplished our schedule, I would like to hear from all of you about how should we travel back home. Basically, should we use full throttle as to arrive on Earth within nine days, or should we use our exclusive plasma-lines and be back – say – four weeks?" Jay rose from this seat to gain their attention. "Well, I speak for all of us who wish only to arrive sooner into our welcoming arms of our families."

Tasha was astonished that he wanted to return home sooner than later; she didn't utter a word of discontent.

"Tasha," Jay said, "surely you agree since we have spoken on several occasions that our families come first." Tasha nodded slightly.

Leo was trying to determine their relationship; seemingly mutual. He shook a thought that they were intimately close. "That's exactly the point!" he said, "the sooner we get home, the better we'll be mentally, physically and in the long run, we'll be with our families."

Jay took the decision to change position, and moved to face his entire crew across the sofa table. "Listen. It has been fun being in space. For me, it's fun to be the first Hollywood actor in becoming an astronaut. Yet, I obey urgency, within us, that we will be home sick the more we just kid ourselves of this luxury cruise in space."

Tasha felt Jay's presence and continued to nod.

"You see, Commander," Jay continued, "even Tasha agrees and I think for the rest of us, that we should hurry back home to our wives; to our loved ones."

"I see the pair of you is being slick," Leo said and was letting his curiosity get the better of him, "to plot a path for all of us. So are you both sick of each other?"

Tasha was a little startled by his remark. "Leo, we've been in space for quite a long while. So, aren't we missing our families?"

"Understandable," Leo concurred, "Tasha, it is understandable."

Emily Walters disagreed, "Leo, it's all good of us to arrive back the sooner the better but I think we're forgetting one thing–"

"Emily," Jay said sternly, "of all the good members of staff on this ship, why is it always you that have to go against the grain?"

Emily stared at him without changing her composure. "What makes you think that I was going to say something negative?"

Jay replied, "Well, isn't it you that shuffle those feathers every time I am near your friend, Tasha?"

"Listen," Leo interrupted, "I do not know what you wish to discuss but this is about the future of the Orion. Therefore, we're not to have a diversion about personal bickering. So, I expect that you all conduct yourselves more professionally!"

"Sorry," Jay said softly, "I didn't mean to interrupt Emily's opinion of things."

Emily resumed, "Now, as you've been made all aware, weightlessness affects our muscular density. So, the more we are experiencing weightlessness, the less dependent our bodies will be to Earth's gravity. So I'll not bore you with further details about how our bodies will get a lot weaker once we arrive back on Earth. On top of that, we'll be required to go through a fitness recovery programme to regain our strengths. However, we can forfeit the fitness recovery programme by reaping the benefits of artificial gravity. Also, since we're a media attraction, I believe its best that we give a positive image that astronauts are physically fit and strong. So forth, it'll ultimately strengthen our relationship with the Supreme Council, NASA and the international community."

"I salute you," Martin agreed, "for you're absolutely right."

"So," Jay said and was still facing them along the middle of the table, "we're more special than the other astronauts orbiting Earth in those space stations? We are not. They spend hundreds of days in space without artificial gravity and they have families too. So, what makes us different?"

Martin said, "What makes us different is the mapping system to determine our plasma-lines. Also, we've the Prima Donna. Basically, what we've here will revolutionize the concept of an astronaut and space-travelling."

Emily nodded. "I agree with Martin that we should lead by example."

"So that's only two people accounted for," Jay said, "I still stand for the rest of us to return a lot sooner."

"Let me remind you," Leo reacted, "that I'll make the final decision for the best course of action; regardless of a count. The point of this meeting is to hear all of your concerns.

"Emily, you feel very strongly that we should continue to use the plasma-lines, for it'll bring us comfort and reserve our strengths. I agree with you that we should display ourselves as being strong when we receive our praises home.

"Jay, we've done what was required from us to reaching Mars for the Supreme Revolutionary Day. Surely, we haven't the need of further delay to get back home to Earth – besides, we didn't need to launch into space four weeks ago but it was to experience artificial gravity – I do expect all of you to understand that all options are open."

"Leo," Jay said bemused, "I'm not sure why you've decided to hold a meeting when it's you and only you, that wants to decide on how we're going to get back home, right?"

"We've been together for the last four weeks looking at the same old faces without really stretching our legs. All I want to do is to continue this great harmony among us. Look, the red flush episode kept us strong to work as a team and I respect our morale, our determination and our initiatives."

After Jay heard his unbiased Commander, he returned to his seat. Emily looked at Martin, with an acute smile, that they had defeated an egotist.

Chris Tallon said, "Commander Rockford may I say a word or two?"

All eyes fixed on Chris because he might reveal something that could turn the outcome.

"Certainly, what's on your mind?"

"Leo, as we aren't to have a vote, I'm a little confused that we're all trying to swing towards a decision. If I can be frank, you're in charge of us all and so it's your call alone."

"Good call, Chris. That's a good call."

"So you're considering a vote on this matter?"

"Not exactly, I'm going to give a final decision but I'd allow ground for anyone to voice their points. Come on now, we're living in an autocratic society, isn't it right?"

"I agree with Commander Rockford, it's his call to sound the horn," Martin added.

"Okay, look then, why don't we go fifty-fifty?" Chris asked.

"You mean that we alternate between plasma-lines and open space?"

"Exactly, it's a win-win situation for all of us and who is to argue?"

"Sounds nice," Jay said and stood where he was before. "But have you ever thought," he went on, "it will take longer to get home that way?"

"We're heading straight to Earth not to the moons of Saturn," Chris replied.

"We're chasing the orbiting Earth around the sun, my little Watson."

"So," Chris reacted and switched his attention onto Rockford, "this get together is really pointless because we still require the thumbs up from the Space Centre."

Leo nodded. "We're forgetting our reliable engine, the Prima Donna; we've a great piece of machinery. We can explore along the plasma-lines and venture out of them and still zoom even closer to Earth quickly. So not forgetting how powerful it is, I wanted this meeting because we had a restraint of getting to Mars no sooner than 13th October. Now we can decide how we're to return."

Jay replied, "Exactly, we have a diva who can sing us all the way home swiftly and efficiently without any fuss whatsoever. So, I still stand by my decision."

Emily said, "It's not your decision to make."

Jay replied again, "Regretfully, my mind is made up."

"What are you talking about *regretfully*?" Emily asked.

"Regretfully, that few people feel differently."

Everybody turned to face their Commander for his final decision on how they ought to return. Leo rose upon his feet and moved along the side of the sofa to face his crew. Also, he pointed to Jay to return to his seat.

"Okay, it's great that we can work together as a team. So as your leader, I'm making the right tactical decision to arrive back to Earth. I have more confidence that our engine may return us back within nine days, and I'm still confident that we'll be triumphant and reinvigorated within twenty-eight days too. Therefore, I've decided that we will return no less than fifteen days.

"The next 48 hours, we will continue to move along this particular plasma-line. After that, we'll experience weightlessness and proceed at a great speed for Earth," Leo said and paused a little. "I value all of you," he continued, "as part of an exceptional crew and I'm certain that you'll all agree on my final decision."

Emily and Jay nodded to their Commander.

"I hope you will excuse me," Leo proceeded to say, "as I require some further rest, and I bid you all a good day."

Chris was coughing politely to gain Leo's attention. "Are you feeling unwell?"

"No just fancy a quiet nap."

"I do as well," Martin said.

The two superior officers received their pardons, and they headed towards the sleeping-quarters.

"Sorry to be a little bother," Chris stated, "but Earth has been waiting for the last four hours on our proposed journey home."

Leo turned around. He gently slapped the side of his face with an open mouth. "How on earth could I've forgotten that? Chris, you tell them that we are to continue along this plasma-line for the next 48 hours, and then we will advise them on our next approach."

"I will do, sir."

The others returned onto the sofa.

"I have never seen them being cheerful together," Jay said.

Chris said, "I cannot help thinking the pair was close to strangling each other's throats. Yet they are the best of buddies now."

"They must have enjoyed the party!" Tasha added jokingly.

"Wasn't there a bad vibe that Martin hated Leo for taking his command? They've got a good groove going on, do we all agree?" Chris asked.

Momentarily, Jay decided to get up from his seat to make his concern heard. "I bet they must have done something together last night: the duo isn't taking a nap in their separate beds."

"You and your theories! So you're just going to wonder into the sleeping-quarters to see them being game?" Emily mocked.

"So what were you whining about, earlier? Don't you like it when I side with your friend Tasha?"

"It's just isn't a personal issue as we're in this together."

"If I may be blunt, we aren't in this together like the time I was socializing with Tasha—"

"Wait a minute" Chris butted in, "why did you bring that up in the meeting about your socializing problems. It shouldn't affect your professional duties, isn't it?"

"Tasha agreed that as a team, we shouldn't cloud our judgments about how we ought to return home, sir!"

"So I need a minder?" Tasha was saying and slightly annoyed, "I can fight my own battles you know."

Jay said, "As I was saying earlier, we're all married adults and we all have responsibilities."

"If you're going to hit on Tasha, your sly stuff doesn't work!" Chris stormed.

Silence followed. Jay, Emily and Tasha were staring upon Chris.

"Do what exactly?" Jay asked him.

"I've seen you trying to canoodle with Tasha on numerous occasions, and you just don't get the message of being rejected. Now your advances appear to be pleasing to her."

"How dare you," Tasha said, getting even more irritated, "share your views. We just had a meeting and our professionalism has nothing to do with starting a romance, dumb drops!"

"You heard the lady," Jay reaffirmed, "so you met your wife under a twinkling star, or is that how you succeeded on gaining your umpteenth divorce?"

111

"I'm sorry. I just thought that I was–"

"Wrong!" Emily interposed.

Jay said, "Goodness me. I had thought that you were to take his side of the story."

"OK, I'm really sorry," Chris said again.

Silence followed in the room again. The only sound being heard was a continuous low humming. An electrical appliance had been left on along the far side of the room. Everybody was drawn to it as somebody left a computer terminal on. The user must had been Tasha or Emily, and they knew it yet nobody really cared.

"I think I check on Leo and Martin," Jay wondered.

He got up to see what the pair was up to. He entered the adjoining section and saw the pair in their separate beds, and they were fast asleep. He noticed Martin holding his pillow tightly in his bed like a teddy bear. Jay returned back to the trio.

"Did you have any fun?" Tasha sarcastically asked.

"I just do not understand the two of them. God, what has the Cold War taught us? That an astronaut and a cosmonaut were racy?"

"They must be tried that's all," Tasha said.

"They've been asleep for over ten hours!" Jay said. "Literately speaking," he went on, "I drank a lot more liqueur than the pair put together!"

"Really, Jay, you're truly good at exaggerating," Tasha said teasingly.

Jay repeatedly pointed at the table. "What I remember late in the party was that Leo had two small glasses of liqueur after we all ran out of drinks! So let me say this, the empty bottles were never beside the Commanders as they were light drinkers, and light drinkers do not drink heavily."

"We all had a fill, Jay. And quit your conspiracy theories that they were abducted by Ming the Merciless when we all got drunk," Chris said jokingly.

"It's easy for you to say, for I sat next to them–"

"No," Tasha implied, "you wanted to sit next to me, remember?"

"Sure, hun. Sometimes having an all-male company can get a little too crowded."

"Oh!" Chris added, "So now you're an expert in social science, bullshit!"

They began their petty arguments about the party at what did take place, also, voiced their concerns at what should have been paramount for space-travelling. Eventually, they realized that their light debate might awaken their senior personnel, and silence followed, once more.

"Have you been thinking," Jay resumed not long after, "about that red chamber, and how it may have affected our superior officers?"

Nobody dared to return with an answer.

Jay wasn't to keep the silence. "Hasn't the pair been friendlier than usual?"

Chris chuckled. "They could," he said, "say the same about you and Tasha!"

Silence did resume—

"I've never seen Martin," Emily said, "being so affectionate for me."

Tasha agreed, wholeheartedly, "He has changed since the party and that's for sure."

Jay with Chris didn't take the news pretty well. "Isn't that" Jay said being contemptuous, "abusing his position? I knew he was a pressure cooker since losing to Leo."

"He doesn't entirely hate Leo. Martin hates his arrogance to apologise that he has taken his position," Emily said.

"Somehow, it now means that they're able to sleep together in the same quarters. That sounds mad if you ask me," Jay said.

Chris suddenly made a move to get upon his feet. He became aware that his departure looked a little rude, and turned around. "I forgot to inform Earth that we will be recuperating for the next 46 hours, and that our flight path will not be formalized until then."

"OK, Chris," Emily acknowledged, "it beats sitting here doing nothing for the next twenty-eight days."

Chris headed for Alpha Control to break the news to Earth.

Meanwhile, Jay helped himself on his assessment. "Can you imagine the expression on Earth if they heard how they hated each other, but to hear of their togetherness by drinking lightly?"

"You can never leave the party scenario to rest, can you?" Tasha rejected smoothly, "what's your concern between Leo and Martin?"

"They were both experiencing red flushes, remember?"

"But they are fine now," Emily replied.

"I'm cool with that but they're behaving more closely than usual. Have you ever heard of then sharing the same bedroom than the cockpit during social hours?"

"We had a party. So you suck if you never had a hangover before," Tasha said.

Jay said sarcastically, "Fine! I just pretend that nothing has happened and when I get back to Earth, I will not say a word that our superiors were red-faced. Then all of the scientists, politicians and the military will leave them alone as they are not a threat to their own good."

"Of course we are going to report it to the Space Centre because Chris had already written a medical log about the two separate incidents," Emily said.

Chapter 16
—Dare to dream—

*A*FTER BEING EXCUSED, Leo retired to his sleeping-quarters. He took off his boots and lied upon his bed. He could hear Martin, close by, creasing his bed sheets; yet, he heard no more. Leo was the only person seemingly awake. He closed his eyes...

It seemed bizarre that an ancient and alien civilization was two light-years away from Earth. Their planet took on the name as Nergal, and they flourished via the wisdom of the wine-coloured water, which was called Zetta. It was only to be drunk by those set to rule, and under their breath, they had high regards of it. Zetta took claim as the creator of Nergal and of the universe. Nevertheless, the alien race considered him a god who drove away oblivion and destruction. He was even praised for the advancement of technological science. Consequently, the Nergalas explored space over the last 12000 years, and Mars was considered a sacred burial site. The dead predecessors were put to rest in the water reservoir, and their genetic make-up, over time, would dissolve; a sacred burial site which was a well of knowledge for future rulers to sip.

Leo felt a tingling sensation rushing through him, and oddly enough, he saw something completely bright white – and of course, it was all happening in his mind while he rested – yet, it dispersed when he became aware that he was seeing through the eyes of those predecessors; he was Zetta taking an interest in a supernova, which lifted his curiosity for outer-space. Moments later, Leo became somebody else that led to their discovery of Mars. The latter ruler considered it divine; the colour of the entire planet resembled the remains of Zetta. Using a large, yet noble, space craft, the Nergalas relocated Zetta's remains. Leo heard thunderous noises; somehow, he knew, robotic drums were installed along the ceiling of the tomb; loud synchronised beats to begin a ceremony. Leo remained overwhelmed, that of a verbal command: Temple dire Zetta mastif. Its utterance would light up the room to reveal its true splendour. All of the predecessors rested there, and their genetic make-up would vitalize future successors.

As he slept, Leo had an unusual nasal sensation: it was the sweet smell of food being prepared for the ruler in the Great Hall – he felt peculiar that he might challenge their power structure, and imagined a communiqué to their culture – As if he already knew, he had breached their fundamental rule; no more than one successor was forbidden at one time. Furthermore, it seemed too obvious that the Nergalas would take some time in accepting him as one of their own. Thirdly, how could he efficiently communicate with them?

(Leo had a bitter after-taste. He took on that Martin MacCormick longed to become a god, yet, he didn't wish to do it alone. He feared little of him wanting to kill him to treasure the thoughts. Leo knew that the water was settling in Omega Control, but could Martin surprise the crew-mates by lacing their drinks? Was MacCormick going to have something in store for Emily? Nevertheless, he wouldn't stir and so continued his dream)

They highly valued the virtue of women. Needless to say, it meant having a family – an unity to better themselves. (Straightaway, Leo rediscovered that the success of Hog's Head was dependent on women, like his own wife, Carly. His wife had been his moral support, and he couldn't accept the American job without her) How silly he felt to not fully appreciate her vitality. Leo understood the wives went side-by-side, with their husbands, to rule the planet. More so, the females consumed the wisdom of Zetta.

His mind took him onto another scenery; he felt slightly cold and numb in a dark alley. In front of him, a Zetta priest, in his black hooded robe, was unmasking an evil; anybody who wasn't willing to declare Zetta was the prince of darkness! Within seconds, Leo was alarmed that the predecessors hadn't any interest in the human race. They saw Earth as a backward society where people fought over ideologies that wouldn't revitalise, and those aliens snubbed the planet and wished less for co-existence.

Through the eyes of those rulers, Leo saw they had a humanoid feature. They contained two sexes and two skin complexions of grey and red. Their eyes were crimson and only females grew hair on their heads. Leo wondered deeper into the females' anatomy: The hair on their heads didn't completely cover from the side and back unlike Earthly women, yet, their dark black hair only grew from the top with wavy curls. He heard his own heart beating fast then faster after beholding their beauty. Nevertheless, he was hurt when the alien females spoke harshly that Earth was a place of rape, corruption and murder.

The Nobilis had the highest authority, and his love of his wife was racy when he took her on public exhibitions, which was similar to two birds singing before they mate; they wouldn't shy away their feelings within a confine space. As if unnervingly, the Nobilis boasted of his genitalia. It was morally accepted for the Nobilis to engage with many girlfriends too. Creamy white; it was completely creamy white as if a jet stream shot out of Leo. A sensation ran through his body, and Leo was very certain that Martin was forming a love triangle with Emily, and of his wife. Leo's body tingled a little with his own desire for a lot of women. He hardly believed how realistic his subconscious mind was portraying. By that, he slipped away the thought.

Nergalas consisted of additional twelve Sub-Nobilis. The planet was split into a dozen sectors, in assisting the rule of the Hierarchy. Yet, every time the ruler passed away, it became a contest to become the highly acknowledgeable one. The Sub-Nobilis had to receive a majority of praises from the senior clergies. Other words, the better they pleased, the better their chances. Leo could only speculate that the latest Nobilis went by the name of Regis; for he had a lot of admiration in the religious sector. Of course, it seemed probable that Regis was escorted to Mars to mark his own coronation by drinking the sacred water.

There was a shiver along Leo's spine, and darkness filled his mind. An evil went by the name as Sabotur. The alien priests were horrified that he deserved any praises as their Nobilis. Apparently, those priests even advised, the late Nobilis Hammad, not to grant his permission to devise a discreet pact on Earth. Sabotur wanted to be the puppet-master in Nazi Germany, Soviet Union and the USA. Of course, his belief was of Earth's complete servitude. Sabotur also suggested hope to promote their god, Zetta, as the true creator of the universe. He also reckoned that Earth had primitive creatures that would be loyal. However, the Priests protested that such a pact was sacrilegious (As the Priests were triumphant, Leo Rockford thought that Sabotur might have blended well in Hog's Head, and took an interest to know more of him). Even if he obeyed his ruler, Hammad, Sabotur had a lust to be above everybody else. It was rumoured that as a Sub-Nobilis, he hated revealing many of his thoughts. He had a tendency to scorn his fellow Sub-Nobilises on many occasions. He had openly argued, to Hammad, to impose a secret police force on investigating the religious sect; all because, they preferred to keep their distance. On top of that, he publicly denounced that Nergala women hadn't the right to drink and gain from the well of knowledge. Henceforth, his opponents were diverse (Leo couldn't believe how Sabotur was similar to General Kaiser. But felt that his General had been more cynical to lead. Leo continued to make comparisons that Kaiser hadn't any idea that the ruby-figurine was only a discarded toy! Leo had thought of Kaiser as complaisant. Now he just saw a child running a nation, not the entire planet).

He was stunned that the Nergalas were under a prohibition to venture the stars, and any rogue would receive the ultimate penalty of death. It was deterrent since a Sub-Nobilis had reached the distant planet Mars; he cheated Zetta and of his teachings. The man returned home to proclaim that everybody might become a Nobilis, and that their ruler was an imposture. There was a disturbance on the planet, which the Nobilis had to silence quickly (It suddenly occurred to Leo that he was a pretender AKA the false prophet. If word reached afar, Leo feared that the Nergalas sought to kill him; the sacred water had to remain his close-guarded secret). The man could feel his heart pounding. Nevertheless, he wanted to understand how those humanoids had knowledge of Earth. He found out that the Nergalas used a high-pitched radio wave that scanned the galaxy for life-forms. After a long while, scanning the vast universe, which seemed dead, they detected the Homo sapiens. Yet, the Hierarchy only thought to snub as too premature. It took another 10,000 years for them to gain new interest; they detected the creation of a transport that could lift into the air. Hammad, the ultimate ruler, had interest in the Wright Brothers' aircraft. For the highly-intelligent aliens, their first attempt was to interpret telegram signals. Unfortunately, their superiority of understanding random signals failed. So Hammad drafted volunteers that would learn the language to achieve a better understanding. Therefore, he sent a small team of scouts to a region, after genetic modification, to pass as humans. The volunteers were sent to North Carolina in the United States in 1904. Their arrival wasn't an easy one as their attempt to speak the native tongue was a challenge. However, they have been made aware that throughout Earth, the best communicator was the distribution of wealth. Therefore, they arrived with nuggets of gold to win the locals' obedience. Leo could hear himself laughing in his own sleep; several thugs made a bid to steal their nuggets by a show of arms. They weren't any match because the alien unit had better armoury and weaponry. The local people thought of them as rich immigrants from Eastern Europe. They taught those aliens basic English, and the direction to their local library.

It took sixty years for the scouts to report back to their Nobilis Hammad, and they still had hundreds of different languages left for interpretation. The Nobilis was horrified that such a planet, which flew a craft in the air wasn't unified. He recalled the scouts back to Nergal. He also perceived that the different tongues were the cause of many bloody and unnecessary wars. Oddly enough, he found Nazi Germany as similar to his hierarchy. They all took on a cultural comprehension on religion, science and on their society. Hammad knew that the German tongue saw themselves much more dignified than their neighbours. Yet, what really disturbed Hammad was that translators were required to decipher scientific discoveries, like the V2 rocket, which compromised Earth to speak only one tongue. He passed a decree that Nergalas were forbidden to interact with Earth ever again. It was the time during the Cold War, and Hammad retracted that Earth would face its own annihilation (Rockford saw a selfish and devious male that only had interest to better himself. He saw Sabotur as the lesser evil who should have been entitled to become the successor. Leo was disgusted, however, Nergalas didn't see the human race was worth saving).

Straightaway, Leo knew that their complacency had led their sacred water being compromised. It wasn't a funny matter because they would pass judgment, against him, for desecrating their well of knowledge. As if feeling guilty, he was now certain that it meant his own untimely death.

Chapter 17
—Regain control—

CHRIS WAS FOLLOWING his instruction to inform the Space Centre of Leo's planned route. Nothing out of the ordinary occurred, as he ventured, to Alpha Control. He sat at a terminal and found a comm. headset under a desk. "This is Capt. Tallon reporting in on the Orion. May you come in please?"

"We copy. This is Kennedy, and how may I assist you?"

"We've conducted our meeting and we're pleased to inform, that we have reached an agreement. We're to continue flying home along this plasma-line for the next 46 hours."

"That's fine, Capt. Tallon. Might I ask the reason why none of your Commanders aren't reporting it in?"

"Rockford had given me authorization to report on his behalf. So is that a problem?"

"Not a problem. Just that you're not second-in-command to report the plot back home. As a protocol, I cannot file your report unless something terrible has happened. Has anything happened to your superiors?"

Chris assumed that he was at a pivotal point to disclose their red flushes, but he didn't wish to spend any time on it — if any. All he could think of was to evade that question. "I have been ordered to inform you of our present situation, and that's what I'm doing."

"May you inform Commander Rockford that he should have personally reported it in, won't you?"

Chris replied firmly, "Of course I will but remember that I must report this, under the order of my superior officer, unless instructed otherwise."

"I understand but—"

"I'll be reporting out!" Chris said quickly and relieved the headset. He decided to check if the ship was in good working order. He started to read the gauges at his terminal. First to see if the fuel reserve had enough to power the Prima Donna engine and it was plentiful. Secondly, he read the hull's integrity, which hadn't any breaches. Thirdly, to see the pathway, along a plasma-line was long enough.

Emily entered into the cockpit and was standing over him as he was continuing his checks. "Having fun?"

"You would have thought I should be the Commander as the pair is totally out of it," Chris said frustratingly.

"So the Space Centre thought that there might be a problem on the Orion?"

"They advised me that Rockford was supposed to give his official report."

"That's true, Chris. Let's face it, they were totally wasted last night."

"Exactly," Chris agreed, "am I supposed to say that our superiors are away for the day because of a terrible hangover? Then report in that they drank something that didn't agree with them too?"

Emily laughed. "We shouldn't," she continued, "have been having our little get-together as people will be talking."

"That's an understatement! They're talking about us right now saying that the Orion is under mutiny, and we're on a detour to the Milky Way."

Emily laughed still. "You're quite amusing when you're stressed," she said.

"Thanks. I've been checking if the auto-pilot is running smoothly, and something occurred to me. What if we had a life-threatening situation to control this ship while our superior officers were sleeping-tight? They're really losing it."

"That's a little harsh, Chris?"

"If you have been here earlier in following Rockford's order, you'd have understood why."

"Wouldn't they buy it?"

"Oh they brought it alright. I think I lost a dear friend at the Space Centre when I was getting a bit harsh."

There was silence in the room as Chris continued to do his checks.

"It's obvious," Emily decided to break the quietness, "that Martin and Leo are not themselves. Do you agree?" After Chris heard her, he stopped. Stood up and asked Emily to sit beside him along the rear of the cockpit. "I'll agree with you. We'll be kidding ourselves that the pair has recovered from the party. I have been thinking that we should perform a psychological evaluation on them, but I doubt that Rockford is willing to volunteer."

Emily thought for a moment. "It will be very difficult to get the pair to volunteer. It all depends if they continue to show weariness."

"That's true, the sooner we report this to the Space Centre, then the better we have a new Commander."

Emily had the giggles. "If those Commanders could hear us talking now, we would look like right idiots trying to break rank."

"It could be for the best."

"It's a long shot," Emily went on, "and this scare mongering is only in its early days."

"OK, I'll keep a closer eye on the pair of them for the next 40 odd-hours. Leo must have known the routine: It can't be the junior staff to report to Kennedy. Besides, I could have reported some juicy information about their party bloopers."

"I think you're right not to go behind Rockford's back about that, and if the pair isn't able to command this crew to its full potential, then we must demand a higher power to demote them."

"It's an awful business having to change the dirty laundry. You would've expected this on Earth not out here."

"Well," she said, "we will be doing them a favour if they continue to under-perform. Anyway, we're speaking of a worst-case scenario, right?"

Chris nodded. "Very true," he said, "I think I'll stay in here to complete my maintenance."

Emily hadn't finished with Chris as he headed towards a terminal, but waited a bit longer. "Since the party, I still cannot believe that Martin is a womanizer."

Chris was bemused. "You're speaking about Jay, aren't you?"

"Who else is there? Martin is a married man with three children. He hasn't been hiding his feelings for me even in the presence of others."

Chris cleared his throat. "Do you fancy him?"

"I'm saying he has changed since the party, he's far more affectionate and understanding than usual."

"But he sleeps an awful lot."

"You shouldn't work so hard," Emily informed and was going to leave him, "because you might end up in the infirmary for showing a little wear and tear."

"I'll be down in a second."

***

Leo re-emerged into the common room after sleeping for six hours; he received a warm reception from Jay, Emily, Tasha and Chris as they were sitting along the sofa and at several computer terminals.

"So you've decided to join us, Commander!"

Leo Rockford did have an incredible dream, but he wanted to silence his crew about his facial flush. "I must apologize for my behaviour earlier as I am not used to drinking alcohol."

Jay burst out laughing. "You mean to tell me that the pair of you is space-cadets still learning to drink cheap red wine?"

"Just because of similar circumstances," Leo said sternly, "between your superior officers, it does not give you the right to take the helm! Look, so I have been feeling a little tried and I hope that you understand that we have seen some strange stuff on Mars, right?"

The crew nodded.

Leo said further, "You all know that our Supreme Commander had enforced a black-out prior to that ruby-figurine, and it's a serious matter."

Chris said, "We do understand you having faith in General Kaiser. Also, we fully understand that the figurine is a threat."

"That's correct," the Commander said warmheartedly, "you understand perfectly well that we cannot reveal our find to the public. I'm going to ask you all another very, very big favour—"

"What is it?" Emily asked eagerly.

"We all know that we aren't to disclose the figurine onto the public domain as it causes havoc. Basically, what we are doing is for the benefit of our Supreme Commander, right?"

The crew nodded again.

"I'm afraid," Leo continued, "of the consequences that might be put in place if word got out that Martin, and I, were a bit under the weather."

Chris asked, "Sir, why do you have no faith in your own medical personnel?"

"It's not you that I'm worried about," insisted Leo, "I've a different concern."

"What might that be, sir?"

"You see, as you all know, our General is a little anxious at not being labelled Ming the Merciless."

"You mean," Jay responded, "if the public became aware of your sickness, that the General will still be conceived as Ming."

Leo nodded. "That's been crossing my mind," he said.

Chris said, "So we are required to sign two classified papers: one for the figurine and the other for our party fiasco?"

"Don't you see?" Leo asked. "If word gets out about our red-faced condition, we could be misinterpreted as collaborating with the Red Resistance Force."

They all believed his artifice.

Jay was shaking his head. "I think I'll hang my boots after this because this is getting far too weird. What you're saying is that since we're contemporary explorers, important people will be too ashamed to associate with us. It's a repeat in history, if we look at Christopher Columbus, for he was the King's idiot by claiming a short trade route to India. Then we have Marco Polo, for his Italian nobles thought he was mad by making up stories on the Far East."

Leo was confounded. "What are you babbling on about, man?"

"Sorry, just that we're not going to be applauded for not being weirdoes."

"Listen," Leo said, "those explorers haven't a say for the present and they shouldn't be role models. All I'm saying is that we ought to be careful, or we might face a witch-hunt."

The crew sat in complete silence as they knew it meant General Kaiser – so they thought.

Chris said, "OK Leo. We promise not to tell a soul."

"That's fantastic. I have been a little tried but I'm good now. So this is what I think we ought to do; we will commence Orion's full capacity within the next forty hours."

"We're to take short cuts for Earth?" Tasha asked him.

"Precisely, besides, I've already taken Chris' advice on looking for plasma-lines every 72 hours – you know, to regain our strengths." Leo turned to Chris. "I want you," he said, "to check that the Alpha Control units are fine."

"I've already done that while you were asleep."

"Eager, aren't you? You will do it again but this time it's with me."

"Yes, sir."

"Jay, wake that lazy Assistant Commander that I want him in Alpha Control."

"Yes, sir."

Eventually, Emily and Tasha were what remained on Beta Control.

"It looks like everything is back to normal," Emily said.

"You do mean that Martin isn't madly in love with you."

Emily shook her head. "Did you know that Chris was thinking to take control of this ship?"

"I wish him the best of luck. Why was he thinking about that?"

"It's because of our Commanders – they've been oversleeping."

"You're serious, aren't you?"

"I'm very serious. He was thinking that our superiors must undergo a psychological evaluation. Of course, to take control of this ship has they've compromised several protocols. He continued saying that it's for the safety of our crew."

"I was thinking of marrying him," Tasha said fondly, "under an alternative reality because of his brunt approach, not his sub-ordinance."

"Looks like you better off with Quency."

"I knew there had to be a good reason why I married him. I think I'm going to send him a lovely email."

Emily halted her. "Have you thought about General Kaiser's paranoia, that he's eavesdropping our messages?"

"That's a possibility, isn't it? If I knew better, I would've sod this fucking mission."

They both remained on the sofa. It was their moment to think of those who were eavesdropping.

"Do you think," Tasha asked, "it should have been professional of Leo to advise us on that?"

"I think he should've made us aware. God! What if Chris is right?"

"I was just thinking not to marry him in a parallel universe," Tasha said fondly again.

Emily got up. "I seriously think," she went on saying, "that we are getting a little too paranoid since finding that figurine. God, what am I doing?"

Tasha got up too. "All I can say," she said, "is that once we get home, we're home dry. At the moment, I'll be writing a—"

Within moments, Leo Rockford made another appearance into the common room. "Oh just one more thing, are you fully aware that all communications are intercepted for security purposes?"

Emily replied, "It's just what we were going to ask you about."

"It's true," added Tasha, "we've been thinking to tell you since you didn't advise us. You did know about Orion's communication system?"

"Terrific!" Leo said without fully answering her question, and returned to Alpha Control.

The two women were left alone again.

"In a parallel universe," Tasha mentioned, "I'm sure I would have filed a divorce against Jay."

The girls laughed lightly.

Tasha said, "Will you be reporting Martin to Leo?"

"Do you really think that he's pestering me?"

"Of course, yes, he's out of character."

"Like Jay."

"That isn't fair. Jay hasn't been holding my hands and looking deep into my blue eyes and saying *Baby! We've been in space for over five sweltering weeks, and today is the only time I'm going to say this, I love you.*"

"That isn't fair. He might have just decided that he fancied the way I looked at the party."

"So you do fancy him?" Tasha asked.

"I've responsibilities back home, and I just cannot jeopardize my family, for a crime of passion."

"It sounds like you've been doing this before," Tasha said jovially.

"As if! I've been reading good romantic novels."

"You do fancy the Assistant Commander. So, you're prepared to commit that crime of passion on this ship, which is thousands of miles from home, isn't it?"

"Look at you! Why aren't you digging the groove with Jay?"

"That's because I'm happily married and so is Jay. Besides, it's not professional to go about sleeping with colleagues in a close-knit community."

"There you said it!" Emily pointed out, "close-knit community! We cannot think straight if we compromise our positions, for a crime of passion."

***

"Can you still not see that there's dirt!" Leo shouted, in Alpha Control, on the dust that settled on the equipment. "I want this terminal unit spotless." He repeatedly pointed to his Commander's seat. "Who has been adjusting my seat? I won't be able to sit up straight!"

Martin and Jay turned to look at Chris for answers.

"I do not know who has been adjusting your seat," Chris responded, "but I do know that I have been evaluating—"

"If you have been doing your supposed checks, you would have seen that those control panels needed some cleaning! Also, you might have caught somebody adjusting my seat – for their own pleasure!"

Chris said, "I'm very sorry, Commander."

"Good, now, if you will excuse me, I'll like to be left alone with the Assistant Commander."

Chris and Jay left them. Leo turned to Martin, shaking his head, and sighed. "I'm going to tell you something that you might not have noticed. You're aware of the Sacred Water of Zetta?"

"Of course, since I'd been suspicious that it was you that spiked my drink. So what of it?"

"Are you aware of the Nobilis status?"

"To be honest, I've been aware of my affection for females–"

"So have I but you should try to fight your sexual desires, and see deeper into the status of the Nobilis. For I believe it's a very serious matter."

"So you want me to rest again and mediate?"

"That's not necessary for now! All I'm saying is that it's a very serious matter that extreme care ought to be taken."

Martin asked, "So you don't like your wife, isn't it? You neither like the Nergala women nor the females here, isn't it?"

"It's got nothing to do with that. Don't you see? I'm the Commander here. So I'm required to maintain discipline in my crew, and in myself."

"Don't I know that? God, you must be sterilized or numb, if not both. If you're worried that I'm going to chase Emily around this ship, don't concern yourself. I do fancy her more than ever and when I'm next to her, I believe she's foxy."

"As your superior, and most likely your Nobilis, I command you to block those temptations promptly."

"You want to make up my own mind, don't you?"

"You need to control that urge and face the Nobilis status in your dreams. You need to understand further the qualities of the Sacred Water of Zetta, and you need to act more human than the crew."

Martin moved a little to the front and laughed. "You expect me to follow your path of a regime?"

"I expect you to understand the Nergalas! Yes, they have a regime and they know about our planet Earth."

"What!" Martin said, stunned, "who are you really, Leo? Are you some kind of power nut?"

"I'm following a discipline that I want you to comprehend. Also, we really should be close friends from now on."

Martin was congenial. "That's very touchy, Commander," he said, "so we may share our mental notes about the Nergalas. After that, we could even write science fiction novels together."

"Martin, you really need to comprehend the Nobilis, the Nergalas and the Sacred Water of Zetta. Hopefully, you'll see the dangers that may lurk if we continue to be impetuous."

"Okay, you amaze me with that heart of yours. What were you again, a stockbroker?"

"I'm recommending that you mediate, some more."

"Fine, I do it later on."

Chapter 18

—Daren't to boast—

*T*HE ORION WAS three days away before landing in Florida. Leo chose routes involving artificial gravity and weightlessness. In that way, the Commander had the advantage of keeping morale. In the usage of artificial gravity, it did bring together advantages and disadvantages. Other words, it made Leo and his crew feel closer to home, it kept the astronauts physically strong, and they had more control on their mobility — than constantly bumping into one another. Nevertheless, there were bad points, such as, it brought boredom in confided spaces, fuel and oxygen levels would drop considerably a lot more, and food would have to be rationized. Of course, Leo was using routes that involved weightlessness in space too. It also brought together advantages and disadvantages. The positives were as followed as that there was hope of returning to their normal lives, even kept the human mind a lot more proactive. However, to highlight the disadvantages, it would make the astronauts weak, by experiencing *wobbly-knees* once arriving on Earth, and to manoeuvre around the decks was rather clumsy, and restraints had to be worn in bed and in the cockpit to remain stationery.

Leo Rockford never flinched. He didn't flinch as he wouldn't vilify General Kaiser. As such, Rockford had prevented the crew from conducting a psychological evaluation on himself. Yet, he did falter a little, amongst the crew, because he hated Martin's flirtatious behaviour. All in all, Leo had to play with his mind that Emily was sceptical that he hadn't any real feelings for her, and maybe, she simply didn't find him physically attractive.

Accordingly, MacCormick did take up Leo's advice, and he was taking the time to understand his alien dreams a bit more. He even portrayed a clearer picture on his Commander: A paranoid man that feared going around corners. He strongly believed that Leo faced being penury, and his family were living on borrowed time. Martin also perceived that the crew saw him as too bossy after that party, and it threatened Leo on getting a psychological evaluation. He had toyed with the idea to round the crew together that Leo suffered from fatigue, which made him delusional that Orion hadn't a fitting crew. Basically, Martin was slightly sick of him.

The two Commanders, in their mind-sets, had possessed an anxiety when having a communiqué with their wives: their loins were roaring for attention. However, Martin was becoming a better man since he couldn't initially handle his sexual desires around Emily. He was able to come to terms of harnessing his urges for his wife, Jennifer. He personally hadn't a problem that he desired both of them but knew such action couldn't go untamed. Martin had thought of himself as a modest monk, obeying his order in continence and perseverance. In effect, Leo Rockford saw himself as his abbot who was proud of his efforts, and saw a great future in his Assistant Commander. He was going to put in a request for him to become a member at the Andrews Clubhouse. Rockford was seeing MacCormick as General Kaiser might see Harry Trump: His bitch – besides, Leo had secured the spatial water within a locker on Omega Control

Martin still had his bitter, after taste on Rockford; he felt certain that Leo wasn't an honest character. On numerous occasions, he would consider him to an alpha-male, yet, didn't see any pleasure in women. MacCormick was very suspicious of his wishes to control him. His curiosity led him to run a biography check, at a computer terminal, he gasped when he realised Leo's first day at work, in America, on 13th October, it was the day when his best friend, General Kaiser, took power. Martin assumed that the two men were using each other to reach higher statuses. The way Martin saw it, Leo was more favourable to succeed Bill Kaiser as the new Supreme Commander of America. Basically, he believed he could achieve that fate if he gave induction to others by using that water. He wondered how he became affluent, and began using an internet search engine. He saw rumours of the Andrews Clubhouse, and speculations were rife that it was a nerve centre for the financial, political, and the religious elite. Martin easily recalled boasting how influential he would become after his water discovery, which had cost him his normality. He continued to detest him.

Leo was re-considering his allegiance with Andrews Clubhouse. He once rejoiced his welcome. Those days, he had the prized green blazer. Not only that, the prayer-room where good-mannered gentlemen were trying to resolve their on-going problems in Washington. They also gave prayer to their patron saint, St Andrew. Yet, there were others that believed in the Serpent of Eden, other words, they mocked the Saint. Such men wanted enlightenment and become one with the beast, and they thought of themselves as knowing the truth behind the existence of man. For Leo, it did seem like harmless fun that the Serpent of Eden was involved in the financial, political and religious areas. But fun it wasn't, it was dangerous. Of course, Martin was still keeping in touch with his wife, and she'd encouraged him to go to Mars, and he loved her for that. He was wishing for her to sip the Zetta to show her the wonders. He felt that sharing his prized drink would be easy; lace her drink. He was going to retrieve the water-flask, from Omega Control, and keep it concealed from everybody else. On the contrary, Leo activated an authorization code to gain access to Omega Control. It meant, of course, relieving Leo his command by undergoing a psychological evaluation, yet, Martin knew, Space Command wouldn't be too keen. Anyway, Leo placed the water-flask, ruby stones and the ruby-figurine under lock and key in a storing cupboard – he had already suspected that Martin was contriving for the water, after which, he considered that it was his own bloody fault for mixing his decent cup of coffee. Leo was keeping in touch with his wife too, and she was writing emails on their family and neighbours. One time, she wrote that Jay Kaiser's cousin had moved next door. Furthermore, their new neighbour was looking forward to invite the entire Rockford family to dinner.

Of course, the Orion was three days away before landing on American soil, and the eagle was travelling along a plasma-line.

Leo was in Alpha-Control, finishing his update with the Space Centre. After Rockford checked that his communication link was switched off, he faced Martin to say a few words. "Wow! They'll know that we've built a rocket to Mars, and they'll know of us entering their temple."

"That's pretty obvious," Martin responded, "you do get a little paranoid about life in space."

"It's not that I'm paranoid. It's the fact that we may have violated their Sacred –"

"Commander," Martin interrupted, "we've agreed since drinking the Sacred Water that it was a violation. After which, it isn't a good thing to boast that we drank it."

"The flask mustn't get into the hands of NASA," Leo said, "so what do you think the top scientists are going to do with it?"

"I've known you for the last eleven months, and I just cannot understand why you're so worried about our –"

"I'm worried that someone might drink it, then, start doing some neurology research."

"I'm more worried about the fact that you may spill the beans to our friends who will see you as a delusional little man. Goodness, no wonder I thought it was you that spiked my drink! Besides, we got the best scientists in the world who will trace the DNA of the water and who knows what? Clone it."

"Look here, Martin, the flask must not get into the hands of the Space Agency."

"I respect you as the Commander of the Orion, Leo, yet, you fail to impress me about the dangers of handing in the space-flask for further study. Just what aren't you telling me?"

"Martin, there are things in this world you may not fully understand concerning NASA, the Supreme Council and the likes. You just got to remember that knowledge is power."

"Like that's supposed to mean anything! What're you talking about? Are you saying that since we can tap into Zetta, we're powerful on Earth?"

"Don't you understand what I just said? You've heard of the rumours of the conspiracies surrounding Andrews, so why are you being a complete dick?"

Martin smirked slightly. "Of course I've heard the rumours, and I've always imagined you being a little paranoid—"

"So you've forgotten already about that ruby-figurine?"

Leo scored a point in his argument that knowledge was power. He felt at peace as he couldn't deny of the black-out. He tilted his seat back. "Like I said, the flask cannot get into the hands of NASA. We need to somehow treat it delicately. We need a ploy and I think I know what we can do."

"We're to dispose it into the sink?" Martin asked.

"No, we're to take the flask for ourselves."

Martin laughed. "You got a very vague imagination when it comes to taking the flask. I suppose you think that nobody is going to notice, that you're adding the flask to your home collection, isn't it? Didn't you think that the Security would just take it away from you?"

"We don't have to worry about Security as what we can do is sound, and what I mean is that we switch the contents."

"Switch it?" Martin asked. "And when NASA realizes it, then what?"

"Who is going to care? If they want to accuse us all, they might as well blame Kaiser the mega-film star too."

"So he's going to be a scapegoat for stealing the water sample from Mars and then what? No, let me guess – you'll be the Zetta."

"You know how dangerous that water can be and we need to keep it safe somewhere."

"So we're to make a treasure map?"

"You know how serious this can get. If you wish to share your comical feelings with everybody; you're as good as dead."

"Why did I take this job as an astronaut? So that I may see that it involves strange occurrences."

"Today, I'll be switching it. Once done, I'll be containing it in my daughter's water bottle where I hope to beat the system."

"That sounds rather ambitious getting your daughter involved."

"This will be like clockwork. I just stroll along to Omega Control, switch the flasks and nobody is the wiser. After that, we just inform the crew to assemble in here to get the briefing about when we're moving out of the plasma-line."

"After tea-time, I hope." Martin said mockingly.

"No, it'll be by supper time to eat my wife's lovely Victorian sponge cake."

The pair laughed at one another's fortunes.

"Leo, you've never told me why you wish to keep it a secret. You say that *knowledge is power*. However, it appears that it's only you and General Kaiser which believe in that type of psyche. So why is it that I feel that you aren't giving me the fuller picture?"

"That's because knowledge is power."

"Let me guess, you're to topple the General without my knowing."

"You've no basis for that kind of action."

"You've no basis that the Nergalas still have an existence, and the reason why the Sacred Temple of Zetta is unguarded is because Nergal is no more."

"Where in your sacred dreams have you come across an epidemic, which wiped out the Nergala people?"

"I haven't, I'm just saying maybe."

Chapter 19
—The homecoming—

*T*WENTY-FOUR HOURS remained on their journey. Leo was in the common room collecting his thoughts. It seemed quite relaxing, floating in mid-air, however, he had been on edge that Martin wasn't sealing his lips with everybody. *Goodness sake*, he thought, *he jokes too much, on his dreams, of alien life forms flying in humongous spaceships, and that Mars is riddled in alien technology.* The Commander's worries didn't end there as Martin believed that General Kaiser, was implausible to silence his critics as Ming. More still, Martin wished to uproot the bureaucracy in Washington. He even acknowledged Leo as amongst the *privileged*, and thought it was self-explanatory why he lost his command. Martin took his views a lot further still, he foretold him that one day, Leo would be confessing of his involvement.

Suddenly, he heard a transmission alert. It wasn't a convenient time but he shifted his attention onto General Kaiser. After he flew across to the upper deck, he passed Chris exiting the cockpit. Leo acknowledged his departure before he emerged inside to take his usual position at the front. From there on, he activated his intercom and it was showing a small visual of his dear friend, the General, standing tall and wearing his military green uniform with his arms folded.

Leo said, "Good day to you."

"Good afternoon, Leo. How have you been keeping?"

Leo raised his thumb. "Everything is going swimmingly."

He nodded his head. "You do know," Kaiser said, "why we're having this conversation don't you?"

Leo hovered in mid-air. "Of course, it's to do with the ruby-figurine, we aren't to admit its existence."

"Will your crew create a problem?"

"Their loyalties lie in you," Leo replied, "and they don't have any issues signing papers of secrecy."

Bill nodded. "It's great to see you again. Things are improving against the Red Resistance Force. Our intelligence is indicating that their numbers are thinning due to you guys. It's a job well done."

Leo turned to scratch his left side, but did an unintentional somersault. In fact, his nose detected something newly worn; the right of his sleeve was directly in front of him. His arms were flapping wildly, like a bird, which seemed to clip its wing in flight. Yet, he regained his balance. "Thank you, sir."

It might seem hysterical but Rockford knew that his crew was hot potato. All because if anyone told the world about the ruby-figurine, then Kaiser would be vilified very easily. He was certain that Bill was going to plant bug devices in their homes, and monitor their whereabouts. Leo was introspective, that it was best to tell him, up front, about the Sacred Water of Zetta. *Of course not*, he thought, *Bill will see me as delusional and a danger – I cannot tell him, just yet.*

"Listen, I think those water samples will be a real treat for the American people," Kaiser said, "so I'm thinking that we should place them in a space museum."

Leo forced himself to smile. "That'll be superb and a real treat."

"Glad you agree," Bill responded, "I suppose you haven't heard about Harry Trump?"

"What?"

"The fucking Red Resistance Force only just bombed one of his offices last week."

"I never realized how desperate they were. Is he alright?"

"Yeah, he's fine and it was only a small explosion that managed to pass our security line, and nobody was hurt. Also, we were able to track down the perpetrators. Of course, we got those sons of bitches, and let me tell you that the Supreme Judges will determine their fates. They just never learn, do they?"

"True."

Bill was standing tall but sensed something odd, and faltered his pose a little. "What's the matter with you? Not happy about the perpetrators being caught?" Yet again, Leo performed an unintentional somersault but regained his balance. "I'm dizzy doing these acrobats. Of course I'm happy for Harry Trump; for he's a good man."

"Harry says *hello.*"

"Great."

"I've been thinking a lot over the last two weeks and it's to do with Martin."

"You mean if Martin will blow the whistle against you?" Leo pretended to ask.

"Well, I don't mind him being under your command, but it's his known frustration of not being the Commander; that's what I'm more concern about."

"Would you believe me that we have settled our differences?"

"How in the world did you do that?"

Leo lied, "It's because Martin is having an affair with Emily."

Bill laughed. "Well," he said after controlling himself, "I suppose that changes things. I always thought a ship having a little too much comfort would result in that."

"That's absolutely correct. You should have seen Jay chasing Tasha."

Bill smirked again. "We all knew that Jay was capable to break his fidelity, but I never saw it in Martin."

"Neither did I...It happened on several occasions."

"There! And I was thinking to send a clean-up team to change the dirty laundry!" Bill said jokingly.

"He's not so hard up after losing his command. I say again, he's not going to cause a riot."

"Leo, I bet he'll turn into an low-life alcoholic and a womanizer before this day is through."

"Who knows?"

"So he has lost the will to be at the top of the tree?"

"Come off it. To sleep with a colleague isn't the best way to climb up a career ladder, isn't it?"

"He's still reckless of becoming a whistle blower."

"I just do not understand that Martin will wake up from his first day back from Mars to make confessions. I think you're being a little too hard on him."

"My God," Kaiser said, "haven't you changed? It sounds like you've been with Emily too!"

"Just because I don't have my wife with me for at least six weeks doesn't mean I'll jump in bed with the first available woman."

"No offence! You need to lighten up and smell the fresh air."

"Erm, yes, of course" Leo wasn't feeling sagacious from the General, "as far as I'm concerned, it's the luxury cruise in space that's the cause out here."

"Okay, but look, I'm sorry, I do not want anybody exposing what you've found in that cavern."

"Understandable since the resistance will use it cleverly against you. God!"

"Leo, I know you think Martin is an alright guy and all. So this is what I will do for you. Do not question my logic that you think Martin's a decent chap. He still sounds reckless that has nothing to lose. Cheating on his wife doesn't show me that he has any loyalty. So therefore, I'll be keeping a closer eye on his activities once he arrives here, and don't you think for a second that you're scotch free."

"Bill, you'll find nothing on him and what do you mean that you're placing me under surveillance? I'm telling you what I know of him – not what I do not."

"Just listen to what I've to say. Martin will be closely monitored and that's that. Got it?"

Leo agreed reluctantly, "Yes sir, is there anything else?"

"Well then, I'll be seeing you."

It took several minutes for Leo to consider that he had better see Martin. He had twenty-three hours to convince him that after they got back to Earth, to act as if Zetta never existed.

Leo heard Martin knocking on the cockpit door, and there and then, the two Commanders were floating in the room to hold their life-changing conversation.

"Martin, we really need to talk and we do not have a lot of time to talk about it. Kaiser sees you as a potential threat. Apparently, you're envious that I took your position, and he speculates that you'll be a whistle-blower. Therefore, the secret service will be keeping an eye on you."

"You mean that you were part of a secret government from day one? And the reason that you're telling me this is because you've flaws?"

Leo shook his head. "Don't you understand the bigger picture? You'll be kept under close surveillance. So if you carry on being casual about Zetta, then they will ultimately think that you are an agent of the Red Resistance Force!"

"So you think I can tell anybody about it? Why do I think it's really you that is the problem?"

"So you think that I'm part of a *secret government* that controlling the American society? So what if I am! I'm telling you as if we are Zetta, there are dark forces on Earth which will not take kindly to the news of an alien life form, and that type of news will be misinterpreted. Also, we'll have to abandon our friendship too."

"If I am Zetta," Martin informed, "tell me who and what is that secret government?"

Leo confessed, "I knew General Kaiser since Turkey. I became tangled, what you call the *secret government*, since the Supreme Council took power. You've to understand the trigonometry of the clubhouse that it runs the American economy, it runs the religious churches in America and it even runs the political arena. It was easy for me to take this Commander post because I am part of the Hog's Head movement, which means that the shortlist was fixed."

Martin was clapping his hands. "So the bird is singing loud and clear. I always thought that you were part of the problem. God, if I wanted to succeed you, I would need your powerful friends."

"Will you stop complimenting yourself and wake up," Leo said and wanted to be philippic. "You'll need," he continued, "to realize that the Hog's Head Order is a potential threat! If they start believing that you're—"

"You don't need to spell out the consequences! We're to return to Earth to live a life like a modest monk. We can neither upset the balance of power, human and alien alike, can we?"

Leo decided to move closer to Martin to pat his right shoulder, but was gripping him firmly. "We've been through a lot together and I just want to say that I've enjoyed having you as my Assistant Commander. Plus, giving me the views on Zetta."

"Yeah, thanks for the insight too."

***

Nineteen hours before Orion's touchdown. Martin spent time alone in the infirmary to contemplate his relationship with his wife, his children and the "secret government" that was going to trail him. As he was floating in the air, it was obvious that the person behind it was his Supreme Commander. Martin imagined that General Kaiser had to be a lot more paranoid than Leo. However, he was thinking that Leo could get close enough to make him understand the potent water. MacCormick knew from experience that it was relatively easy to persuade Leo to have his cup of coffee, so could he learn from that? Martin was still pondering at how long the General's stalkers were going to monitor his activities. A month? A year? Or perhaps more? *As long as the Red Resistance Force is a threat*, he thought.

Before his Mars assignment, the Assistant Commander highly regarded the Supreme ideology, for it removed the economic turmoil, it brought a peaceful harmony, and it was making politics less murky. Now, he hated it. He detested Bill Kaiser breathing closely behind his back, and standing in his way of his career.

Meanwhile in Alpha Control, Leo took time to reflect on his conversation with the General. Of course, he tried to protect Martin, but felt that he had only made matters worse. Leo cursed fate if the General was really going to sound the horn against him.

***

The clock struck 9 o'clock in the morning. It was only six hours ago that Kaiser called. Anyhow, the pair was still trying to resolve it in the infirmary.

Martin said, "Leo, I know you have friends in the secret government, and sometimes friends don't always agree – eye-to-eye – but why don't you tell him straight up?"

"I just told you already about the situation of the ruby-figurine."

"Maybe, but I thought you knew him close up, don't you?"

"I do know him, and the answer is no."

"So why don't you broaden a conspiracy against him?"

"Are you kidding me? You don't just do that just because I've visited the Sacred Temple of Zetta."

"Look at you!" Martin scorned, "you're behaving as if the pair of you belongs to Zetta!"

Leo hovered above him. "Realistically, we can't do that. Looking to elucidate confidants wouldn't be a easy task. It also means that I'll have to be their mentor, and besides, I could easily fold the club if I follow your lead."

"Follow my lead? It beats the secret service peeping through the keyhole of my door!" Martin responded.

"There's nothing else that we can do. Look, I do believe that I can put in a recommendation, to the General, for you to become Major. I could even go a step further and press him to consider a position as Lieutenant-Colonel."

"It's just that my family will be watched by that Kaiser. It isn't right and you know it. That's just terrific, isn't it? I'll be an honoured American, but blemished by the paranoia of him. Leo, so it looks like this will be the last time. We won't be speaking with one another after we disembark, isn't it?"

"Looks like it," answered Leo, "I cannot see it feasible to meet up again."

"Think that your water bottle trick will fool the security team?"

"Yes, the secret service's objective is to obtain the ruby-figurine only."

143

***

It was just hours before the Orion's re-entry.
Chris was in the common room with Jay. He was having a conversation regarding the last six weeks, and what the future might have in store. "This weightlessness makes me wonder the point of having that great sofa."

"Well at least we're arriving back home a lot sooner," Jay said. "Haven't you noticed the two Commanders not killing each other, lately?"

"They both must have realized that they'll be returning to the Supreme Commander: They have to get along."

"Perhaps it's about Emily. I thought Martin was definitely trying it on with her...Maybe Leo disapproved—"

"How's your wife?" Chris asked.

"Great."

"Not much of a talker about her, aren't you? Are you having a marital breakdown?"

"We're fine, just that we have only been married before the space launch, and it's up to us to salvage our marriage. And you?"

"Not married remember."

"You aren't married!" Jay said astonished, "look at the women you could have had!"

"I do have a girlfriend I've been seeing for the last ten years."

"So you think it's a waste of time, marriage?"

"No but we do have a hectic lifestyle. Think about it, before this Mars mission I was doing reconnaissance for the air force."

"Where and whence was your espionage?"

"That's classified information."

"So you think the ruby-figurine isn't going to be classified?"

"The reconnaissance flights were neither governed by NASA, nor Hollywood!" Chris responded, "sorry dude, it's just hush-hush."

"One day, we'll be telling our grandchildren of a paranoid dictator — provided that he passes away quietly."

"That depends entirely on the Supreme Council. What if they elect a new Supreme Commander and he keeps that classified?"

"You appear pretty sure it's going to be a male, aren't you?"

"No! I mean I'm not a sexist!" Chris said, stupefied.

Jay giggled. "Never sure who's going to be the successor. Could even be my wife."

"You're right!" Chris agreed, yet embarrassed. "Your wife may be able to throw punches in the political arena."

"I'll tell my wife about you. You're a decorated captain in the air force. One who sincerely believes that my wife has got what it takes to run the greatest nation in the universe."

"Do you love your wife, Jay?"

"Yes I do. Why else would I be married?"

"It's showbiz!" Chris answered confidently. "You're telling the world that you've found the love of your dreams; your fans marvel you."

"You seem quite perspective of the entertainment industry. Why don't you be my personal assistant?"

"Now you're mocking me. I'm happy with my choice of career so why don't you join the military?"

"I'm happy not too."

Chris asked, "Why were you all over Tasha?"

"She's a very attractive woman with a lucky husband waiting for her on the other side. I could have been her secret admirer but it wasn't to be. Why must you ask?"

"Shouldn't that be obvious?" Chris continued, "your marriage to your wife is a vow. On this ship, you were trying to have a private encounter. You see, Jay, Tasha doesn't want to cheat."

"And I thought you were very perspective about showbiz? I married her recently, and if things work out then things will work out. That means that I may look back on my flirtatious behaviour, and say to myself that I was a jerk."

"There're times when you've been a real sport, and I'm not sure how we as a crew could have been without you," Chris said positively – *Shit! I'm being a little too courteous*, he thought to himself.

145

***

At Cape Canaveral, a welcoming party was expecting the Orion's arrival. After she touched down, there was going to be a fly-over by four fighter jets along with two B-29 bombers. The two large aircraft were to release confetti upon the unsuspected below.

An air force band was set to play the new national anthem. Of course, the crew would be welcomed by their families, the spectators and the media. There were some very important figures, in the welcoming party, being the British Prime Minister, the French President, and of course, General Kaiser (they had attended to a military trade too). The three world leaders were to show their appreciation to the astronauts. Kaiser knew that the crew was the first to land and take-off from the planet Mars, they were the first to experience the plasma-line effect, and the first to return back from the longest journey set by man. Therefore, it was going to be a party he couldn't afford to miss.

Discreetly, Leo was to hand-in the ruby-figurine after disembarking. Then the entire crew had to go through a medical examination, and moments later, sign the paper of secrecy:

I hereby, a citizen of the United Supreme of America, will protect and honour my Supreme Commander; General Bill Kaiser. I'll not confirm the existence of object: Ming's Doll, which threatens the existence of the Supreme Commander and his Supreme Council. I understand that object: Ming's Doll would be manipulated by enemies of the state.

Any perpetrators who wish to violate the protection of our new America will be summoned for a Court Marshall as an act of high treason.

....

SIGNATURE OF ASTRONAUT

***

An hour was left remaining before the astronauts landed on Florida. Despite the hull integrity of the spacecraft, NASA protocol stated that the astronauts must wear their full spatial gear. Commander Rockford was at his usual post with his Assistant Commander beside him. Capt. Emily Walters was monitoring the status of the ship while Chris, Tasha and Jay were in their straps along the rear. Commander Leo Rockford was aware that the space craft was exceeding speeds of 70,000 kph. It looked amazing seeing Earth, which was getting bigger and closer as every second passed by.

"This is Commander Rockford, we are approximately fifty minutes before landing, please advice?"

"This is the Kennedy Space Centre. We will be signing off but Cape Canaveral will be your eyes and ears, shortly."

Leo turned to Martin to gain his attention, then, rolled his eyes to curse the heavens.

Momentarily, the communication channel wasn't active.

"This is Cape Canaveral, and we're glad to be of service. We estimate your arrival within forty-five minutes. All systems go."

"We copy," Commander Rockford confirmed, to his new designator, "we're to make our descent."

"Roger."

Leo brought the nose up to glide along the Exosphere. He had high hopes that the heat-shield should keep its integrity. Since the space craft was exceeding speeds of 70,000 kph on her approach, she hadn't any brakes to decelerate towards ground-control. However, Orion's high speed should take on the atmospheric friction, which should slow her down. Nevertheless, it would be building intense heat around the ship that might cause her to break apart. Yet thanks to the ingenuity of NASA, it was believed that Orion's heat-shield would hold.

Success! The Orion was cruising at a speed of 1000 kph, along the Troposphere. She was heading for Cape Canaveral. To conclude her re-entry, the Orion had no difficulty in her descent and she completed her free fall and weightlessness ceased. Everybody couldn't keep their emotions in check. After all, it was a historical launch six weeks junior.

"This is Commander Rockford, we have re-entered the Earth atmosphere and we're heading for Cape Canaveral."

"Copy, Commander Rockford, the ground is clear for you to touch down."

Meanwhile at Cape Canaveral, General Kaiser was punching the air. His position, as the Supreme Commander, looked more secured. He dashed towards the runway with his Security Detachment. Along the way, he met up with the astronauts' families, the spectators and the media. Over a billion people were watching the extraordinary launch from mid-air, and the Mars exploration. Soon enough, the TV audience was to bear witness of her arrival. The popularity of the hi-tech ship was silencing Kaiser's critics. Therefore, General Kaiser had his own hallmark on the space age. The shuttle was only minutes away, and the air force band began playing the new national anthem, which was, indeed, a cordial tune. Soon enough, the Orion was in full view as she was strolling along the runway to complete her journey.

A lot of people were smiling, cheering and clapping hands loudly as they disembarked with the help of the passenger-stairs. For the first time for over six weeks, they would be able to smell the fresh clean air of their triumph. Leo was holding two items as he took the lead down the stairs. He was looking for his family and spotted his wife and youngest daughter. He was congenial as he revealed his daughter's *lucky charm*. Also, he simpered, to a Secret Service Agent, wanting to shake his hand. The Agent made his request for the key to secure the sensitive cargo in Omega Control. After that, Leo headed straight towards his family and the world leaders. In the process, four fighter jets and two bombers flew by.

Chapter 20
—Not all is quiet—

*L*EO TOOK ON a pleasant aroma: a morning breeze would enter into his home. He had followed it, next door, onto some well-arranged flower beds. His new neighbour was a relative of Jay Kaiser, and Leo couldn't even believe his ears as the sound of birds and insects was livelier in his garden. Already, Leo and his family had accepted invitations to have dinner with Charles Kaiser and his own family. As now friends, Leo and Charles played golf together at the lucrative club nearby. Since Leo was plastered all over the news, his visits made him a recognizable figure quickly. As such, he had the privilege to open a new club bar, and receive a life-long membership at an Orlando golf club.

Leo didn't keep regular contact with his former space colleagues. However, he got word, from Charles, that Jay Kaiser was to direct a Hollywood disaster movie. He had an email once from Tasha that her life biography was going to be published shortly. He also had a telephone call from Emily that she was going to be reassigned to work in Turkey. Furthermore, Leo heard from Chris that he was going to move to Scotland. Despite his updates, he didn't hear any news of Martin.

∗∗∗

It was a Tuesday morning, and Leo felt sanguine. He was alone, driving in his car, to attend a special hearing. The man was summoned to Cape Canaveral; it was about his conduct on the spacecraft.

As he drove onto the site, Leo hardly noticed any media activity outside of the large premise – it was a closed-door investigation. After stopping at the exterior security barrier, a soldier told him the best place to park his car. Thereon, he received a military escort who would be delivering him to his formal hearing. Leo looked at his watch, twenty minutes early, so imagined of waiting in a lobby as he was guided through a series of corridors. His assumption was correct when his escort advised him to take a seat. He sat down, and began to observe the vicinity. There stood a large portrait of General Kaiser on a wall; in his full military dress wear, and his chin was raised to enlarge his posture. There were smaller pictures of famous astronauts close by. One happened to be of Neill Armstrong in his orange jumpsuit smiling. Leo saw a coffee table near his seat, and reached out for a magazine. He was going to read an article on the discovery of the plasma-line universe.

Eventually, a door opened and Harry Trump, made a gesture, to join him. "Good Morning, Mr. Rockford, it's an honour to see you again."

"Adjutant-General Trump, I'm glad to see you too," replied Leo and he entered into the room. He felt his heart pounding slightly. Leo wondered if he should be feeling a little guilty.

Harry Trump was going to sit with strangers along a long oak table. It consisted of microphones, jugs of water and drinking glasses. Nearer to Leo laid a smaller oak desk that had a microphone, a small jug of water and an empty drinking glass. The Adjutant-General indicated to him of where to sit. Politely, Leo calmly took his seat as to face the long table ahead. The room seemed to be a renovated farmhouse as the walls were laid with dark, varnished wooden planks. There consisted of many bookcases which seemed to contain spatial literature. Leo pondered if Tasha's journals were somewhere amongst them.

"This is a Committee Hearing, and we are also the Advisory Panel for General Kaiser. As you may have gathered, it was us who approved to make you the Commander of the Orion. It was also us who devised the Safety Protocols that Jay Kaiser has been known to kick a fuss about," he chuckled, along with others along the huge table. "Anyway, I am presiding this hearing and my name is James Nunn. Are you Mr. Leo Rockford?"

"Yes, that is he," Leo said.

"We've obtained a disturbing report. The content of the space-flask that you alone placed in the cupboard, under lock and key, can't be located. Can you explain to this Panel why you took steps to lock it up?"

"That's simple because I wanted the space deck, Omega Control, to be secured. Basically I feared depleting our food supplies."

James asked, "When you speak of Omega Control, you're in fact informing this Panel about the lower deck of the fuselage?"

"That is absolutely correct."

"Please can you explain to this Panel, that since you had a concern against depleting food, that you enforced strict access to the deck, and placed the extracts under tighter security?"

"That is because I believed that the flask and its minerals were important to the goal of the Orion mission. Since I have such storage to place those items, there and then, I made the decision to secure the cargo."

"You speak of securing the cargo. Are you sure that you've placed the right flask in the secure unit?"

"I'm absolutely and most definitely sure of it," Leo replied.

"Then can you explain to this Panel why we are missing the water from the Mars expedition?"

He sensed that he hadn't thought though the heist properly. He had a slight anxiety that the aliens would soon hear of it! Therefore, they might suspect that it was him. Leo managed to remain composed. "You mean to tell me that you've the wrong flask?"

"I mean to tell you that the flask is missing its spatial water! I must inform you that we haven't disclosed that information with your former colleagues as this is a continuing investigation. So I'll ask you kindly to deter on informing them," James reacted.

"Furthermore," the Adjutant-General made his mark, "that you're not to disclose any information about object: Ming's doll outside of this room. Do you understand?"

"Sure," Leo replied.

James Nunn asked, "Can you explain to this Panel the security lax?"

"Well, all I can say is that I'm very sure of securing the cargo in the unit."

"How sure are you: Out of a score of one to ten?"

"That's a perfect ten."

Another person, to James' right, began asking his own set of questions. "You're confident that you had secured the cargo, isn't it? Then why do you think that I'm seeing somebody that is over-confident? Better still, I'll suggest that you're complacent, isn't it?"

"I'm not a complacent person as that kind of attitude never got me into the position of running the Orion. And that includes being a Senior Astronomer and a Squadron Leader in the RAF."

"You've held some positions of great responsibilities. Surely you're not saying that you didn't realize you were a better candidate in getting our job done?"

"It wasn't my decision to being appointed as the Commander of the Orion."

"You strike me as a very confident individual. Are you certain that we will not accuse you of, let's say, stealing the water for financial gain?"

"Are you serious?" Leo asked, irksomely. "Are you really saying," he continued, "that I'm a crazy fool that had the dollar signs glittering in my eyes? What you're really saying is that there is financial gain in the spatial water, but what of the ruby stones?"

"I'm afraid it's not for us to give the answers but you. Now then, will you be kind enough to answer my original question. Did you see any sense for financial gain?"

"No because I cannot see any sense of a camel trader getting a good bargain for that water!"

Harry Trump was knocking on his desk. "Mr. Rockford, please keep your answers as simple as possible and avoid innuendos. Can you confirm that you saw a financial gain?"

"No, I do not," Leo said.

James Nunn now asked, "Mr. Rockford, do you have any reason to believe that a member of your crew might have taken it?"

"No, absolutely not."

"We've taken account of an absurd incident," James continued, "it's between you and Martin MacCormick." Leo's heart was sinking if the Panel knew of his flushes, however, remained to play it cool. "Listen, it seems like I've came here to help you track down the spatial water, but you're moving into uncharted territory now."

"Not at all, Mr. Rockford, we know that the pair of you was not feeling too well."

"Look, Martin and I were ill. It's not a crime to being unwell."

"But it was your illness that got the pair of you much closer, much closer together, will you confirm that?"

"We had our disagreements before the party. We might have drunk too much as we were in a right state, but it wasn't too serious."

"A little bird told me that you were a bit under the weather. In fact, the little bird informed this hearing that you were looking scarlet."

Leo asked, "So what do you want to know? I accidentally drank the spatial water thinking it's wine, or that I was hiding it for fun?"

"Mr. Rockford," Harry said, "let me remind you again not to bring this hearing into disrepute! Were you looking scarlet?"

"I suppose so...I did look red and I was vomiting that morning."

"The little bird never mentioned that!" James Nunn said, slightly shocked too.

"Perhaps your little bird wasn't there when it happened!" Leo replied.

Harry reached for the jug of water. He was pouring the content into his glass. "Mister Rockford, are you certain that you've been placing the right flask in the secure unit?"

"I'm one hundred per cent certain."

James Nunn sighed. "What I fail to understand is that after the party, you gave recommendation to NASA to place an authorization code. Therefore, only you could allow your crew access on the lower deck of the fuselage.

Why at that precise moment of time would you want to do that?"

"On the way to Mars, I couldn't see the logic to enforce strict access–"

"You don't appear to be worried," a man, from the left of James Nunn, interrupted, "about depleting the freezer on your journey to Mars, can you explain?"

"Certainly, my frame of mind was to be concern about the morale of the crew during the slow voyage to Mars. So therefore, I acted with minimum ship protocols to keep the harmony. Afterwards, the morale of my crew reached a new high as we headed for home. So I decided strict access to Omega. Obviously, we'd have ample supply. I also believed it's a good practice on work ethics."

"Mr. Rockford, will you agree that we do not have any supply of the water?" A question asked, by yet another man, to the left of James Nunn.

"Sir, I do not wish to wind you up. I only wish to apologize for my part in the operation to secure the cargo. All that I'll say is that I didn't see it coming."

James was whispering to one of his colleagues. *What could he be saying?* Leo thought. Needless to say, he then stared straight ahead at him. "It appears that we're going around in circles," James went on, "determining the perpetrator. So can you tell me where you placed object: Ming's doll during this whole operation?"

"Again, it was under lock and key with the spatial water, sir," Leo replied.

"We believe that you are not the type of person to put into jeopardy this Space Agency and the Supreme Council. Yet, we cannot understand how the spatial water is missing. We'll still be asking you of your role: Did you take the water samples from planet Mars, or were you too busy collecting the valuable stones in the cavern?"

Leo was smirking that his crew managed to somehow forget to take a sample of the water: Martin MacCormick was the one who discovered it. Also, the entire crew was wearing video cameras on their helmets. "You know perfectly well from our video footages that we have taken samples."

"I wish that was true but remember that we had a black-out, didn't we?"

Leo's heart was relieved! The authorization prevented visual and audio footages. "I'm very sure that we—"

"I'm very sure that you are an incompetent idiot with his head high in the clouds! You cost us billions of dollars to get your sorry ass to Mars, and in return, you seemed to have left it behind!" James Nunn cried.

Leo stated calmly, "I'm still very sure that I've placed a filled flask in a secured unit on Omega."

"That flask was empty and it's plain to see that you have lost your senses in outer space!" James said contemptuously.

Leo's hearing was quickly coming to a close. The Panel ought to conclude that the crew was terrible at retrieving the spatial water. It might mean another mission to Mars.

"Mr. Rockford," Harry asked, "do you know the actual reason why we installed a secured cupboard unit on Omega Control?"

"Adjutant-General Trump, I never knew that you were part of the Advisory Panel, but could you be kind to give your reason why you are with us now?"

"Please do not be rude and answer my question. Do you know the reason why there's a secured unit in Omega Control?"

"That's because the secured unit holds a weapon."

"Can you explain the type of weapon and why it's concealed?" Harry asked further.

"It's a revolver and the reason it's there is to prevent mutiny taking place on the Orion."

"Very good, Mr Rockford, so is it wrong to assume that you and Martin knew about the secured unit?"

"We've been briefed in our special Commanders training — it was right here in Cape Canaveral — so what're you asking of me?"

"Didn't you sense Martin lacking command on our prized ship?"

"I do not understand what you're asking?"

"I'm trying to understand how is it that Martin MacCormick has a more relaxed mood on his return. His ambition to become Major appears to be distant."

"Harry Trump, I'm not his baby sitter."

"So you've seen him behaving a little odd, yeah? His squadron buddies believed that he has changed: Changed from being an astronaut to an ass. So you haven't noticed a slight change in his attitude?"

"I'm not sure what you're implying? Is this hearing to involve questioning the entire space-wing personnel?"

"I have been reading his military reports to being recommended Major for his services to the Supreme Council. If I'm right on being frank, he isn't suitable to become one."

"Martin MacCormick still wanted to explore Mars, even if you had given him the command of the Orion...Come to think of it, he reminds me when I was a Squadron Leader in the RAF. I turned my back to chase my life-long dream for astronomy. So, if I did get to Martin about it, then I think he deserves a chance to succeed."

"If that is the case," James said, "then why hasn't he asked for a transfer? Plus, why hasn't he made any hints during his annual review?"

"I don't directly work for NASA. I work at an university and I also own a small public relations company. I haven't a clue on how your transfers work. Anyway, we'd only returned from space ten months ago. Surely you're not advising this Hearing, that he should make a quick decision, isn't it?"

"So, it may appear that you've made an impact on Capt. MacCormick, that he's not decisive on his career path," James said, astonished.

"I might've said a few things here and there but I wouldn't describe myself as his personal mentor."

Harry Trump asked, "Leo, do you personally believe that Jay Kaiser is a role model for this space agency?"

"Of course, yes! He's a perfect role model to elevating the space agency, General Kaiser and the American people. He's a movie legend, he has a great complaisance."

"I think you're correct," James contributed further, "still, there seems little evidence, in this Hearing, of your crew extracting the spatial water. However, do you believe that one of your crew members was more than capable of taking it for personal gain?"

"That's absolutely not true. The integrity of the crew had been solid and I would be glad to serve the same men and women at a moment's notice. What we've achieved out there was far better than financial gain but morale. We may have been side-tracked to think that we had secured the cargo, but let me make this absolutely clear, I trust the crew and as I commanded the Orion, so you should too."

"Just one more thing before we close this Hearing," James said, "was it not Tasha's responsibility to take the water sample, or am I mistaken to have heard her during that live black-out?"

"Yes, I gave her the order to collect the water sample from the spring."

"Did she confirm, to you, that she had collected the necessary sample?"

"I must admit that we were close to breaking the Safety Protocols by remaining too long on the surface. Perhaps she thought she took a sample, but object: Ming's doll was a distraction. I'll take full responsibility for Tasha Chayton by not assisting her in extracting the spatial water."

"That we do have a problem," James said. "She says," he continued, "that you and herself, after the Mars expedition, were taking a closer look at the flask. Both of you saw that the water was red. Surely there's some form of irregularity that you've in fact had the water sample. So Mr. Rockford, can you explain to this Hearing, the nature how she made no extraction against the likelihood that you had watched its wonders unfold?"

Leo Rockford got himself into a muddle. At least, he kept his countenance – in must parts – constant. "That is true! We were in the kitchen pouring the content into a cup."

"So my guess is that the pair of you drank the water thinking it's the best drink in the entire galaxy, yeah?"

asked yet another person, along the huge table, to Harry Trump's right.

"You cannot possibly be serious that I and a crew member were taking turns in drinking the content, isn't it?"

"Facts don't lie! The point is that we can establish that Tasha Chayton extracted the water sample from the underground spring. Also, the pair of you made a discovery that the sample had a reddish colour. However, the fact remains that the content in the flask isn't within. Can you explain why to this Hearing, please?"

Leo made himself another glass of water. He wondered if they saw him trying to fix-up Martin MacCormick – that was if the crew made it clear of the apparent hatred between them. He sighed. "I believe in this space agency and this is the best agency throughout the entire world. I thank your Advisory Panel for accepting my application to serve as the Commander of the Orion, and I wish to thank the fantastic crew: Assistant Commander MacCormick, Capt. Tallon, Capt. Walters, Mrs. Chayton and Mr. Kaiser. It was a superb adventure, which I would love to redo with NASA. I only hope that being part of the crew hasn't hampered my relationship, as an astronaut, because of a physical difficulty in tracing the missing water. I'm deeply sorry for letting this Hearing down and I will advise you to enforce a Protocol in securing extraction on future expeditions. Again, I'll apologize in my lapse of judgment."

"It's duly noted," James said, it was the only words to acknowledge his contrition. "You say," he added, "Jay Kaiser is an ideal role model for this space agency. However, you haven't made it clear that you think he's capable of taking the spatial water from under our noses. Don't you have any suspicion against him?"

"Again, I trust the crew and I trust Jay Kaiser isn't selfish to steal our historical find. Therefore, I have no suspicion against him."

"OK, Mr. Rockford, since you and Tasha Chayton were the first to confirm the colouring of the water, will it also apply to her i.e.) Do you think she was capable of taking the spatial water, let's say for her study of plant life, shouldn't we?"

Leo was trying to remain fastidious. He was sure that the Hearing was trying to drop a noose around his neck. Leo coughed. "She is a wonderful member and it will hurt me so much that she had taken the water sample for her botany."

"So you're not certain if Tasha may have taken the water sample? Being that we gave you no incrimination against her. It would only suggest that you have no control over Tasha and of your crew," James Nunn added.

Harry Trump stood up from his seat. He lent forward to say a few words through his microphone. "Mr. Rockford, I would like to thank you in participating in this Hearing and I speak for James Nunn as well."

James Nunn was slightly perturbed by the apparent actions of Leo Rockford. "Given that you're a personal friend of General Kaiser — and that you marked the celebration of the Supreme Revolutionary Day — it's disappointing, to say the least, that you haven't brought back the spatial water. Are you aware that the spatial water would have been significant that planets are so similar to Earth for our own aspiration? It only surprises me that you had succeeded in being appointed Commander of the Orion. Furthermore, given by your lack of judgment to keep the integrity of the crew sound, I would be shocked to put in a good word on recommending you on future assignments. So anyway, I'll thank you for taking part in this Hearing."

Leo replied, almost clumsy, "I thank you, from the bottom of my heart, for having me."

He headed for the exit to found himself in the lobby again. He was through with his Hearing. He knew that they had made their decision that his professional conduct was unjust. Leo was looking at the large portrait of the General; he sensed a problem with Bill looking ridiculous. Other words, the General might scrap his funding on the Robinson Space Observatory and his company too. The only thing left to do was to leave the lobby and hope that his reputation wasn't tarnished.

Chapter 21
—Share his dreams—

*L*EO WAS IN his study. He could hear his clock ticking nearby, and there wasn't much noise trying to drown it. Only his fingers were making an occasional drum-roll on his richly varnished oak desk. His desk was situated against a wall, which allowed him a view, through his front window, of the quiet suburban street. On his desk sat a Banker's lamp that lit part of the room green. Leo was sitting in his swirl brown leather chair too. Anyway, he had a predicament; telling Carly; Charles and Bill Kaiser of his *personal eureka*. He began thinking on his wife, Carly. He believed she didn't deserve the same treatment, like Martin MacCormick, by tainting her drink. *She wasn't going to be anybody's bitch*, he thought, *perhaps, a one-to-one with her on the black-out would do the trick. Carly will be able to understand*. Morally speaking, he saw that it was best to come clean. However, when was it the best time to confess? And where should he do it? There was going to be a lot of ground to cover and Leo felt that his wife would only see him as a strange husband – he couldn't tell her.

After ruling out his wife, he considered telling Charles. He was a very bubbly guy that outweighed his cousin, Jay Kaiser. Leo felt confident. Soon enough, his paranoia got the better of him that Charles would be telling his buddies. Then of course, his buddies would be telling their friends. After all, such a spatial rumour would eventually lead to the media circus demanding confirmation that Leo had stolen the water! Not only would Leo be required to face the *media circus*, it looked likely of being recalled to Cape Canaveral too. Indeed, Leo could tell Charles but could he be able to remain his one and only buddy? Leo had to rule him out.

Last but not least, Leo pondered to confess to Bill Kaiser. Straightaway, there was a problem: The occult created paranoid people. Leo recalled being told, at the powerful clubhouse, of a peculiar man that gained prominence. He was only a grounds-man, yet was once, a monk of the Benedictine Order that was relinquished. His name was Marvin Hooper and he wanted an adaptation to play god. Incidentally, it led him forming his secret society there to perform his *Chaos Theories*. Both the General and the former monk were just as paranoid of external forces (such as the Church, pressure groups etc.) challenging them. So for Leo to confess, of aliens, would be seen as a mockery. He also had to rule him out.

Still in his study, Leo was considering if the powerful clubhouse was meant to challenge the times; for if his alien wisdom were to be accepted, then he would gain confidants. Leo played with the idea that the political, financial and religious inner-circle would benefit by learning his truth. The sheer thought brought new optimism of continuous space projects to Mars. Of course, Leo had reached his conclusion not to tell Carly, Charles and Bill Kaiser. He couldn't inform the three but there was time to form his own fraternity, wasn't there?

He got up from his brown chair to make himself a glass of brandy. He thought fondly of the hot-water bottle placed in the house. Obviously, it had been a present from his daughter, Alicia, for his cold and lonely nights in space. Leo had returned it to her, but she discarded it in the boiler cupboard. Needless to say, the water extract had a new home sitting in a new flask inside his garage. Just what was Leo going to do with the Sacred Water of Zetta? Only God knows.

Chapter 22
—Big brother—

*L*EO WAS IN his study again. A high-pitch metallic sound could be heard. He was reading his diary before looking at the clock across his desk – three o'clock – he resumed to read that somebody was everywhere he seemed to be going. It was rather peculiar, when taking his dog out for a walk, the man was standing along his street taking pictures of him. More so, the man was waiting for him outside the school gates when he collected his daughter, Alicia. Calmly, he pretended not to notice the stranger. He thought that he would go away...It was a disappointment, to say the least, that he wouldn't vanish; so why not make him aware that he could detect his presence, isn't it?...No joy at all, he wouldn't falter. Leo flipped a page of his diary. He wrote that he couldn't report him to the police as the man hadn't made any physical contact. The man had every right to use the public streets, parks and roads. But that man was crude. Leo flipped ahead, he had a reminiscence of having an unusual week; it all started when he was taking lunch outside of his Space Observatory. He saw that man again and he was always wearing his Hawaii-shirt. Instantly, he decided that it was best to challenge the snapper. He asked, in a vulgar tongue, of what the fuck was he doing? He continued to be philippic that he had seen him everywhere, and what the fuck did he want? Still scornful, he implied that he was invading his privacy. The Hawaii-shirt man looked at him and shook his head. The stranger implied that if he thought he had a private life; don't be judgemental about being a member of the public. Leo went berserk on his response and tackled for his camera. It got passer-bys involved in the commotion too (Clifford especially). It might have seemed that the famous Leo Rockford was losing his mind. Yet the Astronomer had a conviction that the man was a public nuisance, and was insulting his intelligence. Eventually, a policewoman entered into the scene to diffuse the situation. She took details of the two men and asked them kindly to mind their own business. Of course, it was a long day and latter diary entries indicated that he didn't see him again. He was returning to normality of collecting his daughter from school, his dog for a walk and even ate outside of the Observatory. Life seemed grand and Leo was certain that the man was only a fanatic stalker. However, he saw a different man wearing the same Hawaii-shirt in the park, outside of the school-gates, and was basically everywhere that he was going.

Leo closed the diary. *Bastards*, he thought. Leo had a glass of brandy, on his desk, and he finished it.

Chapter 23

*L*EO ROCKFORD ARRIVED at Heathrow Airport. He was accompanied by his wife and his entire family. He was going to receive his knighthood to become Sir Leo Rockford. Before receiving his title, he was going to do some sightseeing and shopping around London. Also, Leo was invited to a television studio for an interview.

It was straightforward, but where was his guide on leaving the airport? There were dozens of photographers swarming around him. He tried looking passed them, yet still, nobody wasn't holding a placard with his name on it. After ten long minutes, Leo spotted a man, bearing his family's name, who seemed to be in complete oblivion. The future knight knew that his plane was thirty minutes late and the man didn't seem to realize him standing at a distance. The closer Leo got to him, the more alert he became. Of course, the man began beckoning him over, and gave Leo a set of car keys. He also asked his VIPs to follow him to where their car was parked. Thankfully, Leo drove off to stop at Capital Hotel, which was only a stone's throw away to Buckingham Palace. When they got there, the hotel owners took it on themselves that the Rockfords could stay, for free, in their top-of-the-range rooms, as a courtesy of Leo's recognition of their excellence.

The second day in London was to shop around Knightsbridge with his family, then, attempt to see some famous London sites. Unfortunately, Alicia got tried with the adventure of buying new toys, so they returned to the hotel. By the evening, the family had a special treat to eat, with the hotel owner and his wife, to a small buffet. Leo fondly shared his story when his life seemed to turn its ugly head as he became an Astronomer: His car got stolen, being placed under arrest, and of course, the threat of closure of the Space Observatory.

The following day, Leo paid a visit to Buckingham Palace where he knelt for his KBE, then, rose as Sir Leo Rockford. He attended an evening at the Royal banquet to talk with the Queen and her guests too. After their grand visit, the family returned back to the hotel to end their evening in style.

On the fourth day in London, Leo was shopping lightly in Knightsbridge before his interview that evening. He was a guest on Tara Hussain's show and he felt a little nervous as Tara Hussain was a television mania. She was loved for her down-right attitude to get to the heart of her guests. Nevertheless, Hussain's conduct was pleasant regarding why he went to Mars, and what was it like to command the most hi-tech craft known to man. After his interview, Leo and his family retired to the hotel to reflect back on their stay.

On the fifth day, Leo was to return to Orlando and just before he went across the Atlantic, he took his wife, his daughters and his son to visit a local pub nearby.

Chapter 24

*L*EO LOVED HIS understanding of the early history of Orlando. He noted that the city was once called Jernigan, yet, the reason behind the change had always been unclear. The pleasure was his, he could dream clearly, of the aliens that gave him an unusual insight: It was their regard of Christopher Columbus. Of course, the explorer spoke of a quickest trade route to India than along the coastline of Africa. The aliens were certain that the word "Orlando" was an acronym regarding the Indians:

Or - An alternative European trade route to India
Land - The land of the supposed Indian subcontinent
Do - The people of the Indo-origin that Christopher Columbus wanted to trade with

After he woke up, he was so excited that he couldn't contain himself. Immediately, he headed to his study to write an open letter to the Orlando Sentinel newspaper. At first, it seemed like a waste of time and effort to share his vision, because it took six weeks for the paper to respond. They were going to edit an article of comparing his acronym to the popular folklore of Orlando Reeves: He was killed by Indians after delivering a warning shot.

Anyhow, Leo was content to continue his incredible dreams. Needless to say, the aliens had a very erotic nature. The males had a tendency of relieving themselves at the first sign of dawn. At the evenings, it was time for them to actively spend time with their spouses. They were inspired by a book, which advised the best form of sexual activities for mornings and evenings. The book was devised by Priests of Fertility and there were only few authors, Penii and Somee. Leo stirred from his kip, and something was building up inside of his loins that night. It tingled and he tried to fight the urge but couldn't. In the latter, he thought that he couldn't have prevented Martin MacCormick if he was properly aware of the spatial text.

Leo was still content to go to bed; he was to comprehend on investment. It was Zetta's declaration that the more money you had, then, the more you should be praised. Under Christianity, Leo was bemused that money wasn't a root of transgression (e.g. Judas sold Jesus for thirty pieces of silver). The idea of Zetta promoting money as the answer to their prayers placed him in an awkward position. He also learnt of their recruitment process, which was a single entity: *The Marketeer*. Critics of the Marketeer believed that it took ages for seekers to find work. However, the majority regarded their jobs as satisfactory. It was also the same Marketeer that allocated people to become Zetta Priests – that put forward future nominees as Sub-Nobilis. Leo took on the investment views of Spiciz and Silque. They'd believed that to elevate job performances, avoid demoralization, and you'd create desirable growth. Spiciz and Silque were highly-acclaimed for isolating lurks that were causing havoc. To exemplify, they were musicians that wasn't able to aggrandise. The pair began to appreciate their setbacks and they reinvented themselves. Luckily, their brilliance was recognised by the Marketeer, which earned each of them a role as Zetta Priests. Leo was inspired by his own enlightenment, for he wanted a lot of growth in his Public Relations Agency.

Chapter 25

—Dream job—

CRACKLING SOUNDS OF paperwork was stacked together. Leo was clearing his desk in his study. He was to assess his Agency, and there was a business expert present with him. The entrepreneur wanted to expand the Rockford Group into the European market, and thought of putting his company on the stock market too. Both Leo and his expert agreed that he should use his charisma on winning clients. He was also advised to use his position at the Washington and Orlando golf clubs to attract the hard-hitters to invest in him. Leo was cordial with him. Nevertheless, a stigma seemed inevitable that his knave behaviour would surface by NASA. Obviously, it would turn his heroic image into something else. Despite that dejection, his advisor told him that his business would rake in billions. Leo didn't feel right to inform him on his predicament while he was soaking up the scene at becoming richer. He asked on the prospect of a quick sell-out? His expert believed that the markets would suspect a bad egg. He knew that to secure his riches, he had better seek an audience with the Adjutant-General and the Supreme Commander to bury the hatchet.

Whilst he was troubling himself, his advisor was waiting to hear if he was serious in the Rockford Group expansion—

"As I was saying, Mr. Rockford," Peter said, "this will mean a huge investment project pouring into your business. In addition, I know some private investors who will be keen to take up this challenge. I hope you agree, don't you?"

"I think you're absolutely right," Leo responded, amazed of being praised to become a lot more affluent, "listen, I want you here next week to discuss this further but in the meantime, I will be seeing some old friends at the Andrews Clubhouse about your business proposition."

They both shook hands and Leo led him to the front of his house. They shook hands again auspiciously. Eventually, Leo was standing behind his front door smiling. He returned to his study to make a telephone call. "Hello, this is Mr. L Rockford and I will like to talk directly with Harry Trump."

"Unfortunately, we cannot transfer any calls in the Adjutant-General's Office. Is there anything else?"

"Let me talk to him, goddammit, or do you prefer that I take a flight from Florida to that office?"

"I'm afraid we cannot allow unauthorized persons to see him, unless we've been given strict authorization by the Adjutant-General."

"Tell him that Leo Rockford has called and that I require his company, thank you!" Leo hung-up annoyed. He twirled in his chair before looking through his front window. He thought on Martin MacCormick seeing Hawaii-shirt men. Oddly enough, he scarcely saw any since his return from Great Britain. As if in a loop, he imagined the profitability of a huge business enterprise. He knew that the Andrews Clubhouse was ideal to find investors. However, Andrews was facing a major reconstruction – it was closed. Leo's patience was wearing thin of his misconduct, in space, was going to reach the members already, and investors, of course, were likely to lose faith in his abilities. Leo was desperate to get an answer from Harry Trump on reassuring him that NASA wasn't to jeopardize him. *Oh shit*, he thought as his anxiety was getting worse that the Observatory would definitely lose its funding.

His phone rang and he picked it up. "Hello?"

"This is Harry Trump, what's the problem now?"

"I really need to see you. Basically, I want to arrange a meeting with General Kaiser," he said.

"What's it about?"

"It's about the Andrews Clubhouse, the space agency and my business."

"Well, he's a busy man."

"Busy enough," Leo exaggerated, "to tell you that he's taking in the heat wave in Hawaii?"

"Look, I'm his personal secretary. All I can do is relay the information that you wish to see him in person, is that okay?"

Leo replied, "I'm willing to pay my own expenses to see him."

"I suppose what you got to say is urgent, right?"

"Yes, it's urgent and please could you tell him to contact me on my mobile, will you?"

"Let me see what I can do," Harry said and he ended the call.

Leo sat quietly in his study with much more optimism.

***

Leo's mobile phone stayed relatively quiet for three days. It was Harry Trump and he wanted to arrange a meeting at a governmental building that very day. Leo took a day off from work to drive there. After he found a place to park his car, he ventured into the premise. He wore his dark blue business suit, a multi-coloured striped shirt with a green tie. Inside the building, he saw armed security guards requesting him to be scanned. Speedily, he was walking with a steward that guided him to an elevator.

Harry Trump greeted him on the sixth floor. "Thank you for turning up on short notice."

"Thank you for having me."

The pair was walking along a corridor that led into a large office floor. It was filled with many working cubicles, and it had a bustling atmosphere. Leo and Harry moved along to the other side.

"I'll again," Harry said, as he offered him a chair, in his own office, "will like to apologize that General Kaiser won't be with us."

Leo's heart sank that the Supreme Commander was too busy to see him in person today, tomorrow and in the distant future. He sighed. "I'm sorry," he wondered a little, "for I don't understand what you're saying?"

"General Kaiser will not be seeing you. So how can I help?"

Leo replied, "It's about a significant business venture, my business can double, treble and quadruple within the next twelve months. The point being is that Rockford is the brand name. But there's a little issue regarding a private hearing, last July, on my conduct."

Harry nodded. "Go on."

"That awful revelation will bring more harm than good. It'll affect my clientele. Basically, I'll be forced to lay off a lot of employees, and that Panel will need to find a new contractor in maintaining the public's respect."

"What do you want me to do?"

"I want you to tell General Kaiser exactly what I'm telling you, and I expect him to arrange a meeting in Washington."

"If you really want to see him, tell me again about the spatial water?" Harry asked.

"Look, I'm pretty sure that we had the water in the space-flask. But since that party, things did go a little crazy."

"Go on, how *crazy* was it?"

"Look, we got very drunk. The next thing, Martin was all over Emily. I saw Jay chasing Tasha and I had to tend to Martin's mess."

Harry hummed. "Explain mess?" he asked.

"Martin was sick all over the floor in the common room."

"If he was sick, then how can he take advantage of Emily?" Harry now asked.

"The girls went to the cockpit to keep their distance from Jay. And at that time, Martin just threw up. Afterwards, he was chasing the girls on the upper deck, got it?"

"So you have no recollection about the flask in the kitchen?"

"Well, Chris decided that somebody might've mixed the alcohol by mistake, and to avoid further worry he placed it in Omega Control."

"Chris told us that in the Hearing, Leo, the thing I can't understand is that there was a filled flask from Mars, and you brought back nothing. The General isn't pleased about the outcome, and what makes you think he will be pleased to see you anytime soon?"

"Look, I'm sorry right? I just got a very good business proposition to make with him."

"His business is politics not commercial. I'm afraid he will not be seeing you."

"Worth billions, billions don't you understand my currency?"

Harry Trump laughed. "You say billions, what's in it for the Supreme Commander?"

"If I say billions, I mean billions of dollars and for your troubles – I will slip in an incentive lump sum of one million dollars."

Harry gasped. "Heads will roll if word got out about that proposition you're making. So how sure are you that you can–"

"Harry Trump," Leo quickly engaged with him, "we've known each other for far too long, and what's wrong with a handout here and there?"

"Everything!" Harry said and found it officious, "what you're proposing is that I should abandon Kaiser, but embrace bribery. It's not going to happen. Therefore, I must ask you to leave." He rose from his seat and stretched out his hand to end his appointment.

"So you don't question my membership at the Andrews Air Force Base Clubhouse?"

Harry stood amused. He thought that Leo was mad to change topic from bribery to sport. "Mr. Rockford, let me remind you that this is a Supremacy building, but that–" Harry froze. "You expect me to believe that you've the Supreme Judges and the likes in your pocket?"

"I expect you to arrange a meeting with the Supreme Commander, if you don't mind."

Harry was looking at the ceiling, and gave a sigh. "You're crafty. I'll personally inform General Kaiser that you require his presence at the White House, as soon as possible."

Leo reached out to shake his hand. "Harry, you're superb and studious."

Chapter 26

—Stay or go—

CHRISTMAS WAS DRAWING near. Leo was at home in his garden. He was relaxing behind a shade with a glass of ice tea. He started to believe that he could win his large fortune. As he rested, Leo thought that he ought to move his main business to London and be addressed as Sir Leo Rockford. Leo imagined living a luscious life in Mayfair. *I'll be there*, he daydreamed, *of driving a Bentley in the millionaires' playground.*

Still in the shade, Leo tried to make ready an alternative vision of a richer life in America; he found it too disturbing – regarding Martin MacCormick – to tell Kaiser what he would like to hear that Capt. Martin MacCormick saw him as a scapegoat. If he wouldn't, could the Cape Canaveral Hearing cost him greatly? Obviously, his thoughts of remaining in America only turned over stones of misery. So his best option was to return to Britain.

***

Later on that evening, Leo decided to take his wife out to dinner. They were at the same plush restaurant as before; the first place they ate in Orlando. The couple sat at opposite ends of the decent size table enjoying their meals; each had steamed slice of smoked salmon on a potato cake, with seared lemons with a caper dressing. Also, they each had two semi-filled glasses of Californian white wine.

"Carly, we really have been having many great years together, and I thought this should mark my sincere devotion to you."

"You're so nice, Leo."

"I know," Leo said confidently into her tantalizing eyes, "I've been thinking of our future."

Carly wasn't sure of what to expect from her husband. She held his hand, across the table, to hear what could be better. She waited but he wouldn't respond. "What is it dear?"

"I'm thinking that we should return to London and start afresh."

"I don't understand? Why would you want to return to London?"

"I don't mean right this minute. I mean perhaps within the next ten years. I would love to return with you to a place where we were brought up together."

"There's something that you're not telling me."

"You might have noticed that I've hired a Business Advisor about the fate of the Rockford Group?" he asked and she nodded. "He thinks," Leo continued, "there's real potential for it to become one of the largest companies in North America. Point being is that I've friends who work in the investment sector, that are willing to take a chance on me."

Carly shook her head. "Leo, why do you want to return to Britain?"

"It's because I want to move the main operation of Rockford to the UK. I know, America has been great, but there will be financial cuts to the space agency, which will affect my business alone."

Carly continued to firmly hold his hands. "We'll pull though," she said, "just like before."

"I know, Carly, I know but my Business Advisor sees real potential in expanding my PR agency. I believe him and I will be taking him on board."

"Are you now hiring him?"

"Of course, yes. He has given me so much insight which I believe will determine, and lead my business into a multi-billion dollar establishment."

"Why haven't you been keeping in touch with Bill?" she now asked.

"He's just a busy man but I'll be seeing him shortly. Harry Trump is arranging a meeting."

"What kind of meeting and what are you saying?"

"It's just a meeting about the space agency, dear."

"Will we be invited to his New Year Eve's party, for we haven't been formally invited, yeah?"

"I truly hope so. I will ask him why he has forgotten his old pal."

"Why did he assign you the Mars mission but hasn't invited you?"

"Like I said, I do not know," Leo said openly, "I'll be asking him soon."

Book 2

Chapter 27
—Prominence—

WALLACE HAD SHORT and ginger, but turning, grey hair, clean shaven, and loved wearing Denim aftershave. He could always take a whiff of something when he reached into his workplace: His chambers had leather chairs, old leather hard cover law-books, and his leather bomber jacket on the wall peg. He was one of the most prominent public servants in the Supreme Court. Some people in DC had a view that he had a great chance of becoming the next leader in America. Despite his compliments, he had no desire of running the gauntlet, but to continue his work in the judiciary office. Of course, he swore to serve his country.

Wallace knew his ruler as a friend and colleague. Remarkably, it was due to his determination on the benefits of using a new criminal surveillance system, which was highly controversial. He had a dark humour building within; the Supreme Judge wanted to use a space satellite that could probe suspicious people. The technology was able to tap into their brain lobes, to hear their thoughts, via a microwave frequency. Therefore, it would give law enforcement the edge on anticipating their moves, and the fight against crime was only going to get much more easier. Wallace, being a leading example, on his campaign, saw high-profile suspects were able to walk, scotch free, from court-rooms. It was based on an injustice, of unconfirmed reports, of unimaginable threats being made against key-witnesses. However, there were many protests that saw that technology was an abuse of power in mind control, and anybody stood as a victim in his witch-hunt. One may argue that if a suspect imagined the life of a historical criminal, perhaps, a highwayman, they could merely think on an infamous quote:

Stand and deliver
Money or your life

The sheer impulse would be passable evidence on implicating innocent people as guilty. Of course, they also saw it as an intrusion on civil liberties (even a breach against the Nuremberg Code). Despite Wallace being hands-on, his President required a majority from Congress and even from the Supreme Court to pass the bill. Wallace once found himself in a heated-exchange with his own colleagues because he thought there were good intentions of ridding America of its ills, and in effect, allowed his country to become a healthier and a stronger pillar to the world. Wallace even stated that America stood as an influential nation, which would contribute to a world of becoming a safer place to live in.

Moore couldn't believe it. He felt entitled to procreate in his own country. Other words, he was a very patriotic man who loved America come second to God. One time, he took on a television debate to show his support in the biotechnology. His opponents depicted him as the evil Doctor Frankenstein that was trying to think as a criminal by becoming one. They even described him as Little Hitler. Unfortunately for Wallace, their words had rung well, and his television appearance cost him landmark support (Strong opposition to make the artificial telepathy illegal).

In its aftermath, the President called Wallace to his Oval Office. He was stunned. "That was too embarrassing. How are you supposed to get out of this one?"

"I stuck to my guns but I was being flanked that I was Dr. Frankenstein."

"I saw that but we still need support from the general public to pass this bill. You'll need to understand that I didn't become the President telling the people on what to do."

"I'll agree but—"

"I will have to pull the plug on the initiative."

"Bungles, we still do have a good chance in making it happen. Just remember, your earlier conversation, the Justice Department was mocked by Al Capone."

"That man used the media to drive his sinister image, that he had a champion cause, didn't he?"

"Exactly, the Justice Department was still able to belittle him. We do have a good thing going. To pull out would be a waste of our resources because of a slight setback."

It was satisfactory for Bungles to keep him on. Despite the popularity against the bill, he had a loophole in the constitution; for it would defeat any vote from both Congress and the Judiciary by setting the motion as a national security. Therefore, President Bungles electrified everybody of the dangers of terrorists and drug-traffickers by establishing a new agency. At first, he received a warm reception from the lawmakers. Yet, they had an afterthought of what was really going to happen, and many saw through his lies. So the President tried to make it appealing and promised that the agency would be regulated: It was to publish all criminal investigations every seven years. It might seem the answer but Conspiracy Theorists were portraying him as a tyrant that was trying to put America into submission. Wallace and his President, of course, wanted to see a great future in passing the bill, but they didn't have a clear majority. Worse still, the bill was set to divide Washington. Bungles couldn't afford to be seen pushing his luck, and so he *shelved it*.

Besides the turbulence, Bungles invited his friend to his Oval Office again. "Hi there," he said.

"Good to see you again, Mr. President. How can I help you?"

"It's really nothing but you can help yourself."

"I don't understand? Are you authorising more resources to the think-tank?"

The President laughed. "Not entirely! Have you heard of the Andrews golf course near here?"

Wallace shook his head. "I never heard of it. What is so special over there?"

WAYNE WIGNALL

"Just that it's a good place to relax when work gets too stressful. It's a good one."

"I'm fine, honestly."

"You'll make me a proud leader if you were to join me on the weekend after," Bungles requested.

"Okay."

He eventually began wearing the club colour, green. As a new member, he was shocked to learn that other Supreme Judges were already members there too. Wallace recalled a particular food entering into his mouth. Its topping was the spoiler that richly compensated the chocolate sponge; smooth and explosive ingredients. He had acquired the taste for Black Forest Gateau. Speaking freely, he also enjoyed the club's interpretation on German ideologies in the 19th-20th centuries. The Germans fascinated him as two heavyweights, Karl Marx and Adolf Hitler, changed the country, which changed Europe and even affected the world. He also embraced a medieval German monk, which made him want to get closer to God. Subsequently, he fell in love and married his secretary who was a devout Christian too.

His professional relationship in Washington, and of course, his new membership at the golf clubhouse, drove him to believe that politics could be forged closer together. He despised the majority of the clergy who would be quick to publicly criticize politicians. They were rejecting, in a monotone manner, that politics couldn't be fused together with Christianity. He felt a calling in his heart, to write to the Washington Post. The paper published his views that all citizens testify before God under the judiciary system, and religion did play a significant role in the constitution from start to finish. Surprisingly, he received a backlash from protest groups that he only spoke to limit people's freedoms under his church.

He headed his biotechnology campaign and worked in the Supreme Court. He found himself having a backlog of work. It also affected his attendance to go to church too. Being cynical, he took a drastic step by receiving a planning permission to oversee a house extension. It was to become his new prayer-room situated in his back garden. Furthermore, he took to doing part-time, as a Judge, to continue his work for artificial telephony. In such a way, he was going to be at peace with himself of having enough time between his two jobs. Unfortunately, the news of him building a prayer-room became widely known. Wallace recalled watching the television.

"We cannot live in a society," mentioned the liberalist on the television, "where our lives are governed by somebody that doesn't listen to public opinion. When I heard that he was seeking planning permission, I knew that he was abandoning his church to mad his mind about how good the Criminal Correction Programme really is!"

"Do you think it's wrong," reacted the TV Presenter, "that you're invading his privacy on how he may pray to God?"

"That's absolutely outrageous! I cannot recall a time when someone can accept that the bill isn't in the public's interest. Yet, he wants to push it through. He is a big hermit! How are we to accept that the big hermit is losing track with what is really going on in modern society?"

His new vilification never made him flinch. The new prayer-room was going ahead. It was his place to combine the morals of artificial telepathy into his Christian faith.

The day of the Supreme Revolution was one that Wallace Moore – then again many Americans – wouldn't forget in a hurry. On the fateful day, he was in his Chambers signing his judiciary paper, and not long after, he was watching the news that his judiciary colleagues had supported a military coup.

Wallace handed in his letter of resignation to join a new protest group by the name of *Red Resistance Union.* He attended public events: Community centres, churches and libraries to alert people of his concerns. He warned that the new revolution only sought for soldiers of fortune. Plus, he belligerently spoke that Kaiser orchestrated the whole thing. The People listening felt a positive presence in his rhetoric addresses, yet disbelief that the man once had a vilification as a recluse. In fact, it was Wallace Moore that discredited the Supreme Commander as the infamous Ming. Soon enough, he went on television shows, radio chat shows and was in newspapers. Furthermore, he worked as the Assistant Editor in a political magazine. Wallace had his faith: God wanted him to triumph. His faith was to go through a horrible test. His wife had fallen victim to a plane crash. She was very dear to Wallace, and was always close by to support him against many oppositions. His behaviour became erratic and reckless. Of course, he felt the walls were tumbling around him but his devout faith brought him new strength in prayer. Henceforth, he accepted that he was a widower. His piousness, as a Christian, kept him sound physically and mentally. To put simply, he never liked to reach a life-changing situation without his consultation on the Holy Scripture; it was his own personal salvation.

After a number of public appearances, Wallace received an invitation to a special television programme: The opportunity to hold a debate with the Adjutant-General Harry Trump.

"It was premeditated," Wallace retorted, "I was in the Chambers when that awful day occurred. God sake, man, all of the other Judges were collaborating against the President."

Harry smirked. "Perhaps you have been spending too much time trying to pass that artificial telepathy bill. You should've already known that it wasn't very popular."

"It was unpopular because the democracy system saw it as such."

"Did you know that your former colleagues gave Kaiser the green light? Besides, you were fighting a lost cause."

"I wasn't fighting a lost cause; I was fighting for support in the American people."

"So were we!"

"I might agree with you. However, we can never accept the fact that it was an inside job!"

Harry was looking bemused. "What are you talking about? The American economy was nose-diving, and your former colleagues took our best interest at heart. We want America to remain strong and nothing else."

"I wish that I can agree with you, but General Kaiser is a billionaire isn't he?"

"He does manufacture missiles but you cannot say that the Judges were threatened by his weapons!" Harry said which made a few people in the audience laugh.

Anyhow, Wallace responded, "We had a democracy that was working fine for over two hundred years. That was until General Kaiser entered into politics. I'm slightly suspicious against your leader."

"So you think that General Kaiser dreamt up the whole coup? If so, then how did he convince the Supreme Court, and the entire American military to follow his lead?"

Wallace really wanted to expose General Kaiser, and his link to the golf clubhouse. Yet, he couldn't go ballistic. He sighed. "It's because you followed his charm than follow a man who was supposed to report to the Commander-in-Chief. President Bungles is the ultimate and legal tender!"

Harry Trump laughed. "You're crazy!" he said, "why are you suggesting that?"

"That's because he used his economic influence to drive out the gloom on Wall Street!"

"Are you saying that after he took power, he restored the economy? You should be thankful for the American growth."

As the debate endured a little further, Wallace brought forth a good point. "Since the economy is now in good shape," he continued, "why won't the General consider taking up his candidacy in a democratic way?"

Harry smiled. "The gloom in our American economy shouldn't continue. So Kaiser, quickly, seized the opportunity for a better change."

"Why won't General Kaiser hand the power back down to the people, for the recession had receded. Other words, there are lot of jobs being created against businesses folding. Obviously, the military ought to retreat to their bases."

187

"Are you forgetting your former colleagues already? You've failed to understand, that the Supreme Court gave the ultimate job to General Kaiser. The appointment was set to prevent this country from sinking! Besides, the only person that I can hear complaining is just you."

Wallace shook his head, laughing too. "Just me, isn't it? Are you forgetting that I was a Supreme Judge? I wasn't aware of the development. Therefore, I didn't decide the fate of our country. My former colleagues withheld vital information, which affected the entire legislative, executive and judiciary branches."

The live debate prolonged by thirty minutes, and the incessant exchanges was forced to cut short – by the TV Presenter, of course.

Wallace Moore got struck with a new problem, several agents, working for the new Supreme government, raided his home. He was charged for fabricating information against the Supreme Commander.

In their custody, he was taken to their building to undergo his interrogation. Throughout the process, his interrogators informed him that they had evidence that he was trying to undermine public opinion. They told him that he was going to publish a claim that General Kaiser participated in a paedophile ring, defrauded his own military business, and he was in a prostitution ring that worshipped a biblical demon, Beelzebub. Wallace was aware of a source, in the magazine, that was claiming to incriminate General Kaiser. Nevertheless, it was part of Kaiser's sting initiative. Within seven days, he was facing a court trial, and was quickly sentenced to fifteen years of imprisonment. He turned to prayer and by luck, he got his answer. Frederick Bungles, the former American President, led a public outcry against Kaiser's handling. He was virulent, on television networks, that Wallace was a realist that informed the public what matter the most, not fairy tales. He even took his campaign to Europe to gain support against Kaiser. The Red Resistance Union gained much more popularity than ever before, of its justification. By Frederick's actions, it seemed that international pressure was becoming a little too much to bear for General Kaiser. The General issued a special court hearing that changed Wallace's sentence of fifteen years of imprisonment to suspension, and the incarceration lasted five months. After his release, the first place he visited was his local church for prayer. Moore found the light that it was a heavenly test to get closer to God. He looked for guidance and it seem to be clear, to him, members in the RRU might be collaborating with Kaiser. Wallace was certain that the only person he should trust had to be Frederick Bungles. After all, they had worked together before.

God knows. Wallace faced, yet, another predicament. Frederick Bungles, the former President of the United States, was killed in a skiing avalanche on the French Alps. Wallace knew too well that his good friend and politician stood as the difference of bringing back the true meaning of democracy, and of course, the cause looked lost for good – there was a speck of hope – some of the aides, in the RRU, speculated that Frederick's death wasn't an accident. All because the day before his death, a report surfaced that his car brakes weren't responding, but he escaped with minor bruises in France.

Wallace was in his editorial office talking to Mario.

"I think this whole situation stinks," he said, "just to hear that his brakes weren't working, and then take in the news of the skiing disaster are of wrongdoings."

Mario was pacing around, he shook his head too. "We're losing key figures in this organization. Our founder remains locked up, but most of all, Frederick is dead."

"Don't you see what is really happening? You know I feel strongly that Kaiser used a hidden agenda. I know that he's a crooked man who is enjoying his death."

"We can't really prove–"

"We really need to stay focused, and think of the possible outcomes. I know that Kaiser will be looking to shut us down."

"I agree but there's nothing that we can really do."

"We must change our approach and believe that Kaiser is answerable for destroying democracy." Wallace said. "There hadn't been several similar incidents," he continued, 'where outspoken people have been removed from society, yeah?"

"I know."

"Don't you see what is really happening now? We need to fight fire with fire."

"We've lost, Wallace," Mario conceded, "there isn't a way in winning this fight whatsoever."

"Come on, Mario, we cannot accept that Frederick Bungles died for nothing, can we? We really need to re-organize."

"How are you going to do that?"

"Firstly, we'll need to go off the radar."

Gradually, Wallace knew that he had to leave his livelihood, and go underground as the Union was no more. He was able to sneak out of America to gain his secret asylum in Canada. Moore, and a few others, received new identities to avoid the prying eyes of Kaiser.

So Wallace began running his own business, in fact, a small book store. But it felt – to him who was robust in America – that his own blood, sweat and tears were remote. The new shopkeeper found only emptiness in his work.

Most Canadians were supportive of General Kaiser. However, Wallace knew that many liberal-thinkers saw him as a threat. Therefore, their thoughts of having Wallace Moore, under their kinship, brought them new optimism for a greater freedom. Of course, the bookshop was masking his intention as a freedom fighter.

The Red Resistance Union was branded an illegal organization in America, and hundreds of former members were ordered to attend an interrogation. If they couldn't convince the regime that they weren't against Kaiser, they were charged for breaching the peace. Needless to say, hundreds of former members were incarcerated. So Kaiser appeared to have his own way against the democratic movement, and the union was becoming a distant memory.

Wallace was running a book store to the residents in the small town of Duncan. Strange as it seems, his face was plastered upon Canadian newspapers by Frederick's campaign, yet, nobody recognised him as the former Supreme Judge, or as a political activist. Perhaps so, he had grown a long bread and his hair turned completely grey and long. Wallace Moore took on a falsehood as Regis Wilkins junior from Toronto, that was a reformed drug addict.

As if a déjà vu, one of his employees invited him to her local Baptist church for prayer and spiritual guidance. Bear in mind of his falsehood, Wallace found it awkward to attend any church sermons as his heart wasn't clear on who he really represented: Jesus. Therefore, he lied that he was an atheist. One evening, he was watching an Evangelical Christian channel when a bible teacher informed his flock that to find Jesus Christ, it was only if one sought the truth. Wallace thought of his employee who sought the truth, in Jesus, to inherit the wonders of salvation.

Just as he watched the Evangelist, he felt the urge to cry out against the heavy burden of living a lie—

"I've taken the dark path of the false prophet, Satan!"

Afterwards, he began to attend her congregation to seek personal forgiveness.

It was seven months after settling in his new community when he became a recipient of an important mail:

Dear Regis

Thank you for being patience as I've been making arrangements for you to head our first meeting.

Please arrive in Vancouver in the sunset district at the Warehouse unit 43 this Saturday at 8pm. Please also find attached a ferry ticket and directions to a booked hotel for Friday and Saturday stay.

Thanks

Good old Uncle Sam

He set off late, one Friday evening, to drive to the nearest port. He parked his car before departing upon a ferry, which was heading for Vancouver. It took two hours for the ferry to get him across the Strait of Georgia and it was getting very late, midnight had already approached. It docked in the town centre and the general atmosphere was bubbly. People were coming out of clubs, restaurants, bars, as he was finding a taxi, and the whole process was slow before checking into a room.

The following evening, he was little late for his first meeting. As Wallace approached the warehouse, he spotted security guards patrolling the premises. As he was moving towards them, they assumed that he was a lost homeless hippy who was high on drugs.

"I think that you're in the wrong neighbour," the guard was saying to him, "man, this is an industrial estate."

But a certain person recognized him, and informed them to mind the premises. He greeted Wallace, and him he before heading into a building office.

His entrance received a round of cheers from thirty awaiting men.

Mario Meyer was smiling and shook Wallace's hand. "It's great to see you again," he said, "Wallace, so much has happened after the assassination of Frederick Bungles."

"It's good to see you again, Mario," he replied, hugged his old companion too. "I must agree with you," he went on, "that bastard thinks he can turn the heat against us! He's on the edge for a bloody nose bleed. Sure thing, this has to be the right and drastic step to hide from him."

"Of course, everything is off-record," a stranger said and was standing close to Mario.

Mario took Wallace to one side of the room to introduce him. "His name is Christian McDowell. He's my Canadian cousin who has been helping us to get our papers to settle in his country. He'll be one of your new senior aides in coordinating future meetings."

Wallace looked around in awe, laughing and shaking Christian's hand. "It's an honour to be meeting you, and I'm glad that you're on our side, thank God."

"It's all the same," Christian replied, "we see what is happening in America, which will affect international communities. Canada is slipping into the abyss and I only hope that you'll put a stop to Kaiser's nonsense." Wallace thanked him. Eventually, he observed the room. There were many hung paintings and it was nothing too fancy, nor expensive. A large egg-shaped table was placed in the middle with plenty of seats to go round too.

Moore was going to conduct his first meeting; he cleared his throat. "I hope,' he said, 'that our next meeting will have a much more pleasant scenery i.e.) a mouthpiece!" He heard a few chuckled. "But," he went further, "we must address a great man in our cause for freedom: Frederick Bungles. He has been the heart of our recent operations to wake America against General Kaiser, his Supreme Judges and the state. Without him, we could have easily been losing the battle, for he was the beacon that Kaiser is corrupt.

"I dare say that I'm the most religious man out of all of you here, and I believe God is watching over Frederick in heaven. We all know, from our interpretation that his death is by no means an accident. That wasn't an accident judging by the facts in front of us. That corrupt government took our gem in an attempt to immobilize our cause. Look how swift General Kaiser is at arresting all the members of the Union because of his Kangaroo court. We should see that our brothers and sisters who wanted the truth told have been persecuted. Gentlemen, please, it's why I and a few Americans are secretly living here.

"Again, we've heard how hundreds of former members have been rounded up, and sent to prison to up to ten years. Kaiser wants to silence us as critics against his state. We obviously know that the kangaroo court will never release the political prisoners as that court makes its own rules as it goes along. I just heard from Mario Meyer that my junior administrator is given an extended sentence for not convincing her parole panel! Given by those facts, our American brothers and sisters would most probably never leave their prison cells. Do bear this in mind, it's the Supreme Judges that are creating new powers of extended sentences, the victims of this injustice shall not be forgotten, and we must realise that the injustice was really meant for us." He paused to drink some water. "Since," he carried on, "my assimilation into this country, I've been thinking on who I might be seeing. I've never lost hope in our cause, and I've come to terms that our peaceful measures are being met by a wolf in sheep clothing. General Kaiser seems to think that attacking us will make us futile. He is wrong. We can turn our simple soft words into a hardened sword."

Everybody was ecstatic to his response with Mario being the optimist of them all. He was fortunate enough, to have a Canadian cousin to take care of him and the other Americans.

"As we gentlemen all believe in fair play," Wallace said cordially, "it's now time that we took the shield to protect ourselves from their strikes. Also, it's time to strike the enemy before they try to swerve."

His deliverance looked prodigious. All of the men; Canadian and American alike applauded him. Suddenly there was a loud knock on the door. Mario's cousin, Christian, moved to see what was the fuss. There stood a security guard wanting to report that a participant wouldn't be attending the party. Christian thanked him – it was a deception – that he would have to postpone their get-together.

"I can recognise several, or so people in this room," Wallace continued, "and I hardly know the rest of you. However, I trust you're all Canadians who can see the threat of America turning away from democracy. It'll affect our livelihoods, our rights to stand as freemen like George Washington, our liberal right to decide who shall lead nations, and to have political leaders who will listen to the people, and not fall on deaf ears!

"My Canadian neighbours. Democracy is at stake and Kaiser is the toxic poison we must neutralize. I'll be glad to be marching up Constitution Avenue with Canada by my side because of that wolf in Washington." Few were clapping, others looked nervously of the prospect to march into Washington.

"Listen very carefully!" Wallace said firmly, "the Red Resistance Union is defunct!"

Still some were looking at one another, in disbelief, if Wallace Moore should be heading their meeting. As such, a man stood up–

"We were hoping," said the Canadian, "to have you as a man with a clear vision for our future. So why were you implying to go to war as Canada has a less military might. You've seriously mistaken us as fools!"

"So I noticed we've an impatient individual," Wallace reacted calmly, "one who wants positive action to take place ASAP! For me to run anything, I require loyal people: Brothers and sisters to fight this new struggle ahead of us. The concept of the Union was to bring together democratic parties being left and right. The organization was designed to overthrow that tyrant through peaceful demonstrations. Unfortunately, it hadn't worked and we need a new angle."

"You're a nut!" the Canadian responded, wagging his finger as well. "How are we going to war?" He turned to look upon Christian. "What were you thinking," he proceeded to say, "oh my, Wallace is a devout Christian who believes that God will give him a mighty hand. I do–"

"So you think that it only affects you? It affects us all," he said quickly. "Of course," he continued, "not everybody can see the truth of that alien in America. Otherwise, I wouldn't be conducting this meeting! Besides, Mario and many more would have been with their loved ones if it wasn't for General Kaiser. I expect you to understand that public demonstrations are becoming defunct. I expect you to accept that we've no alternative but to arm ourselves. Also, I expect you to believe that we're now an army that wishes to depose him. Our tactics might be seen dirty, but we represent the ideals of a free America."

The man, that challenged Wallace, gave his pardon.

"I think," Wallace continued, "that we shall change the playing field, and become a new unit as the Red Resistance Force."

Mario clapped. "I'll honour the motion!"

"As do I!" Christian reacted.

Everybody in the room agreed.

Mario asked, "Wallace, how are we going to train an army?"

"Just trust in yourselves," Wallace responded to Mario, "in recruiting new members, and remember that recruiting will not be a walk in the park. Those security agents and their associates will be trying to infiltrate our operations." He turned his attention on everybody else. "If you do not mind," he pressed on, "I'll appoint Mario as my immediate confidant. Therefore, all related information must pass through him to me and vice versa."

"How do we attack?" A Canadian wondered.

"We attack once we mobilized our infrastructure."

"That I think shall not be a problem," Christian responded, "I've some good connections when it comes to hardware but it'll cost."

Mario said, "I do know some good benefactors."

"How are we supposed to know when to strike?" Another Canadian asked.

Wallace replied, "It's all good that we can say this and do that. However, we must get to the heart; for we must sort out our benefactors and our weaponry first. Remember that we're in the early stages, and it may take some time before we are running an effective operation. I suppose it's all that I can say for the time being, and I hope our good man, Christian, will continue to arrange these meetings in good time."

Christian nodded.

Sanjay Patio, was amongst them. He sighed. "I've lost everything back home. All because we're ducking and diving. What am I supposed to do now, while the Canadians muster a force?"

Wallace looked at him and laughed. "Why not wait Sanjay? You're one of my loyalist American aides, and the time will come for you to do us great wonders. You've obviously proved yourself in the Union."

"I know that," Sanjay went on, "but we didn't ask for this to flee America, and to being artificially assimilated into Canadian society. I didn't know what was going on until now. All I want is a system where we've the right to demonstrate peacefully not become terrorists."

"That will be an ugly word to be used by Kaiser!" Wallace said, adamantly. "We're not terrorists," he continued, "we're freedom fighters."

"So I must continue to have this double life and to what end?"

"Sanjay, are you having doubts about being with us? These are dangerous times, which I must stress strongly. Frederick risked his own life for us to being released from prison, and all you're thinking of is to return to a country run by a kangaroo court?"

"No," Sanjay conceded, "you're right. So we must continue our new way of life."

"I'll be expecting you to continue like this for many, many years."

Everybody in the room appreciated the agenda: To depose the tyrant.

By the end of the first meeting, they had set their objectives: to elect Wallace Moore as their President of the militant organization, Mario Meyers was the Vice-President, and Christian McDowell was to arrange further meetings, and all the senior aides were to continue as sleeper-cell operatives.

Chapter 28
—Exposure—

CHRISTIAN MCDOWELL FELT that the RRF outfit was staunch as he arrived home, one evening. His wife told him of a newsflash, of General Kaiser, warning his nation of a new threat. Christian assumed that a sleeper cell had awoken. He stood to watch the news channel, and was a little perturbed by what Kaiser had to say:

My fellow Americans,

These are indeed dark times that I don't enjoy discussing. I've solid proof to inform you, that we must go on a vigil against a new kind of terrorism that is brewing up in this country. We've concrete evidence that the illegal group, Red Resistance Union, is turning the other cheek. I've made them illegal due to our Supreme Agents rooting out their propaganda, that I am not what you're seeing. It was only through the Supreme Court that we allowed them suspended sentences for breaching the peace.

Now, we've just discovered that the same individuals are even more persistent to breach the peace. They're now in hiding to plot bombs at public places: The Supreme White House, our supreme libraries, and other infrastructures. Yes, my American citizens, they've turned to terrorism and we must work together to rid us of that evil. The man behind that terrorism is Wallace Moore and we must find him and try him in the American courts of justice...

Christian took a seat, by his wife, to determine how did the Supreme Commander compromise their sealed-tight operation? He didn't write any unnecessary information on the organization, and his arrangements were strictly confidential. He thought for a further moment that the General was expecting it so, yet, what made the General think that the Union wasn't really defunct? "It's just an allegation, isn't it?" Christian asked his wife.

"You know better than I!" Christina, his wife, said to him and dashed into the kitchen to fix her children their tea.

It made sense to Christian that the news release would be at the top of the RRF agenda. He felt that the Supreme Commander had set the RRF back many years. Basically, General Kaiser had declared that American democracy had a violent past and its future was bleak. Furthermore, he announced that he was a fighter for realism. To add further insult to injury, Bill Kaiser continued to state that democracy lost its sense of direction. Christian smelt a rat.

Chapter 29
—The rat—

*T*HE TREES AND the unkempt grass were swaying in the wind. Wallace Moore could easily hear the ferocious gale outside. It didn't stop him giving prayer quietly inside a chapel. He and a few nuns were the only people present. The ladies weren't accepting anymore worshipers into the building, as it was after public hours. But he was finishing his prayer; facing the statue of Jesus.

> *...The power, and the glory.*
> *For ever and ever.*
> *Amen.*

Christ stood tall looking below onto his flock as the saviour. His arms spread out wide, and his hands had the marks of his crucifixion. Wallace had thanked him for the Red Resistance Force, and for his guidance. Soon enough, he went outside to meet Mario who was waiting for him in his car.

"You've been in there for some time, sir."

"I know, I was praying for you."

"I thank you but the bottom line is that I don't require spiritual guidance. It isn't necessary."

"Maybe, but I still prayed for you. You should have been inside to give thanks."

"I'm not too keen on religion, sir."

"Perhaps so, now let's leave. We must find that rat and flush that out."

Chapter 30
—Premature—

WALLACE MOORE LOVED eating his favourite cake. Nowadays, the gentlemen's golf club was a no-go-area; but his military conferences were always agreeable. He had a stigma when trying to recruit new members into the fold as he was branded a terrorist. Yet, a few of his Senior Aides believed that potential candidates required pay. Wallace warned that money bought traitors, and believed to earn loyalty, the group had be the word of mouth:

One person, one vote

He thought the novelty would reach every American that the tyrant had only empowered himself. Furthermore, even if Wallace was stigmatised, the most talked of comic villain, Ming the Merciless, was his gemstone! Therefore, his Recruiters could easily test the potential of finding new recruits. Needless to say, the candidates that were willing to compare Ming the Merciless to General Kaiser, had passed onto their next test; it was the belief that Kaiser caused the assassination on Frederick Bungles, and his clampdown against the RRU. If the candidate wanted a better future, take the person on. The first breeding ground was universities. The recruiters took on librarians, lecturers and students. The fresh intakes were to attend training centres to become sleeper-cell operatives. Afterwards, the recruiters took on a new breeding ground: Health farms, nightclubs and even a strip joint. The Recruiters did find fresh blood but they still had to be extremely careful. One of them attempted to recruit an undercover agent – off-duty – from a strip club; full of male customers. The Recruiter saw him, a seat along the counter, looking like a despondent, yet, felt a lot better when a girl was touching his shoulder. He wanted to talk to him about the new Flash Gordon movie starring a sex kitten. At first, the agent ignored him, because he was in a trance seeing a topless girl delivering his beer. Later on, he did acknowledge the movie with him. The Recruiter so regarded gorgeous girls, and what nature had in store for them whilst buying him a drink. He continued talking that the Supreme Commander wasn't attractive to any of the beautiful girls, and the agent was accordant by ordering him beer. Again the Recruiter discussed of an alleged prostitution ring, in the White House, and said it were their right to gate crash. The agent was in agreement again, and he bought another round. After several more drinks and lap dances, on the agent's expense, the Recruiter proudly made him an offer—

"Look here," he said, "I know it's fun here. But you must understand one thing: One person, one vote. I'm giving you an invitation to join us. I want you to become a RRF operative, will you?"

The agent had been enjoying himself. Yet, he had thought that his new friend was a little odd: It wasn't a club for male bondage. He was going to make himself on-duty. He hoisted out his automatic weapon to make his arrest. In doing so, his head was swimming slightly.

As the Recruiter realized his mistake, he laughed a little. "I'm kidding, put that thing away!"

"What kind of person would degrade this great nation by destroying our pillars? You're coming downtown with me!"

The agent began to give his suspect the frog march out of the strip joint. As he was doing so, club security approached him, and they were making their mistake that he was the trouble-maker. Of course, the man argued with his badge that he worked for the Supreme government. He also was reaching inside his jacket; for a radio to signal for reinforcement. To the undercover agent, it was a big deal to arrest him because it might lead to the crack down of the RRF. However, he managed to accidentally kill him, in a scuffle, as he tripped him outside. His suspect's head landed onto the edge of the concrete kerb. Of course, it was all in the official's drunken attempt to control him.

Soon as his death reached Wallace Moore, he thought he had better react against the heavy handling. Straightaway, he ordered his first bombing campaign in America.

Kaiser's response to the bombings was to formalize the United Supreme Task Force, USTF. It was basically, a tearaway division from the National Security Agency, and their goal was to eliminate the RRF.

Anyway, new sleeper-cell operatives were to continue their everyday lives until they got the call. It might be several things: Perform an attack on a Supreme building, or perhaps, attend a low-level meeting on the direction of their movement. Besides the scheduled bombings, Wallace recruited – what he described as – *poster-boys* to smear General Kaiser as Ming the Merciless. They were Canadians being sent to America to hand out leaflets. However, for the reckless, many of them were easily caught and tried at the American courts.

Chapter 31
—Counter-attack—

*T*HE DISCOVERY OF the reckless Canadians led to an emergency meeting between General Kaiser, Adjutant-General Trumps and the head of the USTF, David Bruce, in the Oval Office.

"I'll like to thank the both of you for attending," Kaiser said, "I've a few words to say about a new development. That's what the hell is going on regarding those arrested leaflet distributors from Canada?"

"Supreme Commander," David Bruce responded, tentatively, "may I say that it looks like several options. For one, the terrorist group is based in Canada. How they came about doing that will take some time to determine. Another option is that it's a tactical manoeuvre of making us believe that they're not situated in America. The problem with the third option is that they can even be in Europe. Supreme Commander, these are challenging times for the Supreme Order, and my people are doing their best to get to the bottom of it."

"I personally put you in charge of the United Supreme Task Force," Kaiser said, contemptuously, and was pointing his finger at him, "and all you can do is second guess?"

"No, General Kaiser," David replied, "we've been concentrating our efforts against the militants for some time now. In all cases, they were American subjects. What's transpiring now is that this isn't directly related. However, you still have some of the best security servants out on the field; you'll clearly understand the nature of it. Of course, sir, it'll take time."

"Waiting isn't good enough! Just what the hell has happened to Wallace Moore and his top associates? They just vanished into thin air, and another thing, haven't you been interrogating those Canadians?" Kaiser asked harshly.

"Before the USTF was set up, I had incredible leads against the RRU. You know that we were successful against them. Remember, Supreme Commander, our operation has led to their most senior member being placed behind bars."

"Yes, I'm aware of that!" Kaiser snapped, "but what about those Canadians?"

"You see, General Kaiser, we did infiltrate the RRU from the start, and we still have security servants out there since it was defunct. We do have a delicate situation for our people to remember who they are working for. One of our operatives is in the belly of the beast, and it's critical that we do not blow his cover. Therefore, the problem is that we'll need to wait for him to bring us intelligence. I believe that with his information, we can go a step further to dismantle the RRF. But we mustn't blow his cover, or we—"

"I just want to know why — those Canadians! You give me reasons, and I'll be a lot happier."

"In the meantime, gentlemen," Harry said, "the RRF isn't really a well-organized unit. From what I've gathered about them, it's their craze for the Flash Gordon's villain."

"Is this world turning cuckoo? Of course they're an organized unit because how is it we finding those scum in America?" Kaiser asked.

"General Kaiser," Harry continued, "my understanding of social science is that their source of success is to alienate you as Ming. You must admit that the villain has your same facial features. They're using it that you're not who you say you're."

David Bruce was sniggering slightly. "So what you're really saying is," he said, "that we'll need to send our best public servants to Hollywood. From there, we ask the studios, politely, to create blockbuster movies portraying General Kaiser in a good light, isn't it?"

"Look, just think of a world where they're no barriers. What we do in the political arena doesn't mean that we cannot be affected by the cinemas."

Bill was bemused. "I do worry about you, sometimes."

Harry reacted firmly, "What's an arena? It's a place for the general public to marvel or curse the performer.

205

We do have a political arena for the spectators to marvel us. But it's the same spectators that are going to the cinemas watching Flash Gordon. Therefore, the RRF are smearing you as Ming. It's not that I'm taking sides with the terrorists, but the average American doesn't really know you on an intimate level."

David said sarcastically, "So what are you expecting us to do? A reality show about the hard work of the USTF, and it has a special feature of our Supreme Commander?"

Kaiser got up from his seat to make himself a scotch, and was laughing uncontrollably. "We're in a political crisis against a terrorist group that is costing lives, and all you're really thinking about is to escape from reality."

"General Kaiser," Harry continued, "please do not be arrogant with the facts in front of you. We know that the RRF will compare you as Ming. It's that what drove the Canadians south across the border. It's that what sells well with the public."

"So what do you want me to do?" Bill asked bluntly.

"Just acknowledge the facts and improvise. I think that it'll be best to work with the Hollywood studios. Of course, Hollywood is as American as the Supreme White House."

Kaiser gave a sigh. "So I should create a secretary of state for the theatres?"

David Bruce smirked. "That's absurd! You think I'm going to fall for a Propaganda Secretary? I've been working for the NSA before my transfer, and we never heard of a sleeper mending their ways over a bloody movie!"

"Will you add that you never heard of a sleeper winning the hearts and minds of the masses," Harry corrected him. "Besides," he said, "if the populace dictates the RRF then we should mastermind the propaganda."

The General stood up again to make himself another drink. He sat down to look at his men and shook his head. No sooner, he nodded. "Good grief!" he exclaimed, "that Bungles always talked about Al Capone. He always said that he captured the limelight wrongly."

"True," reacted Harry, "but once prosecuted his dignity was swallowed up by the judiciary system."

"Back to where we are, Harry, what do you expect us to do?" David asked.

When Harry heard him asking for guidance, he got up to move to the decanters. He fixed himself a drink of straight bourbon whiskey before returning to his seat. He nodded. "I believe that's obvious, work with Hollywood behind Flash Gordon. We can offer then tax breaks, and we should ask them to produce future movies to give a positive light. Something like Ming teaming up with Flash Gordon against a new deadlier foe. It has got to be simple like saying A*BC*–"

"I just do that?" the General asked, "then all my troubles will go away, yeah? Come on, are you serious?"

"You've known me for the last twenty years and I cannot recall you questioning my judgment, sir," Harry replied.

"Okay, let's do it. Harry, arrange a meeting with some of those Hollywood bosses, and then we can talk business."

Chapter 32
—Threat brewing in the north—

*I*T WAS DECEMBER and bitingly cold in Duncan. Wallace was taking rest, above his bookshop, in his warm lounge. He was watching a TV documentary regarding General Kaiser, his armed forces and his rebels. Wallace was exhausted as the bookshop was busier than usual for it was Christmas. He sneered at the television when the Presenter began saluting the Supreme flag, and it ended with a thunderous sound of drums. Still tired. Wallace thought that the Supreme Council's influence was already working up-north, he had to work quickly, yet, he still lay. He was feeling relieved that his campaign to legalise artificial telepathy didn't pull through. As he continued to be idle, Wallace understood why he was called Dr. Frankenstein, the big hermit, little Hitler and mental. Needless to say, it would have been Kaiser's. *What am I?* Wallace thought, *what am I supposed to do? Share my prayer with him? Oh my God! The protest groups' were right. It was really invading one's privacy.* Wallace was still dormant. But he was thankful that Kaiser wasn't fast enough to take advantage of it.

Miraculously, he rose up to approach a bookcase nearby and returned to his couch. Wallace began flipping through his Bible to find a passage. He thought that he had been complacent, and wondered if General Kaiser was righteous? *No of course not,* he thought, *for the General doesn't respect freedom of speech.*

Wallace did live alone. Traditionally, most people in the Duncan town would be married with children. To his staff, they saw him as a lonely man who wished a simple life of running his bookshop — to put nicely, a bookworm.

Chapter 33
—The hunt—

WALLACE HAD A scheduled meeting with one his confidants at a café in Vancouver. He was early and found it busy. The premise was fairly spacious with two floors too.

Mario arrived five minutes later. He spotted Wallace with a stranger around a small table.

"See you've company," he said.

"It's just busy. Try and find a seat and join us," Wallace said.

The stranger said, "Sorry about this but there aren't any seats. I won't be too long."

Mario made a stop gesture. "Please take your time," he said politely, "I'm early anyway."

The man sat in his position to drink his coffee, and proceeded to read his newspaper. Mario was hovering above them, and informed Wallace that he was going to come back shortly. He left to find the nearest news outlet; bought himself a magazine and a packet of cigarettes. On his return, he found him with new company. It prompted Wallace to take Mario for a stroll around the city centre to a bar nearby. The two men made their entrance inside and they discovered it quiet. They ordered two shots of whiskey at the counter, and moved on to take their seats at the back of the bar, which was lit dim.

"So why do you want this meeting, Moore?"

"Please don't be alarmed why Christian is arranging this, but I wanted to tell you that we've got a new backing."

"So our new sympathizer will bring hope to our cause?" Mario asked excitedly.

"The new backing is directly from Italy."

"You're not suggesting the Mafiosi?"

"It's the Vatican."

Mario confounded. "Why are you telling me this?"

"You must realise that with the Vatican support, we're morally in the good books with the Christian faith. This will be a crushing blow to General Kaiser, that we can champion our cause," Wallace paused for a moment. "The Vatican," he continued, "will be supporting us by enlightenment."

"What do you mean by *enlightenment?* What its significance?"

"The Vatican will allow our message, within the organization, to become much more effective. It'll significantly mean being the torch in the dark. It also means that the Pope will not be renouncing our actions."

"That's all wonderful but what's its significance?"

"Come on, do you not understand? The significance is that the Vatican is going to allow us to co-ordinate with them. Basically, the Church will be giving us a symbolic sign, which can be associated with the RRF."

"You say a *symbolic sign*. Meaning what? I definitely know that you're not speaking of the crucifix."

"That's true. It's not the cross but the Maple Leaf."

"Leaf? What leaf?"

"It's Canada's red leaf," Moore replied.

"What's the significance of the Vatican recognising a red leaf?"

"Mario, just when I thought of you as a full-blooded American. Are you aware that autumn leaves turn red but brown in Europe?"

"Oh my God!" Mario said astonished. "That's beautiful! How did you do that?"

"It called having friends in high places, Mario."

"That alone should surge morale and recruitment. That's wonderful news, Wallace."

"That's why I wanted Christian to make this arrangement – well, let's say in the bar."

"May sound great but there's one snag. Why on Earth will the Vatican take sides in the political debate? What kind of corrupt friends do you have in the Church?"

"I wouldn't say they're corrupt but are just giving their thanks."

Mario mistook a glass collector when ordering a second shot of whiskey. After a little while, he returned with two glasses. "Let's see, you're getting the Vatican to support us, and I wanted to ask you if you trust them to deliver?"

"That's right, Mario. The Vatican is only grateful to my donation of several million dollars. They'll be symbolizing their thanks by a red leaf in their Vatican services."

"That does sound great. So what if the Supreme Commander starts doing the same?"

"Let's just pray that he's an atheist!" Wallace said jokingly.

"I might practice being a Christian," Mario said and was clapping his hands. "I could say," he eagerly continued, "that the drinks are on the house in marking this occasion! God, I never really saw myself being big on religion. That has to be the cherry on the cake. Who else knows of this?"

"To be honest, it's just you from the organization."

Mario attempted to understand how the President of the RRF managed to pull it off. He observed Wallace as a man in hiding, and only a handful of people knew of his undercover name, Regis Wilkins. Still, there was one thing that hampered him as he tried putting together the puzzle. "I hope you'll enlighten me, so how did you get the Vatican's blessing?"

"All in good time Mario. Yet, I'll give you a hint: The Andrews Air Force Base Golf Clubhouse," Wallace replied, laughed lightly too. "You know," he proceeded, "I'm a bit of a religious nut. So anyway, I'm hearing reports of an alarming rise of Americans, in clergy circles, supporting Kaiser and denouncing our RRF cause."

"Wallace," Mario lapsed, "I thought that we've a good relationship, in trusting each other. What you've told me is that you've contrived it alone. Besides, your action isn't political."

Wallace was looking straight at him before deciding to pardon him. On his return, he handed Mario another shot of whiskey. "Mario, I do trust you," he said, "that's why Christian is arranging this meeting. Christian doesn't yet know about the development in the Vatican church, but he'll know once the red leaf is practiced in the religious ceremonies. By then, it should be a nice surprise for our Canadian associates. As you know, I'm the President of the RRF and it's my job to see that it runs smoothly. Yes, it was my idea to approach the Vatican for some time now. And yes, I did put you out of the loop. I did that because I wanted to build new trust, but you'll still remain one of my loyalist lieutenants."

"Okay, I understand. I just hope that you had a little more faith in me."

"As I was saying earlier, I'm a religious nut and I'm testing my faith with others. My faith in you is secured. I was going to tell you about a development in the American churches that supports the tyrant, but you interrupted me. It's a grave area, and I believe it can affect our goal as those churches will be backing the wrong horse. We'll have a difficult ride ahead of us."

"You mean people like Carl Lang, isn't it? He's now at the top of the food chain."

"Exactly, Carl Lang is the person I remember being on the media. He led accusations that Frederick was corrupting the economic system. The next thing, you see that man partying with General Kaiser, the Supreme Judges and the likes. That man is trouble. What he's also doing is creating a swing of the clergy to pledge their allegiance to that bastard. Of course, this means getting the perception that Christianity supports a tyrant in this corner of the world. That's an ecumenical threat, that the tyrant will be seen as the norm in Canada and the world too."

"You just told me that the Vatican is supporting our cause—"

"Of course, yet ours isn't a general awareness. Do you now understand? They've the limelight in getting moral support, and we cannot allow that to happen."

"So you want me to organize his assassination? No problem."

"I just want him to shut up. Look, you're authorized to kidnap him if it's of any good use."

Mario downed his drink, pondered and shook his head. "I can't think of one. We could place a ransom for his safe return? Wait, General Kaiser isn't the type who will let go of his position too easily...re-educate him? He'll not be steadfast for us."

"He'll be steadfast, I think? If we kidnap him, we'll be able to pardon him. Then again, he might even cheat us."

Mario chuckled. "That's a good one. We snatch him from the limelight and he reappears, that he is resilient."

"Well, it was worth the thought."

"I'll lead the shot! Suppose that's it," Mario implied and was making himself ready to depart.

"Just one thing Mario. Make sure you're definite about killing him. I mean that we should give him a second chance on mending his ways."

Mario was reaching for his jacket behind his chair. "What you mean *second chance*?"

"I mean that I want you to take the responsibility of either sparing him or not. I want you to get to know him a little bit."

Mario returned to his seat. "Wait a minute. You want me out there to get to know the guy?"

"That's exactly my point. You're to head this delicate operation. So use your recruitment-skills to see if he could be recruited. From there on, decide if he's worthy of a second chance."

"Why are you being compassionate for Carl Lang? He's just as guilty of killing Frederick Bungles. He's even guilty of supporting the actions of the USTF! He's dirty and his actions speak louder than words."

"It's just that there, maybe, some good left in him."

"Because he works in a church and they're the only people you'll consider a *second chance*," Mario said rudely. "I'm sorry," he now said, "why give Carl Lang a pardon? Good people have died because of him."

"Are you questioning my faith?"

"I'm questioning your strategy."

"You of all people should know. I've been listening to some of his recorded sermons on Jesus of Nazareth, and I just thought the guy is perhaps backing the wrong ideology. The man understands how to paraphrase from the Bible."

"Here I am getting religious as a nutcase! What about the paraphrases in favour of the tyrant?"

"He has given none," Wallace replied.

"Yet he supports the regime."

"If he supports the regime, then why not back the regime with paraphrases from the Bible?"

"Okay as your Lieutenant, I'll see if Carl Lang will use the *good book* on Kaiser, and then I'll decide his fate."

"I want you to be certain about your decision, and I hope that you will relay back exactly what you've found," Wallace requested.

Mario took on his words of wisdom before departing.

Wallace looked at his watch to determine his next appointment; Sanjay Patio was going to meet him within the next twenty minutes. He finished his drink and moved swiftly passed the entrance doors. The bright sun and the fresh air did hit him a little as he joined the bustling streets. Nevertheless, he was set to move onwards. On his imminent arrival, at the café, he found that it wasn't too busy to order an espresso. Later on, he took seat near the large window where a discarded mug and – thankfully – a newspaper were laying. Wallace took great interest on reading several articles. Then, he looked at his watch to calculate Sanjay's arrival and it seemed within four minutes.

It took Sanjay ten minutes to make an appearance as he rushed through the café entrance. "I'm so sorry I'm late," he said hurriedly as he spotted him, "I'm not quite used to seeing two similar cafes on the same side of the walk – I was waiting at the wrong one."

Wallace laughed. "Never mind, it's good to see you again. Anyway, get yourself a drink."

He headed to the counter to order a cappuccino before joining him. "You wanted to see me, Wallace."

The boss looked around before raising his finger. "Please call me dude."

"Sorry dude, so you wanted to see me?" Sanjay said correctly.

Wallace sipped into his espresso. "How are your tearaways coping?"

"*Tearaways*? Oh, my men," Sanjay anticipated rightly, "they're going good. We know that it has been nearly nine years since that setback – of those Canadians being caught."

"I know that," Wallace said scornfully, "I cannot forget, too easily, how you couldn't train them to be evasive." He just stared at him, shook his head too. "Here's a task for you," he continued, "I'm ordering you to send *poster-boys* across the border to spread the word that Kaiser is Ming."

Sanjay said, "Dude, you're telling me to send my recruits to only spread the word? Don't you think that's a little daft? Think about it, let's say the next guy to enter this joint arrives at this table and informs us, that Kaiser is an *ugly motherfucker*. He moves to the next table and says exactly the same thing. Wallace, that's crazy."

"Not as crazy as you allowing them to being caught. Why is that, Sanjay?"

"I've told you already, the Canadians never assessed the immediate danger of going across the border, properly."

"You know that we've been granted asylum, isn't it? Our good friends do understand the threat of tyranny coming to their doorstep, but you seemed to have thought that we have a friend in Kaiser. For crying out loud, if it was up to me, you don't deserve this asylum. Instead, you should turn tail and hand yourself in to him."

"I'm really sorry. But my men are now a lot more evasive, isn't it?"

"So it seems," Wallace replied. "Now this," he handed him a newspaper article, "is an embarrassing matter. It's telling me that Kaiser is deporting them here, in Canada, to finish their remaining sentences; embarrassing that this makes us look-like non-Americans. Let me say this, this is making us look like we cannot fight our own battles. Sanjay, do not upset me again, or I'll be kicking you out off the RRF. Do you understand?"

"Very much so, it can never happen again, and that's a promise."

"Sanjay," Wallace continued, "do send in those poster-boys and leave me be."

Wallace was alone to study his newspaper. Of course, he might read quietly without anybody disturbing him. The man read an article about the RRU having a direct link to the RRF. It was only a speculation and the journalist had an expertise on militant organizations. She theorized that the RRU was governed strictly by Frederick Bungles against an aggressive element. After his death, it brought forth loose cannons. Wallace had a little smirk on his face, as to think, on his earlier days, he once wrote an account titled, *The Loose Cannon*: He had shamed General Kaiser that disregarded the Founding Fathers. Now, he was considered one.

Wallace continued to move along to the next article. It only had a small headline: *Supremacy for Mars*. He read into the storyline that the Supreme Council had drafted their astronauts. It stated that the person to head the mission was Leo Rockford, and he was a former airman in the Royal Air Force. Wallace didn't take much interest on him, not until he casually read further that a star from Flash Gordon was joining the crew. Wallace tried to take in as much detail on the article in a short space of time. He panicked, a little, if he was reading it correctly because his world would crumble on morale. *Surely the space mission*, he thought, *will compromise recruitment, isn't it?* He tried to see pass it as a temporary setback. Nevertheless, how on Earth could he conduct a successful unit for many years to come? He got himself perplexed as he took a breather. He read further into the article and it stated that Leo Rockford was a close friend of the General. Wallace froze, and began to control his own heavy breathing: He wanted to beat him up. The resistance leader moved to the counter to order another espresso. After he took his seat again, he resumed reading, and found that Leo Rockford arrived in America during the height of the Supreme Revolution. Wallace also read that his career accelerated to run his own multi-million dollar business. He wouldn't let go of the article. He perused that Capt. Martin MacCormick was the favourite to lead the mission but was demoted. Straightaway, Wallace assumed he had the Achilles' heel.

He was carrying a notepad and pen in his inside coat pocket. Moore pulled them out to jot some important facts on the six astronauts.

Time was passing by as Wallace studied in more detail about the other astronauts. The actor, Jay Kaiser, seemed to be a womanizer. He knew already of many celebrity photos of him with countless women. Wallace assumed that he was going to bring more harm than good on the General's reputation. He ruled him out that he hadn't any significant role against him. Next he looked into Capt. Martin MacCormick but found he hadn't any direct contact with Kaiser. Moore wrote his name below Jay Kaiser with a question mark for further study. He'd done the same for Capt. Chris Tallon, Capt. Emily Walters and Tasha Chayton.

Wallace started to think on what kind of man Leo Rockford might be. *Surely,* he thought, *one being responsible for the death of Frederick Bungles, because he was reaping his rewards, isn't it?* Of course, Wallace hadn't any doubt that the man was really sidle with the dictator. Nevertheless, he could only speculate on how corrupt Leo ought to be. Afterwards, he casually placed Mario Meyer's name beside him as to select his handler. He then sipped into his espresso but it was cold. Yet again, he pondered if Leo Rockford knew what he was doing. It was either that or he was a recluse.

He stirred a little. The shop was getting a lot busier as a long queue was forming. Furthermore, a lady asked if she could join him as there weren't any seats available. Moore smiled and welcomed her.

"Thank you, sir," she said. "It's never usually this busy."

"I know. It's terrible when people know how good the coffee beans in here are."

The lady giggled. "So you're a trekkie?"

"A *trekkie* did you say?"

She replied, "You know, Star Trek."

Wallace acknowledged the TV show after placing his notepad away.

"Please, I don't mind!" she said.

217

"Not at all, it's just good table manners. You can read this paper if you like?"

"Oh, you're so kind. But no thank you."

Introspectively, Wallace Moore was trying to be critical. He found himself in a difficult position by being beside a beautiful and mature woman of his liking. "What do you think about the Mars mission?"

"I think it might be okay."

From her words alone, Wallace saw a lady who wasn't particularly bothered about America. Hence, he passed his luck to recruit her. "I read," he went on, "that some Public Relations Guru is heading the entire mission than an experienced Astronaut."

"Perhaps a friend of the Supreme Commander, I guess."

Eventually, Wallace introduced himself as Regis Wilkins who owned a bookshop in Duncan, and he was spending the weekend in Vancouver to escape from being a bookworm. She introduced herself too.

***

By the following morning, he woke up naked on her bed. The sheets were lying on the floor and he turned to look for his clothes.

As he did so, Wallace woke her up—

"Hi there, handsome."

"It was a romantic day. I think I just check that I didn't leave anything at the café and in the bar, if you don't mind."

She was purring for him to be near as he was looking for his notepad and pen. Wallace felt guilty, naked and ashamed to spend an evening with her. For sure, she hadn't any idea that he was pretending to be a hip guy that ran a bookshop. It was also a Sunday morning when he attended his local Church. Amazingly, his guilty conscience sidestepped as he held his notepad and pen. He opened it to recall his comprehension on Leo Rockford.

Book 3

Chapter 34
—A day not in the office—

*I*T WAS A Friday afternoon in July. Leo Rockford was standing by his office window taking in the scenery. He was feeling a bit disappointed because nobody hadn't notice his redesigned sign post. It had the word, *Rockford*, written in a paint-brush style, and it was situated on his three-storey building. It startled him that he had lots of attention to venture Mars but it was now diminishing. Despite his observation, he was enjoying his home-made lasagne. Oddly enough, he began thinking of Martin MacCormick, as he ate, he was reaffirming to himself of his dear friend of sharing the same optimism on Zetta. He wondered if the secret police are still monitoring his every move; Leo got slightly tensed that Martin's lust for women may tickle their fancy a little too far. Anyway, things were looking fine as he finished his meal, for NASA was taking steps to arrange a grand reunion. Leo believed that he shall be able to lower Kaiser's suspicion as he seeks his acquaintance with Martin. He looked out of his window for the umpteenth time, he didn't see any Hawaii-shirt men waiting to trail his movements. Still, Leo was a little paranoid that he would need to be careful on how to portray himself. Needless to say, his home might have Kaiser's surveillance devices.

After he cleared his grub, Leo took the comfort of his couch and he just stared at his office ceiling of its rich furnish. He found it beautiful to look upon as the surface seemed to undulate, but turned around as his phone was ringing. He got upon his feet to answer the call. Before he accepted it, he took his seat behind his mahogany desk. Of no surprise of his own, his Receptionist was calling him. "Yes, what is it Lisa?"

"It's Adjutant-General Trump on the other line. He is calling to give you some important news. He wishes to speak to you, sir."

Leo recalled that Harry was to arrange his meeting with General Kaiser. However, it was now taking him six months to get in contact again. He sighed. "Oh does he now? And did he say what it's about?"

"He wouldn't say, sir, but do you want me to patch him through?"

"It must be important. Please send him through."

A split second, Leo said, "Good afternoon, Harry."

"Good afternoon, Leo. I hope that it isn't a bad time to make this call as I know you're a very busy man."

"No not at all, Harry. Please how can I help?" he asked supportively.

"More like I can help you," Harry corrected him, "General Kaiser is willing to see you, in person, on 15th July at his Supreme White House."

"But that's just over 48 hours away. I've an appointment to open a new library here. Surely you can rearrange the appointment?"

"Sorry, Mr. Rockford," he excused, "I meant to call you last week to give you a week's notice, but you may know that security has been tight since the bombing of the Adjutant-General's Department." He continued to say, "God, I've been busy helping reorganize the USTF, and I'm sorry that I couldn't give you the appointment date sooner, please understand."

Leo conceded and sighed. "Okay, I just have to postpone the opening by a couple of days."

"I hope," Harry continued, "you're not seeing this little arrangement as a financial favour between us? I'm doing this in the interest of Kaiser. So again, do you understand that?"

"Of course, Harry, I do not doubt that you've already informed him that I was prepared to fill your pockets."

"You understand well," Harry went on, "I look forward to seeing you this Monday."

Leo, eventually, decided to speed-dial his Receptionist to enter into his office. As she walked in, Leo told her regretfully that he couldn't attend the opening of the new

Universal Orlando Library. His request was for her to immediately relay that information to them.

Ten minutes later, his Receptionist rang again, that the new Librarian Director demanded an explanation. Leo granted the request to patch the call through.

"Mr. Rockford, this is Peter Pliny. I don't understand why you cannot attend the opening of our new and great Orlando library. Surely there's a mistake in your desire of postponing?"

"Not at all, Peter. There's been a drastic change in my personal schedule. I must attend to the Supreme Council this Monday."

"I hope that's not serious, is it?"

Leo laughed. "No," he answered, "I'm not going to face a trial with the Supreme Court. I'm just going to see General Kaiser about the Mars mission. It has been important to the General, the American people as well as I."

"Leo, if you don't mind, you've known the great man before his political pinnacle. I bet you share military secrets together, don't you?"

"No, not really, but we have spoken about the military project of the new assault rifle that's capable of changing its rate of fire. It's universal, and it's amazing for the army, the marines and black-ops. It's nearly capable of all combat situations. Besides, it's not really a big secret when the media is giving it a spin though. Peter, military secrets comes first before the Supreme Commander than anyone else," Leo replied.

"So you do know the General well?"

"I didn't know him at all until a NATO military training exercise. We just happened to have the same interests about the Soviets, and so I got to know him, and he got to know me."

"It must be tough knowing the big boss with all that terrorist activity around you. Ever thought about moving back to England?"

"What I understand about the RRF is that they're targeting people that are the building blocks of the Supreme Council."

"I understand that too, but you know the General at an intimate level, and if those scums get a whiff of that then you'll need protection. God, doesn't it bother you?"

"Life isn't without danger. Look, he wants to see me on that day, and I bet it's to do with the critical funding of the Robinson Space Observatory. I only hope he understands to continue funding."

"Don't mind me asking but can you not fund the Observatory yourself? Especially since your business is becoming a local success story here. Plus, why not arrange funding events for the Observatory as you've a great persona. Surely it beats waiting for the Supreme Council and NASA to renew their subsidy, isn't it?"

"You're right but every cent counts. Besides, if General Kaiser wants to see me, who am I to disobey the Supreme Commander."

Peter laughed. "Leo, you got me! You know the Mayor was looking forward to seeing you in person, and what about the citizens of Orlando? It's going to be a great disappointment."

"Can you not mention the *real reason* why I cannot attend?" Leo asked, "say something like: I got the flu, or something."

Peter was stupefied. "Why lie?" he asked. "You're going to see General Kaiser, right?"

"I think the public," Leo excused, "deserves to hear what they like to hear. Not that I'm bound by chains to front the big man in Washington."

"Fine, I didn't mean to get you paranoid about those terrorists. Leo, your secret's safe with me. Is there anything else?"

"No but I will be able to open the library the following week onwards," Leo replied.

There was complete silence in the office and Leo was still sitting to recollect. He was the Chief Executive Officer of the Rockford Group; he had been on the mission to Mars; above all, he took the wisdom and the knowledge of Zetta. He shook off the thought that life was complicating. Once again, the silence in the room was no more. Leo allowed the phone to ring for a while longer because he never had three consecutive calls during lunch. It was apparent that his Receptionist was intent to press forward something important. "Yes?"

"It's your wife."

"Good, put her through. Did she say what it's about?"

"It's about your children. She wants to speak to you about the children."

Of course, Leo authorized a passage as he quickly thought on who was going to be in trouble. "Carly, what's up?"

"Nothing, sweetie, except that our daughter is on a camping trip with Charles Kaiser's family. It means I'm all alone in this house wearing nothing else than the lingerie you bought last February."

Leo seemed to suffer from delirium. "You're...Saying? What dear, are you saying?"

"I'm saying that you've been working too damn hard for the last six months since that man, your Business Consultant, putting ideas in your head of expanding your horizon. His optimism of turning the agency into a multi-billion dollar one, and making you one of the richest people in North America."

"Honey listen, I've been having a hell of a busy time than I can hardly remember. Just before this call, I've been asked to go to Washington to see Bill Kaiser."

Carly continued to intrigue her husband a little more. She was purring. "So you want to leave me parched? I was trying your Valentines' gift, and I was just thinking about this house being quiet for once, and that you could leave work early to enlighten this afternoon."

Leo pondered on her proposition, and he stupendously reached into his desk draw for his diary. He was now humming as to check any important appointments. Yet, he already knew that he was hosting a meeting with a potential client, which would rocket his revenue. "I'll be home later this evening as I got a big client."

His wife was persistent in her purring. "Listen hun, if I was your Personal Secretary, I give those responsibilities to that damn new Business Consultant of yours, which you've been far more attached with for the last six months."

"Let me get on to it."

Those were the last words before he hung up the phone. Earnestly, he made an internal call to his Business Consultant. The phone tone rang for a short while before hearing somebody picking up the receiver.

Leo said, "Peter Alsopp?"

"Speaking, is that Leo Rockford?"

"Yes it's me, Leo. Listen, I will like you to do me a big favour?"

Peter Alsopp remained silent.

Leo was to continue anyway. "Are you still there?"

"Of course, Leo, what's digging you?"

"As you know, we're to have an important meeting with our client this afternoon. Basically, it will improve our opulence. Therefore, we could be creating a lot more job opportunities in this city. Sealing this contract will be a great boost, not just for our local economy, but will allow more firepower in the boardroom. Unfortunately, due to unforeseen circumstances, I'll not be able to attend this important meeting. As we both know, the last six to twelve months has been challenging in our wake to expand.

"You see, I share your optimism that we can afford to have major offices situated along the west coast. I even share your optimism of opening new ones in Europe. Despite that, I still won't be able to attend this meeting with you. The only reason I can give is that I've got an urgent attendance with my family. I cannot go any further in detail as it's personal, and so let's just leave it as that."

Peter muffled a little. "Erm...I just heard that you're not attending the Orlando library opening. Is everything OK?"

"Has she told you?"

"Yes, she did. I was passing by to have lunch with her but she informed me that she's a little tied up with telephone traffic. Is everything still OK?"

"It's nothing. I'm just going to see General Kaiser, that's all."

"Are you in some kind of trouble? If you aren't available this afternoon, it might affect business."

"No," Leo implied, "I'm attending a national security thing." He said, "Anyway, do inform our client, I've been working a solid forty-six hours each week of seeing important people to opening public places, and fatigue has caught up with me. To put simply, I need to recuperate before I'm able to get back on my feet. Also, you tell Gareth Calvin that you have my fullest confidence in your abilities. Just imagine this, if you succeed in that meeting, it'll only delay my dry ink just by a couple of days."

"Sure," Peter Alsopp agreed, "so you're seeing the big cheese next Monday but it's only Friday afternoon. Leo, the last five weeks has been slow for us and this meeting is our biggest break. Are you going through some kind of family bereavement? I'm sure our client will understand."

Leo was taken in by his apparent understanding. *Empathically, a worthy employee,* he thought, *and very trustworthy. Therefore, he'll sit well on the Executive Board.*

"Peter, I don't know what I would have done," Leo said, "if I didn't recruit you. God, you've gone a long way from seeing me as your client to your employer. I've known you for the last good twelve months and you've even been leaving a positive impression on my wife. You see, Peter, I got a personal engagement with Carly. I trust that you will succeed, for I'm going home to see her."

"Are you serious? Are you having some kind of marital difficulty?"

"Not that I'm aware of. Look, it's just that I'm bringing Valentine's early."

Peter muffled again. "Erm," he tried to be coherent, "I'm not going to tell you. No, I'm surely not going to tell you how to do your job. But we're not going to see our client for another three hours—"

"You mean that I can leave this building, jump into my car, drive downtown, drive up to the drive of my house, enter into my lovely home, run upstairs, bail out of my suit, slip under the covers, do the biz, bail out

– and hope to be back here before the buffet with Gareth Calvin."

Peter laughed. "Sure, you got other executives here that can do the deal. I'm willing to make my mark. I'll say that you're not attending due to an unforeseen situation, and that you've invested your interest in me to conduct the deal."

"You're great! If you secure this, you'll prove to the board that you're entitled for a promotion. It's all because of your continuing commitment towards achieving our objectives."

The call finished with polite farewells and for the CEO, it was going to be an exciting afternoon; he was free to walk out of the building without a lease to hail him back.

He imaged that Carly was in the house pouring a glass of champagne. She was looking through the front window in her lingerie. Leo's mind was set that passer-bys were casually peeking into their home to see her in her semi-naked clothing. She had an acute smile, but only fitting for her husband. In Leo's earnest, he went deeper into his fantasy of his wife wearing just her black French knickers, and her see-through black bra. *I'll be able to give her a good spanking*, he thought. Leo imagined that she was spraying French perfume on both sides of her neck to draw him closer. His body allowed a throbbing sensation pressing against his trousers, and he wished to release his good measure.

As his lust was running wild, in his mind, Leo attempted to be decent before his departure. He stood up to walk towards the door where his double breast coat was hanging on a hook. He wore it to cover his patch on his trousers, and proceeded to leave his office in an orderly fashion.

Lisa saw her boss walking out of his office, and she produced a smile. "Is there anything else you like me to do?" Lisa asked.

"Lisa, you've been wonderful. I'm going out to attend to an unforeseen situation and give Peter the best of luck."

"Sorry," Lisa said perplexed, "but I don't understand what you want me to say *the best of luck* for?"

"Lisa, I meant the meeting this afternoon. I'll not be able to attend so tell him to text me on the outcome." He gave his farewells and so continued to move along the floor towards the elevator. He waited patiently, but felt dirty of having an erection in the presence of the ladies. For the first time, he discovered that his journey home was going to be a safari as he tried dodging them. Anyway, the elevator doors opened and he walked into the lift. Everybody around him was being busy as he pressed a button for the ground floor. In the lift, he resumed thinking of his wife wearing French perfume to signify her sweet surrender, for him, to have his way.

He emerged from the building into the car park, and continued walking to his car. He stretched out his arm to unlock his door to enter into his new saloon. The vehicle itself was imported from the United Kingdom with its manual gear system, and the driver's seat is placed on the right. It was a family car, yet, contained a powerful sports engine. From a starting position, the car could accelerate from 0-70 mph in 7.5 seconds. Besides his love for Carly, he adored his car. It had installed the finest surround-sound system. Also, it did come with a hidden GPS unit of tracking its whereabouts, if stolen. Furthermore, the boot of his car held a hidden chamber where Leo had placed the spatial water, in a flask, away from his family and friends. He opened his driver's door as to enter. Meticulously, he closed the door, wore his seat belt, turned the ignition to start his engine, and began to drive out of the car park onto the main road. As he was driving, he discovered that it was traffic free, and all Leo hoped was to enjoy his quiet drive home.

He was congenially thinking of Peter Alsopp; it was of his professional handling to put the client into their books. He wondered if his Business Consultant was right, that he could easily return to work after romping with Carly. He calculated that it was only going to take twenty minutes to drive home, than double that time - at least - during rush hour. One thing he noticed, rush hour traffic was unpredictable as it could spring up anywhere at any given time. However, Leo's Business Consultant believed that he'd be back within three hours. He could take the chance of seeing to her needs, and return to work.

As he got closer to home, there was some slight traffic and to his surprise, he saw that he was going to pass one of his favourite news stands at a cross section. At the news-stand, a large fat man, in his late forties, recognised the driver, of his new car, and he was waving at him with a newspaper at hand. Leo acknowledged his presence by sounding his horn before the changing traffic lights. As he drove pass, Leo had a mirth spirit concerning his detour; it was supposed to be a quiet drive — but a rather large, and a fat gentleman wanted to change all that! Leo looked through his rear view mirror and saw the same person giving him chase along the street. Rockford had a special calling but to see him running made him conclude, that he still had enough time. As he commenced his U-turn, Leo noticed that the stall-holder was now walking back to await his customer. So Leo drove closer towards the stand and was alarmed to think that he hadn't bought a paper for over twelve months. So the closer he got, the more he was searching for a rational excuse. One reason that popped to mind, that he was working upon a new space project — and it would end the fat man's anxiety, if any. He was still getting closer to the stand, and eventually Leo switched off his engine. Next, he left his car to approach him.

"So you want to see me?" Leo said.

The rather large, yet, fat man inherited a strong Irish accent after catching his breath. "Long time no see...It has been some time since you bought a paper from me...Are you trying to drive my customers away?"

Leo laughed. "You're a funny man! You could've had a heart attack trying to chase me down this road."

The Irishman laughed too on his good fortune. He handed him a magazine and his newspaper — he usually bought. "Nah," he went on, "I always keep fit in the mornings. It's always quiet at this time of day as people are at work, but it will pick up later, I tell ya!"

Leo studied the magazine to see why he's shoving him it. It wasn't what he usually read, but it had a picture of his old crew mate from the Orion, Tasha Chayton. The cover of the magazine appeared to suggest that she was looking directly at you, an air of discontent too. Furthermore, her husband had placed one of his hands on her shoulder from behind. Leo read the headline, which gave him an odd amusement:

Jay Kaiser, the womaniser

Leo looked straight at the Irishman who caught his reaction. "I never saw that coming!" he said, slightly embarrassed. "I was the Commander of the Orion, and I didn't see a sexual predator on my ship."

The Irishman nodded. "Yeah, who would have thought that Jay Kaiser could do such a thing? Couldn't keep it in his pants and trying to get her blindly drunk – I read. That's one disgusting man and I even bet he sleeps with intergalactic aliens – if you gave him half the chance."

"We were all just doing our jobs out there," Leo said. "I'm very surprised because Jay Kaiser is a fine astronaut."

The fat man said, "You mean to tell me that Jay Kaiser is the alpha male than you? Surely you're the captain, and the captain says *keep it in your pants* or face a disciplinary hearing." He paused a moment. "Bejesus!" he exclaimed, "what kind of disciplinary action is available in space?"

"We've been finely selected," he replied to his first, "by the NASA Advisory Panel."

"That's bollocks man!" snapped the Irishman, "it really sounds like Jay has brought a new meaning about space: Being a complete dick! Listen, just watch out for those that are passing the bucket and blaming you for all that mess. Remember this, my boy, that panel will be looking to give you a bollocking."

"I'm a big boy now. I've got my own company."

"You nah hear whatcha I say? They can hang you up to dry because you brought shame to their name! Be careful as you have been a good customer."

"You kind of remind me of my father."

"And you," he said with a wink, "remind me of a son I never had!"

Leo tipped the man for the magazine and the paper and headed straight back into his car. He raced the thought of his wife still waiting for him. Since his journey wasn't going to be a quiet one, he turned the key and his radio came on. It played an old Hip Hop tune, from the eighties, being Ice Cube. It got Leo in an upbeat mood to continue his journey.

***

Leo arrived on his long drive, covered with palm trees on either side. He parked beside his wife's car. Current Affairs was making an unverified report of a bomb blast at a government building in Dallas. The news reporter suggested that many innocent people might have been killed. Also, an USTF spokesman promised swift action – Leo turned off the radio. Just at that moment, he had compunction of going to bed his wife whereas only a moment ago, Harry Trump had just arranged for him to see General Kaiser. He prayed that the report couldn't be substantiated, and that the people would be okay. Leo recalled the USTF spokesman promising swift justice and he told himself that those *bastards* must pay.

He felt comfortable as he entered into his home. He saw some mail upon the hallway table with his name on it. An envelope had a rubber stamp from Beverly Hills. Obviously, it had to be Jay Kaiser and he decided to read it:

Hi Buddy,

Just wanted you to know that you and your beautiful wife are both invited to the movie premiere, in Orlando, Supremacy.

Please find two tickets for you and your wife and three more for your children.

I just thought you should know that my wife and I are separated because of Tasha Chayton's allegations. She seems to think that to drinking alcohol isn't the cause of being drunk, and that I wanted to sleep with her.

Listen buddy, it'll be great to see the pair of you at the premiere.

Your Buddy

Jay Kaiser

Leo laughed, along the hallway, about Jay's separation. It faded after coming to terms that his wife didn't seem to be at home. He looked through the front window to see if any Hawaii-shirt men were doing any surveillance work, and he saw none. He headed into the kitchen but his wife wasn't there. He dashed upstairs into the bedroom that his wife was waiting. He opened the bedroom door and to his relief, Carly was lying upon their bed wearing her black French knickers and bra – she looked stunning and peaceful too.

Leo said, "I got here as fast as I could."

He unfastened his trousers to show-off his glory. *I really want to slip my hardness between her legs into her wide vagina,* he thought, *and be certain to release my seed into her deep.*

As he approached, his wife was murmuring a little. "There's a strange man behind the door."

Leo froze to think that it was just a practical joke, and he laughed. "Do you remember," he recalled, "that Irish fellow? He was giving me such a chase not to get here sooner!"

He took the moment to turn around. It was, to his surprise, that a man was pointing a gun directly at him, while his other hand closed the door.

The intruder said, "Please sit beside your wife."

"If you're after money, check the draws, we got thousands of dollars just stashed in there!"

The man stood there and was wearing a black cap, black sunglasses, black jeans and even a black T-shirt. "I'll need you," he continued, "to face that wall by the bed with your arms and your legs spread. So press against that wall. I'll check those draws, sir!"

Leo looked at his wife whom seemed to find it exciting. He recollected when his Thunderbird car was stolen. He just couldn't help but wonder if the burglar was one of them.

He felt a sharp prick at the back of his neck, and turned around knowing that he was injected with something. "Who the fuck are..."

Leo looked around the room but his eyes were turning watery. He managed to see his wife and still seemed to have a sexual hunger. Also, his sexual hormone intensified, as if, he really ought to jump onto the bed – no matter the presence of the intruder. Nevertheless, Leo found the room going black.

Chapter 35
—Abduction—

*L*EO WOKE UP to find himself sitting on a sofa. He looked around to adjust to his new scenery. He remembered not wearing his bottoms, but somehow, he was wearing them. There was a bright light bulb directly above him without a shade. A secondary light was beaming straight into his eyes. Basically, it was making it difficult for him to make any observation. In the room, there were two men standing near, smirking at either side of the him – both worn eye masks.

One of the two said, "It's nice to meet you! I heard that you're a keen supporter of Kaiser."

A third man was standing behind Leo. "Hello, Leo Rockford. It's a pleasant occasion to be of your acquaintance. I just heard that you've been abducted from your home, and that I got here as fast as I could. People were saying that you're the oxygen to Kaiser; goodness, you've given him life. So you of all people were trying to pull the wool over the eyes of the American people. You know that he's a tyrant, a dictator and a murderer. People were also saying that you were making millions after that revolution of yours. You're out for the money and nothing else, isn't that right?"

Are these the ones that wore Hawaii shirts? Leo thought. He was trying to move his legs and arms but was tightly restrained. "Are you those people trying to see that I'm a mole?"

The man moved in front of him. "I'm Wallace Moore," he said and was wearing a mask too, "if you're thinking that you're a mole in this country then confess it. Are you not aware of the war against the illegal system that you are OK with?"

Leo hadn't any idea who the heck was Wallace Moore, but knew that he was facing tormentor. He sighed.

"You're the RRF, isn't it? Listen, what do you think I
know about the Supreme Council?"

"I want to know why you like being in this country
more than your own. I want to know why you didn't join
the Red Resistance Union, and your reason why you
think that we should spare your life?"

"Where's my wife?"

Wallace moved away to lean against a wall. "She's
fine," he said, "and she is at your home. We've been
watching you for some time now. We know that your son
is in London and your daughters are in Brazil. We
especially know that you've an emergency plan of seeing
General Kaiser. You're an easy target for us. Yet, what
upsets my boys is that you do not travel with any armed
personnel. Are you some kind of super hero?"

Leo could hear the other men laugh. He knew that
the RRF kidnapped people, working for Kaiser, but he
wasn't directly working for him. He sighed again. "I'm no
super hero, I came to this country to fulfil my dream in
astronomy, and it led me to command a mission to
Mars."

"Is it fair to say," Wallace said, "that you and General
Kaiser have the same interests in astronomy? I mean
he's funding the Robinson Space Observatory, isn't he?
There was a rumour that Frederick Bungles was planning
to make cuts, isn't it?"

"You only want to hear what you want to hear!" he
said in a panic. "How am I supposed to defend myself
by your delusions?"

Wallace hummed. "You got heart to turn the tables.
Let me tell you what's really going on. It is I that asks
you the questions and you better answer them. Once I
got enough information from you, then I'll decide your
fate tonight."

"You mean to kill me because I'm funded by Kaiser."

Wallace moved little closer. He nodded. "Why did you
accept the Mars mission? Did you not know the risk
involved like those fabulous engines being out of its line
of array?"

"Why are you doing this?"

It prompted another man to stand to Leo's left side with a gun and silencer against his head.

"You see, Leo Rockford, if you won't co-operate then we're forced to believe that you're a traitor to the true constitution that you've stolen from us. Now, answer the damn question or die right now. Why did you accept the Mars mission?"

"I did the mission because the General demanded it from me. He gave me work at the Space Observatory."

Wallace directed his gunman to move away from Leo, and was breathing heavily. "Do you," he asked, "think that the so-called revolution is rigged?"

"Wallace, I gave you a good answer and you cannot deny that."

He moved in a little closer. "You think the new constitution is a lot better don't you?"

"I think the new constitution is helping the economy and the world economy too."

Wallace said, "Ever since you've been detected under our radar, I couldn't decide to give you the wet works. My senior figures in the RRF still couldn't decide in your fate as well. So you see, Leo, abduction is the only option and it turns out that I alone cannot order him to pull the trigger."

"What you're doing is wrong. Not only are you breaking the Supreme law but international law too!"

Wallace ordered the other person to slap him across his cheek. It was instant and the affect of the pain lingered on Leo.

"I'm considering to spare your life," Wallace continued, "but let that be a warning, and do not try to compromise your abduction. All I ask of you is to make me understand why you're still friends with General Kaiser?"

"OK, you want me to answer? We've been friends since the NATO military operation in Turkey."

"Let me guess, the Soviet threat. As you may know, they haven't been much of a threat for the last twenty years," Wallace said.

"Soviets had its military power throughout the Eastern Bloc. It was the push that was a threat of spreading their

WAYNE WIGNALL

communist views into the West. They might have had
the resources but we had the counter initiative too."
"So you were in Turkey to bomb Soviet targets from
the air, wasn't it?"
Leo lied, "We were based in Turkey due to our
military intelligence that the Politburo might move against
the Glasnost movement in Moscow."
"Goodness sake, are you patronising with General
Kaiser? Was that how you converted him to become a
dictator?"
"I'm giving you the facts for you to play with. We went
to Turkey because of our military intelligence, but it
turned out false – it was before the August Putsch."
Wallace shook his head and returned to lean against
the wall. He hummed a little. "What do you think of
public opinion regarding the Supreme Council?"
"The public supports the change and the fact is that
the international community supports the change too."
"Are you a Christian, Leo?" Wallace asked and he
nodded. "Then," he resumed, "surely you know that the
American people are like sheep that ought to be led by
our Shepherd."
"I don't think that General Kaiser is in the business
of being the Word of God! He saw an opportunity for
reform."
Wallace moved swiftly towards him. He nodded. "So
you're in support of the so-called *reform*? I could now
command one of my boys to take your life for the foul
acts that Kaiser stands for! Yet, I want you to understand
the path that you're taking, which means, your chosen
path was for the disbandment of the RRU by
incarcerating its champion members. Also, it was the
path, which assassinated Frederick Bungles."
Leo was baffled. "It was," he mumbled, "it was a
skiing accident."
"Yeah, I bet you're really sorry that it was an accident.
So you're going to be sorry for your actions, isn't it?"
Wallace said and indicated, to one of his men, to place
his gun on Leo's head.
Leo hadn't any idea why he was place in front of
people who had a demeanour of paranoia. "What makes

you think," he said, "that I had a say in the assassination of Frederick Bungles? I work in astronomy and I look into the skies for answers. I didn't go to university to draft a plan on changing the free world. I went because I loved the stars and its beautiful picturesque. If your organization doesn't share the same idea about the heavens then I suppose you must kill me."

"You got spunk," Wallace responded, "to tell me how to run things. Like I said, if you got the knack on persuading people on their commitments, then it was you that forced the hand in the Supreme Council."

"I've only," Leo retorted, "the public relations agency to thank for!"

"You're something – I give you that. Now I sense that you're a person who likes to back the winning horse, isn't that right?"

"I haven't any real use to the Supreme Council since my return to Mars, and I'm really no use to you either."

"I guess that you may be right. I'm going to retain you here, under guard, and I'll be seeing you!" he said and walked out of the room.

A man took a seat along the large sofa. "I'm Sanjay," he said, "and you're one lucky person to live to see tomorrow, for he could have killed you!"

Leo asked, "Why are you doing this?"

"Well, Wallace says it's for a better America, and you may not appear to fit his vision. If you really must know, your wife is really fine. He did drug her though."

Leo now knew that the other man, on his right, was the one in his home.

The dark dresser said, "Hi, my name is Mario and I had to drug her to keep her quiet! It'll wear off by tomorrow and she'll be absolutely fine. But for you; you're going to face another day in helping us with our enquiries. Oh and one more thing, I brought you here in that lovely car of yours."

It was critical information that his wife was really fine. Still, he had new hope for the car in use. *This should be easy peasy*, he thought. Needless to say, his wife would be able to sound the alarm to the police; and once alerted, they should be able to track his car and know of his whereabouts!

"I like how you stood up to Wallace," Mario said sarcastically. "It was courageous, you know – I thought I was brave enough to enter your home and to wait on your arrival."

"So who told you that I was going to get home early?" He laughed. "I was just following orders. I was told to get to the house this afternoon, and to make myself comfortable. When I saw your wife looking at me, she was surprised and angry that I apparently work for the USTF – she was upset with you. So we did talk a little about how insensitive you've been over the last six to twelve months. She said something that you're hoping to expand into Europe, and that you wished to move there pretty sharpish.

"So I was telling her to stay in America because it's the best country in the world etc. I drugged her and took her upstairs into the bedroom. I just waited for you to turn up. I only waited three minutes and that's a record.

"Of course, we're the RRF and we're neither terrorists nor rapists but good obliging citizens for the American dream, which is freedom."

Leo asked, "Where are we, for I don't recognise these surroundings?"

Sanjay replied, "You're not far from your car. In matter of fact, you'll be free to drive away from here as a participant of the RRF. Becoming one of us will mean that you owe us a debt. Perhaps we'll ask you to donate couple of thousands of dollars and then you're as right as rain."

"You mean that you kidnap people so that they can buy their freedom back?" Leo asked irksomely.

Mario laughed. "You catch on well!" he said, "we recruit benefactors! You see, our benefactors do believe that they're doing this for a better tomorrow, and I hope that you'll agree."

"I told you that we had money in the draw, why didn't you take it?"

"You see, I did take that money. However, if you remain to be a success, we'll still want you to remain our benefactor. Do you understand now?"

"Where are we?" Leo asked again.

"If you must know, you're in the rough area of Orlando, which is known for prostitutes, pimps and drug pushers. Yet, you're in our safe house in Crime Hills!"

From what Leo could decipher, he was in an area near where his first American car got stolen, which was Pine Hills. He knew that the police might track his car but would they be able to locate his exact location? Crime Hills had densely populated areas.

Sanjay moved to exit. "I'm going to get pizza. So what the pair of you want?"

Leo wouldn't say a word, but the other man requested a sea food pizza.

"We've been renting these accommodations for some time now," Mario said. "The landlord here is great after we gave him three months in advance payment. I know that you live in a more luxurious environment, and that this place doesn't quite match your previous comfort level. Yet, you'll find that this will only be temporary and you'll be back before you know it."

"Why do you mock me when you know that I won't be seeing my family?"

"Not at all, I just follow orders and that is what I do. That car of yours was superb and talk about a quiet engine. I've been snooping around and I find all kinds of weird stuff like an astronomy map, and what are you trying to find on the highway?" Mario asked and pretended to think very hard for an answer. "The Milky Way! And why are you hiding alcohol in that flashy trunk of yours, in a flask?" Mario noticed Leo showing a lot of concern for it. "So you're," he assumed, "an alcoholic – and it isn't of any concern of mine – but why have secret stash?"

"If you most know," Leo loathed, "that map holds secret knowledge about outer space."

"I thought I was weird trying to abduct you today. And you mean to tell me that the flask comes from Mars? Just what're you doing with it?"

"I don't have to tell you anything!"

Chapter 36
—Judged—

*L*EO WOKE UP. His eyes were hurting a little as a ray of light beamed down on him. After adjusting to the day, he found himself in the same room as before. He was lying along a red couch. His arms were pinioned. His legs were bounded tightly together too. He even noticed his mouth was gagged, and Leo was feeling the aches and pains of sleeping rough. Leo was alone and could hear the sound of traffic outside. The former astronaut knew that they'd further questions of his involvement, and all he could do was wait. Rockford was sweating because the room was a little too warm. He spotted a single door; which led out, perhaps, to a hallway, however, he was hapless. As time passed on, he just stared at the creamy-white walls as he had nothing else to do.

Sanjay entered the room with Wallace behind him. He was wearing an eye mask, and Wallace a full mask.
"Good Morning, Leo," Sanjay said joyfully.
Of course, Leo wasn't in the best of moods of greeting anybody that had taken away his freedom. The pair picked him up from the sofa to sit him up straight. Sanjay removed his gag.
Wallace said, "I've been thinking about you yesterday but it's appears that we still don't know what to do with you. So let me give you a little story about Flash Gordon. *Ming the Merciless is an evil overlord that wants to put America into submission. He does that pretending to be an Earthling.* Anyway, that evil overlord jumps out of the story book and it's General Kaiser. Guess what? Kaiser devises a plan so that he can pretend to be a righteous American. He does that by hiding behind NASA. Do you see now?" Wallace moved to sit beside him. "Hadn't it

ever crossed your mind that the General resembled Ming?"

"I'm not familiar with your cause, but I can tell you that the General does look like Ming. In fact, my daughter thinks that General Kaiser was a Hollywood celebrity. So what's your point?"

"We had scores of people," Wallace responded, "who understood that Kaiser was masquerading. Now Kaiser sends you to Mars, which is silencing our cause to an all-time low. And that's all thanks to you telling us, ordinary folks, that Kaiser is a true gentleman."

"If you say," Leo said, "that I'm silencing your cause. Then you would have heard it from my public relations company. Earlier, you told me that you've been keeping an eye on me, so perhaps, you should've been keeping a closer eye on my team too."

"Your agency is about space—" Wallace said, a little hesitantly. "I must admit," he continued, "that it seems that you're on the right side of the fence. You could be the first person to succeed in becoming our benefactor. I would like to apologize for taking steps in your abduction. I ask of you to pardon us."

Of course, Leo couldn't believe that he was lucky, that Wallace was going to cut him loose. He looked to stare at the floor.

Mario walked into the room and stood beside Wallace. His boss whispered something to him as he nodded. Then he moved towards Leo. "See that you're successful to join us," he whispered.

"I'm not a bargaining chip!" Leo said, incensed.

"Then you should have boycotted the Space Observatory!" he implied and was revealing his gun.

Leo trembled on his own apprehension.

Wallace was circling around the sofa with his hands behind his back. He sighed. "So you do understand American politics, don't you? So surely you've accepted to being associated with Kaiser. Therefore, you should understand what we do to people that are the real enemies of the state."

"You're questioning my understanding of American democracy, isn't it? I got news for you, that I'd never casted a vote!"

"How dare you!" he said. "Yet again, your British wit wins the day. But remember this," he proceeded, "you're living on borrowed time. I could have easily killed you on several occasions, but that smug face of yours keeps you alive. So from now on, if you want to be left in peace, go back to Britain and leave the fighting to us."

Leo was taken back by his decision – he saw him a bit furious as he was walking around him. "Will you be releasing me?"

Wallace replied, "Did you not hear what I just said? You should have boycotted the Space Observatory."

"Wallace, if you don't mind me asking," Mario wondered, "don't you want me to kill him right here, right now?"

"What's the point in that? We're not murderers. That man was working at the wrong place at the wrong time. We shouldn't kill him. However, we'll hold him here to teach him a lesson."

"Leo, you must realize that you're a very lucky guy," Sanjay said smiling. "I hope," he pressed on, "that one day, we could become good friends and look back at this as a huge misunderstanding."

"So this is just a plain kidnapping against my aspirations?" Leo asked loudly.

"Yeah!" Wallace replied.

Chapter 37
—Hell on Earth—

*I*T FELT LIKE weeks staying in the same apartment. He knew for certain that his wife must have reported it to the police. Then again, they didn't seem able to rescue him. Time and time again, he heard sirens that raged pass. Pessimism was his answer. What really puzzled Leo was his GPS car system; it should have been used to track him down. Leo pondered on the police recovering his car, and if so, would they determine that he was in Pine Hills, or long gone?

Wallace entered the room along with Mario, and two other men. Each of them was wearing eye masks, and was smirking at Leo. Mario, especially, seemed to wish to deliver some unfortunate news to him. He couldn't be condemned to die, could it? After all, Wallace had given his word not to kill him. Wallace was holding a newspaper as he stood in front of him, and Mario removed Leo's gag.

"I've got your morning paper to read," Mario said, of course, insulting his intelligence. "It appears that your beloved Kaiser is cutting you loose."

Wallace spread the paper upon Leo's lap and was pointing at a headline:

Rockford's feud with the Holy Grail

"What do you think it's all about?" Mario asked mockingly.

"What do you want me to do about it?" Leo asked regardless.

"I didn't know," Wallace said, "that you were incompetent on retrieving minerals from Mars. You came back empty-handed. It also states that you deliberately dashed the water to pin the blame on Martin. Is that really true? Anyway, General Kaiser is pissed off with you and is scraping your contract."

The other men were laughing at him.

Wallace nodded. "You do understand," he carried on, "that your biggest benefactor has jumped boat, because you're sinking to the bottom of the sea."

Mario laughed again. "So your American dream," he said, "is up in smoke. I don't suppose you're still interested to be our benefactor?"

Rockford wanted to be contemptuous. But because of his captors, to observe his demeanour, he felt vulnerable.

"It has been interesting knowing you: The Executive Officer of the Rockford Group," Wallace said and was sitting beside him. "It's a pity that your cash flow will be drying out, and your reputation will most definitely be in ruins. So with regards to *public relations* you do leave a lasting impression that Kaiser wants to actually punish you."

There was, obviously, a sinister atmosphere that Rockford's future wasn't fruitful. Leo wished to himself that he was deaf and blind – it would have been much more better than to hear them taunting.

Wallace said, "Altogether, you know that Mario is upset to see you face financial ruin. As we all know, it'll affect you and your family's prospects to remain here. You could work in this neighbourhood to help the fight against crime. Plus, why don't you help old people, like myself, to cross the road. Yet to be frank, you deserve what you get."

Leo felt stupefied. He glanced on the news article, and only comprehended that James Nunn was the spokesman. He sighed. "Why don't you let me leave?"

"That's because you're getting an indefinite sentence for supporting Kaiser!" One of the men said fondly.

Wallace ordered all of his men to leave him alone with Rockford, and the main captor was standing ahead of him. He nodded. "I'd told you that he was trouble. So this is the thanks General Kaiser returns for your service, isn't it? Why doesn't he wait to cancel your contract after your release? Perhaps he's hysterical that you're becoming a benefactor for the RRF, or he really thinks that you're already dead!

"I'll inform you that this is going to be my last visit. As you may imagine, I got a lot of things to do. You should join us in our cause but that may lead to complications."

Leo had nothing more to say to him. *Sod it*, he thought, *I never did like being in America.* He observed Wallace, walking around the room, eyeing the flask.

"Mario was telling me," he said, "that you were hiding liquor under the trunk of your car. The strange thing is that you had a secret compartment to hide your drinks in a cooling flask. Could you be so kind to explain your drinking problem?"

Leo replied, "It was in the car just to avoid a situation with my wife."

"I must inform you that I'm very sorry to have abducted you. It was due to our own suspicion that you were running something with Kaiser. You had a good business, commanded a spaceship and that part-time job in astronomy. Yet, NASA will ruin you. Therefore, I'm glad to say that we'll be releasing you. So you can go, out there, to reunite with your family. After your lovely reunion, you should think on Kaiser that he really regards your welfare; for he'll obviously be seeing you as a treacherous individual. For heaven's sake, man, if you can't convince me that you're his full-blooded supporter then he'll be thinking less of you. You heard of the USTF and the horrible things that they're doing to my boys, haven't you? Altogether, like a father to his son: You are now one of my own boys!

"You can go today but I want you to really consider joining us. Yes, we're a secret organization wishing to enlighten America against the thorn that presses against us. After that, you'll understand the true spirit of being a real American. You may consider your freedom as your first step into rehabilitation. Other words, if you fuck this one up then Mario will be paying you another visit."

Leo couldn't stand being in the same room with him. He thought of returning to his family; receiving a warm welcome from his wife and off-springs; sitting in the lounge watching the television with them; taking the Rockfords on a long holiday; supporting his family via his income. Yet, his business was doomed – Leo wanted revenge.

"Oh God! I never thought that you might understand me," Leo said with a simper. "Regardless of those allegations, please Wallace, could you untie me?" Wallace laughed. "I'm not going to untie you but the police. We'll be giving them a hoax call, which will get their asses in gear. They'll see you like that, and we'll be long gone."

"I just want a cool taste of France that's all. Please join me and open that flask."

Wallace got to his feet to pick up the flask from the corner of the room. He returned, and was being content. "Couldn't you," he said, "wait until the police arrive?"

"Well, I've lost track of time in what's-this-place and I don't wish to spoil one of the finest French wine."

"I think that you know that..." Wallace said and was struggling to remove the cap. "I hate to spoil wine."

"It might be spoilt under this baking heat."

"Drink it and let me see!" Wallace said, and filled the flask cap to the brim. He stood in front of him and placed it straight under his mouth. He tilted the cap as Leo put his head back, and Wallace watched him studiously. "Well, is it vintage?"

It was the first time that Leo drank it pure and it instantly dried his throat, which caused him to choke. "I think it's strong!"

"God damn, what're you, a rookie?" Wallace said and brought it closer towards his own mouth–

Mario entered. "I've got word," he said, watching Wallace lowering the cap, "that we're ready to roll."

"Mario, thanks for telling me, yet, couldn't it wait?" He apologized before exiting.

"Sorry about that Leo. You know that we really sense that you're OK. I only hope that you'll see that our cause is greater, for you are still breathing,"

Wallace began to take a gulp and he coughed loudly. "What the fuck." He caught his breath. "What the hell," he added, "have you got me drinking? Cheap wine?"

Leo was still coughing. "No..." He tried to find his voice. "I got it from an astronaut!"

Mario re-entered the room to see the commotion. He saw Wallace, beating on his chest with the hapless prisoner. He gasped. "Are you OK?"

"Mario, I'm fine!...You wait, out there... God damn it!"

He wanted to stay a while longer why his boss was coughing loudly, but obliged.

Leo coughed, he laughed too. "Will you...Remember me when you think of Zetta?"

Wallace still coughed a little and thought to leave him alone. However, he gagged him tightly. "I've got to get going...In a short while...The law enforcement will be swarming in...Looking for us...You'll remain here until we're long gone!"

Wallace managed to control his coughs. He sighed. "So ass-hole, is that what you like to drink? It's really tasteless shit but has a strange kick. Are you trying to kill the both of us?"

He left. Leo remained sitting there and heard the front door of the apartment open before it closed. It was the only significant sounds but an occasional siren was still screaming pass.

Chapter 38
—Released—

WALLACE MOORE LEFT the apartment. He commanded Mario to declare the whereabouts of Leo Rockford to the police. However, Mario must give himself enough time to make himself scarce. He had driven alone in his car heading north, and stopped at a filling station. It had been a long day on the road so figured to stop the night at its motel.

Later on in the evening, he left his room in search of a telephone booth. After finding one he dialled for a police station in Orlando. The phone only rang briefly.

"Pine Hill Police Station, how may I help you?"

"This is a RRF announcement. I have the location of Leo Rockford. He's alive and well at the Pine Lodge in room 063."

"Do you think I am a twit? Are you trying to waste valuable police time? Just because he was news doesn't give you the right to muck about."

"I'm very serious! He is at the Pine Lodge—"

"Are you aware that the kidnapped usually ends up dead? If you want to waste valuable police time and resources: You'll be arrested!"

After Mario heard the warning, he got furious and hung up the phone. A few moments later, he got himself calm and tried again that Leo Rockford wasn't dead. He only hoped to not speak to the same officer, but it wasn't to be.

"I told you to stop wasting our time for we'll be tracing this call!"

Obviously, relaying important details wasn't going well. It was his second setback and quickly decided to write a complaint, to the Captain, of the outrageous lip service. In addition, he wrote a letter to the landlord:

Dear Landlord.

I'll just like to be urgent concerning my apartment in 063.

It has come to my attention that my brother is left alone, and he suffers from severe learning difficulties. I've informed the local police and the social services but their response is lame

All I ask of you is to check my apartment and you've my permission for full access. If my brother is in there, please tell him to return to our Mother who is worried sick.

I know it an unusual task but I'll be awfully grateful!

Yours truly,

Derrick

PS Here's $400 for your troubles and a spare key

***

It was a sufferance – as the hopeful would say – but Leo felt that his freedom was drawing further and further away. He sat upon the sofa. It was sheer physical and mental torture as no one was able to release him. He thought of Wallace stalling his promise because he had duped him. *This is going to be an eternity,* he thought, *because I'll be suffering from dehydration. Besides, I cannot relief myself.* The mind games by Mario had taken its toll on him too.

The police SWAT team stormed the apartment. The Captain would be one of the first to find him, and saw him hungry, thirsty and in his own filth. He gasped. "My name is Capt. Bangalore. We just got word on your location. It's great to see that you're actually alive. Leo, we'll be taking you home–"

"Please my flask! My flask!"

The Captain was puzzled by its significance. The smell in the room was bad too, and there were cockroaches dotting around.

"Are you feeling okay?" the captain asked, "I think you should be checked out at the hospital."

"My flask. I want my flask!"

Bangalore said, "Fine, we'll send your flask to your wife–"

"No! I want it in my car! I want the flask in my car!"

"Calm down, okay, we have your car in the police lot. I'll place it in there," he responded and noticed something on the window sill. "Oh," he continued, "I suppose these are your car keys?"

"Oh God, yes!" Leo said, delirious, "please return car home!"

The Captain granted Leo's wishes and made certain that he got checked-in at the local hospital. He received, of course, medical treatment as a precaution, and not much activity occurred around Leo's hospital bed – besides few police detectives, his family and friends dropping by to pay him a visit.

Chapter 39

*T*HREE DAY LATER, Leo got the all clear to check out. However, the USTF wished to escort him to their local office on helping them with their own enquiries. Leo returned to the same building where he tried to bribe Harry Trump. He sat in the waiting room with one of the USTF agents. Not long after, the Agent beside Leo made a dash towards his colleague whom approached him. Leo could overhear his protégé receiving his order that other agents were to collect him to the sixth floor. Shortly afterwards, Leo found himself in the company of three enormous men that led him onto the elevator.

At the entrance of the sixth floor, Rockford was welcomed by a stranger.

"It's good to see you, Leo," he said, "I'm David Bruce. It's good of you to pay us a visit, that you can help us in our investigation."

Leo hesitated to shake his hand, as he recalled, it was just over 72 hours ago that he wasn't clean, nor was he fresh—

"Sorry, just thinking back on the time that I left that dreadful flat. God, everything is moving very fast."

"No matter," David continued, "I'm the head of the USTF. As you may know, we're a newly formed unit to combat militia crimes. Obviously, our main focus is the RRF, and we're very fortunate to be with you."

David led him along the corridor into one of the empty rooms.

Harry Trump stood up to shake his hand—

"Leo, it's great to be seeing you again," Harry said. "I never thought those bastards had any logic, that you weren't a key figure in the Supreme Council. We've brought you here for we're hoping that you can give us a substantial lead." He then reclaimed his seat.

Leo looked to his right to see a large photographic portrait of General Kaiser. The picture was hanging above Harry's head with the Supreme flag close by. It was a large room with ample space for twenty persons to seat around a magnificent table.

"What do you think I know?" Leo asked him.

"You're lucky to be still alive, and we want to know why?" David asked bluntly.

Harry was slightly embarrassed. He sighed. "Leo, please excuse the abrupt behaviour of David Bruce. He's a lean, mean machine but the finest around."

"They strongly," Leo said, "believed that I was pulling the strings against democracy—"

Harry sniggered. "I'm sorry, Leo, they thought that you were a threat to their existence?"

He took a seat near Harry and nodded. "They informed me that they were considering taking me out, but only wished to understand me first."

David paced around the large table, he hummed too. "What you are really saying is that they were thinking of killing you?"

Leo nodded. "Yes, so they took me to that apartment for answers."

David moved closer to Leo and took a seat – still he hummed. "You said to the Orlando Police, that their questions were erratic. Yet, they conformed not to kill you, isn't that right?"

Leo nodded again. "Look, they wanted to see if I was a major player—"

"You're the proprietor of the Rockford Group, right?" David asked abruptly, and he agreed. "Please excuse me, for how could they be at ease since you're Kaiser's success story."

"I told them that I loved space and I've always loved space—"

"You loved space and so the RRF shared in your fulfilment?"

"Are you accusing me of staging my own abduction?" Leo asked.

"We're basing it on the fact that it's a rarity. To hear of the RRF, giving a pardon, is the first of its kind. So on that basis, what deal did you strike with Wallace?"

"Lord!" Leo exclaimed and stood up to leave, "you've no right to believe that that the RRF has turned me against Kaiser. What they saw was a citizen that isn't involved in the corridors of power. So that is that!"

Harry said, "Leo, we got a very good chance of ending them for good. We need to believe that you're on the winning side."

Leo said, "Winning side? Of course I am. I came to this country to become an Astronomer, and now look, I run my own—"

"Just that the only reason," David rudely interrupted him, "is that the RRF wants to release you, for you're a potential asset."

"I did not give any funds to that organization, and if you must, you may bloody well check my business trading accounts! You're wrong to believe that I'm a sympathizer, and I haven't made any clear intention to them that I will!"

Harry said, "So you were sly but we still believe that they will be recruiting you to topple us. We do have reliable intelligence but their infrastructure is rather murky."

Leo now stood by the window to face them. He sighed. "What you're saying makes no fucking sense! They took me because they had a paranoid belief that I was pulling strings in Washington. When they understood their mistake—"

"Come on, Leo!" Harry butted in loudly, "didn't you realise why you went to space in the first place? To make General Kaiser as humane as possible! You supported us and the RRF saw your actions as a direct threat."

"Yet," Leo wondered a bit, "I'm a member at the Andrews Club—"

"So was Frederick Bungles and look at him now: Dead," David said sarcastically.

"So I commanded the Orion and I own a company - so what the fuck is that to do with in-stabilising Kaiser?"

Harry rose to his feet and headed swiftly towards Leo. After he got closer, he patted him on his shoulder – Leo wasn't really receptacle to it.

"You do appear a little naïve," Harry said passionately, "but it's to do with public opinion – I'm surprised that you do require a crash course on it – besides, you're rather foolish to run a public relations agency funded by Kaiser: It's hideous."

"Look here," Leo reacted, "I never asked to be in space, nor to owning a multi-million dollar business. Just because I happened to team up with Kaiser, in our quest against the Soviets, doesn't mean that I can change the balance of power in America. It's obvious that the RRF would be put in jeopardy if they killed me."

"Look," Harry implied, "they kidnapped you for two months and we didn't know if you were dead or alive. We didn't know squat until the police gave us the call of your whereabouts."

"I don't think I like the way that you're looking at me," Leo said to David who seemed to be suspicious. "I've won my freedom," he went on, "and if you must know, you're giving me the creeps. It's best, it seems, that I should really consider moving back to Britain."

"We know all that," David reassured him, "your wife has been very helpful about your desire of expanding the Rockford Group. Nevertheless, losing the spatial water made us really think, that you really do have butter fingers. Those butter fingers must have cost you dearly."

Leo was angry and approached him, but Harry was in his way–

"It's not worth it, Leo!," Harry told him, "he may be hiding behind his Supreme badge but you cannot attack him. Kaiser didn't give you immunity."

"All I'll say is that you're a bastard," Leo remonstrated, "God! If it wasn't for Harry, I would have beaten you down so silly."

David wouldn't flinch.

Harry said, "Leo, I have a car waiting that will take you back home to your family. Also, we'll be putting a watch on your house 24 / 7. We do like to thank you for taking the time to come here. David, over there, was curious how you cheated death. Anyway, we'll like you to identify a specific person for us," he moved, a short distance, to his briefcase and returned with a photograph. "Do you know that man?"

Leo looked at it. He recognised him from the nose down, and gasped. "That's Sanjay! He has been helpful and supportive during my captivity!"

"Good!" Harry reacted, "he must be our ticket to bringing down the RRF."

Leo asked, "Might I ask how I'm going to help you in your investigation? I was the victim here, isn't it?"

Harry replied, "Well, all that I can say right now is that he is what we're looking for to flush them out. I hope that you'll honour my little revelation."

Leo now asked, "I've been kidnapped by the RRF for over two months, and just before my release, I nearly died of dehydration. However, where's General Kaiser?"

"He's at the Supreme White House," David informed, "under my advice, to re-evaluate this situation regarding you. I know that you were friends and all but the fact remains that the safety of the Supreme Commander is paramount."

"He is paramount? So you're not under the watchful eye of the RRF and what if–"

"Enough, Leo," Harry jumped in, "he's doing his job that's all! General Kaiser is totally aware of this developing situation, and he sends his regards."

"He should have sent a card."

Harry and David laughed lightly.

"I'll pass on your message," David advised, "and I'm sure the General will enjoy seeing you again. Anyway, if you haven't realized the point of this little get-together: Sanjay is the target. So if you get any new information, approach us and we'll do the rest."

"I think what you're saying is that you're expecting them to contact me, isn't it right?"

David nodded. "You're going to have a new friend from now on and his name will be Howard Giles. He'll be your direct contact from now on, and we'll go on from there."

"You mean that I've a minder, right?"

"Of course it isn't!" Harry responded, "you got a special contact whom will introduce himself as such."

Leo nodded. "OK, you got my word."

The two men were grateful and David showed him the door. There was a Supreme Agent waiting outside–

"Mr. Rockford, if you'll follow me, sir."

Leo acknowledged and followed him into an escalator, which took them to a parked car in the basement. The whole journey was a quiet one, and Leo was finding it a little weird–

"Are you usually this quiet?" Leo asked.

"Well, I'm your driver, sir!" he replied – and the last thing he uttered. After they arrived, there were several police officers standing watch along the street. Furthermore, it was getting late in the evening as the car rolled up onto Rockford's long palm tree covered drive. Once the man parked near the front door, Leo thanked his driver.

Chapter 40

—Unmasked—

*M*ONDAY, EARLY SEPTEMBER. Leo had booked lunch with his Marketing Director, Peter Alsopp. He was eating a light meal, while Peter took on a lobster special. It was a magnificent place and as a customer; Leo was sitting in a bustling, expensive, yet small, restaurant. It seemed odd, to him, that the Chef had a grand park garden around the building, however, hadn't considered expanding it.

Anyway, Peter said, "It's a blessing in disguise that the Rockford Group is still afloat on the stock market, and your release has soared its business value to an all new high."

"You kept this business running smoothly during my absence." Leo responded before taking a swig of his wine. "I just," he added, "want to thank you for being a positive player."

"Just a little curious," Peter asked and used a napkin to wipe his mouth, "but what was it like when you realized that you were taken away from your family?"

Leo laughed. "If you must know, it was shit."

"I know that you've befriended General Kaiser, but how did you convince the RRF that you're not a worthy target?"

"All I said was that I love astronomy and when the astronaut opportunity was available, I took it."

"And they really believed you? Don't you find that a little weird?" Peter asked. He had enjoyed his meal, and was pouring himself a glass of wine.

"To be honest, it did seem weird but what can you do."

"Have you heard of the conspiracy theories, that it was Kaiser behind the kidnapping to test your loyalty. All because the real RRF are known to torture and kill their abductees."

Leo was irritated a bit. He also sighed. "Please," he said, "knock it off as those theories have no place in here, or anywhere else for that matter."

"It's in the morning papers; that a British Conspiracy Theorist believes that your abduction was staged."

"Don't make it harder than it really—"

"That won't happen again," Peter quickly interjected. "But" he continued, "am I wrong, that General Kaiser is an asshole for not seeing you lately? I mean, it's nice that you've your own highly-trained bodyguard, but Kaiser is supposed to be a close friend of yours, isn't he?"

"I know what you mean," Leo replied before a waiter approached the table. "Harry Trump," Leo continued regardless, "keeps telling me that Kaiser is a very busy man. I reckon I'll be seeing him again at the New Year's bash."

"I met your wife several times, at the office, and she always wanted to believe that you were still well. She thinks that he was a complete bastard whom was only using you for his own self-esteem; Carly told me that he didn't take any further interest in you," Peter said and was finishing his last fork load of lobster meat.

Leo asked for the final bill since the waiter was waiting patiently for further assistance and she left. Then he observed Peter who found the food quite dainty.

Peter said, "It has such a succulent texture. That's beautiful."

"I'm really thinking of going back to Britain in the near future. It's far too risky here."

"I could understand your concern but isn't that just going over-the-top?"

"Not at all, the terrorists were speculating that I am some kind of powerbroker in the Supreme Council. Now the Supreme Council is making their own speculations that I am coordinating with them. Staying here isn't going to do me any good. I'll take the chance of moving back to England."

"So you're going to leave America," Peter said and was readying himself to leave. "But what about your business interests in Orlando?"

"Well, I do have a soft heart; for I'll be keeping the Orlando office open. Of course, I'll be expanding my operations to London – and like you said – the Rockford Group will be sitting on a *gold mine.*"

"You're right, Leo. There'll be less suspicion after you've returned to England. Yet the villains will start believing that you were mad, for concerning yourself of the heavens. Look here, we're all Americans and you've taken a vow as a citizen. You might be holding two passports but you're an American citizen. I understand the danger of being affiliated on either side, but it's the risk that every American must take.

"I must admit that I wake up every morning not having any true feelings on today's politics. I put my family first, and obviously, my work too."

"Oh what the hell," Leo reacted, "I'm going put word out that you should be the new Operating Chief in North America. It'll mean a lot to me."

"You mean to leave very soon?" Peter asked.

"I think it'll be in the next fortnight, how about it? My wife agrees and I'm sure my girls and my boy will also agree."

"Goodness, you don't really feel safe under Kaiser, isn't that right?"

Leo nodded. "As I was saying earlier, the brutal truth is that I got a bodyguard who is really keeping surveillance on me."

"You sound pretty shaken. Please don't encourage me to meet up with General Kaiser, any time soon."

The waiter returned with the bill. Leo paid and tipped her before standing up. His driver was waiting in the car park, and he was fortunate to have Howard Giles as his bodyguard too: A former Special Forces soldier.

Peter held him back by his arm. He sighed. "Boy, there's something that I must tell you which may shock you a little. I know the buzzword – Zetta."

There on, Leo looked on at who he really could be. All he saw was a white male with short ginger hair, and freckles on his cheek. He gasped. "What did you say? How do you know about it?"

"You're supposed to know what it is. Frankly, I was told to tell you, in person, by your Zetta friends. Just what the fuck is it?"

"Just who the hell are you really?"

"God I could kill Mario—"

"God, it really was you!" Leo said, astonished. "You put me up to being abducted, didn't you?"

"No I did not! All I said is that you were not directly involved with the revolution. Yet, my superiors were finding it hard to believe."

"You allow those people to drug me and my wife. You knew that I was going home early and you were spying on me."

Peter signalled for him to occupy his empty seat but loath he was. "I'm just like you," Peter insisted, "because you love the adventures of space as I love making money. I've only been a sleeper cell agent over the last six months. You really do have a neutral stance on politics, and it's the only reason why we're eating together."

Leo was staring at a crook. He burst out laughing. "How could you do this to me?" he asked, controlling his composure, "I'm your boss for crying out loud."

"I wasn't running the gauntlet but you do remember Mario, isn't it? He was calling the shots and he could have got you killed but he didn't. It's because he believes in you," Peter apparently said, feeling uncomfortable also. "The motives," he resumed, "of the RRF is the soundest and the greatest for this country. However, I had some doubt in that buzzword, but you understood it instantly. So what the hell is it?"

Leo recognised his position: He was his employer. Much more, his answers to making him understand. He sighed. "It's just an ideology which Wallace obviously shares."

"I was under orders to inform you of Zetta, and to give you this," he handed to him, mobile-phone. "Wallace will be making his call any time soon. So please don't get pre-occupied. Also, only answer that phone in a private place, not at your home.

"God, I'm really sorry if you think that I'm responsible for your abduction. Look at this in another way, you obviously an interest to Wallace, and he does require your services. I know it's not my place in asking but I don't suppose you could tell me a bit more about Zetta?" Leo replied, "Zetta is a buzzword you should never, never, never try to utter beyond these walls. Listen, I know that it may be difficult for you, yet, that buzzword is something you should keep quiet at all times. No matter the outcome."

"So you'll be helping us?" Peter asked, still perplexed.

"I'm helping a friend in need," Leo replied and stood up. He thought to himself that his life must be becoming less complicating. "Peter," he went on, "I know that you're probably the best employee at the executive level. So despite your beliefs, I'll still require you to be the Operating Chief here."

Chapter 41

—Grand opening—

STILL IN ORLANDO, it was the morning of mid-September. Leo was trying his best, but in a mess to sort out his silk tie in his bathroom. It was an important day to officially open a library. It had been delayed since he was abducted, however, the librarians had a garden vigil for his safe release; now, of course, he'd be opening it. It was exquisite, the garden, it had many beautiful tropical plants; Moss Roses to Calla Lily from around the equator.

As he straightened his tie, he was running late. Hurriedly, he put on his suit jacket, but dropped his wallet, picked it up before shouting through the bathroom door if his wife was ready. She informed him of her readiness.

However, Carly was looking for something which Christina, Niobe and Donno had bought her on Mother's Day.

"It's in here!" Leo told her as he splashed lotion on his face, "I'll bring it out!"

Howard Giles would be taking him, his wife and their daughter, Alicia, to the event. He waited patiently outside, inside of their BMW 325i estate car. It was a gift from General Kaiser and it was specially built: It had bullet-proof windows and could hold out against a small car bomb. Anyway, the family were prepared to move out and their driver opened the car door as he greeted them.

***

At the new library, lots of people were standing outside. Unmistakably, the library itself was already opened to the public, yet, the luscious tropical garden remained closed.

"Mr. Rockford, it's finally great to be seeing you," Peter Pliny said, the Library Director, as they were climbing out of the vehicle. "Also, it's an honour to finally meet your wife and your young little daughter."

"It's nice to see you in person."

The spectators cheered him on. It was hardly difficult to notice that Peter Pliny was very tall. He had short ginger hair with freckles upon his cheeks too. Of course, Leo was the attention as he waved to acknowledge the crowd.

They were all cordial as Peter guided him and his family into the edifice. Leo felt that phone vibrating in his pocket. It could only mean that Wallace Moore wanted to speak to him, but he ignored the silent-mode.

Along the corridor, Peter Pliny couldn't help but inform him of other guests in the library. He mentioned that the Mayor was in the courtyard, and science fiction writers wanted to see him too. Then he went further that a very important person was amongst them.

As Leo heard him, he peeped from the corner of his eye that General Kaiser was walking straight towards him.

"Leo Rockford, it's an honour to see you again!"

Leo looked around the vicinity to see if David Bruce was also lurking around, but he wasn't. The two men were grabbing each other's shoulders as an act of warm affection.

"And I thought you never cared!" Leo said jovially.

"You of all people should know that the RRF has been a serious threat against my safety and of others in Supremacy. It's absolutely amazing that those scums can see the errors of their ways!"

"Have you been planning this for some time now?"

Bill shook his head. "No, just that Harry was telling me that you'll be opening a grand garden and I thought about coming."

Strangely for Leo, he felt distant when he saw his old friend again. Nevertheless, Peter was keeping them amiable as he described the layout. The sight was surprisingly pleasant to the eye too.

Leo said, "It's great that you're here, Bill Kaiser. It's a great surprise to see you."

The General agreed. Altogether, they walked, along a long corridor, which led them into a large courtyard. It was, of course, a garden and it had its own large fish pond. There consisted of a bridge which went across to the other side of the court. Before the bridge stood a small curtain that covered a plaque; a red ribbon that spanned the breath of the bridge and a dug-hole to plant a small palm tree.

Peter continued leading his company to the mouth of the bridge, and in doing so, he seemed nervous – his feelings that the Supreme Commander, and the Mayor were superior.

"General Kaiser, will you please, stand with the Mayor at the other side of this plaque," Peter asked and he obliged. He turned his attention onto Leo. "Please will you," he pleaded, "can you be just here. Thank you."

Leo got himself familiar with his new surroundings. He was standing behind a stand box with a microphone fitted into place. He also saw people ahead of him cheering him on, and through the windows of every floor. Leo felt sanguine and prepared to start his speech:

"People, it's an honour to be with you," Leo began to announce, "this is an unique garden, which will be the beauty of–"

Peter grabbed him by the arm and was frowning too. The Library Director insinuated that he was to use the puller to open the curtain, which was near the stand-box. He also indicated that he also cut the ribbon and plant the tree.

Leo apologised for breaking the *customary way*.

"Ladies and gentlemen," Peter said through the microphone, "I knew he was eager to open this garden but not that eager!"

The crowd were humorous to his quick gab–

"Ladies and gentlemen," Peter continued, "it's an honour and still a great honour of having the three finest men here today. So please give a warm welcome to Leo Rockford, Ted Simpson and General Kaiser."

The atmosphere went ballistic for the three men. There were children shouting at the top of their voices on recognising General Kaiser – not certain if they really thought he was Ming the Merciless – and the adults were showing their appreciation.

"We know that it's been a difficult time," Peter said and was being appreciated, "for Leo to open our garden last July. However, there's no time like the present. Of course, I would like to also thank the Mayor and the Supreme Commander in showing their support for this superb library."

Peter looked onto Leo and signalled that it was his cue to make a speech–

"Americans, please excuse my behaviour," the General begged to differ, "in making an unannounced trip to the new Universal Orlando Library."

Leo felt slightly embarrassed on how he had conducted himself. His wife, amongst the crowd, was pretending that she didn't notice him being pulled back. Her countenance wasn't joyful, nor morose, yet stunned.

"If there was room at the Supreme White House ground, I'd move brick-by-brick this entire library into my backyard. Americans, today we're here because the RRF couldn't break a good man of his spirit to regard our great nation. He's the finest example on what a good American ought to be. We all know that at opening ceremonies, it's usually the most important person that is designated on officially opening things, but Leo is no ordinary guy. He's an American who believes in me, and an American who believes in the continuing growth of the new America. Do bear this in mind, Americans, it means that we're the number one force to reckon with."

The General's address made everybody ecstatic – Leo's wife was still stupefied if he was impertinent.

During the climax, in the applause, Leo thought that it was best to open the curtain rails by using the puller, he revealed a bronze plaque with its inscription:

Universal Orlando Library
Space Garden
Opened by

Leo Rockford on the 19th September

Rockford proceeded to cut the ribbon and to plant the small palm tree. Of course, the spectators continued applauding his actions; for he had officially opened the library.

Peter escorted the three men, into the building, to an astronomy book-section. There were light refreshments, and in the background, a stereo was playing Jazz music.

The General was in the mood to talk to Leo alone. He led him to the farthest corner, away from the refreshments, away from the other guests, away from Leo's family and away from Peter. Leo was holding a plastic plate which was full of sandwiches in one hand, and orange squash in another.

"It's nice to see you again, Leo. I was horrified that the RRF weren't selecting supreme servants. It is the foulest act yet to date."

"They were certain that I played a significant role in Washington."

The General laughed. "I never thought of you as a master of disguise," Kaiser said, "but how did you really do it? I mean, David reported that you told them that you went to Mars because of your love in astronomy, and nothing else, isn't that right?"

"It's true. That's exactly what I've been telling him."

"I never would have believed it! So you didn't tell them that you weren't too keen to go on a spatial adventure, but I persuaded you. I told this to David. Yet he seemed tacit. He kept on thinking that you'd already rediscovered yourself in your ordeal. Do you know what I'm trying to say? He thinks that you might have become a terrorist!" He said laughing and nudged him hard on his side.

"I think David saw my release having a slim chance of occurring. However, I proved him wrong."

"David is considered *the finest men in Washington*. I mean, I do hope he is wrong – I don't know why I put up with him though – still, what I cannot understand is his belief that you've grown an interest in American politics, like you said, you love astronomy a lot more."

"Kind words for an egg head, kind words."

They both laughed loudly, as if arrogant that the library was a place to keep quiet.

"I'll be leaving here to return to Washington within the next ten - twenty minutes. Yet before I go, I wanted to point out about the NASA reunion at the Kennedy Space Centre next month. I hope to see you there as I'll be attending. And between you and me, I think another mission to Mars will be exceptional."

"That will be great news."

"Just one more thing, I'll be selecting a new crew on this mission with the exception of you as the Commander. David Bruce was telling me that you were thinking of moving back to the UK due to safety reasons, is that true?"

"What! I would but—" Leo said hesitantly.

"I know that the RRF really has an interest in you. You see, their problem is that you're a dear friend of mine, and one with a well-balanced belief. When I say well-balanced, I mean that you haven't made an affiliation for Supremacy, nor the old Federal system. Don't you see, Leo? David and Wallace don't really know what to do with you – what am I talking about – if you feel less safe, more security can be arranged. However, it'll be considered that you are siding with us."

It was too good to be true. Leo didn't doubt him, and he sighed. "Bill," he said, "you're right. My family have been thinking about returning to the UK since it's scary here. I'll only say at present that I'll need to pass your proposition onto my wife."

"This is truly a remarkable find," the General said as he was looking around the room, "I never thought that you could complete these bookcases about space, the stars and its planets. I bet you'll be spending a lot of time in here, isn't it?

"We for one, I want to see more of you in Washington by taking a seat within the Supreme Council. Anyway, I got to get going."

The General moved onto other matters, and Leo returned to his wife. After spending twenty minutes in the refreshment area, Kaiser left the library.

Leo thought on how persistent Kaiser wanted to be. It seemed apparent of soaring Kaiser's popularity, and would it undermine Wallace Moore, yeah? Anyhow, Leo was still in the library, and he took a moment to explain his experience as an astronaut to the people around him.

***

Later on in the afternoon, Leo was in the car and was thinking fondly of the library. As such, Leo had the urge to speak to his wife.

"The General is hoping to arrange another Mars mission."

"Leo," she replied, abhorred too, "I thought we were returning back to Britain after the NASA Reunion?"

"I know that we've original plans, but the General will love to see me back up in space. As you know, it was he that has been supplying us with our driver. Besides, he's even thinking of arranging a political seat on the Supreme Council. We'll be having a bigger house, better security and a much more promising future for our children."

"You'd been kidnapped," Carly retorted, "because they thought that you had a say in the Supreme Council. Now you're going to assure them that it's the case!"

"Carly, I promised the General that I'll be discussing this with you."

"Goodness, Leo. You could've refused his offer, and that would have been good enough for me!"

"Just remember this, we got three options: Option A is to return to London, and hope that my business will boom; Option B is to continue my work in Orlando. Option C is to go to Mars which will land us in Washington."

Their driver was hearing all of the commotion before parking on the Rockford's drive.

Leo praised Howard as his family climbed out of the car. Carly was holding her daughter, pondering quietly, on starting anew in Washington.

"Look, just keep an open mind," Leo said as he was following her into their home. "Yes, I do want to go to London. But I don't want the RRF to think that their actions can undermine us. It's not why I married you."

His wife won't say another word and she moved into the lounge to watch television with her daughter. Leo, on the other hand, moved quietly upstairs to the bathroom. He reached inside his trouser pocket for that phone, and it had a text message:

We need 2 talk - Zetta

Leo had a recollection. He knew that tampering with Martin's drink got his spiked. He now might be able to tête-à-tête with Wallace – but he was a terror. He thought on returning to Britain, and leave him behind. *Danger,* he thought to himself, *Wallace will – somehow – be chasing me for his troubles.* It dawned upon him that to detest Martin had only made him a good friend. Sooner or later, Leo would see what was to become of his relationship with Wallace Moore, wasn't it? Leo loathed to make a response for how secure was it? After all, Harry Trump had already informed him that the RRF was within striking distance. Strangely enough, Leo thought of his business associate, Peter Alsopp. His heart went soft and he began to text him back:

How R U going 2 meet me?

Just as he sent it, he almost got a very quick response:

Business Convention in Canada - Peter has details :)

Chapter 42
—The plot—

*P*ETER ALSOPP WAS more than happy in his preparations: The rendezvous of Leo and Wallace – he was making the arrangements before being given the go-ahead. At the business fair, it was enormous; the building that is, nearly all the floors had a high ceiling, very spacious, and its entrance was enough for anyone to gasp that Olympian gods did reside there, of course, floor spaces were being booked for entrepreneurs.

Wallace was the least of Leo's concerns. The fair had been lasting for three days and rumours were rife that Leo Rockford was signing the Canadian hockey team – which wasn't the case at all. He found it exciting when potential clients were seeking, on his expertise, to improve their own image. His engagement was highly-regarded: Eager, Inspired, and Empathetic.

"He's waiting for you at the left-wing cafeteria," Peter said on the final day.

"Why does he pick the most conspicuous places here? That's implying that he can just walk up at this stall to publicly justify the need for arms. That's rather stupid!"

He headed straight towards that location. However, along the way, he was greeted by fans and was signing autographs – that took up some time. Once he arrived, he ordered a fresh cup of coffee, sat alone at a table to face everybody coming and going. So far, it was an easy affair to order his coffee and to select a table of his choosing. But where was Wallace Moore? Leo continued to look around and there was no sign of him. He stayed put and hoped that nobody else wished to sit next to him.

Five minutes later, a man stood in front of him. "Zetta" he said, "is the best business opportunity."

Leo recognised the gentleman: Wallace Moore. He had his grey hair tied back, and bread trimmed. He was dressed in a business suit to fit the occasion, and it appeared that he was wearing eye make-up to enlarge them, along with, a fake tan.

"I'm sure," Leo responded, "it could rake in trillions of dollars."

Both he and Wallace were now facing the comings and goings.

"I had to see you for I've a lot of questions to ask—"

"The Supreme Council has no knowledge of the spatial water. There are only three people on Earth who are aware of its potential. That's you, myself and Martin MacCormick."

"Why do I get the impression that you didn't start on a good note with Martin, isn't it? So you made him drink that stuff, but how did you became aware of its potential?"

"I accidentally slipped Martin the spatial water, and he returned the favour."

"So you like slipping the potent stuff into people's drinks just because they happen to have a bit of friction with you, yeah? Then you expect us to give you a pardon, isn't it? So from what I can gather, I bet that you're in the *good books* with General Kaiser. Am I right to assume that you haven't made him your little number?"

"Right you are. So may I ask why you wanted to meet up with me?"

"It's that knowledge of the alien god. I must admit that Zetta is quite an amazing deity. Yet, I still have a commitment to fulfil; I want to bring down General Kaiser."

Leo just looked at him while he was drumming with his fingers. He sighed. "After you got some insight about Mars," Leo said, "haven't you noticed that there's a more advanced society out there, but you prefer to divulge into something primitive, right?"

"If you got a better idea on how to use my time, let's hear it!" Wallace replied and stopped drumming too.

Leo laughed. "How about this," he said, "you should join us on a Mars expedition."

"You're not taking this matter seriously!" Wallace replied. "I still want to bring down Kaiser, and I think you can have an important role – I believe you're a very discreet person – I'm going to tell you that General Kaiser will be dead real quick."

Leo laughed again. "You're fine about that?" he asked. "So," he continued, "why are you're telling me that? You expect that I just lie back, and watch it all unfold in the newspapers, right?"

"I'm telling you because I want you to become part of a better cause. It's us that is Zetta. It's apparent that your friend, Martin MacCormick, gave you a pardon.

"Am I wrong to think, that you ought to do something similar to General Kaiser? Obviously, you don't have a special bond with him. Leo, you're quite eccentric when it comes to taking sides, because that is a wolf, and you're a merely a sheep – I fully understand where you are coming from."

"I've a wife, a child and three young adults. I've a happy family and I'm thinking of expanding my business into Canada. So how does my career path fit into your master plan?"

"Everything it seems. We've the advantage and it'll mean the end of tyranny. I want to tell you more but I don't trust you, really."

"Look, I don't want any blood on my hands!" Leo said and got up to leave.

A person from a nearby table was looking at Leo. He seemed to register what he thought he heard. Both Leo and Wallace returned their glances at him. The eavesdropper looked away.

"I don't believe that your bombs," Leo whispered and took his seat again, "will be a credit to my involvement. I've a business to run, and quite frankly, I'll require that you end further contacts with me.

"Make no mistake, I'm willing to make sacrifices to see that you honour my request. Just because Peter Alsopp is one of my best executives, it doesn't give you the right to start killing people for me. Also, I'll consider this meeting as an one-off. If you ever attempt to approach me, or my family again, I'll report Peter Alsopp to the USTF."

"You're not into politics. You're an astronomer who is taking advantage of Kaiser. I haven't come here to argue with you. I came here to make you aware that you're backing the wrong horse. That horse in Washington is a corrupt bastard that has ruined many people's lives for getting at the truth. Peter has a high regard for you. God, if you're prepared to stand to your threats—"

"So Peter's ideas were big bucks," Leo interrupted him, "but you think that you can obtain my forgiveness? No! You, he and the RRF know perfectly well that you were trying to ruin my wonderful career. You may think that I'm a little eccentric, but what of Peter? He thinks it's all weird that you want to see me."

"So I was dirty at abducting you but you do play dirty too. If you wanted to get Kaiser involved in your alien conspiracy, why haven't you done it already?"

"I don't want to see you again," Leo stood up, "and I respect that my position is final."

"I respect Zetta!" Wallace shouted – it got the attention of the eavesdropper again and he left. "Anyway," Wallace went on calmly, "you haven't convinced me why I should let go of the RRF."

"Doesn't Martin the astronaut," Leo excused, "have a say in any of this?"

"You want Martin to have a voice? Then why haven't you brought him here?"

"As you know," Leo said happily, "Martin and I had taken a sip of the alien water, which has given us Zetta. But you must remember one thing that the Nergalas take a great pride in their secrecy. I fear to expose their—"

"Why are you so paranoid? Don't you believe that you could change this world by bringing it out to the open?"

"I've degraded and tormented the Nergalas by drinking it! We'll face persecution if the truth becomes fully known."

Wallace laughed. "I find it funny that you're more afraid of them than me! It's OK. I'll not tell a soul as it would jeopardize my position on running the RRF. On a serious note, I'm grateful that you wanted to see me, yet, why haven't you seen Bill Kaiser about it?"

"As I was just about to tell you, the Supreme Commander is very difficult to meet with."

"Basically, you're waiting for the right moment where I cannot kill him," Wallace said sarcastically, "otherwise, it's his own fault if he doesn't have the time to see you in person. Anyway, I'd thank you for your complimentary drink – you're a son of a bitch."

There was silence around that table.

"Are you ever going to see Martin again?" Wallace wondered.

"Yes, there will be a reunion. It's set in the Kennedy Space Centre, and it'll happen in a fortnight. I only hope to gain his acquaintance."

"I bet your pal, General Kaiser, will be making an appearance, isn't it?"

"I don't have time to talk of the political implications with you. I'm here only to expand my business in Canada, and to give you any guidance concerning Zetta," Leo said.

"That's what you're saying but the truth of the matter is this: We're on the same boat. Yes, I do want to dispose him but I must find the right circumstances for that to happen. Anyway, if you won't be cooperative, I'll inform NASA of a footage, which may suspect that it was you who took the water. You see, Leo, I've a good eye to see that the water came from that water bottle. If word ever gets out that you were trying to be discreet–"

"What makes you think," Leo interrupted, "that you can make idle threats? You're underestimating Kaiser!"

"Maybe, but I may allege that it was you that had flushed it out into space, and you hadn't come clean about it. I've good contacts that will put you on the radar for being too suspicious."

"I've been under suspicion already," Leo said. "If you've *good contacts* in NASA," Leo mentioned fondly, "explain those agents in holiday shirts, will you?"

"Basically, I'm right," Wallace conjured, "I could've gone mad by exposing you as a sleeper cell–"

Leo smiled. "So you're willing," he went on regardless, "to ruin Peter Alsopp, and what was his crime?"

"Didn't I say *mad*? I could expose you as our sleeper cell that wishes to exploit the Supreme Council. You've stolen the water and it was in that flask."

"Look, you know that I'm planning to expand my business into Europe, and to re-start my life in London within the next fortnight or so–"

"That's why Peter was ordered to declare Zetta. I want you to remain in America until the dust settles. Your presence here will wake the American people on the assassination of Frederick Bungles."

"Why are you still insinuating that I should make a confession?"

"You're something. It wasn't wrong when Kaiser offered tax breaks for the Flash Gordon movies, isn't it? I mean if you cannot see that coming, then you should believe that the Orion is a warplane."

"I don't want any part in your decision-making," Leo continued, "so if you want to expose me over a flask, that's good riddance."

"You're surely stubborn. A nightmare of an ass-hole," Wallace said, virulently. "I just don't understand why you did that thing in that apartment. I can only imagine that very soon, that you'll be giving David Bruce your shock treatment.

"You haven't any appreciation for Zetta. The worst thing about you is that you throw his ideas around like confetti. You don't even care about America. It's only your selfish and curious desire to better yourself. Like I said before, you're living on borrowed time."

"What's going on?" Peter asked, of course, he was making an appearance, yet no one answered him. "I don't suppose," he carried on saying, "the two of you have sorted out your differences."

Leo laughed. "Look, I'm a businessman," he reacted, "and I'll remain a businessman – and even an astronomer – to the bitter end. I'm not one to become an ideologist."

"Look at the pair of you. You can get along, for the both of you treat that buzzword heavenly. So let me guess, Wallace is coming on hard, but Leo doesn't share his views."

"So what are you expecting of me?" Wallace asked. "Why not have me as the middle man? Otherwise all bets are off. Think about it, I'll have to resign from the Rockford Group, and that will mean that Wallace had compromised his best opportunity by far."

"You expect far too much," Leo disagreed, "I'll not walk along the corridors of power by giving Kaiser a sending off."

"We don't want you to do anything," Wallace said calmly, "all we want is justice in the proper courts."

"You were suggesting some kind of street justice, and I want no part in that!" Leo said vehemently.

"It's only an option. I'm not certain if it's credible," Wallace said.

"Not credible because I want no part in it. Besides, I think it would be best that I return back to Britain within the next three weeks."

"That's after the reunion at the Kennedy Space Centre?" Peter asked.

"Very much so, Peter. I do not wish to get my hands any dirtier."

"I cannot understand," Peter continued, "how you're planning to be evasive, if you're admitting that your hands are already dirty, wasn't you?"

"He's right!" Wallace said, "explain why your hands weren't clean?"

As logic seemed to be dictating his actions, Leo had a prescience of becoming a bomber. He wasn't jovial and remained silent.

Wallace laughed. "I should've got Peter here earlier!" he said, "for he's right about you."

"It's great that I've reconciled your differences," Peter said. "I believe," he carried on saying, "that we may have a golden opportunity to take advantage of Bill Kaiser. Anyway, I'll be shooting back."

"He's right," Wallace said quickly, "I hope you don't mind us targeting Kaiser."

"Peter made a bold move," Leo said, of course, he was adamant to circumvent, "but I don't want any part in it."

"Like it or lump it. Yet you ought to imagine that David Bruce will be gathering his intelligence. Basically, what is to stop him knowing of our little meeting? He'll crucify you."

"Making threats doesn't change the fact that I participated in your militia."

"That's fine. You'll not be playing any direct roles in our operations. Therefore, I just hope that you'll see to some packages being placed in the Kennedy Space Centre."

"You want me to smuggle a bomb, isn't it?"

"It'll not cause a large radius of destruction. It'll be used only in line of fire."

"There is another way."

"That if you can make him step down, but you don't realize how ruthless the General really has been. He has truly given riddance to one of our best rejuvenators. Don't you get it? We had to disband peaceful measures because of his deadly threats. It's the only reason why we went to arms. That man is only using you."

"Listen," Leo said and gestured a hand, "all I desire is a peaceful life in England. I do not want to associate with you any further." He looked at a picture of a space shuttle hanging on a wall. "Only if I'm convinced," Leo resumed, "that the General is really ruthlessness, then, and only then, you'll have my full support."

"Peter was right about you! You really do understand the seriousness of our situation."

Chapter 43
—The spy—

SANJAY PATIO HAD had Kaiser constantly on his mind; especially after the death of Frederick Bungles. It seemed unlikely that it was an accident, because outspoken dissidents were more than likely imprisoned, if not killed. If he was driving alone to work, or returning home, he would stop halfway before continuing against his fear that somebody was tailing him. However, residing in Canada kept him calm.

He was now working for Christian McDowell — one of Wallace's lieutenants — in the national intelligence service as his assistant. It was strange, for Sanjay, that Canada was a world leader in intelligence and counter-intelligence. There was a lot of confidence in the MI6, CIA and the KGB being the best of the best, and anybody else's envy. But it wasn't for Canada. The rise of fascism, the Cold War and Colonel Gadaffi's Jihad call, had seen their agents in the thick of it, which led to the Normandy landing, the probability of a Soviet push, also being involved against a Jihad outfit. Canada wasn't generally considered a pace-maker on espionage, but that's its secret.

Sanjay was Ubi Mahal; his falsehood of claiming to go, head-on, of removing security threats. His role wasn't as macho as James Bond — a good old action hero. He was a pencil-pusher. All he only did was file reports from a special police branch, and from the public on suspicious activities. It was tedious, boring and perhaps the worst job given to boast morale. Of course, Sanjay was living a lie, and had a girlfriend who was an Indo-Canadian. Both he and she shared a two-bedroom apartment, which faced the Ontario Lake. The view, from their front window, always welcomed the rising sun, and the scenery of the bright rays reflecting the crystal blue water was a wonderful sight. His girlfriend was Amala

Kaif, exceedingly fit and was very spiritual. She was a type of girl Sanjay wished to wake up to, and held the belief that the world was only waiting for him. She had a slender build and her breasts are her greatest assets. The woman enjoyed wearing upper-tight clothing and loose-fitted bottoms. Sanjay loved her dearly and Wallace Moore was aware of it. More still, he wanted to leave the RRF. Nevertheless, Wallace kept him on a straight and narrow path. One time after a top-level meeting, Wallace was completing his briefing when Sanjay approached him—

"Wallace, I really need to get something off my chest."

Wallace nodded.

"As you know," Sanjay said, "my life is too complicating since being with Amala."

"So you prefer to turn your back on Frederick Bungles? He did so much for our country," Wallace said.

"This is getting far too complicating—"

"It'll continue to get far too complicating with that kind of attitude! As you know, we're going to capture Leo Rockford. So I expect you to come with me, Mario and a few others, got it?"

Sanjay obliged to his request.

Nowadays, Sanjay was on holiday with his girlfriend in California, and it was their third year together. He was going to ask her for marriage. Before doing so, he took an early jog, alone, in Los Angeles along the South Beach, and he got to see the rising sun along the inland sky-line. He was wearing his sunglasses, a black Adidas tracksuit and a headband. He was trying to keep himself fit, but found it heavy going as the beach drained him – every time his trailing foot sank into the sand. He had already burnt a lot of energy, and the heat wave was now starting to wear him down. Sanjay found a convenience store to buy a cold drink. Afterwards, he saw three benches of different colours. He chose to recuperate on the orange one. So while he sat, he reflected back on the time when he was at university to being graduated...

His upbringing had been vibrant. His parents were both medical doctors running a private surgery in Miami. They also came from the Caribbean islands of Trinidad & Tobago.

He went to Harvard University to study Pharmacy. On his first year, he had a room-mate named David Jones at the university campus. Oddly enough, David had a strong interest to tackle drug traffickers from Latin America, and he was passionate, ambitious and well-organised to earn his Criminology degree. He had shared an unfortunate incident, after the police were knocking on his mother's door, as a child—

A police officer asked if she was Mrs Jones? But she was concerned that her husband might be in trouble. The officer responded that he wasn't yet now insisted to come inside and she obliged. The police in the house continued asking for all of them to take a seat and David's mother ushered them into the lounge. The comfortable seats brought no warmth in the news that her husband was killed in a cross fire between rival gangs outside a convenience store. They promised her justice.

The murderers were never brought to justice, and David lost a dad who would always take him to the Red Skins American football games. His bereavement couldn't go unnoticed on Saturday afternoons – he was gone. Despite the enormous heartache at an early age, his heart quickly hardened with the desire for state justice. He told his mom that he was going to enforce law and order in Washington, and his mother believed that her son would grow up to patrol the streets. Yet, her son perceived a greater ambition of fighting crime. As an undergraduate, he longed to join the Drug Enforcement Agency.

The two undergraduates had formed a special bond together. They would talk openly about recreational and medical drugs. The former was the most talked of. Soon enough, they were consuming hashish, it had a strange scent, as if, an ancient use to disguise body odour. Of course, considered illegal – not the smell – the product itself. It instantly dominated the air in their bedsit, and *they felt an insecurity of the authorities: The wardens and police. They always kept the door locked as a precaution, yet, nobody disturbed them. To inhale the potent drug, they believed it gave them new freedom. After which, they took on their new feelings to push for world peace and equality, and considered that hashish didn't cause violence, unlike alcohol. Much later, in David's studies on drug barons, his views differed that they were killing anybody in their path i.e.) police and the local populace near the cultivations.*

Nevertheless, their love for narcotics drew them closer to a new circle of friends at university. Immediately, they took on an interest into the effectiveness of Marxism. Of course, its ideology that equality was righteous for humanity. They also dabbled, a little, on capitalism too. For the two students, the communist model worked for billions of people from Eastern Europe through to the ends of Asia. Still, it suffered self-denial on the economic growth in the United States. Of course, economic growth, in America, brought about the success in the space race, bigger cars and better financial markets. Mikhail Gorbachev collapsed socialism, in his own bid, that capitalism maybe beautiful. So the West won their ideology against the East, yet, there was a new student thinking that Marxism might still work. Such curiosity led the room-mates to join a discussion-group. They believed that they were able to make America a fairer place. It was a radical group that had a firebrand that the upper-class only wished substantial control over others. Sanjay and David could easily recall their attendance at a debate between two hard-hitters: A communist and a capitalist supporter. It was in the student assembly hall, and the building was ideal for graduation-day due to its sheer size. The stage had enough space for a hundred people to stand upon. There were many ground and balcony seats, which were richly put together, and polished oak cross-beams along the ceiling. Incidentally, a small audience were taking turns to question the two speakers. However, their questions were getting drowned as the two, Carl and Richard, were arguing amongst themselves.

"America today is not about lining the pockets for the average worker, but to turning out their pockets! You expect me to believe that if we just turn off our televisions, radios and other propagandas, that we as the people won't see through your lies! That success that you are really speaking of, is just you jangling your coins, for what a lucky boy you are!" Carl said loudly.

Richard didn't nod. "You've no idea what you're talking about," he said. "The idea of capitalism was a social science; it identified our natural abilities. For argument sake, you're out of line by exploiting the sweetness of an orange to a grapefruit. Plus, we do trade with foreigners with our common denominator – money. You apparently speak that capitalism belongs in a pig-style, but do you not see it rejuvenates our knowledge, science and our economy? Is the recognition of capitalism not to acknowledge the Industrial Revolution? How about man striving for new and clean energies for our expanding population? What you represent offers nothing but a flat line."

"You speak of a social science that only identifies gold. Your social science fails to identify the disadvantages of it!" Carl replied.

"You've failed to answer my question in its entirety!" Richard said harshly.

"Carl!" the moderator intervened loudly, "you haven't been answering his questions correctly. I've been assessing the both of you: It's a complete shamble! Therefore, I expect you, Richard, to answer Carl's earlier question. Will you identify that capitalism is responsible for turning out the pockets of the poor?"

"Not at the least," Richard answered confidently, "in fact, that's called robbery, and the system doesn't force the working-class to turn-out their pockets. Carl also mentioned that I was jangling coins, didn't he? He's absolutely wrong to make accusations on a social science that isn't his expertise. I therefore expect a formal apology from that pea brain."

"I speak from experience! He's either blind or dumb, if not both! How can he not recognise a fat cat on our streets to a starving one? You do not need an expertise

to identify the faults of capitalism, because it worked for those that want to be richer than the rest!"

His opponent laughed. "So looking back over centuries ago, what if some rich kid wasn't bothered to identify capitalism? Are you just going to be some kind of sperm whale waiting to find an existence in mankind?"

"If it wasn't for the development of the welfare benefit system," Carl said, he also knocked him out too, "our iron fist speaks for a classless society!"

After graduation, Sanjay joined a pharmacy company in Jacksonville, whilst David took on his training course in the DEA, and their times together seemed to be their last. Sanjay lost a friend, but gained a new one. It was Carl Simmons: The one that supported a classless society in a violent manner. They enjoyed each other's company to discuss the past, present and future of the United States.

Much later in his life, Sanjay was driving home from work when his mother called him by phone.

"My dear, I don't mean to surprise you. It's about your old friend from university. He called here wanting to speak to you," she said and was exceedingly jolly too.

"Did he say who it was?"

"Oh, he's such a nice and well-spoken boy. He told me that he had finished his course regarding drug enforcement. He even told me that he was running his own task force."

"Surely he isn't with you now, is he? I mean, you've forwarded my telephone number to him, haven't you?"

"Sanjay, what kind of mother do you think I am? Of course I've forwarded the details to him. Anyway, you must come down here for Sunday dinner."

"Sure Mum, I come round this Sunday, and thanks."

Later that evening, Sanjay was relaxing in his condominium. He was watching the Red Skins play a tense game against the Cowboys. The game appeared to be one sided for the Redskins in the opening, but their opponents were coming close to steal a win. Sanjay was sucked into the action and his door-bell rang. He suspected that his mother had forwarded his home address to David Jones, and was slightly frustrated. He *didn't want to budge, and the door was ringing again. The referee called for time-out. He was determined to have enough time to answer that door and drag him in.*

"I just had to come here to see you, Sanjay!"

"I haven't seen you for years and there's a terrific game on! Do come in quickly. Surely you haven't come all this way to talk about drugs, yeah."

"No," David replied, yet, he got a sensation of seeing his home team looking victorious. "Is that," he asked, "the Redskins winning?"

"Just about winning but those Cowboys are putting up a hell of a fight! Now David, I haven't seen nor heard from you for years."

"Sorry buddy, it has been a bitch doing some undercover work. I just wanted to come here to clear my head."

"Don't you have psychologists for that?"

"I don't think it's related to stress."

"It must be important if you aren't watching it," Sanjay said and gave him a can of beer. He asked sarcastically, "What have you found? Something much more appealing than that social class system?"

"It's my Dad," David replied sternly.

"I don't understand what you're saying? I thought you said that your father was shot by a stray bullet, isn't that right?"

"Yes, that's true, but it's my mum as well. She has just found out that my father was having an affair with some high-class mistress, and she lived near that crime scene. His late night shopping was his excuse."

"So what makes you think what you're saying is true?" Sanjay asked.

"It's because my mother, just recently, has been doing a little investigation on some unusually high-transactions from his business bank account. She got the bank, the police and then eventually a private detective to look into the matter and guess what? It turned out that he was paying substantial amount of money to a high-class brothel that evening. That creep was sneaking around to fetch grocery. He was cheating my mother!"

"You've pursued the DEA to honour the memory of your–"

"That," interjected David, "is exactly that!" He said, "I was doing this career thing for my mom. I had to see that transaction myself to believe my own mother. He was killing us."

"So are you're going to chuck away the last six years, of your life, because of your father?"

"I won't quickly excel in the DEA, that my law-abiding father had cheated my mother, and was shot by a thug. Nevertheless, I really do want to work in the federal government."

"So your dad's a creep but how are you keeping anyway?"

"Fine I guess. I took annual leave to comfort my mother. I cannot justify staying in the DEA. Sanjay, what have you been up to?"

"I work for a pharmacy company. It's really boring but pays well. You should continue working for the DEA, isn't it?"

"Well, I don't have the drive to better myself. Think about it, you do have a career, which may lead you to run your own lab, right?" he asked.

Sanjay nodded–

"My job," he continued, "holds annual appraisals and what am I to say? That I love working in the DEA to honour my dad, yet, my lovely daddy was a love rat."

"Surely you don't have to tell the whole truth?"

"The truth will catch up with me in the DEA. It'll happen and it won't look pretty in the long haul."

"Your father was a bastard but you shouldn't–"

"If you were thinking," David said abruptly, "I've put in a request for a transfer to NSA."

"Why would you want to work for the NSA?"

"I want to continue working in the federal government, and it beats honouring that filthy man."

"Just don't rush into it. But I'm happy for you."

"So, you're following the steps of your parents. Do you enjoy working in the healthcare sector?"

"Love it."

"I'm happy for you too. Anyhow, since my father was shot by some kind of divine act. I'm going to officially disown him. I'm going to make a recommendation to my mother to officially disown that creep too. The time has come that we change that marital name to her maiden one. I'll no longer see myself as David Jones but as David Bruce."

"I'll second that motion," Sanjay said and pointed at the television. *"Oh my, the Red Skins have won!"*

Sanjay was sitting on the bench drinking his cold drink. He knew that Kaiser was hunting him down, but what were the odds of being tracked down on the beach? There was hardly anybody around him. He was still panting little, and decided to look back on the Supreme Revolution...

Carl Simmons, was the founder of a magazine which resisted Kaiser. He got Sanjay the role as the Assistant Editor of Red Resistance Union. Carl Simmons only took him on because he knew David Bruce, and it was his belief that he would cripple Kaiser as a whistle-blower.

The magazine gained a lot of attention when Frederick Bungles joined the fold. Before all of that, Sanjay was working in his office when word reached him that Frederick was in the building. It was his birthday so thought of his colleagues arranging a surprise – which it was.

"I know you! It's Frederick Bungles!"

"It's nice to meet you," he said, shaking his hand, *"you're inspiring to restore hope at this dark time."*

"I thank you, sir," Sanjay responded, *"and you're here to see Carl Simmons?"*

"Who else do I need to see than Carl Simmons? Where is he?"

"He's on lunch. I don't think that he was expecting you to turn up, and to show your admiration to our worthy cause."

"I came here to show my approval to your work. It's a fine magazine for people of all ages and classes. You've illustrated Kaiser's destruction. Of course, he's a

king without a legal crown! Oh Sanjay! This is my good old friend, Wallace Moore."

"Nice to meet you," Wallace said to him.

"What the f–" Carl said as he returned from his lunch break. "Glad to meet you."

"It's an honour to serve," Frederick acknowledged and was shaking his hand, "to serve for my country which believes in the American way. I've come here to show my gratitude and support. All I want is for you to ask for my help."

"I'm just as patriotic like everybody else here. Not forgetting the readers too."

"I'm serious. I want to help you," Frederick insisted, "and I want you to help me."

"I'm sorry, Mr. Bungles," Sanjay said, "he's a little taken back that a VIP is in his office."

"Of course, I want you to help me; by making me your icon to reinstate democracy. I therefore ask to take full ownership of the Red Resistance Union."

"What!" Carl could hardly believe it. "What makes you think," he went on, "that I'm willing to let this one go?"

"I've been reading all of your articles, and it speaks only for a democratic society. A society where we tolerate equality and freedom. If these are the words that you solemnly believe in, then believe in me as the new Editor and owner."

"Can I refuse?"

"You may but think of the mockery once I leave here: Democracy only works for the selfish. Listen, I'll hand you a buyout of $1.6 million. Take it and work as my Assistant Editor."

"No! You work for my magazine."

"Are you thinking that I'm trying to worm my way back into the White House? It's the house that the Americans had placed their faith in me. Do you understand, that it has been taken away from them?"

"Mr. Bungles, I don't think that you're hearing me right. The magazine is only for the people. I do acknowledge that the Supreme Judges made a vote to throw you out of the White House. If I do recall correctly, you were starting a campaign to be re-elected. Therefore, you're

wrong to come in here, and throw your weight about. You haven't the foggiest idea on what you're asking for."

"Look here son," Wallace reacted to his harsh remark, "I know from your stance that you didn't vote for Frederick Bungles. Quite frankly, I could fathom you demanding a recount from the last elections. But the point is this, we all got screwed. I was a Supreme Judge and I didn't contrive that Kaiser could fuck this country over."

"I won't be selling my business to anybody. However, I'll show support that Frederick Bungles should be reinstated to finish his term. That's my final offer."

"You're a hard man to bargain with," Frederick said and was about to depart.

"Are you really so tight-fisted!" Carl exclaimed, "to recognise that we'll be supporting you?"

"Aren't you rather annoying that this country shouldn't evolve around your magazine, but around the President?"

"Can you not be reinstated without me?" Carl asked sarcastically.

"Listen, why don't we just cool off," Sanjay said, hoping to reconcile, "as we're all on the same team, right?"

"And what do you have in mind?" Wallace wondered, "you do have a fabulous formula to open the public's eye."

"That's simple. We invite Frederick to voice his concerns."

So it was set into motion, Frederick Bungles was going to share his political opinions as a guest writer, and Wallace Moore became a columnist on legal matters.

Sanjay was still recuperating on the bench. The weather was getting a lot warmer, and it was forecasted to be the hottest day for the year. He seemed lazy not continuing with his morning jog. However, he began thinking of David Bruce. He was, after all, the head of the USTF. Sanjay didn't believe that he was in danger, and looked back to consider him when he visited his home...

"Nice to see you again, buddy!" David Bruce said cheerfully.

"We've done this before during an American football game."

"Can I come in?"

"Of course."

Sanjay ushered him into his stylish lounge. From there, David took a seat and gave thanks to Sanjay's hospitality. The host moved into the kitchen and returned with two cans of beer.

"What's digging you?"

"You!" David replied after receiving his drink. "A little bird," he said, "was telling me that you're doing a hate campaign against General Kaiser. And another thing that I'll sidle against the General."

"I might have said that—"

"Have you lost your mind? Or are you getting dopey on dope? We follow the rules of the constitution, and since there's no technicality against the transition, we recognize that General Kaiser is a legal subject."

"You're becoming a lot more politically driven. Wha—"

"And you joined the Red Resistance Union," David said quickly. "I thought you left the student days behind, but you brought it with you."

"I didn't bring the student days with me. I met up with Carl Simmons one evening," Sanjay said.

"So you told him that I'll be an insider for the Red Resistance Union, isn't it? An insider! Are you mad? That's called being a threat to national security! Did you know that your magazine – which speaks for potty flower power – is now on our grid?"

"You're taking this far too seriously."

"I shouldn't even be here," David implied, "discussing sensitive matters. However, after I heard it was you, I just had to see you for myself."

"I only said that we were friends, and that we used to be political un-deciders. Anyway, you should meet up with him because he'll love to meet you."

"Why aren't you listening?" David asked and shook his head. He now asked, "Why are you in that political cult? Why are you being mad? I mean, can you understand

that you are now being monitored by NSA? I'll be monitored if you spill the beans, that I came here to warn you. As a friend, I want you to stop spreading rumours that I, David Bruce, will become an insider against Kaiser. Otherwise, I'll come back here with an arrest warrant."

"OK, I get it. I shouldn't mention about you at all. Otherwise, the NSA will be seeing you as a threat!" Sanjay said sarcastically.

"Well, you're putting my career at stake with those wild allegations, and all I want is for you to stop doing that."

"Stop doing that? How can we give up doing something which is right?"

"Sanjay, things always change. Like the time when the British Empire ruled America, and communism in Asia. You'll just have to adjust, man."

"Adjust to a tyrant that—"

"Adjust for a better society!"

"I know what you're imposing, that the economy is now in better shape."

"That's right. Look at the economy as it works for the people, and our constitution really does look out for the 'little guy'. You just have to accept the hard facts of life that tyranny actually works," David said smiling.

"I bet you got Carl Simmons under surveillance, isn't it right?"

"I couldn't tell you that he is 'under surveillance', for that will mean that I'm breaking the Secrets Act. Look, that publication that you're doing is really trying to slide this country backwards. Sanjay, why don't you just leave them be and restart your career in pharmacy?"

"Why don't you try your persuasive skills on Carl?"

"Perhaps if Carl realized that he was in the wrong, he might give me that sucker punch."

"He's a great—"

"So is General Kaiser!"

"Look, I'm still going to work for the RRU. So I think you should better leave."

"You can be rather harsh when you want too," David said sincerely. "Besides, did Carl give you that Assistant Editor position because of me?"

"Look—"

"Then how did the little bird inform me that I might become an insider?"

"What do you want?"

"What I want is for you to stay out of trouble; I want you to work for me."

"Like I said, I believe in Carl Simmons. I'm not willing to jeopardize everything because of your whim."

"You're not hearing me right, if you work for me then I'll work for you. Everybody, including Carl, will be happy."

Sanjay sighed. "In that case," he went on, "we're friends to the last."

"Good to see that we can still remain friends. I suppose I could go home, and not lose any sleep – in fear of you talking trash. I'll be seeing you."

Sanjay had just recuperated from his jogging. He could now set off along the beach and return to the hotel. He wouldn't budge. He stayed to ponder when Kaiser – his men –incarcerated him...

Men clad in dark-suits and an armed team, in black combat wear, stormed into his office.

"This is the NSA! We're taking control of the situation! So please don't panic!"

It abhorred Sanjay what the NSA were doing. He looked around to see if David Bruce was amongst them, but he couldn't spot him anywhere. One of the Agents placed handcuffs on him. The next thing, he was in the back of a van.

"What the hell is going on?" a detained employee asked.

"I do not know but really do want to find out," Sanjay replied before the vehicle was moving off.

Sanjay thought that the vehicle must have been driven for over two hours, until it reached a complete stop. The door suddenly opened and men in sky-blue uniforms dragged the pair out. Sanjay observed his new surroundings as he stood inside a court yard of a newly developed seven-storey building. He and a few dozen

others were escorted inside. Quickly was his frog march
after finding himself alone in a holding cell, and two
officers removed his handcuffs. His freedom was gone
and he cried out against the regime.

Several hours later, officers ordered him to stand up,
and proceeded to place Sanjay's ankles and wrists in a
shackle. After which, he was on the move onto a narrow
white corridor - it was a long walk that seemed to go
on for ever - one of the guards pointed to him to enter
into a room to his right. As he entered, Sanjay noticed
a desk accompanied by a female and male in black suits
facing the door.

"Please take a seat. I'm Agent Gilani and this is Agent
Davies," she said.

Sanjay didn't wish to take up on their offer but hadn't
a choice. The guards forced him to sit and attached his
shackles onto a bolted chair. "What is this?"

"Please let's not make it any difficult than it is," Agent
Davies said.

"We haven't broken any laws!"

"That depends on the activities that you were planning
to mastermind. Do you recall a guy proclaiming that he
knew some dirty secrets regarding General Kaiser?"

"Some guy who was in the air force. He was telling
us that Kaiser was a paedophile. He kept on saying that
Kaiser was a member of a ritual circle that worshiped
Beelzebub. We understood that he had some proof of
his attendance."

"Exactly what proof were you expecting to hear from
a Special Agent? Your magazine was under surveillance,
because of the threat that you were willing to portray.
It turned out that Carl Simmons was very excited at
getting those false allegations out upon the printing
wheel. Other words, he was to stir the American people
into hating Kaiser. It was his desperate act to slander
General Kaiser."

"Yet, we didn't make any attempt to publish an article
on those false claims. All we wanted was to restore
democracy."

"You ought to wise up. Do you deny that Carl Simmons was extremely excited, in seeing it set into motion?" Agent Gilani asked.

"We were all weary at first. But it seemed authentic. He kept telling us that after he left the air force, he was appointed to work in Washington. He knew of the location where they..." Sanjay stopped and became hesitant – an entrapment.

"What were you going to admit, guilt?" Agent Davies asked.

"I want a lawyer."

"This is regarding national security, and I'm afraid that you'll not be allowed a representative. Look, you could be serving a very long time behind bars because of that offence," Agent Davies said. "Why not," he continued, "do the right thing, and tell us everything about Carl Simmons. He wanted to run the article, but couldn't verify it. You were only following orders, and he could have fired you if you didn't comply."

"Just think on it," Agent Gilani joined in, "if you help us then we'll put in a good word to lessen your sentence. You saw that we took thirty suspects in for questioning and all we're asking is for the truth."

"I know nothing but the truth as Carl Simmons is a great man. He is highly regarded by his staff."

The composure of the agents expressed disbelief, that they couldn't crack him. They retired and silence consumed the room. Sanjay was expecting those two agents to continue their pointless questions. He hadn't done anything wrong. He thought that the undercover agent could have easily been anyone - a fantasist, perhaps. As he was waiting, he observed that the room was small, and the ceiling above had a bright light bulb that was blinding him. He saw that the walls weren't properly finished as freeze blocks were visible. Also, he noted the thick metal door was the only way to enter or exit. The door opened and an officer came in with a plate of plain sandwiches. He placed it in front of him—

"Take this as you may get a little hungry later."

The detainee reached out to eat his cheese and onion sandwiches in his shackles. As he ate, another man entered into the room and sat opposite him.

"Sanjay, I told you that the Red Resistance Union was going down, and now look at you."

"David, what are you doing?"

"I'm trying to save your ass," David said warmheartedly.

"What do you want from me? I told you that I'll be considering your proposition. I don't believe that you would stab me in the back, will you?"

"I'm moving up in the world. Adjutant-General Trump has just given me his authority to head this task force. Its primary goal was to monitor your magazine, and I gave the order to start making arrests. I believe that we've a very strong case against Carl Simmons, because he's desperate to reinstate Frederick Bungles. You do remember that little bird telling me that I'll be a whistle-blower, don't you?"

"Are you implying that Carl Simmons will be sentenced?"

"It could have been the death sentence. Listen, he'll face a preliminary hearing tomorrow. He'll be charged with conspiring against General Kaiser."

"So what is going to happen to me?"

"Unfortunately, I must follow protocols. You'll remain in here until those two agents believe that you'll do the right thing. You'll be helping us to imprison Carl Simmons."

"That's if I help you but Carl is a good man."

"We're not asking you to lie. Do you not understand? Tell the court exactly what you've told me. Just say that I work for Kaiser, and that I was supposed to break my allegiance to him. Just do the right thing."

Sanjay was astonished. "I cannot believe it," he said, "I haven't any intention of lying."

Soon enough, the two previous Agents entered into the room and David beckoned them to take his position.

"You're siding with the winning team," David continued, "and I'll be catching you later than you think."

The Agents were waiting for him to exit.

"As you may know, I'm Agent Gilani. We do have some damning evidence against Carl Simmons. Will you now co-operate?"

Sanjay was waiting for his contact who was ten minutes late. He was ascertained of his rendezvous. Yet, nobody seemed to wish to see him. He saw a man jogging with his dog and a police officer. Yet there wasn't any sign of his intentional contact. Sequentially, that person was late by over fifteen minutes. He continued to tolerate it, and thought that that his contact had deplorable time-management skills. Anyway, he was wearing his walkman, and placed his headphones on. Oh the music soothed him.

A lady, short-cut blonde, in her jog wear, wanted to take a seat beside him—

"Good morning!"

Sanjay had a conjecture that she wanted his attention. *Who was that women*, he thought, *and what is she trying to say?*

The girl touched him to get a little bit friendlier.

"Can I help you?" Sanjay asked after removing his headphones.

"You don't remember me don't you? It's Agent Gilani."

"So you're my contact. We'll need to talk which will affect America—"

The girl raised her hand to slow him down. "I think," she said, "it's best if you take a ride in my car, and we take it from there."

The pair got up to head to a car park nearby and it was quite empty. She started her engine and it moved forward, away from the convenience store.

"What was the delay?" Sanjay wondered.

"I'm just new here, I was looking for the goddamn car park but it isn't situated on my map. I mean it's new, isn't it?"

"I was told to meet near the convenience store, and I hadn't any problems. I even got there early and still I found it," Sanjay said smugly.

It was only a short drive and she stopped at a multi-storey car park. The pair walked together into an elevator. She pressed for the ground floor so that they may enter into the hotel, which was next door. The hotel looked like a blue skyscraper. Being in Los Angeles, many rich and famous people had booked their stays there. Anyway, it was straight for the fifth floor, and it was a quiet affair. They entered the room where David Bruce was watching the news.

"Sir, Sanjay Patio has arrived!"

David changed his view towards the pair and stood up to greet her. "Thanks Doris," he said and turned his attention to Sanjay. "It's actually quite nice to be seeing you in the flesh. Please do take a seat."

"Thanks," Sanjay said kindly and sat right across him in an armchair.

"Would you like some breakfast?" David asked magnanimously.

"No, thank you."

"I believe that you have some pressing information. Could you enlighten me?"

Sanjay was looking at Doris Gilani – watching him.

"Please Doris, leave us," David asked and she obliged.

Sanjay said, "Something big is going down. It's very big."

"Is it bigger than that poster-boy programme?" David said jokingly.

"It's big and it has everything to do with Leo Rockford."

"We know that Wallace had already kidnapped him, but what makes you think it's him again?"

"Yes, we'd abducted him, yet, released – Wallace couldn't justify any harm on him. You know that–"

David smirked. "Well, I'm not responsible for directly changing the federal government into supremacy! My point being is this that I don't think Wallace could ever pardon me!"

"He's a little different. I do suppose it's because Leo thinks too much on astronomy. It was that reason why he left Britain. I can only imagine that Wallace kind of felt sorry for him."

David laughed again. "You've said so yourself," he said, "Leo Rockford is a space-cadet and he isn't in touch with society. So how can he be a problem?"

"You know I would tell you everything, but I've got this strong feeling that it does involve him. Besides, Wallace told me."

"Great! So Wallace told you already. Anyway, may I ask why you didn't relay details that you were going to abduct Leo?"

"Look, I told you that Wallace was only considering it. I didn't know then that he was going to take out his order."

"How did you run off to Canada?" David asked erratically.

"It's a little complicating. But I'm telling you now that the RRF is mastering something huge, and it concerns Leo," Sanjay said repeatedly.

"Sanjay, you've been a great help in bringing down Carl Simmons but this is ludicrous. I must admit that I was a little suspicious about Leo Rockford. But boy, isn't he a space-cadet."

"That's kind of true but the RRF has its concerns with him. It's because I've been asked to see him in person."

David froze. He asked, "You're seeing Leo Rockford? So what's it about?"

"I'm supposed to see him to give him some reassurance to work for the RRF."

David was speechless. He was surprised that Leo hadn't informed his driver – one of Kaiser's Agents – of it. His eyes lids rolled back, as if, window blinds. His eyes enlarged as he sat opposite him. His countenance was expressionless after he shook his head–

"Reassurance, what do you mean?"

"I know that Wallace and Leo didn't see eye-to-eye on things, but he's now considered an asset."

"That doesn't make any sense. So you seeing him to reassure that everything is going fine. So what's going on?"

"All I know is that I'll be meeting him within the next two weeks. Yeah, I'm stopping here with my future fiancée before I'm heading out to Florida. Wallace feels that I'm good at making people commit to his cause."

"This has to remain between us. I don't want what you told me to be out in the open."

"Are you going to do nothing?"

"I suppose I could scramble a team and place him under surveillance. Besides, I was hoping that you could give me some clarity on how you managed to go off-the-radar?"

"Sorry, I just don't know the full details," Sanjay said – an excuse as he was still slightly paranoid of Kaiser.

"It makes no sense. Sanjay, you'll need to get as much information as possible. So where will you be meeting him?"

"I don't know yet. I'll be advised shortly. As you can tell, it's the only reason why I'm in America."

David hummed. "It still doesn't make any sense," he mentioned and got up. "He could either be playing ball with Wallace or General Kaiser, isn't it? Since he is an odd ball, who do you think he's siding with?"

Sanjay hadn't a reply.

The door was being knocked upon and David went to it. He thanked the maid for his breakfast before taking a seat.

Sanjay asked, "David, are you seriously going to eat–"

"Just leave it with me," David quickly answered, "for I know what I'm doing! I know that Wallace Moore is the top dog, but I don't want him to become a legacy. I mean that I've brought down Carl Simmons, and I even been keeping an eye on Frederick Bungles – we didn't suspect Wallace to be much more demanding. To take Wallace out of the picture, I've only got one shot at that."

Sanjay nodded. "You could take him out of the loop, but it may risk somebody else taking his place. It should be noted that his replacement might not be so forthcoming."

"I could lose Kaiser's complete trust."

Sanjay asked regardless, "I didn't know that you were responsible for the surveillance on Frederick Bungles?"

"As you are my friend, he wasn't on my surveillance list."

"Why are you telling me this?"

"Because it'll make a real difference, if I don't get definite results. You see, Harry Trump is the one that had recommended me to lead the USTF. However, Kaiser isn't impressed that the editorial can slip off the grid, and re-emerge as terrorists."

"What you really saying is that for the both of us, this is going to get real ugly."

"I should conduct myself more professionally. I shouldn't be talking about my superiors like this."

"I suppose you'll be keeping a tab on Leo?"

"He does have one of our Agents with him at all times. I should request a report from him. Perhaps he noticed something out of the ordinary. Also, I could take Leo in for some routine questions, and try to get as much information from him."

"If you do that, you must get me out as I won't be safe any longer. I'll need a new identity and a new life."

David nodded. "Suppose I should ask for a transfer too."

"I always wanted to ask you this, but do you think that Leo Rockford is considered one of the new founding fathers of America?"

David giggled. "I never looked at it like that before," he said, "haven't you asked Wallace about that?"

"No."

"Surely it's his desire to eliminate the new Founding Fathers, isn't it?" David asked.

"It's just that I don't like where this is going. There are too many dangers lurking. David, Leo Rockford is a serious threat."

David nodded again. "I'll be keeping a tab on him."

"I'm pretty sure it has everything to do with the NASA reunion."

"Impossible! General Kaiser will be having his own security team, and the building is under a military protectorate. It has got to be a long shot. I can only suspect that you'll be discussing about that with him."

"We've known each other since university, and Rome wasn't built in a day," Sanjay said. "Wallace," he continued – being excursive, "Wallace, sees him as a

---

space cadet that loves space. A space cadet who befriends General Kaiser, a space cadet that moved to America. A space cadet who happens to own a public relations agency, and a space cadet to gossip at."

"Sanjay, that man is a headache," David confirmed. He also said, "I don't suppose you knew that your *space-cadet* is leaving our troubles behind? He's going back to England?"

"Never in my years have I come across such an enigma!"

David stood up and moved across the room to reach for his briefcase. He pulled out a notepad and sat down again. He was quiet whilst Sanjay was bemused, watching the news too. "Obviously," he said after a quarter of an hour mediating, "your new friend knows something that we do not know. The information that he holds must be of significance."

"It has everything to do with that reunion. That's what I'm sure of. It's no secret that General Kaiser will be–"

"The biggest threat was Carl Simmons," David said and was trying to humour the situation, "he must be pulling the strings in prison."

"I don't really find that funny. I got sucked into this political fiasco, and I could either be facing prison, or get myself killed."

"Nada! You worry too much," David Bruce said. "What does the RRF know about us through Carl Simmons?"

"I just want out."

Chapter 44
—Debrief—

HREE OF DAVID Bruce's agents were on a covert surveillance. The rooms of Leo's home and his car were installed with listening devices, and nothing seemed out of the ordinary to incriminate him. David wanted to go a step further to bug his own office, but Leo's own security was patrolling the premise 24/7. So he tried to arrange an appointment for an undercover agent to plant a bug, yet, Leo wasn't available.

In the meantime, Sanjay got his marching orders, directly from Wallace, to meet Leo Rockford in his office. He'd be reassuring him to support the cause, and make his own assessment on him. Accordingly, Leo Rockford's fate laid in his hands on Friday 11th October, and he was masquerading as a potential client.

On the morning of the farce, the day was very hot and sunny. Sanjay was wearing his sunglasses, chinos and white short-sleeve shirt as he entered.

A man approached him on his arrival.

"Good morning, Mr. Mahal," he said with an extended arm to shake his hand, "we've been expecting you."

Sanjay nodded slightly. "Sorry but do I know you?"

"Of course not," he replied, "but I do work for the Rockford Group, and I'm here to lead you to the founder of our business. My name is Peter Alsopp."

Sanjay shook his hand.

Peter led him away into the elevator, which was going to take them to the third floor.

"Mr. Singh, we're having an expansion of operations for Canada and Europe. It will make this company one of the largest multinational public relation agencies in the world."

Sanjay hummed to his presentation as the elevator ascended.

The doors slid open. Both the visitor and Peter saw a Receptionist on the hallway.

"Welcome, Mr Singh," Lisa said and was shaking his hand too. "Mr. Rockford," she continued and was leading him to his office, "is expecting you."

"Mr Singh is here, Mr Rockford."

"Lisa, thank you and that will be all," Leo replied. "Mr. Mahal, will you join me at my desk, please?"

Sanjay said, "What a nice office you have."

"I recognize you. That voice. You're that guy in that apartment," Leo said, pointing at him a little shocked too.

"Don't be alarmed. I'm just here to check on you, and see that you're OK."

"Will you like a drink?"

Sanjay shook his head. "I'm good. Now, I know that you and Wallace weren't seeing things eye-to-eye — especially after we took you by force. Yet, just treat this as a formal appointment, as we get to know each other a bit more."

"You expect to come here when it suits you? And return to Wallace and say that I'll shoot the General. Listen up: I ain't going to do that because he's not an asshole!"

Sanjay was in the dark. *What is he trying to say?* he asked himself. He gasped too. "Aren't you," he anticipated, "prepared to get your hands dirty? You must understand that the General had murdered one of the finest Presidents in the United States."

"All I'm going to do is return back to Britain and forget about this whole mess! Wallace thinks too much of me since he has given me that pardon. The only favour that I'll return is not to kill him."

"All I know is that you're not going to shoot anyone. All Wallace wants is to know of what I think of you. I do recall that you stood up to Wallace — and nobody could've had your defiance and lived to tell the tale. Guess what? That's the only reason why you got the pardon. He really does respect you, and he doesn't believe that you'll be affiliated with Kaiser."

Leo smirked. "Great speech but I won't be killing him."

"Did Wallace want you to kill him?"

"Look, if you want to talk to anybody about taking the upper hand, then you should talk to my colleague."

It was, of course, a revelation that somebody else, inside the building, was definitely a RRF Operative. Sanjay dug a little further for the truth–

"So you want me to talk to your colleague?" he asked.

"What're you talking about?" Leo wondered frustratingly. "Don't you understand?"

"Not at all. But Wallace sent me to comfort you."

"What the hell is this? You coming here to see that I'm fine, but you haven't the foggiest idea about a RRF member working here, isn't it?"

"I'm here because Wallace sent me to comfort you. I need to succeed before I go. I only hope that you're OK with the RRF man working here. I gather that you're OK with the hit?"

"You're suggesting that I'll make the hit, isn't it?"

"Why aren't you inspired that the other guy won't be doing it?" Sanjay asked.

Leo hummed. "Ever since I've spoken to Wallace," he said, "he wanted me to believe in his cause. Why don't you believe that he wants me to blast the General's head off!"

"Wallace isn't like that and I've known him for a long time."

Leo was agitated and got up to look outside of his window. "So what," he inquired, "do you want me to do?"

"Just remain calm and tell me more about your colleague who works for us?"

"I'll call the operative in here, yes?" Leo now asked and returned behind his desk.

"No, I'm good!" Sanjay replied – he knew that he was breaking his need-to-know protocol.

"So why ask?"

"Leo, I was asking you."

"Then why don't you want to see him?"

"Wallace has given me direct instructions to see that you're fine," he said and objected modestly.

"I'm fine, thank you," he said, "but please will you leave."

"I know that you care for the welfare of your employee, or you would've told me already. That's a good sign," Sanjay said. "All I want to do," he carried on, "is go home, and tell the big cheese that you're—"

"Why do you obey orders blindly?"

"I've faith in him and if it wasn't for the likes of Wallace then I'd have been in a prison rotting away. Just like Carl Simmons."

"Who's he?"

"Haven't you any idea how the Red Resistance Union became a force?"

Leo had enough – of his presence. He reached across his desk to make a call. "It's me," he pressed on, "and this isn't going smoothly as I thought."

Eventually, Leo's office door was knocked upon, and he gave permission for entrance.

"Is there a problem?" Peter asked.

"Mr. Mahal thinks that he deserves the lion's share in my business," Leo said sarcastically.

"Mr Mahal, I can assure you that you're a potential client, but I'm afraid that we won't be able to take you up on that offer."

"I've no idea why I came here in the first place," Sanjay said. "This is ridiculous!" He stormed out, leaving the two men behind, to head back to his Orlando hotel.

***

He saw his fiancée greeting him, and she gave him a twirl in her new clothes. As not to complicate things, even more, Sanjay kept his cool by complimenting her. Earlier, he had excused himself that he was out to surprise her: He gave her a ring for marriage, and she accepted. Later on, he moved quietly into the bathroom to call on his assessment.

"It's me, Sandy. Listen up, are you sure this is the guy?"

"That's what Wallace is saying."

"If I'm serious, I don't see how that guy can be of any good use; it's his arrogance. Wallace didn't put that into consideration. I mean, what am I doing here in

Florida? I mean, what if my mother recognised me here?"

"But she didn't and she doesn't live in Orlando. So is Leo OK with it?" Christian asked.

"What the fuck is he supposed to be OK with? And why are you stalling on the finer details?"

"I told you what you need-to-know, and I'll pass on your assessment to Wallace. Good work," Christian said and hung up.

As far as Sanjay could tell, it was abstruse.

***

Later on that day, he took the liberty to see Doris Gilani. Sanjay's rendezvous was at a small casino hotel nearby. As he was sneaking around, behind his fiancée's back, he was going to buy tickets for a night-out at the dog-tracks. Miraculously, Doris had a pair of spare tickets, and she was going to trade his information for hers.

It remained a sunny day and he was heading towards it. After he arrived, he sat at the reception area being several minutes early. It was a small building and the foyer had enough seats for only several visitors. There was white marble statue of Venus nearby, and he hardly waited long. Doris was wearing straight-fit blue jeans and a plain white shirt.

"Hope you can recognise me now?" She asked.

"Yeah."

"How did it go?"

"Well, the big boys aren't telling me anything. All I know is that I was given a so-called assignment, to see that Leo will be committed," Sanjay said tentatively.

"What's critical is that Leo is collaborating. That's enough for us to continue our close monitoring on him. You feel that there's something going down at the NASA reunion bash, any idea what that is?"

"I don't think Leo has any idea what is going on. To me, he's just a dummy. I still believe that Wallace will be doing a hit at the reunion."

"Do you think that David Bruce understands what you're saying?"

"Bruce does understand me, but wants solid proof. My solid proof is that I did meet him at his premises."

Doris sighed. "We're keeping a close eye on Leo," she continued, "yet, we haven't found anything to foil him. So what did Leo say when you met him?"

"I asked him about his involvement," Sanjay said and was rolling his eyes, "but he wants nothing to do with it. It's similar to his abduction as he wanted nothing to do with us either.

"I know there's something going on between Wallace and Leo, for Wallace is taking a keen interest in him. As you know, Wallace had asked me to dig details on him, but he's clean as a whistle. Let me put it simply, I feel as if I'm in the dark."

"Have you ever bothered asking Wallace about it?"

Sanjay sighed again. "I have, yes," he said, "but its air tight. Let me tell you that I'm supposed to be one of the senior figures."

"You appear not to know the inside-outs, isn't it? You don't know what the right arm is doing with the left."

Sanjay was confounded. He stared at her — *was it blatant?* he thought — "Right arm?" he asked.

"I guess that's Wallace being the left arm, while you're the right," Doris replied, and was abhorred by his stupid question.

"I've checked-out Leo," he said, "and he obviously doesn't fit the bill. I know that there's something else at play."

Doris was waiting on it. His valuable intelligence to rely on David Bruce, yet, Sanjay paused. He was looking around at the richly-decorated reception foyer. Of course, the Venus statue was close by, and a water fountain contained tropical fishes.

Doris coughed. "Who was it then?"

"There's some guy that works at the agency who has been behaving somewhat strange. I think he's the real deal. He's some kind of side-kick to Leo."

"He must have a name?"

"It's Leo!" he exploded. "He got me so mad," he continued, "that I kind of stormed out of the building.

That guy appears to know something about my visit, and he knows about the hit!"

"Calm down, this is a public place. Look you must remember his name, or what he looked like?" Doris said. "I would have brought a sketch artist, but this will have to be done quickly. Meet me here tomorrow."

"But I'm heading back to Canada."

Doris found Sanjay too difficult to work with, and decided to obtain a description of him herself.

"What did he look like?"

Sanjay replied, "All I know about the guy is that he has short ginger hair, and has freckles on his cheek..."

Chapter 45

*T*HE ONLY PEOPLE who knew in-depth of the assassination were Wallace Moore and Christian McDowell. Wallace named the operation, *Superseded*. He had definitely had his hopes on setting it at the astronauts' reunion. Wallace Moore was smartly dressed to prepare for his confession on a recorded video:

"My name is Wallace Moore, and I wish to speak to the American people.

As you'll probably know by now, General Bill Kaiser is critically injured, and is presumed dead. You'll be hearing news of Canada's involvement in the plot of ridding us of a tyrant that was opposing free-speech, and our right to be the electorate.

"America must not mourn him but Frederick Bungles. We've damming proof that his alleged accident was sabotage via the Supreme Council. The truth has been concealed inside the White House, and we'll reveal those destructive documents to the American people. Unfortunately, the truth will hurt us that General Kaiser was playing us as fools.

"Some of you do think that the Red Resistance Force is a violent, cruel and cold-blooded organization that wishes to undermine the economic and political growth of America today. What I can tell you is that we've no intention of having any influence upon the economy, but to maintain its success. We must realize that from time to time, our economy will always have bad patches, and Kaiser isn't fool proof.

"Ask I speak for the RRF, we only wish to roll back the times where our grandparents, parents and young adults will be able to determine the future of America. The point why I'm making this bold statement is because I want to believe in America, which has the Founding

Fathers being the likes of George Washington, Benjamin Franklin and Thomas Jefferson in her bosom. What George Washington had done was to bring us together, that we're stronger than being alienated. The fact, my good Americans, is that we've been alienated by General Kaiser.

"As you may already know, I was once a Supreme Judge in Washington DC. I had a proud career in the Department of Justice until that unfateful day. It was 13th October when the President of the United States of America, Frederick Bungles, was removed from the Oval Office. I was unaware of this horrific crime to illegally remove the President. If I had known, I would've opposed the motion. Anarchy is responsible and our Founding Fathers would have scorned upon that. I remember America being built for freedom, and it wasn't to enslave its people.

"I stood up to expose him and I've made new friends on my journey too. These are great people who hold a devotion to uncover the evils of Kaiser. Therefore, I worked for the Red Resistance Union. All we wanted to do is bring a peaceful end to that illicit government, but they wanted to subjugate us. We were facing imprisonment, yet, Frederick Bungles gave our freedoms back. Thanks to him, we had new hope that Kaiser will bow down.

"You may remember that Frederick Bungles got involved in a skiing accident. We were told that it was an avalanche that took his life. Please wake up America! It was a small bomb that triggered the devastating avalanche: It wasn't a natural disaster.

"Evidently, I had decided that the best course of action was to fight fire with fire. Therefore, I'd reassembled the union into a militia. Our goal was to strike the tyrant that took the life of a humbled President. Today, we've succeeded with the death of a tyrant. Therefore, I'll disband the Red Resistance Force as from today. We'll no longer be the thorn to the thigh but a flower!

"Before the bud becomes a flower, I'll ask the Supreme Judges to realize their mistake to approve

General Kaiser. We must never turn away from the Founding Fathers, because of the evil he offered. Once again, I demand the Supreme Judges to correct their ways, and look forward to a democratic society. I can think of no other man for this transition than the former Vice President of Frederick Bungles, and he'll make a formidable candidate.

"Once more Americans, I've full confidence in the transition and may God bless America!"

After he finished, Wallace Moore believed that the Supreme Judges would come to their senses; there wasn't a plausible alternative. Nevertheless, Wallace had a prescience that Harry Trump may stand as the alternative. David Bruce might also hinder Wallace's framework. Thirdly, the Supreme Court could even nominate one of their own to become the new Commander.

Chapter 46
—Ace in the hole—

*L*EO WAS GETTING ready for the big event. He straighten his bowtie as he saw himself though his bathroom mirror. It was a huge one that was hanging on the back of the door.

Leo left the bathroom in search of Carly, and saw his son and daughters, in the lounge, playing a video game console. Leo stood in front of the television screen—

"Where's your mother?" he asked.

"She's in the bathroom!" Donno replied.

"I was just in the bathroom."

Carly walked into the lounge, and spotted their annoyance. She shook her head. "Leave them alone."

Of course, he was fond of his family. He took a moment to kiss them all on their cheeks, and Carly found it rather amusing since their game seemed more important. "I thought," she said anyway, "you wanted to get there early?"

He turned to inspect his wife and she was wearing a long silk red dress with a split along her right leg, and looked fabulous—

"You look good!"

Carly accepted his compliments and they said their good nights, for the long evening ahead.

The couple wasn't driving; for they had Howard Giles. He helped them take their positions at the back of a black limousine. Inside there was enough space to tightly fit a dozen passengers, it included black leather seats, and a glass pane that could wind down to talk to the driver — evidently, it may go up for private conversations too. Anyhow, Howard began the long journey to the Space Centre.

Carly knew that Leo wanted to get there a little early to inspect his recording crew. She was looking outside of her side window, and the scenery kept changing. "Are you going to take the job?"

Leo was also looking out from his car side window but turned to his left to face her. He giggled lightly. "We can scrap this chauffer, if we leave America."

"What's that supposed to mean?" Carly asked astonished.

"I mean that there's no rush returning to a life in England. Why not stay for a couple of years or so."

"I thought you wanted to move your business to London, but you're hesitating."

"That's still in the pipeline. However, why should we parachute back as I haven't nowhere to conduct business?"

"What about the kids?" she cried.

"We're not the only people in America getting this type of treatment. Look at the families within the Supreme Council; they too do have the same level of protection like us."

"You mean to tell me that General Kaiser only has one driver, and his home security system to fight the odds? He does have the USTF for that!" Carly said, disdained.

"If you want me to complain, we'll get the USTF too!"

"I just don't want anything happening to our children, because of your work."

"I do understand dear," Leo replied, "I won't be making any hasty promises about going back to Mars."

***

He arrived at the space centre, and inspected the crew in their broadcast trailer. They reported that everything was in order – there was a slight scare when a microphone, for Kaiser speech, wasn't working. Soon enough, he and his wife entered into the Training Centre with fifteen minutes to spare. He found himself agreeing to smoke a cigarette with a man from the Security Detachment. He excused himself, from his wife, to go outside for a crafty one. As the two men were outside,

Leo wanted to discuss security. The Agent was just about to reassure him that everything was fine, but received a radio check-in. He answered and politely left him. Leo Rockford was now feeling sorry of his involvement to kill his old friend Bill Kaiser. As he smoked, he prayed that General Kaiser would walk out unscathed. Additionally, Leo had sensed that the best way to circumvent was by not granting Peter access to the do.

Now he was getting wired that Wallace Moore shared his comprehension of the god Zetta. He considered his own actions: His selfish satisfaction against unsavoury characters. Leo then pondered on slipping the General the spatial water, and imagined that Wallace Moore would see the errors of his ways — which was very unlikely. As he thought on, time was running short, and something was lingering on his mind that Peter was the hit-man. If it could be, then why would he give up anything: Family, friends and his work. Sure enough, Peter wasn't permitted to go to the function. He allowed a small crew that consisted of two camera men wearing their tuxedos. Apparently, they were to take their orders from Peter Alsopp, as their Executive Producer, on who, where, and what they ought to do — by an ear-piece.

Leo couldn't picture himself being wrong; for it meant warning General Kaiser. *Two wrongs*, he thought, *doesn't make it right*.

His wife joined him outside, and was surprised when she caught up with him. "Leo," she said, "you're crying. I thought you wanted to stay in America, isn't that right?"

"Carly," he excused, "I'm just going through some emotions. I cannot tell you how much this event really means to me. It's going to be exquisite."

"Honey, I know you went through a lot in the last four months, but you were once a serviceman; you were trained against extreme difficulties. So that kidnapping shouldn't break you."

"You're right," Leo said, and had a pretence, "I should be headstrong."

"So you'll decide to return to Britain?" Carly asked.

Leo stubbed out his cigarette and coughed. "Of course," he said, "but I want to arrive in Britain knowing something; of having my business up and running. Otherwise, it's a bad practice to turn tail and run." Carly hadn't the desire to hear another word, but moved quietly back inside with her husband right behind her.

***

David Bruce was at the space complex, sitting with Harry Trump in a canteen. He had ten minutes remaining before the grand dinner. David was wearing his two button dark grey suit, clean white shirt with a black bowtie. Across the table, Harry had on his light green military clothes. He was displaying his honorary medals pinned to his chest as well. Unfortunately, for David Bruce, he didn't receive an invitation – General Kaiser's wasn't satisfied on his regular briefs against the RRF.

"As I was saying," David said after a sip on his coffee, "one of my most trusted assets had already told me of a hit, tonight."

Harry hummed as he basked on his intelligence. "There's always a threat against General Kaiser, but what makes tonight any different? Still, why haven't you told this a lot sooner?"

"Adjutant-General Trump, we only learnt about this within the last three days. Yet, I must put it to you that it's credible now. The RRF is placing all of their hopes in taking him out, tonight."

Harry Trump sighed. "Listen, you're the head of the USTF because you brought down Carl Simmons. He was the real threat to the stability of the Supreme Council, and you're now reporting that you cannot take out his pups?"

"All we know is that the RRF is headed by Wallace Moore. He wasn't considered a threat. So my question is this, what makes that organization stick? What I'm saying is that I don't believe the RRF is really an independent body."

"You told me that already! Yet, what I'm discussing is of your incompetence. Why didn't you decipher that intelligence a lot sooner? So what am I to do now?" Harry asked.

"Ideally, I would like General Kaiser to abandon his attendance this evening. After that, we can concentrate our efforts for a specific target." David replied.

"Who is it?"

"What we have is a key description being a Caucasian male with short ginger cutback hair. He has a slim build and wears red thin glasses. By that, I do have the best people circulating the whole perimeter. We're on top of this, Adjutant-General Trump."

"I just hope you get that bastard!" he said and rose up to leave. "If I were you," he continued, "I wouldn't be near this vicinity as the General will be passing by."

David nodded. "He still isn't satisfied that I brought down the RRU?"

"You've done well. The fact is that you've an informer in the RRF, and that's why I'll be still recommending you as the chief."

"I'll be in the trailer monitoring the situation. So if you require my assistance, that's where I will be," David responded.

***

The function room was going to be the dining hall, and it included expensive oil paintings of past American Generals, to photographs of astronauts. Obviously, they'd be hanging on the walls. Between the paintings and photographs were large marble statues of Roman deities. Light entertainment was to be performed by a small orchestra band.

Five minutes before the evening dinner, Leo and Carly found their table. A steward had already ushered them to the front near the stage. There was quite a number of guests arriving too. As the hall was becoming lively, Leo and Carly had drunk a couple of Alice Paul cocktails. Leo spotted a camera man dotting between the tables, which seemed a nuisance to some of the guests. As Leo thought to humour it, he spotted a peculiar figure standing near the statue of Mars along a distant wall. Leo focused on his face; it was the man that had followed him in his loud Hawaii shirt. His face dropped in horror; the man had picked him out of the guests as he raised his right hand. Leo was ascertained that he wanted him to acknowledge, and so he raised his flute in full view of his wife.

"Who is that?" Carly wondered.

"He's just one of General Kaiser's men," he excused, "from the Supreme government. We met several times through Harry Trump."

The room looked half full as people were trying to find their tables with the help of the stewards. The atmosphere was getting livelier, and as it was picking up, Martin MacCormick got in front of Leo.

"I bet you haven't been missing me you dirty dog!"

Leo got onto his feet to shake his hand then he hugged him.

"Long time no see! How are you keeping?" he asked.

Just as he is speaking, Jay Kaiser made an appearance. "God!" he exclaimed, "it's good to see the two of you again!"

The room continued to get a lot livelier and Leo was happy to see his former crew mates. It was becoming obvious that they were all taking front row tables.

Martin pushed himself forward on Leo. He coughed slightly. "I'm sorry to hear about that kidnapping. I bet that was terrible."

"It was! They were accusing me of being responsible for the Supreme Revolution—"

"So you did," Martin whispered jokingly, "fix their drinks?"

Leo laughed. "I'm glad to see you again. It has been terrible not able to talk about our unique experience."

As the two former space commanders enjoy each other's company, Jay was finding his girlfriend a seat before returning—

"What're you two talking about?"

Martin replied, "It's just that party we had in space. You know, the one when you were flirting around."

"That party cost me a divorce," he said joyfully.

"I never knew," Leo reacted fondly, "you could buy a wife!"

Martin gasped. "How many," he pointed at his drink, "have you had?"

"It's OK." Leo said. "So me and my wife," he proceeded to say, "had a couple but no harm is done."

Jay giggled. "I think I'll join ya."

However, Jay found himself being accompanied by Chris Tallon.

Leo was still standing with Martin. It didn't seem strange to them that they would become life-long buddies. Whilst in admiration, Tasha entered into the scene. She was wearing a red evening dress–

"Nice to meet you, Leo," Tasha implied, "this is my husband, Quency–"

"It's nice to meet you," Carly said as she got up. "Oh, you must be her husband."

Tasha and Quency were courteous.

"It's great to see that you're alive and kicking," Tasha continued, "I was afraid that the RRF wouldn't get you released. You're a brave man."

"That's why I married Carly. She says the same thing, thank you!"

The room itself seemed to peak at its liveliest level, yet the guests were continuing to find their tables. Harry Trump was suddenly amongst them–

"Leo Rockford," he said, "it's nice to see you once more in pleasant surroundings."

"It's so nice to see you too!" Leo shouted.

"I'm here with my wife, Debbie," Harry said.

She had a radiance of being the spouse of one of the most powerful men in the world. She had bright light blue sparkling eyes, and long ginger hair set up in a simple braid.

"It's very nice to be meeting you," Harry's wife acknowledged, "it's a good thing you're here as I hear so much good stuff about you."

"It's nice to meet you too, Debbie," Leo said and kissed her on the cheek, whilst Harry done the same kissing his. The Adjutant-General and his wife moved together to one side of the room to find their table.

General Kaiser laughed loudly. "I'm glad that you can make it!"

Mr Rockford hugged and shook his old friend's hand. "We for one, Bill, we for one."

The General was looking around and saw a sea of people flocking in to hear his speech. He said, "This is going to be a night I won't forget in a hurry!"

About that time, Leo, Martin, Jay, Chris, Emily and Tasha found their seats as the General was here—

Leo was becoming a little tipsy but still found his friendship with the General a little weird. There were times that they would talk on the world's problems for hours, over beer, but that looked remote. However, Leo admired him as a man who only wanted to serve his country the way he knew best.

Carly asked, "Are you sure that Bill Kaiser wants you to go back to Mars?"

"Remember, he did tell me only a short while ago."

Carly now believed that she was drunk. She belched quietly. "I suppose your abduction has been doing you some good! NASA had you on their black list!"

"It's showbiz."

Carly nodded and the pair was waiting for General Kaiser to deliver his speech.

The General received his warm reception, and looked tall upon a constructed stage with the diners below him. Everybody was cheering him on. Now he made his way to a splendid podium, which had the seal of the Supreme Commander – and a strange looking red carved leaf below it. All of the guests were cheering to show their devotion, and one of the guests was pretty enthusiastic as he shouted, clapped and gave a standing ovation. It was Jay Kaiser, and he reached out to his girlfriend to show her support. Harry Trump rose too, in slight embarrassment; for he thought that it had better been him to lead the applause. It didn't matter as everybody believed that Kaiser deserved a marvellous complaisance.

Bill Kaiser was still soaking up the scene in front of him. He knew that he was the most memorable person in history, and they favoured autocracy. He waited and waited for the cheers to cease, but the noise was inexorable. The General saw two cameramen at either side – near his security personnel – since they would be broadcasting the event worldwide. Of course, he was the first to authorise a hi-tech spaceship to Mars, and brought economic prosperity to his nation. Eventually, the guests allowed their host to speak. The General cleared his throat:

"Please my fellow and lady Americans. I welcome you all in here to mark this anniversary of our Supreme Revolution. I thank you all as tonight is a special night. We've the finest astronauts that mankind has to offer. These are brave men and women who had taken the chance of flying – perhaps – the most beautiful craft of modern time. The people that are sitting with us today have done us proud by providing us images and samples from Mars. Therefore, it has brought us closer to the planet with our own Mars Gallery in this very centre. So let's give a round of applause to Leo Rockford, Martin MacCormick, Chris Tallon, Tasha Chayton, Emily Walters and Jay Kaiser."

All the diners showed their appreciation. Some stood up and others didn't. Leo saw it as another welcoming back from Mars. A tear was streaming down his cheek, and he was kissing his wife too.

General Kaiser continued, "I thank my Adjutant-General for being here tonight. It was his call to advise the adventure amongst a lot of other things! I believe that space is like a vital organ – a heart – which keeps America strong. In addition, I know that the world looks on, to this evening, wondering why I wanted to host our national anniversary at the Kennedy Space Centre. That's because I do respect my predecessors. As well as our Supreme Judges who took the decision, that it was time for a change, and it's a change for a better and not for the worse. I don't usually do grand speeches, but I want to tell you good people that things are only going to get even better.

"Earlier today, I've given authorization for NASA to receive thirty billion dollars from the Supreme Treasury. After all, I own a business called Aries, and I know it's wrong to splash money where it's not wanted. So let me tell you the real reason why we should go back to Mars.

Yes, it's true that having another Mars mission will create more jobs in this sunshine state. It'll also generate new businesses, and even enable us to have closer ties with our foreign neighbours. Think about it, it's what this country really deserves.

"I want to tell you that those fine astronauts couldn't have done this without the expertise of Leo Rockford. I've known him since my time with the US Air Force, it was a joint operation during the Cold War. It was in Turkey where I met him, and we got on like white on rice. I do remember his first career choice was to be in space, but such opportunities were hard to find in Britain. So when one was available here, he quits the Royal Air Force to start his dream job. Leo came to America when there was an economic heartache: Wall Street was collapsing, there were job losses, our borrowing was increasing and things weren't picking up. Leo came to America not to rescue us from our turmoil, but to chase his dream to be a space guru, and I do respect him! I remember doing him a favour to work for a space observatory post, which did coincide with the Supreme Revolution. Leo is not a man of politics, but a man who has his head in the clouds. Goodness me! When I asked him if he wished to go beyond the clouds, you guess it folks, he wanted to!"

Giggles were heard all around the dining hall, and Carly gave him a sarcastic smile – Leo wasn't drunk enough to think that the General was exaggerating a little.

"Since our successful expedition to Mars," the General continued still, "we can conclude that America is the first of its kind to go into deep space. This craft has revealed the secrets of artificial gravity. It's even the first to ever use the new type of fuel which is cleaner and safer to use. As General Kaiser, we're the first to contribute in this hi-technology. All what needs to be said is to confirm another launch.

"I ask politely that Leo Rockford could take the helm once more! This man isn't out there for a political gain, but he is out there to improve mankind's understanding! Please, Mr. Leo Rockford, will you honour us by joining me up here? Please come here to confirm that this day will be the day that we can look, beyond the clouds, knowing that we're in good hands!"

Leo hesitated, for a moment, to kiss his wife, several times on her cheek then slowly rose up. He looked ahead and saw the General beckoning him to speed up. Yet, for that specific moment of time, he looked around to see if either Peter Alsopp or the camera crew were holding any concealed weapons. Leo saw all of the diners were getting upon their feet to show their admiration, and they broke into a cheerful song. Leo was slightly drunk, and made an unusual attempt to calm the desperados. Nevertheless, the atmosphere was going to take a horrible turn...

As Leo was facing hundreds of guests, he heard a strange loud thump of a noise coming from behind him. He panicked and landed on his front in a surprised fashion – he imagined that Peter Alsopp was right behind him to declare his allegiance. Leo's wife screamed whence the sound came from, and everybody else had stopped being cordial. The camera crew were filming the stage ahead of them, and captured a bright flash, that was followed by a small ball of smoke hovering above the actual stand – the General was down.

Leo feared for his conscience. *Is the General assassinated,* he wondered to himself, *and is it my fault?* He turned around to the incident behind him, and saw at least three security personnel. Leo still looked on and hoped that his fears couldn't be true. Of course, he was on his feet and walked steadily to the stage.

"What's going on?" Leo asked Security.

No response.

Harry Trump was looking at him and headed his way–

"Take the astronauts with their husbands and wives to that extension room over there!"

Leo obliged and requested his former crew members and their spouses to the other end of the stage.

"This is bad," Martin stated to him. "How can the Supreme Council be shattered like that?"

"I've no idea. I only hope he's OK."

David Bruce had already stormed out of his USTF trailer. He headed straight towards the hotspot. He strongly believed that the man that fitted Sanjay's description had to be responsible. As he eventually got closer to the box stand, he found Harry Trump waving him over.

"How could this have happened?" Harry asked.

"I'm not sure! I'll be getting the forensic team to examine this stage."

"Do that now and don't allow anybody to leave this complex."

All of the guests were told to enter the gymnasia – that would have been the ballroom. Some of the guests presumed that the General was dead, and their evening ruined. At times, people were shouting to comprehend on the situation. Harry Trump was the only person to keep the people calm.

"People, please listen," he spoke into a microphone, "there has been an incident in the dining area. I must ask for your complete cooperation. We're investigating where General Kaiser got injured. I'll like to thank you and you'll all be able to leave eventually."

Some speculated that General Kaiser's death was at the hands of the RRF, and were trying to gain his attention. But the soldiers refrained them. Others were trying in vain to speak to Harry, yet, he swiftly left the gymnasia. He was making his way towards the extension room. Harry was certain that he must have quick answers, or America would slip into a state of anarchy. David Bruce was also with him. Harry opened the door and saw Leo. He proceeded to ask him to follow him out of the room.

Leo recognized David as the man who had accused him of making a deal with the Red Resistance Force. At first, he loathed to follow them, but volunteered against his own will. The three men made their way from the extension room, with an additional Security Detachment, to the USTF trailer. Sure thing, the trailer was the nerve centre of keeping the General safe, but it was a danger room now. David ordered his men to wait outside. The three men took their seats inside the front of the trailer.

"What can you tell me about the bomb?" Harry asked.

"I know nothing of a bomb until now! Why are you waging your fingers at me? Are you suggesting that I'm the terrorist?"

Harry Trump replied, "We're just following up on a credible lead. It was pointing at a gentleman who was under your wing."

Leo's anxiety was kicking in. It appeared, all along, that the USTF had infiltrated the RRF, and they knew about Peter Alsopp. Yet, he thought of their sanguine behaviour was no more. After all, Kaiser was dead.

"Are you're implying," Leo now wondered, "that one of my employees was responsible for that attack, then why didn't you act upon it sooner?"

"Leo Rockford, I'm placing you under arrest for further questioning."

"That's ridiculous! I've done nothing wrong. You of all people saw what was happening, and I could've got killed myself! What you're really saying is, your selfish pride to run this country."

David shouted for his men to enter the trailer. On their arrival, he made a formal request to arrest Leo.

"I'll be placing you under arrest, Mr Rockford," David said, "you're the suspect that we were looking for, and make no mistake that your actions is of high treason."

Chapter 47

—Aftermath—

*D*URING THE EVENING to early morning, a forensic team found that the microphone at the podium was the actual weapon. Their discovery caused further shock that before the General's speech, there were several security sweeps throughout the entire function room. The security team deployed bomb detectors, and sniffer-dogs; they never imagined complacency.

Luck belonged to the RRF that evening; for they knew that there were two sweeps by two separate teams — Beta & Alpha. The Alpha team verified the work of Beta before the area was considered safe. After the Alpha team gave their clearance, Peter Alsopp ordered a sound check to find that the microphone was defective. Obviously, the faulty microphone was given a replacement, which had concealed a controlled device. The bomb itself had a small radius of damage. However, it was enough to kill, or maim people. Peter Alsopp, of course, was the bomb plotter, but he wasn't anywhere within the dining hall. Yet luckily for him, Leo Rockford gave him the role as an Executive Producer, and so was in charge of the camera crew that gave him the necessary sight to push the button.

***

Leo quickly ended up in Washington, and the Adjutant-General made a declaration that Leo Rockford was formally charged with high treason, and faced the death penalty. Plus, the acting Supreme Commander announced national mourning.

Shortly afterwards, his stability to rule was put into question by a televised announcement by the Canadian Premier! It was of shock, disbelief and awe that he knew of the attack beforehand. The Premier called for America to cherish democracy, and he ended up saluting the Maple Leaf! Furthermore, Wallace Moore made it official to disband the RRF. In all fairness, it made Harry Trump languid.

Herbert Engels quickly started his petition for the devolution of the Supreme Council; for he was the Vice President under Frederick Bungles. He became the successor and was going to be the last. He immediately reformed the Supreme Court to not hold any power to select future leaders. By his show of strength, he'd be allowing the American people the chance to decide on who should become their President − one day. He also offered immunity to people in the Supreme Court and the Supreme Congress, in exchange, for their complete cooperation.

***

Much, much later in Washington, Herbert Engels gave his decree to release Leo Rockford and Carl Simmons. Leo was imprisoned for nearly a year before he could return home to his family.

Chapter 48
—The interview—

ON SCREEN, TARA Hussain had her own political show, and she was known for making her guests reveal more than what was known. Hurrahs were going her way by exposing the Prime Minister to admit his incompetence, which caused a string of resignations in his Cabinet, and losing his residence on Downing Street. It was also she who publicly speculated that Jay Kaiser's sexual hormones would get the better of him. And finally, she was the last British person to interview Leo since his return from Mars. Basically, the bets were on, if she could still deliver? Tara was going to host a TV show with Sir Leo Rockford as her main guest after his release.

Tara had once conjured that Leo was a monomania during and after the Supreme Revolution. However, she knew, full well, that Leo was going to be her focal point of radical changes in Washington, future missions to Mars, and his business. She recalled the first time when her Agent rang her. He recommended that Leo Rockford should be invited on a political edition. At first, she thought of it as a sick practical joke, because Leo was thousands of miles away, and he hadn't any political status. It was a paradox but he shed some light, that it would give a whole new meaning in the way the British people were watching the tube. He argued that Leo Rockford was an ethnic minority who befriended a tyrant, and America was making lots of headlines in Britain. So to allow Leo Rockford to sell himself on her show would boost ratings to a new high. Her Agent continued that the viewers did show an interest in Leo Rockford as the man who chased his American dream, to become a successful entrepreneur. His nationality, as well, had an underdog status that stormed America — there wasn't many British people making such an impact. Her Agent also told her that to miss such an opportunity was surely insane. So through his persuasive skills, she agreed to do it – he made a confession that it was already in motion!

Off-screen, Tara Hussain was a Londoner, and she hailed from Tottenham. Both her parents emigrated from Asia. Her mother was from Sri Lanka whilst her father, Bangladesh. Tara took on a degree in Journalism too. She possessed a light-dark complexion. Her eyes were dark brown, she had long jet black hair and a toned body. She had a spouse being Stanley Prince who was one of Cambridge's finest students: He had won the boat race against Oxford, two times over.

On-screen again, she had a highly acclaimed mother working in the fashion industry. Therefore, she could easily find a job on a news network, which offered fashion content. Contrary to her prominence of hosting political shows, she took the position as a Celebrity and Fashion Correspondent. As such, she was interesting, to her audience, as she covered celebrities that were train wrecks. From time to time, a famous model, or television star went off the rail as they were drowned in alcohol and drug abuse. She would expose them, but it was an interview on their struggles, and how they were overcoming them. Her image took on the political stage. It was all because of a substantial increase of young politicians in Parliament. Soon enough, she became a household name from a girl presenting fashion to a woman who was making politics a satire.

The way she conducted her political interviews, Tara quickly addressed their credentials to make her guests comfortable. She then threw in a question, which triggered a series of other questions. All in all, it usually raised the temperature of her guests. To reveal one of her splendours, she was chatting to the British Prime Minster about the government's handling on the Church. He had a reform that churches should acknowledge other faiths. The proposed bill was that within a sermon, the clergy who wished to bless God via Jesus Christ should be humbled, and give thanks to other religions–

Tara said, "Eric, you're a man with a set of principles: Procreative, approachable and adapting to the changes in Europe. I'm saying all this because of your career record. You've been tackling to restore the health in our society, for example, the tax breaks for businesses to invest heavily in science. It's your belief that tax breaks will create jobs for school leavers. If I may say so in your own words:

We must find the team spirit to lead this country forward, and to continue our growth and prosperity.

"Also, I think I fully understand your commitment to integrate Britain into a multicultural society. Is it therefore necessary to put forward this Inter-faith bill?"

Eric replied, "Of course it is! You know perfectly well that we live in a British society that strives making exports to our neighbouring countries, which aren't necessarily Christians. I mean the Church have been living in the dark ages, like not allowing homosexuals to have marriage to banning contraception. That's why we'll set the right balance for Britain. Look, my mother is a devout Christian and every Sunday, we go to our local church to learn about Christ. The problem lies that we've a narrow-minded view on other faiths like Judaism. What I've noticed since attending Sunday-school is a sense of believing that we're better than other faiths that led to world problems like Ayatollah Khomeini to those Christian cults. Therefore, it's time to allow a new theology that Christ is about loving thy neighbour. By making the Church accept other faiths, we'll have a new generation of people that will interact without any sign of prejudice."

"I understand" Tara said, "since my mother and father are of opposing faiths, but their love for British society drove them together." She asked, "To put simply, allowing the Church to acknowledge different faiths will open new channels of communication, wouldn't it?"

Eric nodded. "Of course and all I want is a Britain being good for everybody."

"I understand the difficulties of discrimination, and we must stop it for an utopia. If I daresay, it sounds like your government should only ordain the vicars, priests and reverends, wouldn't you agree?"

"Look," Eric responded, "you're not tackling the heart of the problem. The law will be there to make sure that everybody isn't above the law."

"What you're implying," Tara said, "is that we should remove our uniqueness as it hinders our social development. From what I've gathered about the Church; it's there as a guidance to understand God. It's a historical fact, that the Church was persecuted by the Romans for not elevating their gods. Could it be argued that you're putting the government above the Church?"

Without the Prime Minister mentioning another word, his political ambition was to head to complete failure. Many people in Britain had accepted that such elevation was the work of Lucifer the devil. His mistake, in front of millions of television viewers, was being more important than God himself. After which, Eric only had one option and that was to hand in his resignation – it was a vain attempt to give the political party a fighting chance in the elections.

Before that, Leo Rockford was aware of Tara Hussain. So imagine his surprise after he took a prank telephone call, in his Orlando office, of her Agent masquerading as a potential client–

"Good morning, Mr Benson," Leo said.

"Hi there, as you probably just realized from my accent, I'm a cockney geezer with a business interest regarding you; you being the head in your particular expertise."

"Hello there, I'm Leo Rockford and I'm the current CEO. I've gathered, from Peter Alsopp, that you've a *sharp eye* for success, and you require us to deliver it to you?"

"Listen, some people think we cockneys are blooming pranksters trying to swindle others their livelihoods. Just want you to know upfront."

"Sir, I believe your name is Gordon–"

"Ain't that the truth!" he interrupted, "listen up, since you visiting us for your knighthood, I gonna make you a lot of quick dosh, and I mean in London town. So why don't ya suit up, and see me with all expenses paid. Plus, I want ya to go through my process team. I hope that you'll accept our interview to get the wheels turning, Guvnor!"

"That kind of sounds fabulous. So when do I leave?" Gordon gasped. "Listen up," he continued, "I'm sending you British Airway tickets, and a car to drive in. Gordon Bennett! Where are my manners! I'll also splash in some money for your family to have a nice stay in London. So are you up for it?"

"Sounds prom—"

"I'll say that again," once more he cut him off short, "you must see my team, and it has to be the day after your knighthood."

"Don't mind me asking but I find your approach somewhat misleading. I do have a public relation agency, and we do accept clients to market their brand name. Usually, it's us that will do the wining and dining."

Gordon reacted, "So ya know that I'm a serious businessman, and I see a promising future for you, myself and the team. Listen, I'll be sending my courier today to deliver those tickets."

"I'll need to talk with my wife."

"I know that you left the air force to chase an American dream, and look what it got you: Fortune. So I want you to remain fortunate."

"I'll still need," Leo reiterated, "to speak to my wife. You're asking my entire family to accept your gifts."

"You should accept it cause I also want you to spend an evening with one of my closest friends who's Tara Hussain," Gordon admitted — not fully though.

"I hardly know you, and you're expecting me to be spending time to meet her. So why would she want to meet me?"

"Let me come clean. I'm Gordon Benson her agent, and I would like it very much, if you'll allow her to interview you. It'll be for her new show this season, and I'm really begging you."

"I'll still need to talk to my wife, but all I'll say is that she's a big fan of hers."

"Gotta dash but expect the gifts within an hour!" Gordon said and hung up. Of course, Leo did accept the invitation to attend her TV chat show. It was all because the news pleased his wife about the chance of meeting her off-stage. Furthermore, Leo was able to be at peace from those men in loud Hawaii shirts.

**

The show was to feature Leo Rockford's second appearance. There was to be a live audience, and the studio was huge to seat several hundreds, and the layout had a theatre setting. Contrary to her popularity, the stage itself took up a rather bland arrangement. Quite frankly, an uplifting atmosphere, from the audience, would make an outsider believe that they were drunk. Nevertheless, the chemistry between the Presenter and the lively audience created vitality.

The stage had a large brown mahogany desk with several brown vases. The laid carpet and along the walls were rosy red. Therefore, it consisted of two primary colours, to create a clash, between the table and its surroundings. Pictures are also hanging on the walls and it looked bland too. One picture had big brown spots within a red background. Another picture was displaying a check sequence, whilst the third contained thick and thin stripes of red and brown. Tara's leather chair was bright red, and three empty brown chairs were across her huge desk too. The two other brown chairs might suggest additional guests, but it was going to be a surprise.

A small orchestra band was at the corner of the studio. The musicians were wearing their casuals. Also, they were to play a number that would bring life. The music was to create an anticipation of something beautiful might occur: It was Beethoven's Allegro con brio.

As the orchestra played the tune, Tara got a terrific reception as she stood at the side of the stage. She smiled onto her audience, and was very confident that her show would aggrandise her status. Despite the primary colours of the set, she was wearing a V-neck multi-coloured pullover with a light blue shirt underneath.

Also, she wore a black loose puff frock and red high heels. It took a while, for the audience to settle down, as she began her introduction. "Good evening all! It's nice to be with you all again. Please calm down!'

Few people saw her stunning; and were wolf-whistling inexorably. Yet, a security man faced them directly from below: He was tacit of removing them from their seats, unless they'd keep the peace.

"As we're starting, yet another brand new season," she went on, "I thought why not have someone that has always been on the news. If we cannot have tea with the Supreme Commander Engels, then why not get comfortable with the former Orion Commander who will be sharing his thoughts and views on America. So please give a warm welcome to Sir Leo Rockford!"

It was Leo's cue to join her from the backstage. He had a stage-fright on how to present himself. He thought that some might be hissing and jeering on his entrance, because he had supported a dictator. He marched instantly to Tara, kissed her on the right cheek, and attempted to shake her hand too. For Tara, the kiss was suffice. Momentarily, Leo stood to look onto the audience; he saw hundreds giving him a marvellous reception, and he was cordial too. Tara showed Leo his seat, which was the middle brown chair across her desk. As he continued to be jovial, he saw himself as an astronomer, an astronaut and a world-class businessman.

"You looked surprised coming out from the back," Tara said. "Weren't you expecting this level of support?"

Leo shook his head. "It's been far too long since my last visit here and I love it!"

"Surely you've been seeing your parents since your return to Britain?"

Leo laughed. "Of course," he continued, "my parents are a bit like yours! My father was from Kenya and my mother is from Britain, and that's how I forged a great relationship with the British way of life. Are yours—"

"Yes," she anticipated very quickly, "you could say I'm from Sri Lanka, and I was supposed to be a spoilt little girl who went to a posh public school."

It took a while for the audience to settle down, and Leo was waving both of his arms in an ecstatic fashion. Tara said, "I remember the last time you were here, I had a little soft spot about that fantastic spaceship."

"It's rather a high-altitude aircraft," Leo corrected her, "it can take off at any airport, visit the moon, and she could land at a different airport."

"Now that the American government has grounded further flights, how do you feel about the Orion?"

"Engels sees that such a technological advancement shouldn't be used to determine the future of the American people. He did say that the Orion is a constant reminder of the late General Kaiser, and he thinks it's best to bury his legacy."

"I understand that General Kaiser gave you an American citizenship," Tara said. "May I ask," she now wondered, "that if Engels wants closure, do you believe that he'll ask you to leave?"

"Engels only wants what's best for the American people," Leo responded, "I moved over there to follow my dream in astronomy. As an American, I respect its constitution and the law of the land."

"You know from our previous interview that I was taken back by that spaceship. Oh boy! I must be mad not to think that General Kaiser, is a powerful figure, who heavily invested in you to command the spaceship. So surely, you're not ashamed about that?"

"I wasn't ashamed about General Kaiser being the dictator in North America," Leo replied and was sanguine, "however, I was very anxious to understand if his new found power wasn't corrupt."

"What and how," Tara inquired, "could you tell that it wasn't corrupt?"

"That's because I asked him in person. I paged him that evening when he became the new ruler, and it was written to say: *Bill, are you feeling OK?*"

Laughter erupted by his description, and Leo was again waving at everybody.

"Where was I?" Leo said, "Oh yeah, I write: *I think that me and you'll need to talk.* Afterwards, he offered me a visit to his White House. There then, I was trying to detect if he was a good egg, but I got blasted off to Mars."

"Do you think that the Orion mission was really a diversion? That's to say that Kaiser was really a despot?"

"The science behind Orion was terrific, and Kaiser's seeds were watered well. Once the roots were strong and in place, the new constitution was stable."

"That might be fine. So let's look at the finer details that the roots weren't really for the American people, but for Kaiser's personal gain. Since his death, we've found his political ideology crumbling away, don't you agree?"

Leo replied, "The General will always be something for historians to mar or marvel. I find some good things in him and heard some disturbing things too."

"The Red Resistance Force saw him as a despot, and they claimed that General Kaiser took the life of Frederick Bungles. However, in your own personal opinion, do you think that's true?"

"I know that since the wake of Kaiser's death, nobody has been able to trace any documents that Bungles was assassinated. However, it's still only early days."

Tara asked, "Do you believe that General Kaiser ordered the killing?"

"I knew him as a good man – I had thought. He's the same man who had given me a good word to Orlando University. I think I know what you're really trying say, that the Supreme Court wanted him to lead, yeah? So the answer is no, he didn't ordered the killing."

"Don't you believe that the RRF was right: General Kaiser did rub him out?"

"As I was trying to tell you, I knew nothing about the revolution, and it did take me by surprise. So the answer will be no, that I don't think General Kaiser is a murderer."

"Sorry, it's just that I never had the opportunity of interviewing General Kaiser," Tara acknowledged, "and you're probably the only person who can reveal his tendencies."

"I understand."

"Have you heard Engels' view that after General Kaiser's death, former government agents could've destroyed the incriminating documents?"

"I know that American politics is a major shockwave on these shores. Yet, I haven't the slightest interest in backhand dealings, nor if there were blackguards in the White House."

She hummed. "If Engels believed that there are documents; he must have heard about it beforehand?"

"I absolutely agree with you."

"I'm thinking-out-loud that Engels might issue another commission hearing, to investigate Kaiser's dealings. Basically, do you think that you'll get summoned to attend?"

Leo nodded. "I absolutely think so. It's only early days after the Engels supremacy. Of course, he's to restore the beliefs of the Founding Fathers. It's likely that he'll be asking me on my work in the Rockford Group."

"Would you consider that the Rockford Group is ethical? I mean its existence is through a deceased despot?"

"The Rockford Group's main focus was to fascinate the world in the wonders of space. As its CEO, I think we've done good."

Before the live interview, Gordon Benson, Tara's agent, researched into Leo; he noticed his visit to Canada, and suspected that Leo knew a lot more than he was letting out. He had passed it on to Tara and she also agreed that Leo Rockford wasn't a simpleton, but sedulous. She wanted to reveal him as the man behind the assassination. However, she felt that her spotlight would make her seem hysterical—

"The Rockford Group," she said. "You do have plans to expand its operations abroad, isn't it?"

"Of course, I've a good management team that sees a promising future. We do have leading experts who will be able to work in the wider market."

"So you're bringing your investments to Britain?"

"I hope that London will be our HQ."

"I know, deep down, that the Rockford Group is an important pillar in America. Without it, things would've never been aspired like your Mars expedition." Tara stopped talking. She leaned forward to pour herself some water, and smiled too. "So what I really would like to ask," she carried on, "is that of the Mars expedition itself. I was watching the whole expedition, and you were entering a long tunnel. There's a glimpse when I saw a red figurine made of clear rock. So the point I'm getting at, was that a farce?"

"Did you say *farce*? You mean a practical joke?"

"Of course, I mean that I remember a blackout. Not only that but conspiracy theories on a deliberate attempt to cover the truth. You've heard of them in America, yeah?"

Leo cracked up laughing. "Indeed there was a blackout," he said, "and I had heard about an alien life form of high intelligence co-existing with us! Tara, you do understand that General Kaiser had an interest to reach for the stars. His point of view was to make the Supreme Council stronger and sound. Without that expedition, he feared failing in his junior years. I think it's best to say that he didn't take kindly to innuendos – like the ones where General Kaiser is an alien from Mars that wished to take over Earth for his own demise. The mission to Mars, from the General's perspective, was to enhance our human technological achievements than suppressing them."

"I must rush you!" she said, "will Orion's technology be shared with the rest of the world, or will it remain classified?"

"Sorry but I cannot answer that question. It's not my decision to make."

"Did you not sign papers in not revealing certain details about the Mars trip?"

"Yes," Leo said and leant forward; he had his legs crossed but now apart. "All of the astronauts were compelled to sign papers," he added, "it was to uphold sensitive information for national security. It's understandable."

"Is it still understandable?"

"I don't fully understand what you're imposing? What do you think is *understandable*?"

"It's no secret," she explained, "that all of the six astronauts, including yourself, sworn not to reveal sensitive details under Kaiser. My point is that devolution is now taking place, so are the same details as sensitive as ever?"

"It's still only early days of the Engels Supremacy, and he may choose to disclose the files regarding the blackout, as well as Orion's technological components."

Tara believed her show was going nowhere fast, as Leo was withholding information on the blackout. "Will the Rockford Group be having full access in what you describe as sensitive information?"

Leo shook his head. "Initially, the Rockford Group was a medium to handle press releases for NASA. It's still only early days, and Engels will be considering long and hard about what is safe, and not safe for the American people."

She coughed. "Do you miss going to Mars?"

"Mars is a dream for human beings to see their potential in this lonely universe. You must agree that Mars doesn't limit our abilities to better ourselves, and the same goes for the Rockford Group in searching for new opportunities."

"OK, you and your wife are happily married for over twenty years. Therefore, have you ever been tempted to go into detail, with her, about that Mars blackout?"

"It's still only early days if I'm permitted."

"You've been married for over twenty years, isn't it? General Kaiser had demanded your silence on the Orion expedition, but bygones are bygones. We've a new sheriff in town so Engels will most likely be relieving your gagging order. Nevertheless, will you be sharing any details with your wife?"

"I know it might sound silly but to be a decent good American, one must oblige to follow the legal requirements from Washington."

Tara nodded, and glanced upon her studio audience—

"Thank you, Leo. Now for my next guest may be considered a class-act, for he won't be holding back any punches. So please give a warm welcome to Jay Kaiser!"

Leo felt agitated. He gasped. It was a state of shock from her announcement. Leo couldn't find a reverie, because Jay knew of his red flushes. He turned around and saw him, approaching, in his light blue double suit. Jay Kaiser was pointing his finger at him, kept a prolonged wink, and was even congenial. He took a seat after kissing Tara by her right cheek too.

Tara asked, "You don't mind that I have Jay Kaiser with us this evening?"

"No, not at all!" Leo replied.

"Jay Kaiser, you're probably one of the greatest actors in the world. You even took the leap into space. How does that all feel?"

"Boy, it's great! I never knew Leo had a soft spot for the British! May I say what a wonderful jumper you're wearing, Tara."

"Sure Jay," she reacted, "as you may know, Leo Rockford is thinking about moving his operations into Europe. Any advice you like to dish out?"

"Leo is a dark horse."

"Say Jay," Tara swiftly moved on, "do you think that the late General Kaiser will continue to have a presence?"

"Categorically, it's a big no! I was listening backstage about that *gagging order* and it got me thinking—"

"I do respect," Leo intervened, he saw Jay was now more trouble with the General dead, "I do respect Engels pushing for devolution, and I'll still respect him to lift that *gagging order*. To be frank, Jay ought to button it."

"*Button it?*" Jay asked. "And what is that worth? That we found a ruby shaped figurine just laying there in the cavern." He looked upon Tara. "Oh yes," he recounted, "General Kaiser ordered the blackout because he thought it was his doom."

Leo shook his head. "Jay, you are too bold for your own good."

"If I was to say that, three years ago, I would be locked up in a high-security prison. All because General Kaiser was a little paranoid how the public perceived him. I mean, I'm an actor who plays a hero in Flash Gordon, and I know deep down that Kaiser did resemble Ming the Merciless. It was considered impertinent to share that view to him, or with others. Anyway, check him out that it isn't just visual but characteristically too.

"For Kaiser to die like that makes me think a bit, that Leo was responsible against the delusional despot!"

"Why do you say that?" she asked and was very intrigued too.

Jay laughed. "Tara, it's just a joke."

"Jay, this is supposed to be my show," Leo responded, "so why are you the one for drama?"

"You should have seen Leo feeling space sick," Jay continued, "he turned into a roast."

"Did you say *space sick*?" Tara asked.

"We were drinking wine cocktails, champagne and beer, but Leo here got the bug. We had to take him into the infirmary for treatment, and that was only after Martin MacCormick had the same symptoms too."

Again, Tara asked, "Did you say *space sick*?"

"This place reminds me of the pubs here—"

"You're drunk like the last time in space!" Leo said, presumed by his inability to be fully responsive. "I can imagine you having a stiff pint before stopping here."

"I'm surprised the pair of you didn't gel together," Tara said. "As our main guest, Leo, do you believe that your surprise guest is a socialite?"

Leo loathed. He felt as if he was a loiter in the studio. He wanted to storm out. However, he wished to remain etiquette.

"I'm just thinking," Leo said politely, "about my personal experience, but if Jay is happy to blurt about my health scare, let him."

Jay reacted, "I don't mean to be a nurse, but we did have a good time."

Tara asked, "Jay, what are your thoughts on the death of the former President?"

"I met General Kaiser," Jay answered, seemingly suffering from delirium. "On several occasions too," he added, "he didn't strike me as capable of killing people – not in power."

Tara asked, "Where have you been drinking?"

"I was drinking in my limo on my way here!" Jay replied.

Leo with Tara had something in common as they're looking at each other. "I think he had one too many!" Leo said.

The audience were finding Jay Kaiser a little comical. Tara sensed that Jay was only going to be an embarrassment to himself – she expected little from the celebrity that went out into space, and returned out-of-his-face.

She asked, "I never had the chance to ask you, Leo. Did you really hate your time in the RAF?"

"I kind of enjoyed being the Squadron Leader," Leo said smiling. "But my love for space is deeper."

Tara now asked, "You do have a very supportive wife. How did she cope with the ventures in America?"

"She's a rock! When she heard about the astronomy job in America, she knew straight away that I wanted it so bad. She was like saying, *let's do it* and I was like: S*uperb*!"

"You must've felt that you owe General Kaiser a debt. Yet, did you have any negative feelings towards him that cheesed you off?"

"What I hate the most was that he was always too busy. I must I've sent him piles of messages, and he only replied to several of many. Also, he had a mediator that he was using for recreation. He was the kind of fellow that drank his drinks and put his shots at golf."

"Adjutant-General Trump," Jay answered quickly.

Leo nodded.

Tara now asked, "They say that he's in hiding in Mexico, what do you think?"

"I think he could be anyway in Latin America, because there are a lot of backhand dealings."

"There're assumed backhand dealings everywhere," Tara said, "we had a tyrant in America and the rumour is that he was a corrupt ruler."

Jay concluded to say, "I just love my country being the world's political battlefield. I mean Washington is the talk of this town and where else is there?"

Tara hummed. "This is Leo Rockford being the main guest, whilst you're the surprise guest from America. So please contain yourself."

Leo agreed, "America may have the best political arena in the world, but this is my show."

"Leo," Tara continued, "I think I was cut-short in asking you, but what is your religion?"

"My family are Catholics and what's yours?"

"Mine," Jay interrupted, "is Methodist."

Tara replied anyway, "I don't really practice a religion, but I think I'm drawn to my mother's side on keeping an open mind."

"I don't think I understand what you're saying?"

"It's a personal development to understand God. So I'll keep it as that"

Leo said – dazzled by her remark, "Both my parents are Catholics and so they raised me in that fashion."

Hussain only thought to conduct her show in a professional manner. She moved onto her next question–

"This may sound a bit strange, due to your unforeseen abduction, but what did happen to the spatial red water?"

"That red water," Jay responded yet again, "is only red because it got mineral red bits mixed in to give it that look."

Leo replied anyway, "I know it may sound strange, but I'm pretty sure that the samples from Mars are somewhere on the Orion. I mean, I left it there, and NASA was unable to find its whereabouts. Of course, I'd heard that some people were implicating me as irresponsible."

Tara agreed, "Oh yes, NASA said that you'd lost the spatial water – on purpose – that's what the impetuous ones were saying. After all, you were the Commander. How did it feel to lose your high appraisal with the NASA Advisory Panel?"

"It was a difficult time of having that accusation. All that I will say is that I was wrong to throw a party in space."

Jay nodded. "He's right! The discovery of plasma-lines might have allowed us to party. Nevertheless, Leo and

Martin were lightweights when it comes to handling beverages."

Momentarily, the studio audience giggled on his remark.

"Leo," Tara pressed on, "Jay says that there's a ruby figurine. Will you concur?"

"There was a strange looking mineral that resembled a humanoid, but it wasn't! Just imagine the fear of lions seeing flowers looking like themselves, but we humans justify them as dandelions."

Tara laughed. "That's a nice way of putting it, Leo. If we imagine General Kaiser looking like a notorious lion, he would be very upset to finance a space project that brought home a flower!"

Leo nodded. "That's why it was supposed to be a secret."

Everybody was in uproar. It lasted a minute – exactly on the mark, and of course, it waned.

"Knowing my luck," Jay added, "General Kaiser would have sent us to Kensington Gardens!"

Yet again, everybody was in uproar. Only, this time, it lasted twenty seconds, and of course, it waned.

Tara said, "Behave the pair of you, because this is not supposed to be a sitcom!" She took a sip of water. "Leo, we know that the figurine is accounted for but not the red water. Do you think that NASA will be re-launching another batch of astronauts into deep space?"

"Leo drank it thinking it was wine!" Jay snapped.

For the third time running, the whole studio was bubbly.

"Of course I do, but I don't think Engels will be sending me out to space," Leo said momentarily.

Tara asked, "Leo, do you think that Engels might consider another space mission beyond Mars?"

He replied, "I think it's merely early days for any leader to consider shooting us into space. I understand what Engels is going through, and that's a healing process. Afterwards, the country can consider taking the initiative for a new space programme."

"But surely if Engels takes that initiative, he'll embark upon a quick healing process for the American people." She added, "It won't reflect badly, won't it?"

Leo agreed, "If I knew Engels a lot better, I would've put what you said to him."

Jay now concluded by saying, "Tara, you're amazing. I should put in a good word on your excellence. You ought to think about hosting a chat show in America."

"Thank you but I'm happy to stay in London," she answered and took another sip of water. "I wonder why," she continued, "I have another empty seat there, it's reserved for Engels to whet our appetite."

Leo said, "I met the Supreme Judge, Wallace Moore, on several occasions. I could pass on your thoughts to him."

The chat-show host nodded. "You'll do that? That's great! I would love to hear the outcome! It'll be a pity if Engels doesn't select you in commanding another space mission."

Jay said, "Leo is right that *it's early days*. But make no mistake, if Engels lifts the grounding on the Orion, it'll most probably boost Engels chances to stand as President of the United States of America."

"You're both too sweet!" Tara Hussain said complimentary. "Jay," she dabbled, "would you consider living in Britain?"

"Only if Hollywood is relocated."

"Leo, will you be returning back to the UK, or stay in America?"

"Well, my wife loves this show, and she's always watching your programmes. So, I cannot see why I shouldn't be able to relocate to London."

"So what will you be bringing back from America?"

"I'll be bringing the Rockford Group, and surely my family."

"Are you leaving America because there isn't a future for you anymore?" she asked.

"During the time of Kaiser, I've talked with my wife about returning to the UK. It's not new news to us."

"Why would you want to leave the present America?"

"It's the kidnapping."

"I understand," Tara said – conceded that she wanted to sing aloud of the link between the RRF and the Rockford Group, "I understand why you want to leave America behind. It's the constant reminder of the RRF that saw you as a potential target, and they were an extremely dangerous group. Leo, since the formation of the freedom fighters, how did you manage to cope with that constant threat hanging over your head?"

Leo replied. "I always had armed personnel with me at all times, since regaining my freedom."

"After that release, have you felt a lot more secured under Kaiser?"

"Well, the USTF is a reconstruction of the NSA. Obviously, it was a dangerous political battleground, but I could hardly see how I was a threat to anyone."

Tara coughed politely. "I said did you feel secure under Kaiser?"

"I thought that if the USTF can protect General Kaiser, then they can protect me."

"How did you feel once General Kaiser was struck by that bombing device? Did you feel insecure?"

"I was surprised like the rest of the diners that evening about it."

"So it did cross your mind that General Kaiser was the target?"

"I knew he was a target but I didn't know he was going to be the target that night!" Leo lied – unintentionally.

"Would you feel safer living in Britain today?"

"I do feel safe in America as long as my family does as well. I can only imagine of living here will be a life of tranquillity."

"Britain does have a serene feeling than anywhere else I can think of," Jay acknowledged.

"Leo, would you ever consider moving into the political arena?"

"I never consider it as a goal. I think the first thing to do is to expand the Rockford Group, and after the ball is rolling in London, I can't see why I shouldn't consider being a candidate."

In the studio audience, Tara's Agent, Gordon Benson, saw himself all becoming. He stood up and started to clap his hands in a timely rhythm. It got several other people joining him. Soon enough, a standing ovation. The audience saw a man that could make the world a better place.

"Leo, my good man," Jay said after the awe calmed down, "you should consider being the next Prime Minster."

The room wasn't as ecstatic as before, and Jay thought of Washington as superior.

Tara laughed. "The only thing what happens in the Houses of Parliament is the debate about foxes, badgers and moles. We don't have the American drama of intrigue that I think Leo seeks!"

The audience were cordial on her assessment.

She concluded to say, "God. We're running late! I would like to thank the both of you in your precious insights." She turned to face the studio audience. "Of course, you, the live audience." She changed her posture onto the cameras. "And for you," she finished, "watching and good night!"

Epilogue

*T*HE MOMENT THE Canadian Prime Minister admitted his awareness of the assassination plot, Harry Trump's call to rule was haywire. Obviously, his hold on Washington wasn't plausible – he was what the Judges would call a *dead-man-walking*. Since Harry was becoming an anachronic; he had to be evasive. He left behind his wife, his children and his home. Failure to perceive his predicament meant that Engels would've arrested him. He was more than likely of facing the death penalty too.

Harry Trump managed to escape Engels but for how long? He knew that any attempt to contact his family would be an entrapment, and the all new CIA was trying to trace his whereabouts.

David Bruce was also hunted for his acts against democracy. Engels had made him public enemy number two, behind Harry Trump. According to the intelligence, the agency knew that David Bruce with Harry Trump had made his escape through the American-Mexican border but the trail went cold. The CIA dedicated a team of fifty Agents that were trying their best in tracking them down. They were allegations that their targets, had re-established themselves, to become high-profile drug barons in Latin America. Of course, such claims were questionable that the tyrant's lieutenants could just vanish, and re-appear as drug lords. All in all, the CIA wasn't able to substantiate it.

David had a favour returned by a Columbian drug cartel, and was ingratiated for his work in the DEA. He had an unethical strategy when fighting a single drug cartel; he aided another by promising them immunity, as long as, they would play his game. He worked in the Vigilante Detachment of the DEA, and his job appraisals were measured through US government statistics:

Drug-related gun crimes, police stop and searches, and drug raids. When the stats fell, in certain states, it was interpreted that his task force was winning the fight. David Bruce had condescended a Latin American vigilante group to become a drug cartel, *Los Mendellas*, and he was a close friend of the Drug Baron, Carlos Colain. Needless to say, his escape to Mexico City was the help of the Los Mendellas crew. Nowadays, Harry Trump was overshadowed by David Bruce, as they both, took up the Los Mendellas' courtesy. It may seem that the Cartel's main turf was in Columbia, but Mexico was their trafficking point into America. David bore the nickname, the *Latino Gringo*. He had controlled a street corner, after which, the entire slums that consisted of his Cartel soldiers. Then David was promoted to cultivate coca plants in rural Colombia and he had a guerrilla army.

Now Harry was observing the view of the valley ahead of him, and everywhere around him was vegetation: It was a jungle. As he did so, David Bruce was fixing himself a drink from behind. He had a Latina woman in her bikini standing beside him. The woman offered a massage to David, and they returned to his own bedroom. Harry was basking quietly under the sunny sun with a gorgeous escort, which was after all, seemed to defeat the purpose of how a fugitive ought to live.

The Los Mendellas Cartel owned an escort service in the city of Medellin, which was sixty miles away from the jungle. Some of the girls accepted to be despatched to the jungle villa. From there, senior crime figures would enter to enjoy their company. As it's out in the jungle, the girls were assigned for three months before returning to Medellin. Before Harry heard of the brothel, it got some guerrillas suspecting him a homosexual. Andres Ramos was one of David Bruce's soldiers, and he spoke fairly good English to raise his concern.

"David," he said, "so you relax tonight on marijuana?"

"Sounds like a good idea," David replied.

"Don't you like being horny with women?"

"I do have a wife back in America, and I really do miss her. What are you scheming?"

"You have no lady friend for long time, and you have not think to please your body. So, you should go freestyle to the villa wing."

As he was a top-rank soldier, David accepted his offer and bedded a Latina woman for the rest of that evening. The following day, Harry Trump was informed of it but he didn't take the news very well.

"It's was a living hell in Mexico, and this is how they reward you?"

"I went through a Supreme Revolution, and it doesn't make you any much better!" David replied, and the pair now visited the brothel.

Harry really wanted to return to his family. Henceforth, he detested how the RRF managed to swindle Washington. He had been running back and fro, in his mind, about what could be his last days, and it was really tough for him as he tried so hard in coping with his losses. None of the working girls knew of his true identity, but they obviously understood that he was an important American that worked for the criminal world. Strange as it might seem, word on the streets in Medellin was swift that the Latino Gringo was making a big name for himself in Mexico. Few of the girls assumed that Harry Trump was that very dodgy person who would kill anybody that stood in his way. By the way, they would speak little of him because they feared his fury.

Of course, Harry Trump was basking under the sun with a glass of iced Tequila. The drink itself should aide him to lessen the troublesome heat wave. After all, he was viewing the marvellous sight of the valley ahead of him upon his sun lounger. He was on a spacious balcony, and its wall was crafted low. Harry wore a white trilby hat, beach shorts, white unbuttoned shirt and in his sunglasses. A woman was behind him carrying several folded American and British newspapers. She approached him.

"Here are the papers that you've requested," she said.

"Thank you."

As she left him, he began reading about America. It was abundantly clear that Engels wanted to accelerate the devolution, and the paper reported new Directors in the CIA, NSA and the FBI. In another news article, it gave word on the continuing manhunt to find him. However, Harry was feeling relatively safe, and he switched to a different paper with the headline:

Rockford Sights the White House

He started reading on Tara Hussain's chat show: It praised her professionalism, and the paper saw her as the most proficient presenter of modern time; it also mentioned the impact, that Leo Rockford, would make if elected as the next President of the United States of America. Harry recalled how he used him as a scapegoat, but Canada dashed his hopes. He also thought of General Kaiser when Leo hesitated to reach the podium before detonation. Drastically, he stood up from his seat, and he was pacing along his balcony that Leo really did kill Kaiser. Harry might be living a life of luxury, but at the expense of losing his wife, his family and his great career. He knew that David Bruce was lying low inside a villa wing, and he was going to confront him. Of course, Harry walked inside from the balcony to pass his bedroom onto a long corridor. From there on, He headed straight to David's bedroom. Without a knock, Trump entered his room—

"That bastard is all over the news!"

David Bruce was lying upon his front, along the massage bed, while a woman was tendering his back. It seemed rude of Harry to intrude his moment of peace, and he couldn't understand what was upsetting his former boss.

"What's up?"

"That genius is considering running for leadership. It's the same traitor saying that all is well!"

David asked, in Spanish, his massager to stop as he changed his posture to read the article. With a bath towel around his waist and just before he read it, spoke again for her to leave.

Harry said, "I always thought he was up to no good! I mean the moment that the RRF released him back to society tells its entirety!"

"We've been through this conversation before. What do you expect me to do?" David asked.

"That man was the conspirator! Both you and I know that he's a member at the executive golf club. Call me paranoid but he'll be using his influence to become a billionaire! He's also thinking to dabble in the political arena. He knew that General Kaiser wasn't keen on anybody being his equal, so he disposed him! Leo was coordinating with the Canadian government and the RRF!" Harry said astonishingly.

David shook his head. "You're truly getting a little delusional. Imagine what Engels will be thinking regarding our actions? He'd think that we were poisoning America, on drugs, during the high heights of Kaiser's supremacy. That isn't true."

"You're missing the point. I knew Leo Rockford from the moment of the Supreme Revolution. Therefore, I think I know him more than you. When I say that Leo Rockford is the guy that orchestrated the whole—"

David coughed loudly. "So you don't think the brainchild is Wallace Moore, so how you figured?"

"Is Wallace Moore considering a campaign in becoming the next President of the United States? That's a negative! Wallace Moore," he went on, "has his seat in the Supreme Court, and he'll most likely be endorsing his support in Leo. That's because who else can there be?"

"There's Engels too, and he'll be standing for the Presidency. So your theory doesn't hold up."

"It's him, David."

"So what if it is? And then what?" David asked.

"Just look at what seemed impossible," Harry said, "Leo Rockford is planning to storm into the White House."

"I wish I could help you big guy, but how can we take on the might of Engels?" David now asked.

"All I want is for you to accept that Leo Rockford is responsible for the whole fuck-up!"

"Harry, when I was the head of the USTF, we didn't consider the media circus as an intelligence source. We had people out on the field to collect that. We went

353

through this a thousand times about one of my prized agents that was able to determine the hit. You know the outcome; we didn't have enough detail on who was going to be the smoking gun."

"I don't want to argue with you, but where is that prized agent? Why isn't that person with us?"

"He's in America and I told you that—"

"You told me there weren't any implications that could link him to his work with you, but why is that?"

"I don't like how you are treating your stay here, but the fact is that you didn't have a contingency plan," David answered and paused a moment. "I'm making," he added, "all the necessary moves of keeping us from harm's way — you don't have to imagine Engels hunting you down, while you're chasing butterflies. Remember, Harry, it was your own fault for getting too cosy with the General."

"You remind me of a cocky guy, I used to work for, and he thought that he was invincible: General Kaiser."

"You remind me of not blowing your horn!" David shouted.

"Sorry, David," Harry regretfully said, "all I want is for you to make some recognition, that Leo Rockford is a serious contender."

"It's done! Today, I wish to relax. Tomorrow, I'll be supervising the export of some uncut cocaine to Europe. The following day it's supervising exports to America...Can you not see that I'm a very busy guy?"

Harry still wanted to protest. "I had blown my trumpet at him on many occasions, but he just had to be right. Look, General Kaiser was a great man, and historians will just have to accept that he sacrificed everything in bringing a lot of good. Without being too cocky, I've accepted that Leo masterminded it."

David shook his head. "I can only accept that Rockford didn't kill General Kaiser. I've been hunting the RRF for many years — not to be funny, I heard that Leo was under suspicion for quenching his thirst in space. Seriously, you should be implying that your main target is Wallace Moore."

"Perhaps my judgment is clouded because I've known Kaiser more than I've known you. However, all that I ask of you is to recognise that Leo Rockford is a suspect that caused the assassination," Harry said repeatedly. David agreed sarcastically, "OK. Oh my God! I could imagine you, in Washington, organizing witch hunts for any discrepancies in every other American."

"Did you once say that you were looking for a man with short ginger hair, and freckles on his cheek?"

"He was nowhere on sight. To be honest, the only person with ginger hair and freckles was your wife. So imagine if we pulled her to one side, and asked her about being a threat to national security? Surely you wouldn't be amused."

"If we had that information a lot sooner, I'm sure we could've neutralized that threat."

"I'm sure you're thinking the right course of action, but licking our wounds will not bring back General Kaiser. He's dead and we're officially fugitives." He added, "Do you remember when we were in Mexico sorting out the turf war?"

"Yes, of course."

"I got labelled as the Latino Gringo and that was part of a stigma. Word on the street is that the Latino Gringo is a top senior member of the Supreme Council on the run. Now that was just a rumour by our rivals that were trying to outmanoeuvre me. Nevertheless, those rumours attracted the witch-hunters."

"They'll probably believe that we're roaming around graveyards," Harry said jokingly.

"Point is that the Los Mendellas is a well-organized group. You may already know that a Spaniard is in my place in Mexico – a decoy."

"So that's why we are here?" Harry asked.

"In some parts yes. Carlos Colain was a very resourceful guy during my days in the DEA, and he's still a great man."

"I understand but will you accept that Leo Rockford is the suspect who killed Bill Kaiser?" Harry asked for the umpteenth time.

"OK, I'll accept that Leo Rockford may be responsible."

Harry beckoned David to walk outside upon his own balcony, which didn't have the view of the valley but large fields of coca plants that ran for miles.

Harry said, "We should at least consider killing him."

"Have you lost your mind? How are you going to get that in motion?"

"It just isn't right," Harry responded, "what Leo Rockford had done to his old friend. He's a traitor and we shouldn't ignore that fact."

"You'll be attracting too much attention just to kill him. Again, you'll be making a confirmation to Engels that the Latino Gringo is really me."

"So we must live like this because that traitor wants to live a lavish lifestyle."

David was delineating with his hands; everywhere around him—

"So this is how it feels to have a lavish lifestyle that we're living as kings? I suppose to go on my knees and beg Carlos Colain for a bigger favour, and that's to kill Rockford. Oh and if all goes well, he'll grant your wish and then I can take another long massage – until you barge into my room to say thank you!"

Harry said, "So far, you made it easy for us to live this lavish lifestyle, and I cannot see why you find that a problem?"

David laughed. "Have you not been listening to a single word what I've just said? I got lucky here because I helped a vigilante group to succeed in the drugs trade."

"I do understand how faithful you're with Carlos, but that doesn't change the fact that you'll always be an American."

"Of course I love my country!" David said, "why would I work up a sweat to secure the stability of Kaiser? Lets face it, the Supreme Court doesn't believe that autocracy is the answer anymore."

"Are you not willing to use your power, to bring about some kind of street justice against Leo Rockford?"

David sighed. "OK! But first I'll be resuming on my massage and who knows what. Later on, I'll be cultivating and when I get the chance to speak to Carlos Colain, I'll mention that Leo Rockford is the reason why we're here."

"I wouldn't put it like that," Harry implied, "you make it sound like Leo Rockford was righteous; a God send."

"I should..." David said and stopped all together. "Wait! I can't just go up to Carlos, and say that Leo Rockford is the culprit that brought down Kaiser; for I'm working for a Marxist group."

"Not even a favour?" Harry asked.

"I could try to get really political, that Leo Rockford is a hungry capitalist machine. But the bigger picture will always be General Kaiser."

"I don't understand you? Were you a supporter of Carl Simmons?"

"Whilst I was at university, I did join a socialist movement — and it's not what you're thinking — I watched Carl Simmons in action; he had fire in his eyes. Obviously, I locked him up because he did pose a threat to Kaiser. Yet, we failed to neutralize an even bigger problem: Wallace Moore."

"The only people, left in this world, that endorsed Marxism are in this villa alone. You've exotic girls running around in their bathing suits with greasy old men chasing them around. Are you really expecting me to believe that?" Harry asked.

"You were always a hard worker for our former boss, and now you're asking me to approach Carlos for a dare."

"Amigo, call it jungle justice as it's the way out here."

"Well, it won't be today but maybe within a fortnight. Can you imagine reading those newspapers that the Los Mendellas Cartel killed Leo Rockford? How can we triumph when who-the-fuck would want to kill Leo Rockford?" David asked a little harshly.

"Why not? Don't you think you're being complacent? After all, Engels is struggling to implicate us as the culprits that killed Frederick Bungles?"

"Implicate is a good word, so who would be clever enough to implicate us on retaliation?"

"Engels."

"So who are we trying to avoid?" David seemingly asked.

Harry shook his head. "Could make it appear that it was a robbery."

David left the balcony to lay upon his cypress double bed, in frustration. Harry followed his new master into the bedroom.

"If you don't want to do it," Harry continued, "then why don't you say so? It was only a suggestion, and that's that."

"It just wouldn't work, Harry," David replied.

"Martin MacCormick!"

"That's an astronaut that went to Mars."

"He's the answer for he hated Leo Rockford for ruining his career!" Harry said.

David changed his position to stare right at him. "What can you do?" he asked. "Make him join the Los Mendellas to serve our own amusement?"

"David, you're the closest thing to understand the CIA's mind control—"

David laughed. "It's really a load of crap! Put it this way, you get a human test subject that is short on political and religious ideologies. You make him consume certain narcotics and shock treatments, and that person would be under our control, apparently."

"So you don't think Martin MacCormick is a good test subject? If we give him a spin, he would most probably kill him," Harry said passionately.

"I thought that the old CIA, testing human subjects, was heading for failure from day one. Besides, you aren't sticking to reality that you cannot induce bullshit that Martin won't be willing to comply to."

"I'm just keeping an open mind—"

"No you're not! If you were, then you would've seen that this whole episode is real bull! Anyway, I'll speak to Carlos about your opinion, and let's leave it as that," he said and was making his way to the door.

"You've known me for over ten years, and I never said anything wrong to insult your intelligence, nor status. So when I say that the culprit is Leo Rockford, I mean that! Nothing else holds up. The RRF hadn't any direct access that evening but Leo Rockford. You said so yourself, that Leo knew something was going down, and he just let it roll out on stage."

"I'm tried Harry and that mind control tactic isn't going to stick. I've told you earlier that we need to keep a low profile, as long as possible. So your idea of jungle justice will only backfire. And another problem, since the Supreme Judges won't be supporting supremacy, are you just going to pop into their chambers and request for street justice? Come on Harry, these are hard times."

"I'll admit that the General thought of himself as an elitist."

David was still standing by the door, not opened, with the knob at hand. "You don't know how lucky you are," he said, "these guerrillas would have killed you already. If they just stopped to think, for the slightest moment, that you're the suppressor of Carl Simmons…It's bang! Bang! You're dead! So you think that Martin MacCormick might be interested in your scheme. So why don't you just go on the next plane and head to his home?"

"I know these are difficult times, but you've been a terrifying enforcer for the Los Mendellas. You're a lieutenant of the biggest drug cartel in the world, and before that, head of the USTF. Since you've a strong will, you can easily claim—"

"Inspiring but you sound like a crazy scientist who thinks that he can change the world, through mind control. Look, I don't want to argue with you but you're really pissing me off — just drop it."

"I would if you just listen," Harry said adamantly. "Through this little clatter, we've managed to understand that we cannot make the hit on Leo, but our only best option is Martin MacCormick. Therefore, all I ask is that we send word to him."

"We're on the wrong side of the law, and Martin MacCormick may not like what he finds, if we can magically approach him. So how are you planning to do that?"

"That guy of yours that already infiltrated the RRF."

David said, "He's a little difficult to get hold of right now." He froze in thought. "My God!" he exclaimed. "He's a useful asset inside Washington! He'll be in the best of positions to know the efforts of the new Supremacy!"

"So we've somebody who might detect what's going on in the CIA. Yet that doesn't change the fact that we shouldn't locate Martin MacCormick."

"You're missing the point for my *somebody* will most likely become a highly-decorated citizen. If he plays his cards right, he'll know a lot more what's on Engels' mind!"

"So we do have eyes inside Washington, but I want our eyes on Martin MacCormick."

David sighed. "Once I figured out how I can re-establish my link with him," he said, "I suppose it's probable that he could approach Martin MacCormick."

"I just had a thought that he will surely be holding a different worldview?"

David now paced around the room. "I've known him, as a friend, before the founding of the USTF. It's fortunate for me that he was in Carl Simmons' movement. After the assassination, I alone knew that I had to make myself scare."

"It's unfortunate that your friend wasn't able to warn us of the bombing sooner, and how are you planning to contact him again?" Harry asked.

"Don't be too concern about how I can contact him," he said and was returning to the door. "He can be approached but it will take some time."

"Are you just going to pick up the phone and call him?"

"That's possible but not the best option. It'll have to be done with prudence," David said.

"What do you mean *it'll have to be done with prudence*?"

"If it wasn't," David excused, "for Andres Ramos forwarding your newspapers here, you would've kept yourself cosy, on your balcony, admiring that valley." He asked, "Why can't you just let it go?"

"Letting this go is like forgetting that the world out there is hunting us!"

"Have you not heard yourself lately? You're making it appear that Leo is the main figure in Washington. He's not—"

"He'll become the next President," Harry detracted quickly, "if we continue to play pocket billiards! I bet that in America, there are pockets of people that still support the ideals of General Kaiser. Basically, all we got to do is stimulate their desires, and the world will be within our reach."

"I think that you've got the wrong end of the stick. First you were trying to win me over, that I'm not in touch with today's America. Now you want to get in touch with people stuck in the past."

Harry said, "If we learnt anything about history, then perhaps, we should learn that Carl Simmons' ideas was from the yesteryears. Let's just keep our options open."

"I do respect you," David now moved to the bed to find a pen and paper. "Look, I'll be trying to re-establish my links with an old friend, and I'll mention to Carlos about the kill. So are you happy?"

"I thought we agreed that the Los Mendellas Cartel isn't to kill him, is it?"

David replied, "I bet you'll be telling me to get my informer to kill him."

The room stayed silent as Harry contemplated. David, yet again, moved to the door.

"I do appreciate what you've done. God, who knows if we could do the impossible in America?"

David shook his head. "We haven't really a basis to form a conspiracy."

"I'm open to opinions, and our *conspiracy* can start here."

David said, "Our conspiracy wouldn't go well with the Supreme Court, Congress and what about the White House. I cannot understand why you think that the Los Mendellas Cartel will have any influence in Washington. Surely you aren't saying, these Marxist guerrillas will make an impact on the left-wing Americans? That's nonsense!" David said and he started to turn the door knob – he was going to bid farewell.

Harry knew that he had out stayed his welcome and so made his exit. "Just be prudent about the outside world," Harry said, "I will say no more."

"Just don't babble about our conversation beyond here."

***

Three days later, the pair was observing work done on the coca plants in a jungle glade.

Harry said, "I know we haven't spoken to each other, for a while. However, can we talk some more?"

"Go on. We aren't really doing anything," David replied as his watch was extremely boring.

"I've been thinking a lot about America. The fact is that the Supreme Court did support our revolution. Now, they've turned to the whim of a minor — Wallace Moore. So can we agree that they're all traitors?" Harry asked.

"Suppose so and what are you trying to scheme?"

"Of course, it's about Leo Rockford and his Rockford Group. He clearly has an ambition to win the Presidency. You see, why would he make a move like that without showing any regrets? I daresay, he's responsible for Kaiser's death."

"Hmm, I suppose so. You do know that I'm supervising, in this jungle, don't you?"

"Of course I do. If it could be feasible today, will you consider ending that farce?"

David laughed. "You make me think," he said, "that you should've been the leader of the Supreme Council than General Kaiser. Why is that? No wait. The Supreme Judges didn't wish to side with you on saving the economy. You don't really think that you can win over the Supreme Court, and make them take our side on the drugs trade, don't you?"

Harry replied, "It doesn't change the fact that you worked under General Kaiser: He was your employer."

The guerrilla lieutenant said, "I knew him as the man that didn't want me to run the task force. But all thanks to you, he takes your view that I'm the best candidate. He always wanted to overturn your recommendation. Perhaps it's best that you just drop it."

"General Kaiser didn't know a lot of potential candidates for the USTF post," Harry said scornfully – forgetting his place. "I'm sorry," Harry continued, "Kaiser wasn't as narrow-minded as you're trying to make out. When he wanted advice, I gave it to him. He might have thought openly, but he always kept his options open. You were the best man for the role at that given time. So if there were better candidates, then let the best man win."

"I'm sorry too, it's just that we're lucky to escape Engels."

"But for how long?" Harry asked. "What I know about you and Carlos Colain is what Washington should already know." He said, "You were leading a task force to take out the drug cartels. I also understand your success in the DEA is due to the lesser crime waves on the American streets. Oh wait a minute, the Carlos vigilante group, you were sponsoring, is now the largest trafficker – it's ironic that Engels cannot understand that you're under his wing – surely, you're not suggesting that this new life will see us into retirement?"

David was finding the heat wave too much. He walked a short distance under a tree shade. "This place," he said, "will have to do for now. Think of it this way, we do have enough influence to forge new identities."

Harry replied, "So our documents can be forgeries, isn't it right? I just find that hard to believe that this Drug Cartel is able to create new birth records, and link us to a Spaniard family, or whatever. What you're suggesting is that this Columbian government is corrupt too, isn't it? And if that is the case, then why have guerrillas guarding our livelihoods?"

"You're not hearing me. We can forge passports to move around Latin America, which will make us a difficult target for Engels. Besides, all that we must do is to convince Engels that the late Kaiser had a contingency plan."

Harry nodded. "This might sound a little odd," he whispered, "but you do recall your crackdown against Carl Simmons?"

"That's how I became the head of the USTF, so?" David asked rudely.

"Frederick Bungles was winning a public opinion that the Supreme Council was an illegal government; an illegal government that hadn't any true reflection on the Founding Fathers. He was also winning over some Supreme Judges for the release of the former members in the RRU."

David said, "We did capture Carl Simmons and that was the goal, and nothing else."

"Obviously, Carl Simmons was in our sights, due to his propaganda, and holding him down was to prevent further impact.

"There was still another problem, and it's Frederick Bungles. He claimed to have won the hearts and minds of the Supreme Court. He was affecting the ongoing status of Bill Kaiser. So think about it, we had overlooked to release those prisoners. Don't you see? Bungles was clowning around with the media circus; he had earned the respect of the Supreme Court. Therefore, his return looked in earnest."

David laughed. "Kind of funny."

"Well not for General Kaiser. He needed the support of the Supreme Court and Congress to continue running, and Bungles was his obstacle—"

"So, it was you that gave the order."

"We were able to anticipate, with pinpoint accuracy, Frederick's whereabouts: He goes to see his mother, visits that communist publishing house, the Andrews Clubhouse and the French Alps. We chose the Alps and we despatched a three-man team to set a small charge, which was enough to start that avalanche. Before that, they tampered with his car too,"

David shook his head. "I suppose you'd destroyed any evidence, isn't it?"

"What do you think? I'd deleted all of my accounts on the event, and the three-man team will be silent," Harry confessed.

"Who and what were the team? In the army?"

"They were black ops."

David said, "So that's how the RRF began to be set into motion. I suppose there was a leak in the crack team, wasn't it?"

"No! Those were loyal soldiers who strived to protect our interests, for the sake of national security, treason isn't an option."

"So the RRF," Davis said, "made allegations that the autocrats were responsible for his death, without a shred of evidence. He ends up getting killed and we're on the run."

"Engels won't be able to implicate us to the assassination of Bungles, and it's only his guesswork. However, we still need to be a lot more careful from now on."

"Since you just told me your dirty little secret, I suppose that Leo Rockford also knew about that as well?" David asked.

"I know it sounds messy but action speak louder than words. He's in the American and British tabloids, and he's considering leading a democratic constitution. He alone is penalizing our chances for the right Supreme Commander. He'll also be signing our own death warrants."

David nodded. "You got me thinking," he said, "we must have propagandist who will spread our own firebrand."

Harry asked, "How are you supposed to firebrand in America?"

David smirked. "Not quite! We don't actually do it there."

"We'll establish it here, in Columbia, isn't it?"

David nodded. "Exactly," he said, "we start it here but I wouldn't recommend it nearby. Now the point is that we can open shop anywhere in Latin America, and I think the best place will have to be Cuba."

"Why must it be Cuba?"

"The fact is that Cuba has a proud history regarding Fidel Castro's defiance against American imperialism. We can easily firebrand there that the new America is just like the old."

"We're gringos in this part of the world, and what I've noticed is that we stick out like a sore thumb."

"I still think Cuba is the place to start our propaganda. Of course, we shall be nowhere near there. Harry, we should support some of the Marxist ideas – the redistribution of wealth etc. We should allege that the Supreme Council had nearly endorsed communism, but Engels wouldn't allow it, isn't it?"

"Yeah," Harry said, bemused.

"The Supreme Judges," David continued, "realised the flaws of capitalism, but Engels denied them any substantial power."

Harry hummed. "Sounds like you're a pretty good shit-stirrer," he said, "but who is going to make those allegations?"

"I'm pretty sure Andres won't have any problems finding us some suitors that America is still corrupt."

"This is getting too confusing. What you're saying is that we slander against Engels, but not Leo Rockford, right?"

David nodded. "I'm not exaggerating when I say Cuba," he said, "than your original plan."

"We don't have to do anything in Cuba. Also, there are those Conspiracy Theorists, in America, who will be more than happy. Your suggestion seems pointless."

David disagreed, "But Cuba is the–"

"You of all people should know that slander caused the death of Kaiser. The point is this, why don't we just fuel the fire in America?"

"We could."

"Good."

David said, "I must confess that I'm not too familiar with Conspiracy Theorists. So who is going to fuel the fire? Such a person will have a tough task in disputing Engels."

"That's true."

"So Cuba is the more feasible option."

Harry said, "Cuba is asking for trouble. Haven't you considered that Engels will be taking measures?"

"You mean that Engels will try his hardest to sabotage it?"

Harry replied, "That's always a possibility."

"I think you're right," David agreed, "we should use the available Conspiracy Theorists to fuel the fire. If we're able to succeed, what are the benefits?"

"Perhaps Engels will think twice to implement his international manhunt, or Washington will see the errors of their ways. Maybe it will just fall on deaf ears."

"I'm certain that our message will not fall on deaf ears."

Harry nodded. "I concur with you. So do you have anyone in mind?"

"The same man that was warning us of a hit on Kaiser," David said to insinuate.

www.ingramcontent.com/pod-product-compliance
Lightning Source LLC
Chambersburg PA
CBHW020820180626
46814CB00001B/49